"In *Alaska Justice* Mike Kincaid has created a masterpiece of adventure, suspense, intrigue, and humor. His writing style reflects his warmth and dedication to his fellow officers and his work; it is hard to tell which he loved most—his life as a law enforcement officer for the great state of Alaska or his writing. *Alaska Justice* is a must read book. You will enjoy it from its exciting beginning to its surprising ending. Truly unforgettable." —*Sandra E. Graham, author of Amos Jakey and Nicolina.*

".... Trooper Blake braves the bad weather, worse flying weather, killer rivers, plane crashes and living quarters not fit for animals—on snowshoes, running behind dog sleds, flying a variety of bush planes and float planes, sometimes with the assistance of a Fish and Wildlife trooper, the beautiful and able Jet Torsen. Alaska Justice is a fun, hard-to-lay-it-down read and I recommend it to anyone who is looking for a measure of good, adventurous diversion."—*Charles L. Lunsford Author of "Departure Message" and "Boxcar Down: The Albanian Incident"*

"One adventure after another after another. Whew! Definitely action. That was just like Indiana Jones with no time for popcorn or restroom breaks." —*747 Captain Dave Glasebrook.*

"It rates right up there with 'Wager with the Wind.' Fantastic book and very well written." —*Dave Linde, pilot*

"The best book I've read since high school. I couldn't put it down!" —*Gary Conner, Pleasant Land Books.*

"... This is one of those books that you want to read in one sitting and then are sad when it is over."—*Sue Harvey, Seattle schoolteacher*

ALASKA JUSTICE

A NOVEL BY

M.D. KINCAID

Adventurous Books

Copyright © 2007 by M.D. Kincaid Adventurous Books

Illustrations by Briana Murphy, Matthew Nipper, and Mike Kincaid. Cover design by Tom Latham, Signal Point Design.

4th Adventurous Books Edition: August, 2008. ISBN 978-0-9796693-0-9 The Library of Congress has cataloged the paperback editions as follows: Kincaid, M.D. Alaska Justice.

To purchase books, visit the www.AdventurousBooks.com website, or ask your favorite bookseller.

Acknowledgments

My deepest thanks to dedicated and insightful editor Kitty Fleischman, whose keen eyesight and incredible patience kept me straight. Kitty, a former Bush Alaska teacher and journalist, now is the publisher and editor of *IDAHO Magazine* and received the 1st place award for magazine editing from the National Federation of Press Women in 2007. If the reader finds any errors in this book, it is all on me, as Kitty would not have missed them. Also great thanks for the efforts and encouragement of technical editor David Schuck. Thanks also to aircraft and firearms technical advisor Ted Herlihy, medical advisor Dr. Mark Manteuffel, food and wine consultant Chef Alex Mayberry, mug shot by Julie Kerr, and to proofreaders Jill (my supportive wife), Rich Emery, Trooper Kevin Murphy, Gerry Clark, and many others who helped with this project. Thanks to the Troopers who shared their stories. Thank you to Megan Peters and Sandy Belcher of the Alaska Department of Public Safety for their assistance with photographs.

This work is dedicated to all the hardworking Troopers and support staff of the Alaska Department of Public Safety. Special dedication to my friend, Alaska Trooper Troy Duncan, killed in the Manley incident. Also to the other Alaska Troopers who made the ultimate sacrifice protecting the rest of us: Dennis Cronin, Larry Carr, Frank Rodman, Roland Chevalier, John Stimson, Robert Bittick, C.E. Swackhammer, Bruce Heck, David Churchill, and James Moen.

The main character is named for Jack Blake, my wife's father, whose final dog–sledding race was his final day on earth.

ALASKA JUSTICE was inspired by actual events.

"Moral excellence comes about as a result of habit. We become just by doing just acts, temperate by doing temperate acts, brave by doing brave acts." —Aristotle

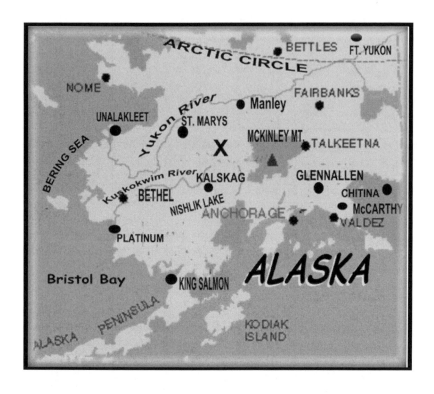

About the Author: M.D. Kincaid survived a rewarding, and exciting, career with the Alaska Department of Public Safety. He has lived in McKinley Park, Talkeetna, Valdez, Glennallen, Fairbanks, Bethel, King Salmon, Girdwood and Palmer, where he hiked, fished, hunted, skied, snowshoed, mushed dogs, flew Bush planes, chased bad guys, and built log cabins deep in the woods. He now shares his passion for seaplane flying with students from around the globe in his restored Piper J3 and writes when the weather grounds him.

PROLOGUE

Jack Blake, Alaska Trooper and pilot. My job is to serve and protect the citizens in one of the harshest environments in the world. Over a half million square miles and more than forty-four thousand miles of coastline to patrol with too few personnel.

You can see more women dancing at the annual Trappers and Miners Ball in Anchorage than there are troopers in all of Alaska. No police or sheriff departments for backup—often no backup at all in the Bush.

Funny how I got here, fighting battles so far from home as a Bush Trooper. Now it seems this is all I ever wanted to be. I'm not the hero type. Just an average guy, looking for justice. Nothing special. No tougher, no smarter than most, in love with a wonderful lady who I probably don't deserve. Seems like my life has been charged with circumstances that were far over my head. But, now, that's okay, because it's my duty.

Being an Alaska State Trooper is a unique, exciting, sometimes dangerous profession. So is being an Alaska Bush pilot. Since the Bush has no roads, you need to fly to get where you're going. Not all troopers are pilots, just the lucky ones. Which makes me lucky, I guess.

I don't feel lucky right now. I feel hurt, and cold, and bone-weary. There are some days when the job is so great that I feel I shouldn't be paid. Other days, no pay in the world makes it worth it. Today falls in the latter category.

CHAPTER 1

FIRE! It's coming into focus now. It's—well—it *was* an airplane. Now it's just twisted and broken sheet metal in the snow. More a burning trash pile than an airplane. But the tail is still there, pointing at the sky. Painfully, I turn to the crackling on my left. Black smoke, billowing, smelling, and tasting strongly of burning plastic, oil, and something like overdone backyard barbeque—all marinated in highly explosive aviation gas. The morning winter sun is painting the frozen landscape gold-orange and the little sparkling crystals dancing over the ice somehow makes it all look kinda pretty.

Focus Jack, *focus*! Squinting, I'm trying to make sense of what I see—the sky is sideways? Wiping away blood to clear my eyes, I see something familiar just above the wrinkled registration numbers—a shiny Alaska State Trooper decal.

My neck is jammed and why is the ground filling half my view? I'm lying on my right side with my arm pinned under me shivering uncontrollably. Shivering and hurt badly, deep inside. Think, c'mon, *think*! Shake it off! Wake up, get your bearings— evaluate the situation like you were trained. It's cold though. So cold, and the only hint of warmth I feel as I turn my head is the blood running from under my fur hat and down my face. I wipe at it with my hand. Blood? Great. Just great.

I half sag, half roll, onto my back and lift my throbbing head until my chin touches the rough fabric of my survival vest.

I'm trying to focus, but the blood in my eyes is now crusty and starting to freeze-dry. Painfully, purposefully, I look around, finding more bits and pieces, and….a pile of clothing? A wolf skin? No, a wolf skin *parka*. Something, no *someone* inside the parka. Crawling and sliding on my hip and elbow, I force my way over to the parka as heat from the fire just above bastes us with greasy fumes like salmon in a smoker.

He is a dark-skinned man and lays half out of the wreckage. About fifty years old, maybe five feet eight inches tall and two hundred twenty pounds with thick black hair. There is a big seeping hole in that hair near the right temple. The seepage is dark red blood, flecked with gray and white, and mixed with clear fluid. He stares in terror at nothing. Though I already know, I reach for his right wrist, hoping for signs of life. My frozen fingers sting when they strike cold steel, not the still-warm flesh I expect. Raising the sleeve of the fur parka, a black Glock semi-automatic pistol is still firm in his grip. Something is familiar about his hand. A tattoo of some sort, smeared with blood, concealing the pattern.

Who is this guy? Why does he have a gun? Why are we here in what appears to be the middle of nowhere? My mind slowly grinds through the possibilities. Something wanders just out of reach through the fog in my brain but I'm sleepier than I've ever been. The heat from the fire is strangely comforting—even though, in the back of my mind, I know the gas tanks could blow whenever they get the urge. I should move, but the warmth makes me want to curl up and take just a little nap here in the snow by the nice fire. Maybe with a little rest I will be able to figure out what happened, why I'm here and how to get home. Wherever home is.

Before I pass out or die here, I'm going to make a record. A record for myself if I survive or, if not, for somebody—anybody—who cares. I fumble the little tape recorder and a couple extra tapes out of the inside pocket of my parka. A Bush trooper never knows when he might need to interview a suspect and it's senseless not to record it, so I started carrying this around early in my career. I write investigative reports, so this isn't going to be like a best-selling novel with lots of pretty language or prose, just my words as I remember the facts.

Testing, testing, test. Okay here goes.
My name is Jack Blake. I'm an Alaska State Trooper. Note: my life isn't normal. It never has been.

Have you ever wondered how you arrived where you are in life? How something in your original plan didn't quite work out and now you find yourself in a career, a relationship, living a life you never would have imagined way back when you were, say thirteen–years old? Well, that's me now. Wondering how and why I ended up here—in the middle of what looks like the most remote part of Alaska in a tough spot. It's odd how coincidences seemed to collide and, all of a sudden, people and events are thrown together—sometimes with tragic results.

At thirteen years old I never thought I'd have a career where it's not unusual to be dragged out of bed in the middle of the night to jump in a Bush plane and fly through some of the worst weather in the world. Then, after fighting through the scud, snow, or whatever else nature throws at me, having to land on some of the shortest, crappiest excuses for runways man has carved out of the frozen ground. Next the fun part—dealing with a complaint, which usually involves booze, drugs and guns—often, being abused simultaneously.

It's said that near-death experiences cause your life to flash before your eyes. Not for me. Mine have been bittersweet: sheer terror with quick flashes of people and events most important to me thrown in. If those experiences, minus the terror, could be bottled and chugged down like juice every morning, I imagine life would be a little more focused.

There wasn't time for my entire life to flash in front of me when I've been on the sharp edge of death. Unless you're an infant, I don't see how there could be. But now, after the crash, time has slowed down and I can think about it. Wonder about it, marvel at it, really.

CHAPTER 2

Leaning against the rough bark of a towering live oak tree, I was thinking only about the present—the first day of eighth grade. Wiping sweaty hair off my forehead, I gazed over the school grounds. I was a shy kid, but I forced a smile at some old friends and some of the new kids.

It was an early September Indian summer morning. That's a nice name for a hot, sticky, still, Dallas day. Dressed in purple and gold wool uniforms, the marching band looked miserable struggling through "Flight of the Bumblebee." Hundreds of teenaged voices blended into a burbling hum, almost—but not quite—complementing the wavering band. The smell of fresh cut grass, the American and Texas flags hanging limp on the flagpole, kids wearing brand new school clothes and carrying colorful notebooks were signs that things were getting back to business. Summer was over and class work would begin as soon as the bell rang.

Going back to school was an easy break from a summer of cutting brush, carrying lumber, and "go-foring" for a construction company in the unrelenting Texas sun. I had earned a few bucks, got a good suntan on my lanky frame, and even lighter blond hair. I now wanted to learn something more than new cuss words I'd heard from the older laborers. Now I could concentrate on school during the week and only work on weekends. Maybe this would be the year my life would be normal. Things were looking up. I felt at peace. The "Bumblebee" was almost soothing. And, who was that cute girl with the ponytail wearing the short skirt? She looked like she should be dancing on American Bandstand.

POP! I jumped involuntarily. Jerking my head toward the noise, I saw Bill McGrady, a ninth grader I knew only because of his talent on the football field. He grabbed his chest with both hands, teetered, and fell straight backwards onto the school lawn with a thump. The kids around me laughed—it looked just like the old-time cowboy movies when a gunslinger gets shot. Then their laughter choked into screams and I saw the gun.

Felix Rodriguez was holding the black, short-barreled .22 caliber revolver. Standing over McGrady, he turned the muzzle to McGrady's teammate, Bubba Franks, who stood frozen in his tracks. "Please, please don't shoot!" the crew-cut two hundred pound lineman begged, but Felix's finger tightened on the trigger.

I had no delusions about being a hero—heck, I was the *shy* kid—but I could only focus on the gun and all I wanted to do was grab it and stop this madness. Pushing off the tree, I closed the five yards to the shooter. Rodriquez' gun hand came into clear focus: the white lines of knuckles, the red swelling in the joint from the pressure pulling on the trigger. And a strange little tattoo on the back of his hand—a box filled with stripes and a triangle with a star inside it.

Diving the last yard, the gun filling my vision, I saw the finger involuntarily move away from the trigger when the shooter's peripheral vision warned him. Time slowed, everything got quiet. Then contact: with both hands I slammed the tattoo. The pistol flew from Felix's hand.

Looking up from where I landed face down in the dirt, I saw brown khaki pants, a white t-shirt and black shoes as Rodriguez ran away across the schoolyard. Kids were screaming and running everywhere and a teacher was hurrying towards us. Rising to one knee, my young mind examined the wounded boy with curiosity.

Blood. Thick, purple blood was quickly spreading from the center of McGrady's white shirt. The gym teacher skidded to a stop and knelt beside the fifteen-year old. Blowing air into his mouth caused the purple blood to bubble from the wound at a faster rate. The teacher kept blowing, but McGrady's blue eyes rolled back and the color of his face faded to gray, a color I had seen once before on another face. When I was only six–years old I saw that same color on my father's face when he was pulled from a wrecked airplane.

Suddenly, I was hauled to my feet. "Thanks, kid," Bubba said as he picked me up and dusted off my white shirt. I was dazed, looking around, looking at Bubba and the dark wet spot on the front of his pants, and looking at McGrady. The gym teacher stopped blowing in his mouth and the boy's curly black hair slumped back into the dirt. A crowd of students and teachers gathered around the body and me, their voices raised in confusion and fear. Sirens in the distance grew closer and closer, warbling over the excited voices and confused sobbing.

A Dallas Police detective, two television station reporters, and a radio anchorwoman interviewed me, all asking the same questions. I watched the way the other kids looked at me as they passed; some seemed in awe, while others stared as if I was some sort of freak. The principal cancelled the first day of school, so at least some of them were pleased.

"You're a dead man, you know it? Why the hell'd you want to do something so damned stupid?" My big brother Rick was a senior in high school and knew about gangs. Gangs of angry young *white* kids wearing blue jeans with *their* white t-shirts. Gangs of angry young *Mexican* kids wearing brown khakis with *their* white t-shirts. Gangs that, in 1963, didn't have much to fight about except imaginary territorial lines and equally imaginary possession of girls. It all went way over my head. I had lived and played with Mexicans since I could remember and didn't understand what the fight was about.

Rick forced me to walk on the opposite side of the street from him when we went to the corner store on an errand for our mother, yelling, "In case some Mex-gang members drive by and blast you away." That made it clear he didn't want to be in the line of fire.

I didn't know why I had done something as stupid as jumping into the middle of a gunfight. Maybe I'd seen too many cowboy movies on our black and white television, but I wasn't about to admit that to my brother. I didn't respond to his repeating how stupid I was either. I knew better than to challenge *anything* my brother said. He was bigger and stronger than me, and the physical consequences could be worse than the verbal abuse. The next day at school, his point was made.

I was in shop class, momentarily forgetting the shooting, the gun, last night's dreams of the purple blood, the gray face, and the stares of students. I became lost in the simple task of sharpening the edge of my metal shop project. Working material from the chisel, the whirring of the grinder's motor, the smell of hot metal and the sparks flying at the safety goggles took me away from the bad stuff.

Without warning, I was hit hard in the middle of my back. Falling into the grinder, the sounds, smells and flying matter all changed. Dropping the chisel and breaking my fall with the spinning wheel, my right index finger spurted blood. Pieces of skin flew into my goggles. Jerking my hand away, I hit the off switch. Someone put an elbow to the back of my neck and held me from turning to see their identity. But the whispered words were clear: "Amigo, you'd better not be testifying against Felix, you have no idea who that hombre is."

Grabbing a greasy rag to stop the bleeding, I watched brown khakis; a white shirt and black shoes quickly shuttle from the room. What did he mean I had no idea who that "hombre" was? Rodriguez was just a kid. A bad kid in my view.

"Jack, let me see that." The shop teacher reached for the bleeding finger. Wrapping the open wound with gauze and tape he looked sternly into my eyes. "You'll need stitches; do you want me to drive you to a doctor?" I knew that wasn't going to happen—doctors cost money—and we didn't have any to spare.

"Thank you sir, but this will be fine, the bleeding has almost stopped." Blood seeped through the layers of white gauze and the stern look continued.

"How did this happen?"

I lied, "Just got careless, I guess."

The pain in my finger was bad, but worse was trying to figure out why all this was happening to *me*.

I would think about that for more than a month. A long time to think, especially when wondering what was coming next and from where?

"Jack Blake! Report to the principal's office!"

Grimacing and pulling at the gauze that had grown into the new skin of the wound, I replayed the past month in my mind. I closed my eyes and shook my head, listening to the message repeated over the school's public address system. Threats and occasional rough treatment in the hallway from Felix Rodriquez' friends, several whom I had *thought* were also *my* friends, abruptly ended when the police finally found the young felon hiding in a city park. The court accepted his guilty plea and "juvie hall" was his next stop. Rodriquez would be out in three years when he turned eighteen. He'd live a full life, doing whatever he wanted. I was only thirteen, but I had a hard time accepting this as justice for the cold-blooded killing.

"Jack Blake! Report to the principal's office!"

Beads of sweat formed on my temple as I swore at the still-painful wound on my finger, muttering, "what now?" under my breath.

The heavy black walnut door closed firmly behind me as I walked into Principal Fredrick Jones's office. He was a stout man with gray hair and mustache, and black horn-rimmed glasses that saddled his prominent nose. Perspiring from the heat in the airless office, he nonetheless forced a smile while ordering me to sit. Easing into the big green leather chair, I looked at the school's ultimate authority figure with concern and maybe a little fear, as I mentally practiced my lines: "Yes sir, I know it was stupid to grab the gun and yes, it was careless of me to slip into the grinder and no, I won't cause any more trouble."

I wondered why it had taken the principal so long to summon me to his office.

"You've been through a lot in the past month and you're a good student, I want to reward that." Surprised, I shifted around in the big chair, trying not to squeak in the mushy leather. Possibilities raced through my head.

The only good one was a doctor appointment for my finger. My brother told me it was going to get infected and fall off in my sleep—an outcome I feared deeply.

Clearing his throat and straightening his red and blue striped bow tie, the principal rolled his chair closer and leaned forward for eye contact. He had something else in mind: "I have decided that you will be one of three students to represent Alex W. Spence Junior High School for a very special event. Next month, November twenty-second to be exact, the president of these United States will visit our fair city. You will take the bus downtown and have the honor of seeing President John F. Kennedy in the parade. Congratulations." We both sat back.

What about my finger? I wondered, as I pulled at the gauze that had grown into the wound.

Political science wasn't even a school subject yet, much less an interest of mine, but I kind of liked what I had seen of JFK on television. I even had a dream once of sitting next to the president at a football game, like he was my father. I grinned, the first smile in more than a month. I was excited. This would be the first parade of my thirteen-year-old life. Now, maybe now, my life would be *normal*.

"Thank you, sir." Still grinning, I shook the hand he stretched across the desk. The handshake hurt my sore finger, but it was worth it.

"You should see a doctor about that," the principal glanced at the gauze, raising his eyebrows.

I did see the President, and Jackie Kennedy, and the governor of Texas, that day in Dallas. My first parade was one I never forgot.

CHAPTER 3

IDAHO? Why *Idaho*? The worst school year of my life was about to end and my mother had just announced my summer plans. I had my *own* plans. I was planning to again make big bucks working construction, maybe even learning a few new cuss words in the process. I started to argue, but the quick glare from my diminutive mother reminded me that, although she loved her sons, she ran the household with authority, regardless of her stature. I knew better than to argue. She gave us a lot of leeway, which probably helped make me the independent cuss I am today, but she always seemed to know what we were up to, no matter how far away she was. To my brother and me, she was the law.

"Your uncle J.D. in Idaho needs help this summer and he knows you're a good worker. You'll learn a lot and it will be a great experience." She said nothing about me earning wages and I wasn't sure what her idea of a *great* experience was.

The last I remembered of my uncle was the day my dad was pulled from the airplane wreckage.

Well, at least it wouldn't be hot and humid in Idaho, like Dallas summers. And deep down, I knew my mother was doing this for my own good. I'm sure that, at that point in my life, I needed direction, and she was probably more than a little concerned about my welfare with all that had been going in Dallas.

Two days, three stinky Greyhounds and four Louis L'Amour shoot 'em up stories later, I was in McCall, Idaho. It was June 6, 1964. Throwing my army-green duffle over my shoulder, I began the mile hike from the little downtown grocery store/bus terminal to the airport, in the crisp, pine–scented mountain air. Besides the deep blue skies and the imposing, rugged mountains surrounding this hidden village, there was something else. The locals smiled and nodded, acting as if they were downright pleased that I had dropped in on them. Not at all like the big city where people are in such a hurry and avoid eye contact. Before I had a chance to take it all in, a green US government pickup truck, loaded with groceries in the bed, stopped and the driver offered me a ride. The Forest Service smokejumper was headed to the McCall airport, hauling supplies to the base and seemed happy to have company for the short ride.

The McCall airport hadn't changed much in the eight years since my last visit. There was a fleet of fire-attack aircraft on one end of the field and a tiny log cabin flight office on the other, where I was supposed to meet my uncle. Standing in the middle of the wide gravel ramp, I took in the surroundings—the airport, the mountains, the colorful little airplanes—it all seemed so peaceful. That peace quickly ended.

The snarl of a racing engine and the growl of tires skidding in the gravel made me try to dash for the safety of the building. But my course was cut off and I had no place to run, so I stayed right where I was—in the middle of the parking ramp. Raising my duffle in front of me for protection, I braced for the impact. A small plane, which I had thought was crashing, skidded right up to me in a turn, spitting rocks from the gravel taxiway and slid to a stop in a thick cloud of dust.

Something was familiar about the silver plane with the throaty engine, but before I could decide what, the door kicked open and a pair of worn work boots popped out.

"*Jack!* Jack Blake, you little bugger, get your tail over here." Limping through the settling dust, a man—dressed in jeans, a blue down jacket and a tattered, stained, once-red cap—waved. Although a little shorter than my five foot ten inch frame, the forty-something man with the tanned face, white beard and kind, blue eyes, spoke with a voice that commanded attention.

Texas-stained, but without the drawl I was used to in Dallas, his accent was just recognizable.

"Hello, Uncle J.D.," I said, extending my hand for a polite shake. Ignoring my outstretched hand, he grabbed me in a full bear hug, lifting my one hundred sixty pounds off the ground with ease.

"Welcome to God's country, Jack. Throw your bag in the heap and let's blow this place before the flies do. And drop the 'uncle,' you can call me J.D."

At the same pace as in Uncle J.D.'s arrival, we raced to the runway and took off in a few hundred feet, banking steeply toward the big mountains. Before I could answer the rapid-fire questions thrown at me about my Greyhound excursion, J.D. began a narration.

Looking first at the grizzled face of my uncle for reassurance that he knew what he was doing, I turned my attention out the airplane's window. I didn't have time to think about being afraid of flying, as I had thought I would. I'd had seven years to consider the horrors of small planes since my father's death in one. Instead, the beauty of the rugged green and gray terrain entranced me. Except for the one trip I made here with my father when I was only five, my wilderness experience was a tiny, damp spot called Turtle Creek in Dallas.

As we swept along, J.D. offered a story for each point he thought worthwhile. Lick Creek, Idler Lakes, Nick Peak, "that's almost nine grand elevation," Wildcat Creek, Deadman Bar. I wanted to know if more than a dead man was found there, but there was no break in the travelogue. Fish Lake, The Pinnacles— "that's nine g's for sure." Bear Lake and Cougar Basin, "good hunting spots," were tossed at me while we bounced over threatening rocky peaks. "Okay, hold on, we're going to pop through Bear Trap Saddle, drop down along Rush Creek and we're home."

Home was a little section of land, cut out between big rocks and a creek. I was sure there was no way we were going to get down between the canyon walls, land on the grass, and stop before careening off the end to certain death. Banking sharply, simultaneously pushing, twisting and pulling the controls in the airplane, J.D. swooped low over the end of the runway and, with a buzzer screaming, eased onto the grass. Stopping short of the halfway point of the field, the airplane skidded to an abrupt halt, pushing me forward into my seatbelt. Taking my first breath in a long time, I released my death grip on the instrument panel. I was simply relieved I was alive. Regaining my composure and remembering my manners, I complimented the nice landing. "The beauty of the Cessna 180," responded my uncle.

The main lodge building was constructed of sturdy logs. It was imposing, but at the same time, welcoming. The south wall was almost all windows, overlooking a grassy meadow leading to a creek with rugged mountains looming in the distance. A massive river rock fireplace dominated the north wall. Log furniture, padded with heavy dark leather, encircled a red Oriental rug in front of the hearth. An elk-antler chandelier hung from the high ceiling and a rock and wood bar divided the great room from the kitchen. It reminded me of the Ponderosa from the television show "Bonanza." I expected to see Hoss and Little Joe walk in any second. Instead of the dead animal heads one would expect on the walls of a rustic lodge, there were mostly photographs. Black and white photos of people, animals and scenery, which I would study later.

Something took me to a glass box, mounted between the photos. Behind the glass was the most amazing display that I'd ever seen. Green leaves surrounded a five point gold star with the Statue of Liberty in its center. I couldn't make it out for certain, but what looked like an airplane with arrows was attached to the star with "VALOR" written above it. All this hung from a blue ribbon and the centermost part of the ribbon was filled with gold stars.

"Come on Jack, I'll show you your room." It was the first room of my own, complete with a log bed, a soft mattress, and colorful handmade quilt that my uncle said was a "Log Cabin" pattern, made by his mother. The bathroom was down the hall, but hey, I had my own room.

Supper was elk meat, fresh vegetables, and homemade sourdough bread with huckleberry pie for dessert. J.D.'s eyes became misty when he spoke of his wife Betsy who had died in a rock-climbing accident four years earlier. Originally running the ranch as a base for hunters, J.D. found guiding wildlife photographers and fly fishermen, running raft trips on the Salmon River and flying government biologists for wildlife studies was more to his liking. He kept eight horses and hired four guides for the season. My job was to help the guides, care for the horses, assist with the haying and the "hundred or so," other duties as assigned.

Sitting in front of the big fireplace after we cleaned the dishes, J.D. entertained me late into the evening with stories of wolves, elk, bears, bighorn sheep, moose, mountain goats, cougars, deer and a bunch more critters, along with the occasional big fish tale. Then he threw in a short, but fascinating, history of the ranch. Built on land once roamed by the Sheepeater Indians, the site was homesteaded in 1911. "Cougar Dave" hunted cougars for bounty and also trapped, prospected, grew crops and guided hunters, selling it in 1934 for a guest ranch. Later, in my room, I fell asleep thinking of my uncle's stories, wondering what adventures lay ahead for me.

"Breakfast!" J.D. bellowed. Looking out my window, I saw it was still dark. "Let's go, we've got a busy day!" After the best breakfast of my young life—sourdough pancakes with huckleberries and smoked elk sausage—I was led to the barn, introduced to the horses and was getting detailed feeding instructions when a skeleton in the rafters surprised me.   The carcass was made of metal tubing and loose fabric. It was an airplane. The faded yellow color pulled feelings from deep inside me as I stared, motionless, until J.D. spoke. "Ah, I see you found it. That was your dad's Super Cub—the one he crashed."

"He was loaded with elk meat, the wind was really blowing and he got into trouble turning to final in the turbulence," J.D. spoke, nodding towards the airstrip. "He spun in. Didn't have a chance."

My father's gray face of death flashed before me, but for some reason, the skeleton intrigued me more than causing me grief. I would see Dad's gravesite, alongside my aunt's, at the end of the airstrip on another day. "Can we get it down, so I can look at it?"

I just realized that it's cold, the fire is almost out, and I better shake this off. The heat of Texas sounds good right now. I better pick up the pace and keep talking if I'm ever going to get to Alaska in this story.

"Hold the wingtip on that elk. Yank it around in that canyon, right up against those rock walls. Don't be afraid of tearing the wings off, this is a Cub. Okay, now let's do a four rotation spin. Anybody can recover from a stall. Now, land on that gravel bar and stop this thing in two hundred feet!"

My uncle took me in like a son and I learned about the wilderness and airplanes and life. Together, we rebuilt the Super Cub and he taught me to fly, without the benefits—or hindrances—of a city airport.

Although not legal, I soloed at fifteen. I got my private pilot's license at seventeen, and the commercial rating at eighteen, all thanks to my flight instructor/uncle. I earned my keep by taking guests into the backcountry, first by horseback, then in the Cub and then the 180. After seven hundred hours of flying, I made my first landing on pavement when I took the 180 to Boise for a new engine.

Except to visit my mother at Christmastime, I didn't go back to Dallas. J.D. had taught school in McCall before buying the ranch, so he was my home-schooling teacher, with curriculum from the State of Idaho.

A believer in physical conditioning, J.D. insisted we start the day with a vigorous run, or snowshoeing and Nordic skiing in the winter. Next was a session of Kalaripayattu—an ancient martial art, of which my uncle was a master. The Kalaripayattu discipline taught that there is nothing more worthy than a battle fought in the path of duty. Earning merit badges of bruises, I learned how to defend myself with my hands and various fighting tools, including my uncle's favorite, the tonfa. Fashioned from local hardwoods, it was basically a thick stick about two feet long with a handle protruding from the side near the top. J.D. cut grooves into the handle for gripping and sanded the end into a knob. He taught me how to block blows for defense. Better yet, he also taught me how to strike blows, setting up a practice dummy fashioned from an old duffle bag.

When I questioned the value of learning self-defense way out in the wilds, J.D. explained that martial arts develops coordination and good coordination makes for a good pilot. He sold me on that and I began to see the control stick in the Cub as my "airplane tonfa." Another of J.D.'s interests was shooting. Long rifles, shotguns and pistols—it didn't matter. He was a master with all. Using his .308, he taught me how to dial in a target, compensating for wind, terrain, and bullet drop. After a season of tutelage, I could repeatedly hit a small can from the length of the airstrip.

"Church of the Woods." That's what my uncle called his inspirational talks to me. His belief was that a person could have a church wherever he wanted and that a formal facility was not needed. That was appropriate, since there was no church structure within an hour's flight of the ranch. J.D. would quote scripture, always relating it to our current situation, like the day of my first solo. *"And he rode upon a cherub, and did fly: yea, and did fly upon the wings of the wind,"* J.D. said as he climbed from the backseat after we had made three touch and goes that morning. I had no idea what that meant until he added, "take it around the patch."

Pouring the coals to the 150 horsepower Lycoming, the little plane performed much crisper without the weight of a passenger and it jumped off the grass runway. Breaking from the ground, I realized I was on my own. There was no one to urge me to add rudder, or to lower the nose so I wouldn't stall. I was full of fright, full of thrill, full of freedom—all at the same time. Making a climbing turn, I looked back at the ranch. Climbing higher, it now seemed tiny. I looked between the crossbars to the blue sky and understood the scripture.

CHAPTER 4

Leaving the ranch wasn't my choice, but J.D. insisted I give college a try. "It wouldn't hurt you to learn something from the smart guys at the university." I enrolled at the University of Idaho in Moscow in the fall of '68. J.D. arranged for me to room at a friend's farm in exchange for taking care of the livestock. There was a nice pasture, making a decent runway for the Cub. I'd fly back to the ranch on weekends, when the weather permitted and J.D. could clear the airstrip of the deep snow.

I worked summers at the ranch, but it wasn't the same being there only part time. Then in the fall of 1970 my life changed again. J.D. announced he was selling the ranch. "I'm tired, Jack, worn out and not up to chasing horses around the mountains anymore." I suspected there was more to this rash decision, but he wasn't talking and I knew better than to probe. Although he had plenty to say, my uncle spoke little of himself.

Talk about wanting to "find yourself" in college, I had no idea what I wanted to do. I found myself studying just to pass tests. Passing those tests would only earn me a degree to qualify me for a career I didn't want. I could leave school and get a flying job somewhere, but the military draft was looming. I was considering enlisting in the Air Force, hoping to fly an F-4—my vision of a hot rod Super Cub, and the only thing the military had that I wanted to fly. Then one evening the phone rang.

"Jack Blake? This is Bob Smith. Your uncle gave me your number. Can we meet?" Curious, and not wanting to offend a friend of my uncle, I agreed.

What harm could come from a simple conversation?

Studying a cup of coffee in a little café off campus, the hard features on his face looked out of place with the mostly longhaired students. Flavored with a slight Spanish accent, Smith spoke briefly of his relationship with J.D. "We served in Korea together. He was quite the hero. Medal of Honor, you know. Too bad he got shot down." I never knew my uncle was in Korea, much less a hero. "J.D. wouldn't want me to talk about it, but I'll just tell you, he saved my ass and a lot of other guys', strapped in that F-84. Man, can he fly an airplane—any airplane!"

Smith focused his dark, close-set eyes on me and I knew the chat about the old days was over. His face turned from the friendly, war buddy of my uncle's to that of a warrior, a killer. Suddenly, it occurred to me that I knew nothing about this guy. I started to wonder if Smith was his real name, but his next words broke that thought. "I have a proposition for you."

"J.D. told me that you are a helluva pilot, so how about flying for our little company?" Before I could answer, he went on, his posture and stare even more intense. "Pilots working for us are exempt from military service, as our flight operations support the troops. The pay is tops and so is the adventure. The fleet is pure Bush stuff and you'll like that. And, if you want, I can arrange a job for you in the real world, once that mess in Nam is over."

It sounded great so far. I asked about the downside. "It can be dangerous and, well, you are limited about what you can talk about after it's over."

I studied Smith. I thought about what he said, and thought about the ranch and my uncle. I knew there was a reason J.D. had sent Smith—he wanted me to have something now that he was giving up the ranch. And he probably didn't want a kid following him around in his new life.

Making a quick decision, I reached out and shook Smith's hand, asking the only important question: "When do I start?"

CHAPTER 5

Stick it on the ridge." It was my first flight with Ace Jackson, the tall, thin dark-haired pilot from Oklahoma who looked like he should be roping cows instead of flying airplanes. After an hour of steep turns, stalls, chandelles, and three touch and goes, he ordered me to land the Helio Courier on a little piece of dirt cut out of a mountaintop. It was a one-shot deal—cliffs at the end meant a go-around attempt was impossible. I had studied the flight manual and memorized the short field landing procedures, but didn't feel ready for setting the big plane down on the four hundred foot strip. But at least I had a high-time instructor at my side. He'd certainly take over if things went badly.

After saying my goodbyes to J.D., I threw some tarps over the Cub and stuck it in the back of a faded red barn on the Moscow farm. A month after first meeting Smith, I was in Laos munching down on spicy sticky rice and laap, a mixture of chopped meat, spices and uncooked grains that are dry-fried and eaten with raw vegetables. My new home was a base camp with a collection of ramshackle hangars and Quonset huts on a dusty strip lined with short take off and landing aircraft—Helio Couriers, Beavers, Turbo-Porters, Otters, along with C-123 and Caribou transport aircraft.

Instead of a comfortable room, like on the ranch, I bunked with eleven older men. The barracks were littered with beer cans, clothes, girly magazines and trash.

It was always too hot and everything smelled like dirty socks, but I was in the presence of an impressive group.

Ace, Batman, Big Daddy, Grits, Nuts, and Viper—the other pilots, were mostly World War II vets and all were high-time pilots. Their attire ranged from mechanic's overhauls to leather flight jackets to shorts and baggy shirts. Because of my youth and the Idaho connection, I was tagged "Kid Spud." Sure, "Ice Man," would have been cool, but I was still wondering how I could have possibly been chosen to join the ranks of these highly skilled aviators and was glad to be called anything that didn't involve a cuss word.

A little high on long final....cut power, good, now a little low...add power and ease the nose up. Was I set up right? The landing zone looked really, really short. Was I going to overshoot the strip and crash into the cliff? We were a half-mile out and my hands were rubbing the controls. I could feel Ace watching me wipe my palms on my pants. Now on short final—I wasn't sure—was my speed too high? "*Click*." My head jerked to the right to the source of the distraction. Ace was unbuckling his seatbelt. "Good luck," my instructor said, sliding his seat back and folding his arms.

I guess I didn't scare Ace too badly. He signed me off for the first phase of my training. After ten more hours of dual instruction by two more of the old-timers, I was cut loose in the Helio Courier, known as the U-10 in the Air Force. Designed by M.I.T.-trained engineers, the high-wing tailwheel Bush plane could fly into the shortest strips and get back out with a big load. It could hold up to six, but we usually flew with the backseats out to haul cargo.

When he recruited me, Smith hadn't bothered to tell me that I would be flying for Air America, with more than two hundred other pilots, and that it was operated by the Central Intelligence Agency. He also didn't tell me about the nature of the missions in this land of the monsoons and that I would be shot at—and shot at often. Nor did he tell me how it would feel when I shot back, but I got over that. He was right about the good pay though, and there was plenty of action. Air America was a well-kept secret for years and there are still things that shouldn't be discussed, although most are now de-classified.

Smith didn't run my outfit, but dropped in occasionally in a C-123. The word among my bunkmates was a hard-core Special Ops guy called "F-Rod" ran the show. No one I knew ever saw him, although he handed out assignments. I would have liked to personally thank him for some of the ones I drew.

One of those assignments marked the turning point in my Laos vacation. I was dispatched with the Helio Courier to a "Lima Site" to pick up a couple of Special Ops guys who were survivors of a rough attack. The rest of their unit was wiped out. We were just breaking ground from the mountain top strip when we came under heavy fire.

Forcing all 295 horsepower out of the Lycoming engine, we clawed for the sky at the max climb angle. I don't know how high we were, because the familiar scary sight of tracers searching for the Helio commanded my full attention.

Rap, rap, rap. By then, I'd been shot enough that I knew the sound of bullets hitting aluminum. Before I could ask the G.I.s if they were okay, the right-seater yelled.

"*I'm hit! I'm hit!*" The soldier screamed.

Blood, first in a spray, then in spurts, flooded the inside of windscreen and the instruments.

"*Da ya think?*" Snorted his companion in the back seat, followed by a vicious laugh. The significant amount of blood did make the injury apparent, but that humor at that particular moment seemed out of place. Suddenly, the injured man began violently convulsing, and then went totally rigid. The seizure forced his right leg solidly into the airplane's right rudder, while he jerked back into the seat with both hands grabbing the control yoke. Fortunately, the unique aerodynamic design of the Helio Courier prevented the outcome expected of most airplanes subjected to such abuse—it didn't spin. But, considering the added threat of the unfriendlies on the ground, I still had my hands full.

"Get him off, get him *off!*" I yelled at the comedian in the back while slamming my right arm across the injured soldier, fighting for control of the airplane. It was too late. The plane began a sickening slide to the ground—and we were still taking small arms fire.

The back seat soldier lunged forward. With a chokehold, he yanked his buddy away from the control yoke. I smashed the power in and jostled the control wheel forward to gain flying speed. Glancing out the right glass past the dead solider, I saw the shooters scrambling for cover. They were probably thinking we were going in for a Kamikaze attack.

I finally got the shaking bird back close to level, but we were far too close to the ground. Hitting hard, we bounced sideways back into the air and wobbled, barely gaining lift, chewing through the brush on the side of the airstrip like a chain saw.

Managing to climb about three hundred feet above the ground in the struggling, damaged airplane, I sensed for the first time since the initial gunfire that we were going to make it. For a moment, I thought of my father. I now knew the fear he must have felt for those brief seconds as he sped uncontrollably, face first, into the earth.

"Do you believe in God?" The rear seat soldier yelled. Before I could answer, he went on. "Why not believe? If you're right, you will end up in a good place. If you're wrong, at least you've led a good life." That little piece of wisdom took my mind off the shaking airplane as we limped back home.

Landing back at base in a shot-up plane with two grunts, one dead, we pulled off the taxiway. Jumping, no falling out of the wreck, I took note of shrapnel wounds to my right arm and the multitude of holes in the Helio. Looking up to the sky, I muttered a "thank you," and promised to give up flying forever.

Okay, this story is in Alaska, finally. My arm is numb, but the shivering has lessened and I'm sitting up now. I just have to flip the tape over and continue. The wind is picking up and, damn, it's cold! Chuckling, then a soft whistle, drew my attention to the brush behind me. My mind told me at first it was a rescuer, but then I saw the bird.

Chapter 6

Splashing into the current of a fast running stream, the little plane wobbled onto the rocks with the brakes locked. It wasn't a landing technique—it was a crash that ended well. Nick Rotner logged his flying hours in P-47 Thunderbolts during WW II. While he still had the fighter pilot's attitude, he had lost the skills and the eyesight required to fly in the Bush. Sitting in the backseat of the Super Cub, I kept my mouth shut, even though each landing made me cringe and hang on for my life.

A man shouldn't make promises he can't keep. I should have known that to hunt and fish in Alaska, you've gotta fly in small planes. Smith, with authorization from "F-Rod," got me out of Laos and into a totally different world as an assistant big game guide in Talkeetna, Alaska in June of 1972.

Rotner, master guide—and my boss—was one of the most miserable, disagreeable characters I'd ever met. He knew nothing about my background, other than that I did some flying overseas and worked on a ranch in Idaho. He didn't ask more and I didn't offer more.

Rotner worked his crew hard. In between hunts, I was assigned to run his homemade sawmill. It was a big blade powered by a long belt attached to the drive wheel of an old pickup truck. The one pleasant thing about our base camp was Lisa Rotner. Somehow, Nick convinced her to marry him, and then he dragged her from Anchorage to his camp in the Talkeetna Mountains. She prepared the best meals she could with what she was provided.

Among her specialties were cold moose heart sandwiches on homemade bread and meatloaf featuring half moose meat and half sawdust from the mill. The crew was so hungry, after twelve hours of backbreaking work, that there was little complaining about the menu.

The learning curve to becoming an Alaska big game guide was steep, but my co-worker Ray Genet, a great guy with a mischievous sense of humor, led the way. Ray was a McKinley mountain guide who was so strong that, while marching across the tundra stalking game would often carry his out of shape and spoiled hunting client's pack along with his own. Ray was the only one who could call his own shots while working for Rotner.

"Fair chase" wasn't a concept practiced by Rotner. After a full season of what seemed like the endless slaughter of moose, grizzly bear, caribou and Dahl sheep, with Rotner employing all the illegal means known to unethical guides, I was ready to try something different.

A team of seven sled dogs, along with an oak sled and all the harnesses and rigging, set me back three hundred dollars. The dogteam led me to the hills to "live off the land." Living off the land actually meant busting my tail creating a tiny log cabin out of the forest. The few harsh winter daylight hours were spent searching for firewood to feed the potbelly stove, keeping the cabin temperature just above the freezing mark. Instead of living off the land, I lived off my savings to feed my dogteam and myself and pondered what I wanted to do for the rest of my life. After half of the winter had passed, I knew it wasn't being a hermit in the woods of Alaska.

CHAPTER 7

Talkeetna's parking meter didn't work—some local character had stolen it in Anchorage and planted it in front of the bar
as a joke—but it functioned well as a dog anchor. I was tying up
the dogteam when a familiar rumbling sound above the trees
grabbed my attention. The rumbling suddenly went silent and a
gleaming aluminum plane descended over the downtown street
and gracefully landed between the old buildings. For a second, I
forgot J.D. had died from cancer while I was in Laos. This Cessna
180 looked just like his.

"That's Don Sheldon, the Bush pilot," offered a trapper,
noticing my fascination. After cramming the sled's ice hook into
the snow to ensure the team wouldn't follow, I walked across the
street to the snow-covered airstrip.

Simultaneously killing the engine and popping open the
door, a man I guessed to be about my uncle's age, slid out of the
plane. He was dressed in a bulky down parka, wool pants, and
heavy winter boots. A red stocking cap sat on top of a polished,
smiling face. Almost running, he grabbed an engine blanket from
a box near the edge of the runway and in one quick swoop,
secured it over the engine cowling. His grin, his demeanor, and
maybe the airplanes on his ramp, made me want to get to know
this guy better.

Like my uncle, I knew this pilot had it together. He
worked fast, but with precision. I said nothing as I watched the
post-flight procedure, which he had obviously done many times
before.

Finally, the pilot noticed me. "There you are, let's get going, time's a wasting. Jump in the Cub, I'll be right there." Sheldon pointed to a ski-equipped red Super Cub perched in the snow next to the 180, and ran into the house.

I started to protest, but I'd heard a lot about this famous pilot and knew he must have a mission that needed immediate attention and, hey, who was I to argue with a legend?

The door slammed as Sheldon ran out of the house. He smiled and stretched his hand out, saying, "Don Sheldon, good to meet ya. Did Trooper Daniels send you?"

"No, I just…" I tried to answer, but Sheldon interrupted.

"Well, no time for chit chat, let's get up to the mountain."

Bouncing from the crusty snow after accelerating for just a matter of seconds, Sheldon laid out our flight plan as he turned the Cub towards Mt. McKinley. "Don't know how much Big Dave told you, but he got a report that some climbers may be in trouble up on the mountain. We need to take a look-see and make sure they didn't fall in a crevasse or something. Here, take the stick for a minute and point us to that big white hill while I grab a bite."

After a few minutes of munching on jerky, cheese and a mixture of what looked like grains and nuts; Don grabbed the microphone and called his base station. "Roberta, we're headed up to the mountain, probably will start around Ruth, then wherever the trails and winds take us, see you in a couple." I kept the little Cub, now buffeting in the winter winds, pointed at Mt. McKinley, which, at over twenty thousand feet tall, was hard for even a rusty pilot to miss.

"Say, you're doing good on the stick. You must be a pilot," said Sheldon as he finished his meal and sipped tea from a red and silver thermos.

"I was, but since riding in the backseat with Nick Rotner, I pretty much stopped flying."

"Heck, flying with Ol' Nick would make me give up flying too!" Without detail, I explained that it wasn't Nick's flying, although I admitted that didn't help.

"Well, that's too bad, 'cause a guy needs to fly to get around in this country," Sheldon offered. "Now, how did you hook up with the troopers?"

Before I could try to explain again that I wasn't with the troopers, Sheldon shouted and jerked the left wing toward the glistening ice and snow of the glacier we were now over. "Look! Right down there. Climbers!" I counted eight on mountaineering skis, all wearing bright colors, contrasting against the icy white. "There should be twelve, so four are missing. We're going to have to land and check this out."

Land? Land where? I quickly scanned the surface to find a landing area. The skiers were in an oval-shaped bowl. One end of the bowl rose straight up, continuing a climb to the threatening ice peaks of Denali. On the sides, steep, jagged cliffs with knife-like points seemed to want to impale our little plane. The other end of the bowl was just a nightmare.

Skimming the rock wall on Denali—so close that I was sure contact was imminent—Sheldon whipped the Cub into a modified chandelle aerobatic maneuver and dove back to the bowl. Sinking lower and lower into the snowfield, the bright white and lack of contrast prevented even the most experienced Bush pilot from knowing how high we were above the surface.

"Seventeen hundred RPM and fifty miles an hour. That will get us down," shouted Sheldon, focusing on the tach and airspeed indicator. Silently gliding in the white soup for what seemed forever, I involuntarily calculated the remaining length of our landing area after we would finally touchdown. Could we stop before dropping into that nightmare at the end of the bowl?

Maybe Sheldon was overrated—maybe he had lost his touch. Our little world inside the cockpit got very quiet. Even though I couldn't see ahead, my other senses became more acute. I could smell the tea in Don's thermos. I could hear one rough cylinder in the Cub's engine. With the plane's nose pulled up to the sky, it seemed to be taking forever for the skis to find terra firma. Finally, with a slight bump and an explosion of powdery snow all around us, Sheldon yanked the throttle back and we settled deeply into the fluff.

I was pretty sure we had escaped the nightmare, but was anxious to confirm that as soon as I could. The skiers arrived as Sheldon and I began pushing on the Cub's clamshell door against the pressure of the snow. After their digging and our shoving, the door opened and we were extricated from our craft, which was listing in the snowfield like a beached sailboat. The extreme cold and thin air were tangible as I sank to my knees in the fluff and my nose hairs froze.

"What brings you out here on this beautiful day?" one of the skiers asked in an Italian accent, half laughing.

Sheldon explained the call he had received from the troopers about overdue climbers and since we only saw eight of the party of twelve, he thought we should "drop in."

"Well, that explains our pilot circling yesterday. That was kinda chicken of him calling the troopers instead of landing and checking on us. The other four are bivouacked with a touch of the flu up on the hill. They should be here in a minute. I appreciate the concern, but everyone is okay. If it makes any difference, I argued with our sponsor to use you, Don."

With a knowing smile, Don graciously answered, "No problem, I'm pretty busy anyway," and shook the climber's hand. Before I could do the same, he offered, "and this is Trooper… what did you say your name is again, trooper?"

"I'm Jack Blake, good to meet all of you," I said, noting that now all twelve of the climbing party were present.

"Now that we know everyone is okay, how about you fellas giving us a hand getting out of here?" Don requested.

"Okay, men, let's get on the snowshoes and make an airstrip. I'm sure Mr. Sheldon doesn't want to spend the night on the mountain," yelled the head skier.

Sheldon tossed me a pair of snowshoes and, strapping a pair on himself, the fourteen of us began stomping out a path in the bowl. From the ground, the bowl—with mountains on three sides—seemed much bigger than from the air. Then I remembered the nightmare departure end of what was to be our runway.

Not more than three hundred feet away, the glacier bowl came to an abrupt end, terminating in a ledge. My first snowshoe tracks were laid directly to the ledge and my fears were confirmed. The glacier broke straight off into space and there appeared to be no bottom as I peered over the edge, feeling the air rising from the depths. Rock ledges stuck out from the sides and way, way, down in the depths I could barely make out what appeared to be trees. Ghost-like wisps of fog rose from the bottom. Looking back at the Cub, I knew in this deep snow there was no way we could get airborne before the drop off.

"How far down would you say, maybe a mile to the valley?" Sheldon, now standing next to me, asked.

Stunned at his estimate, I wondered if he was joking. But, in no place to argue, I nodded in agreement. "Well then, if we make it, this should be interesting." he mumbled.

Make it, MAKE it? What does that mean? Did he really think the two of us, with all of the gear in the Cub, dressed in those heavy winter clothes, in the very thin air, could somehow plow through that heavy snow and get airborne?

In Laos, I'd had plenty of near bowel-loosening experiences, but there I was the pilot and I had some control over my fate. No control now, but the alternative of spending the night on the very cold mountain without gear was not a desirable option.

I watched in wonderment as Sheldon compacted the snow into a little ramp at the ledge. Was that tiny bump supposed to stop us if we lacked speed for liftoff? Had the pressure of his intense Bush pilot schedule finally driven him crazy, or had the altitude starved his brain of the oxygen required for rational decision-making?

Smashing snow for an hour left all of us in a sweat, even in the minus twenty-degree temperatures. The sun was rapidly abandoning the mountain on this short winter day and, whether we liked it or not, the runway was the best it was going to be. We had to go *now*.

Don asked the two tallest climbers to grab the wing struts where they joined the wings and the fastest climber to push forward from behind the port side strut. I tossed my snowshoes into the baggage area and started to join Don in the Cub, but he had other ideas.

"Jack, I need you to push on that strut and run alongside until we get some speed," pointing to the wing strut next to the open door. Before I could question the sanity of this plan, I heard "CLEAR."

The engine roared to life. Don waved frantically at the ground crew to push. It took a lot of muscle power, but the Cub finally inched forward onto the compacted snow and slowly gained momentum. The pushing got easier and I began pumping my legs, now a fast walk, then running as quickly as I could in the snow. I wouldn't be able to keep up to the accelerating plane much longer. I assumed I was going to be left behind. The ledge was coming up much too rapidly.

"Jump in," Don yelled, "jump in *NOW!*" jerking his thumb towards the backseat. My heart pumping, I took one last glance at the rapidly approaching cliff and dove into the back seat of the Cub. Hanging onto the seat frame, I hurriedly rolled over, facing the skylight with my legs dangling out into the cold air.

Don yelled, "Hang on tight." Then, "*Yippee!*"

A flash of panic hit me as the Cub's skis catapulted over Don's ramp, flipping into the air. Then *weightlessness*. Hanging on the best I could—contorted legs still dangling in mid-air—we raced towards the valley floor, far*, far,* below. The Cub screamed through the air in the narrow canyon for what seemed an eternity. I could only pray that the wings stayed on.

Don eased the stick back and we soared into the wide part of the canyon. I took in a breath of the cold mountain air rushing into the cockpit and realized how he earned his reputation.

"Great job, Don. And by the way, I'm not a trooper."

"Yeah, I know," answered the Bush pilot.

That was the scariest flying experience I'd had since I left Laos, but it was exhilarating and I felt alive again.

At that moment, in the middle of the canyon, looking up through the skylight at the mountain we had just leapt off, it hit me—*this Alaska flying could be fun!*

CHAPTER 8

Waiting for us back at the Talkeetna airstrip was one impressive-looking man. Standing next to a shiny white pickup truck adorned with intricate door badges, the Alaska State Trooper wore bright blue wool trousers with a gold and red stripe, a dark blue parka with a gleaming .357 revolver sticking out the side, a fur hat with a badge in the center, and tall wolf mukluks. The lawman's bushy mustache smiled as he waved at the plane. He had to be at least six and a half feet tall. He looked like he had just stepped from a recruiting poster.

"Sorry my man didn't show today, Don. He got the 'Oil Rush,' and up and quit without notice." The trooper explained that, like many other State of Alaska employees, troopers were leaving their jobs to work for the high-paying oil companies building the Alaska pipeline.

"Is that right?" Don asked, shaking his head.

"It ain't right, but it's so." The trooper laughed.

Chuckling, Don admitted that he had assumed that I was the new trooper—I *was* wearing a blue parka like troopers—so he took me along. "Boy, can he mush fast in deep snow," Sheldon added, winking at me and offering an introduction: "This is Jack Blake."

"Jack, good to meet ya, I'm Dave Daniels. You want a job?"

"When do I start?" I was half-joking, but my mind was still rehashing the excitement of my recent introduction to what I thought the job could be. Then I remembered that I'd said the same thing a couple of jobs before, maybe a little *too* quickly. The conversation became serious when Daniels spoke of the fleet of Super Cubs, Cessna 185s, and other aircraft operated by the troopers. Heck, I was living way out in the wilds with a pack of dogs at the time, so it sounded pretty good to me.

Earning a commission with the Alaska State Troopers wasn't as easy as getting a job flying in Laos, but after months of filling out forms, suffering through interviews, a thorough background investigation, a somewhat embarrassing polygraph, and a written test filled with—of all things—algebra, I was in.

While standing by to be called for duty by the troopers, I flew with Don every chance I could, paying him an unusual tariff. Don's hobby was woodworking and he was a true artist. Fortunately for me, the trees around my cabin were loaded with burls, an abnormal growth on birch trees. Don turned these freaks of nature into beautiful bowls and other collectibles. I'd haul the raw material into town on my dogsled, trading each burl for an hour of flying. With Don's help, I found a good home for my dogteam. Strawberry, my lead dog, ran in the Iditarod a year later.

When the days got a little longer, Don flew me in the 180 to Anchorage International, where I boarded an Alaska Airlines 727 and headed back to Idaho to pull my Cub out of the barn. Accomplishing another goal I had had for a few years, I spread J.D.'s ashes from the air over The Pinnacles near the ranch.

After six days of fighting weather following the Alaska Highway, I was back in Talkeetna, putting the flying lessons learned from Sheldon into service in the backcountry. As soon as the ice melted, a local flight instructor introduced me to the fun of water flying. I got a seaplane rating in his well used, but air and seaworthy, J3 Cub on Talkeetna Lake. During that training, I learned the true meaning of the philosophy that it's the journey, not the reward at the end, which is often the most gratifying.

The Rock," as Sitka was called because of its remoteness in Southeast Alaska, is home to the Alaska State Trooper Academy. It was the opposite of the Air America barracks. The building was spotless and the recruits were responsible for keeping it that way. If an inspector found one cigarette butt on the grounds, or one hair in the lint screen of the dryer, the entire class would be forced to do a hundred marine-style pushups—and that was for the first offense. Recruits were assigned four to a room and each bunk was inspected daily for proper condition, by bouncing a quarter off the bedspread. Our blue recruit uniforms had to be perfectly pressed and our leather gear and brass highly polished.

Unlike college—where I forced myself to study for classes in which I had little interest—every bit of the academy training fascinated me. Instead of liberal instructors droning on, trying to impress naïve college students, the instructors at the academy had lived what they were teaching. The three *months* of training provided me with more practical knowledge than my three *years* in college.

The intensive one hundred hour EMT course, along with case law, Alaska statutes and codes, crime scene investigations, and the other police curricula during the six-day workweek at the academy, caused many long nights of cramming. But I wanted to learn and I looked forward to studying for the first time in my life.

Firearms training was the easy part, for unlike hunting game or returning fire from an airplane, the targets didn't move and they were much closer. Physical fitness and hand-to-hand combat were fun, thanks to the ranch workouts with my uncle.

The colonel of the troopers, a distinguished gentleman, with a shock of white hair and facial lines indicating years of hard duty, greeted all the recruits just before academy training was over, asking each his wishes for a training post after graduation. The choices were Anchorage, Fairbanks or Juneau. These were all detachment headquarters where recruits could get on-the-job training with seasoned troopers before being trusted to go out on their own with a gun, a fast car, and all that authority. My answer was Fairbanks, thinking it the lesser of the evils when having to work in a big city. Anchorage was like any major metropolitan area, referred to by Alaskans as "as close as you can get to Alaska without really being there." Juneau is the state capitol and full of politicians. Fairbanks was the smallest town and close to the Brooks Range, where I imagined flying my Cub on my days off. Plus, it wasn't too long a flight in the Cub to Talkeetna.

For reasons unknown, I didn't get to join any of my classmates in the cities, but was ordered to show up in the very remote post of King Salmon a week after graduation.

CHAPTER 9

Just a "sleepy little post," the colonel had said of King Salmon—a fishing village three hundred miles from Anchorage on the Alaska Peninsula. By the colonel's description, King Salmon was the sister city of Mayberry and I would be Andy Taylor. I guess the post woke up for my benefit.

All one hundred of the bright blue seats were full on the Wien 737 from Anchorage to King Salmon. Captain George Clayton played "Springtime" on his harmonica over the jet's PA system. I enjoyed that unique bit of entertainment, but the rest of the passengers—mostly loud, rough looking, foul-smelling characters sporting caps with the names of canneries, didn't seem to notice. I wasn't in uniform, but being clean-shaven and wearing clean clothes must have made me stand out.

I asked the Native man sitting next to me about his "sleepy town." "*Sleepy?* Maybe sleepy in winter, but not when fish come." He explained that the towns of King Salmon and Naknek, connected by a 13-mile road, grew from about five hundred residents in the winter to about eight thousand during the summer and fall fishing seasons. "Fishermen and cannery workers are everywhere—the docks, the stores and especially the bars. Then the town is sleepy no more," he sighed.

Peering out the small, foggy window as the jet touched down at King Salmon, I was surprised to see menacing gray Air Force fighter jets. F-4 Phantoms were lined up in front of a big hanger emblazoned with "King Salmon Air Station." It was news to me that the U.S. Air Force was in King Salmon, but I would be reminded almost every night—every time the F-4s scrambled to intercept an unknown threat along the nearby border with Russia.

Walking down the air stairs gave me a chance to survey what little I could see of the town, which seemed cold for June. A fleet of Bush planes, mostly Cubs and Cessna 180s and 185s, were lined up next to the Wien Air Alaska terminal. Three bars and one store provided background for the busy airport hangars. The dusty gray skyline was otherwise uncluttered.

The crew of a battered C-119 "Flying Boxcar," a World War II cargo plane parked near the jet, was unloading familiar cargo. My Jeep, with most of my boxes, was at the bottom of the old beast's ramp. The pilot was throwing more from the cavernous fuselage. After helping unload the rest of my belongings, I thanked the combination pilot/co-pilot/baggage handlers.

"Good luck, Trooper, you'll need it." The old pilot snorted. A hand-drawn map, attached to my transfer orders, led me to the trooper-housing unit and I spent the rest of the day and part of the night hauling the boxes in the Jeep.

I was hoping for a cozy Alaska-style cabin, something fitting for a state trooper in the Bush. What I got was a tattered turquoise and white "Royal Court" singlewide trailer. Jiggling and shaking the broken screen entryway, I had to use the full force of my shoulder to open the warped front door. Stumbling over a wadded-up throw rug and into the metal box, the stench of mildew was overwhelming. Orange countertops and avocado green appliances sulked in the tiny kitchen. Brown lines of mold ran down the walls and the faces of the kitchen cabinets from a leaky roof. The fake walnut paneling bulged and was covered with hairy mildew caused by frost permeating the thin walls in the frigid winters. Pushing on the rotting paneling in just the right spot somehow turned on the kitchen lights. The orange-brown shag carpet smelled of urine and was matted with white dog hair, courtesy of the previous occupant's Saint Bernard. The teal toilet looked ready to surrender, slouching lopsided on the gold vinyl bathroom floor. A torn shower curtain sporting what may have been a tiger—the mildew made it impossible to identify for certain—partially hid a soap scum-encrusted pink tub. Chalky toothpaste stains, peppered with bits of tobacco chew spittings, covered the sink. All of the interior doors showed heavy dog-scratch marks, except for the bathroom door, of which the canine beast had apparently eaten away the bottom six inches. The dark brown bedroom drapes were half torn from the rods. One window was broken and there was a fist-sized hole in the drywall.

Little sparkles from the water-stained ceiling snowed onto the bed when I pulled at the closet door, which fell off its tracks. The place sounded haunted as the wind whistled through unseen holes.

Unpacking the boxes and organizing the dump tired me enough that I became immune to the smell and sounds of my new quarters. I fell asleep about midnight.

I dreamt of flying the Cub over snow-packed mountains and landing on a long, sandy beach. Arctic char attacked the fly I tossed into an ocean-fed stream.

Just as I was landing one of the red-sided beauties, I was blasted out of bed. The whole tin can of a house shook, sounding as if you were in a metal trashcan and people were beating it with hockey sticks. My heart raced to the roar of powerful jet engines. It was as if they were in the living room. That's when I remembered the F-4s and the King Salmon runway, less than a half mile from my bed.

The bedside clock read 2:45 a.m. as I pondered the F-4s racing off into the night to intercept MIGS, dancing along U.S. airspace playing war games.

Glancing at the clock between bouts of restless sleep, I finally rolled out of bed at 5 a.m. The mildew stench reminded me where I was.

CHAPTER 10

The trailer door slammed behind me with the vacuum force of the wind. I eased down the splintered steps to follow the battered roadside sign I had seen yesterday: "Al__ka __ate T_oopers." Wind-driven snow must have eroded the rest of the letters, but the arrow still pointed down the road toward some buildings, so I walked in that direction. After about a hundred yards, something made me turn around.

Silhouetted by the rising sun, a figure strode quickly towards me, kicking up dust on the unpaved road. Squinting into the bright morning sun, visibility limited by the blowing sand, I could make out a brown, flapping, long-coat. Sunglasses hid the eyes and a gun protruded from the side. Bulky, knee-high boots and a Stetson hat completed the outfit of the thin figure.

From a distance, Clint Eastwood in spaghetti westerns came to mind. But it was too far away and the sun was too bright to tell more. I couldn't tell if it was friend or foe. Like when scratching at a fresh mosquito bite, without thinking, my hand moved to the firearm on my hip. Standing still, I waited until the figure got closer. Then I saw the hair.

Coming into focus, the curly blond locks gracing her shoulders, highlighted golden by the sun, flowed beneath the Stetson. "Morning, Trooper, you look lost," a sweet voice sang through the wind. As she came closer, I recognized her uniform as a fish and wildlife trooper. Known as FWP or "Brownshirts," they received the same training at the academy and had the same authority as "Blueshirts," but their focus was primarily on protecting the resources.

In some posts, FWP troopers were the only law enforcement, doing both jobs.

"I'm Jessi Torsen. Everyone calls me 'Jet.' You must be the new guy." She removed her sunglasses to reveal the most amazing deep blue-green eyes. Her upturned pink lips slightly opening to a bright white smile, olive complexion, that very blond hair, and a figure that was not at all like Clint Eastwood's, were pleasant surprises. Rather than an Eastwood western, I thought of the young Daryl Hannah in Splash, only with a better tan and even prettier face. Immediately rendered stupid, I at least managed to get my name out as I shook Jet's soft hand and didn't want to give it back. Mumbling something about how I just got to town and was looking for the trooper office, it must have been apparent how taken I was with her. Until then, I didn't know troopers could be pretty.

"I'm headed down to the river where the Cub is beached, so I'll walk with you. Oh, and excuse the silly hat, I just came from court so had to put on my Sunday best. And the hip boots—I'm traveling by floatplane today. One question for you, Jack, who did you *not* impress at the academy to be sentenced to this hole?"

Shaking my head and smiling, I probably looked like the village idiot at that point. "Someone at the top must have wanted you here, Jack, so watch your back. This is a wild post. Excuse me for saying so, but not exactly a *training post* for a rookie. The colonel is retiring soon and taking one of those high-paid jobs with pipeline security, so he probably could care less. Who knows who pulls the strings these days?"

Fortunately, we arrived at the office before I was required to speak again.

The building was long and skinny. Just inside the entry was a counter that stood in front of a row of desks where a serious-looking clerk with gray hair and granny glasses was typing. Several young guys were scurrying about and a bearded man sat in a corner reading a newspaper. The salt and pepper beard was well trimmed and matched the man's hair. I guessed him to be about fifty and he looked somewhat familiar. Looking over his reading glasses, he yelled in a baritone voice, "Jet, what are you up to? It's been a while." Pushing the swinging door of the counter side, he came around and gave Jet a bear hug.

"Just out protecting your fish and running the poachers into court, Governor." Then I recognized the bearded man as Jay Hammond, Alaska's governor.

"Good for you. *Good* for you, Jet. And who is your new boyfriend here?"

I think it was safe to say Jet blushed as she answered, "this is the new King Salmon trooper, Jack Blake."

"Good to meet you Jack. Welcome to King Salmon. I don't get back here as much as I'd like these days, but I run my set net for a week or so every year. And, please, call me Jay." I was proud to meet the man most Alaskans thought of as the perfect fit for governor. He was a Bush pilot, big game guide, and all around nice guy who cared more about his beloved state than politics.

Jet spent a few minutes filling the governor in on the current fishing season. He spoke about his net site and the fishing run prediction until we were interrupted by a phone call.

"Wow, a clerk, a bunch of assistants and the governor, all here to help me in my new post. This is great." I attempted humor, probably failing.

"Not quite Jack. This is the Fish and Game office, the only state building in King Salmon. The governor sets up shop here when he gets a break from Juneau. Against the wishes of most of the free-spirited biologists, the troopers managed to wrestle away a little corner. We can thank the governor for that."

Offices poked out of the long corridor on both sides. We passed rooms with bearded biologists sitting at their desks, several with fish or furry animals mounted on the walls. Some looked up and nodded, then continued their busy work. Others frowned and turned the other way, as if I was an encyclopedia salesman. "It's red salmon season, so don't expect much of a house warming," Jet explained.

In the middle of the corridor was a closed maple door with a state trooper decal stuck on the wood. Jet unlocked the knob and opened the door to my new office. Papers, books, unfinished reports, a half full cup of moldy coffee, and an ashtray full of cigarette butts littered a heavy gray metal desk. A black chair with a broken back support was plopped in the corner. A clipboard holding wanted posters hung from the wall, next to a photo of a trooper truck in deep snow. The cramped space smelled like an unheated bowling alley.

"Sorry, this place is such a dump. I haven't been in here for a while and didn't know you were coming today or I would have tidied it up a bit. Joe Slovak was a real slob so I avoided this place. The pressure got to him, I guess, and he left on very short notice." Jet grabbed the ashtray and set it in the hall.

Jet gave me the lowdown on the post. The first was the worst news: she wasn't stationed in King Salmon, but in Dillingham, almost an hour Cub flight away.

I was the only trooper on the entire Alaska Peninsula, which extends five hundred miles toward the Aleutian Islands. Part of my work included city police–type duties for the towns of King Salmon and Naknek. And if the district attorney, couldn't, or didn't want to make the trip to our remote and rustic court facility for arraignments or misdemeanor trials, I would fill in for him, but I wasn't allowed to cross-examine witnesses.

I also would be the "jail supervisor." That meant I would book prisoners, and then try to hire a temporary guard. If no one wanted the work, I had to guard the prisoner myself, sleeping on a bunk outside the cell. The prisoner had to be fed, so, if I was lucky, I could buy meals at the local lodge. If they were closed, I had to fix the meals myself.

She added that the local bars were the only watering holes for the entire region, enticing villagers to come to town to whoop it up after trading fish for cash from the canneries, usually causing a sudden increase in my business.

"Okay then, is there a *downside?*" I tried to make light of this gloomy news.

"Well, occasionally I ask for a little help, like right now. Are you up for a flight?"

CHAPTER 11

The blue Super Cub, adorned with Trooper badges on each side of the fuselage and under each wing, was beached just below the Fish and Game building.

Jet popped the floats off with ease on the Naknek River and pointed the Cub downstream. From the air, King Salmon looked much tidier than at ground level. Fishing nets were strung from the muddy beaches into the river between King Salmon and Naknek. Dipping the right wing, Jet explained the short road between the villages was paved right on top of permafrost.

"The first spring after paving, it heaved, and now it's a mess," she laughed. Naknek lacked King Salmon's government buildings, looking much more Alaska-like. Multi-colored wood-plank houses dotted the tundra. Busy canneries lined the beaches.

"The Bristol Bay red salmon fishery is the biggest in the world." Jet's voice flowed through the intercom like one of those female nighttime disc jockeys on a jazz radio station. She went on to explain that greed drove many of the commercial fishermen, especially the non-residents. "The bad guys will break every law to beat the legit fishermen to the run."

Passing over hundreds of thirty-two foot fishing skiffs, the Super Cub zoomed in on one boat a mile past the rest.

"That guy is deep in closed waters," Jet said as she descended toward the boat. "Here, get a shot, please," she asked, handing me a Minolta 35mm. I slid the window back and snapped photos as Jet set up for a landing.

The sea was a lot rougher than it looked from the air. Landing between swells, the little floatplane splashed hard in the saltwater. Water enveloped us as the horizon disappeared. It looked as if we would sink to the bottom of the ocean. Then we had a view of the world as the swell popped us back up. Floating up and down like a cork, with prop spray covering the windscreen and waves breaking over the floats, Jet taxied to the stern of the big boat, motioning to a crewman to throw us a line.

Sliding out of the Cub and onto the float, she tied the rope to the prop hub, and then pulled the plane to the boat. Following Jet's lead, I climbed up the boat's ladder to the deck as the Cub floated back to the end of the line.

"Trooper Torsen, what brings you out for a visit today?" The captain grunted with a scowl.

"Well, let's see, could it be you have your gear out more than a mile into closed waters?"

"Yeah, I guess maybe we drifted past the line a little, but you know how swift the current is here in the bay." If the fish boss was looking for compassion, he wasn't getting any.

"Funny how the other three hundred or so boats out here are less affected by the current than you. Pull your gear and deliver your catch to the tender. Thanks for your cooperation." Jet handed the captain a ticket as he muttered something under his breath. She thanked the crewman for helping us board, and that was it. Short and sweet.

Just when the Cub popped on top of a crest, Jet slammed the throttle forward. After a series of hard skips on the tops of the swells we were airborne in the strong wind. She explained that she tagged the same boat with the same captain, two seasons ago.

"Just like any area of law enforcement, you have crooks," she explained.

As we flew over a tender boat, Jet called on the marine radio, telling them to hold the records for the fish sale from the illegal boat. "You got it, Jet," was the response on the radio. They knew the drill. Jet knew her job and was good at it.

"I'd like to take you to dinner, or maybe *cook* you dinner in Dillingham, but it will have to be another time. I have reports to do and the fishery starts again at six-tomorrow morning. I'll drop you off back in King Salmon."

I had just met Jet, but I knew I wanted to spend more time with her. Our first day together was ending much too quickly. Was it possible she could look like that, be that good of a trooper and pilot and *cook* as well? I'd have to find out later. After docking the Cub on the Naknek River, she spun it around in the water, and then jumped on the right pontoon while floating downstream. She shouted thanks and waved as she climbed into the cockpit. As I watched the little blue plane fly low down the river, I already missed Jet. I'd had a few flings in college, but my life never seemed to be in the right place or running at the right pace for a long-term relationship. Maybe this would be it.

CHAPTER 12

Sweeping low under the sunny skies over the forever glassy waters of majestic Lake Iliamna in 'Ol Yeller, my Lockhaven Yellow Piper Cub, now atop a pair of silver floats, we glided to a smooth landing at the mouth of Talarik Creek. After beaching, Jet tossed me a pack and I unloaded our picnic lunch while she laid a red blanket in the sand. Jumping rainbows in the creek were inviting me to toss a fly just above the clear water, but Jet had my full attention. This was my chance, the setting was perfect and so was Jet. I went in for a quick kiss, to be our first. Just as our lips touched, bells rang.

"Ring, RING, RING! The phone blasted me awake. Jet was gone. Now just the smell of mildew and a screeching, demanding voice on the other end of the phone.

"Trooper, we need you over here at Eddie's, there's a big fight!"

In less than five minutes, I was dressed in full uniform and inside Eddie's Fireplace Inn. Not really an inn, just a long wooden bar covering one wall of a smoky, low-ceilinged building. Booths with torn orange plastic backs lined the opposite wall. There was an empty stage at the far end. Lighted beer signs hung crooked along the walls and the booths were full of what I guessed were fishermen—the same rough type of characters that were on the Wien flight into King Salmon. A drunken couple was shuttling on the dance floor to the honky tonk tune from the jukebox.

Standing behind the bar was a tall and wide redhead. Think Miss Kitty from Gunsmoke, add seventy pounds, double the makeup and triple the red hair, and you have "Big Red."

"Over here honey," she yelled in my direction. "Wow, we sure got an upgrade with the new cop in town, dear."

"Thanks, what's the problem?" Tired, I just wanted to resolve the complaint and get back to bed.

"See those two yahoos over there?" She pointed at two bloodied men slumped back in a booth. "Crazy Mark kicked both their butts."

Walking towards the men, I looked over my shoulder at the barmaid and asked where Crazy Mark was.

"He's right behind you," she squealed with laughter.

Wild-eyed, standing about six four, and weighing at least 260 pounds, wearing a red checkered shirt and sporting a brown beard, he looked like the Bounty paper towel man with a hangover.

In his right hand was a .44 Magnum revolver, pointed right at my chest. Wrapped around his left arm was a dark-haired skinny girl with a broken lip. She barely looked old enough to be in a bar. She was his shield.

That caught me off guard. The academy did a great job of instilling too much confidence in us gung-ho troopers. Some of us came away with the foolish attitude that people respected the troopers and wouldn't *dare* assault one. It surprised me that some dirtbag would have the audacity to pull a gun on one of us wearing this impressive uniform. That feeling lasted about a second.

Troopers were trained to take our chances if someone had the drop on us. After much practice, a recruit could draw and fire before the recruit playing the bad guy could react and pull the trigger of his already drawn weapon. I was ready to put all that practice to practical application. But, Crazy Mark had the shield. A bullet aimed between his eyes would miss the girl—if she didn't move. I wasn't going to take the chance she wouldn't.

"I'll be leaving now, Pig," Crazy Bounty Man snarled. I could only watch as he trudged out the back door of the bar, dragging the crying girl.

Rushing out the front door, I watched an old truck burn out of the parking lot while the hysterical girl was pushed out the passenger door.

"He's going to kill Leroy," the girl sobbed. I asked her for directions as I led her to my state–issued pickup. It took a bit to collect her thoughts in her drunken head so we could find the right trail.

I expected to find two big drunks slugging it out.

Crazy Mark's truck was parked in front of a small house trailer. A wheelchair, with an American flag painted on the back of the seat, was overturned at the bottom of the trailer's stairs. A broken pair of black GI-issue eyeglasses lay next to it.

"No, no, please *no!*" The pleas came from the other side of the shack on wheels. I ran through the darkness in that direction.

"I'm going to kill you, you f...ing little freak!" Crazy Mark's gravelly voice blasted into the night air.

The quadriplegic, all eighty pounds of him, lay defenseless in the dirt. His face was broken and bloodied. His assailant was now working on his ribs, kicking with full force.

"State Troopers, don't move!" I yelled, hoping to stop the beating. It worked. Now Crazy Mark came toward me, raising something over his head. It was too dark to tell what he was swinging, but he kept coming even after my second order to stop.

Trooper Dave Daniels's words of wisdom flashed into my brain: "My goal is to retire from this job without getting shot or having to shoot someone—one really hurts and the other involves way too much paperwork."

My side-handle baton caught Crazy Mark in the right knee, popping his kneecap to the seam of his jeans. That would have taken the average man down, but dragging the crippled leg, he kept coming. Swinging the tonfa back along my arm, I stabbed the end into his soft gut. Apparently strung out on PCP or some other drug, he felt no pain. The air puffed out of him, but then he straightened. Raising a baseball bat over his head, he began an overhead strike at me.

Spinning the baton's handle in my grip, I took out his other knee with a satisfying thud. He went down in a pile. I slapped the handcuffs on and asked him to lie there nicely, or something like that.

Cussing and thrashing in the dirt like a wolverine in a steel trap, Crazy Mark was otherwise immobilized. I quickly moved to the injured one who mattered.

"That maniac dragged me out of my house, saying he was going to beat me to death! *Why?* What did I ever do to *him?*" The victim moaned, drooling blood and a couple of teeth into the dirt.

I assisted Crazy Mark into the truck. Okay, maybe it was more lifting, shoving and pushing. Bouncing face first in the truck bed, I clicked his handcuffs to another pair anchored to the side rail of the truck. He was now secure.

Carrying the victim, now identified as Leroy Taylor, I carefully sat him next to the girl in the truck's front seat, making him as comfortable as possible. She mumbled that the only clinic was at the air base, so we hurried there.

Dr. Kris Shewmake examined Leroy, stabilized him with a sedative, and told me that he would have to be transported by plane to the Dillingham hospital for surgery, *immediately*. He suggested calling the local air taxi, Bristol Bay Air Service.

Once Leroy was feeling no pain, I tended to the still-thrashing load in the bed of my pickup. With resistance from Crazy Mark, the medic and I delivered him to the doctor who, by this time, knew the story. "Doc Shew" promised he would treat him with "kid gloves," then added, "Welcome to King Salmon."

The note on the door of Bristol Air Service directed me back to the bar—"I'm at Eddie's. Pete."

"I can't believe that jerk would beat up on poor Leroy. Here are the keys—it's the 207 on the ramp, gassed and ready to roll." Built like a bull, sporting a balding head and a beard, it was clear that Pete was as drunk as the rest of the bar's patrons, but he did the best thing he could in offering me his plane.

After the medic and I loaded a heavily sedated Leroy in the back of the spacious Cessna 207, I took a quick look at the checklist and chart and then we made a beeline for Dillingham with the morning sun just peeking over the hills. Unfortunately, Jet was away on a field assignment, so after ensuring Leroy would get good medical treatment at the regional hospital, the Air Force medic and I returned in the Cessna to King Salmon.

That was my unofficial checkout in a Cessna 207, and my even more unofficial beginning as a pilot with the Alaska State Troopers.

CHAPTER 13

Under the dark cap, the short and thick bill contrasted with the white forehead. It was a Gray Jay, known as a camp robber to Alaskans. A bird of opportunity, it preys on anything it comes across—whether food left laying around by careless campers, or carrion left from the efforts of another animal or a hunter. Today, it seemed to be more interested in feeding on my former passenger. I crawled over and closed his eyes, which must have been tempting snacks for the bird.

Forty below is cold, especially where you're not moving much. I'm still in a lot of pain, but my mind is kicking into gear and now my thoughts are about survival. All trooper/pilots are required to attend annual safety seminars in Anchorage and part of the training includes a survival refresher. The first element in the winter is to keep warm, so it's good I grabbed a down sleeping bag from the wreckage before the plane totally burned. The bag isn't keeping me toasty, but at least my shivering only comes in waves now. We were taught another thing that surprised me at the time—a common factor among survivors was that they kept a sense of humor. So I'm going to try and remember something that happened in this often-miserable work that was funny. It might hurt my broken ribs a little if I laugh, but if it helps me survive, it's worth it.

Willie the Weed and the Yapper-Snapper

By winter I had become accustomed to responding to Eddie's on at least a semi-weekly basis to break up bar fights. After a few of these untidy events, I had learned to slow down the response. Rather than racing to get to the bar, I'd have a cup of coffee and take my time. When I arrived the fight was usually over and the slobbering drunks were now best friends. No need to join in the fracas, and paperwork was rendered unnecessary.

One cold Friday night, awakened from a sound sleep, I responded to Eddie's, but found no bloody faces, no overturned chairs—just a few customers hunkered over their drinks. By then, Big Red and I had developed somewhat of a working relationship.

"Hey Sweetie, did you come by for a drink? I get off at 1 a.m." She seemed far too calm. Then it hit me—the wakeup call wasn't from Eddie's, my usual complainant for bar fights but, for the first time, the Fisherman's Bar in Naknek. So, driving as fast as the bumpy thirteen-mile road allowed, I arrived at Fisherman's.

The troublemaker had left. The bartender, who was also the mayor's wife, identified him as "Willie the Weed." Willie had tried to steal money from the bar's cash register, becoming hostile when she stopped him. A couple of the patrons tossed him out in the snow. While I was taking the complaint, the mayor telephoned the bar, reporting that he had been called by Helen Rose, who lived just down the street from the bar. Mrs. Rose's husband, the local preacher, was out of town. She had heard her bedroom window breaking.

Walking unannounced into their living room, Willie attempted to steal a television, which Mrs. Rose was watching at the time. When ordered away from the TV, he tried to steal a lamp, a painting, and various other fixtures in the house.

Each time Mrs. Rose yelled "No, Willie!" he would drop the item in hand and move on to the next choice. Willie finally settled on Muffin, the diminutive poodle-mix that was yapping and snapping at his ankles the whole time.

Mrs. Rose last saw Willie as he stumbled down the snow-covered street with the yapper-snapper under his arm.

Willie the Weed was an easy suspect to find, even for a rookie like me. Wavering along the middle of the road, his ear was bleeding from a snapper bite and the yapper was latched onto the cuff of his pants. He seemed glad that I came along, pleading with me to relieve him of the canine.

Readily admitting that he was trying to steal something to trade for his namesake—weed, he extended his hands for cuffing. After returning the dog to Mrs. Rose, I booked Willie into the basement jail and told him to empty his pockets.

The first evidence spilling from his pockets was broken glass. The second was Mrs. Rose's wedding ring. Knowing I wouldn't be able to find a guard at that late hour, I trudged upstairs into the court office to do my report.

At 6 a.m., I walked down to see if the prisoner had slept off his drunkenness, but there was no Willie. Turns out that his rail-thin frame allowed him to slip between the bars and escape. Following his tracks in the snow, I came to the road just as a sno-go raced down the main drag with Willie on the back. The driver told me that Willie had jumped on his snowmachine, ordering him to take him home to his village. Instead, he simply made a big turn around the town, bringing Willie back to the courthouse. The driver introduced himself as the mayor.

Back to Crazy Mark, legally known as Mark Morgen. I forwarded a complaint to the Dillingham district attorney, which included attempted murder, felony assault, and assault on a police officer. All were straightforward, basic charges. The district attorney ignored all counts and filed only one felony charge: "burglary in a dwelling at night."

"The *lawrr* reads the crime is where the *offendoor* forcibly enters a residence to commit a felony, the *felony* in this instance being the assault." With the superior attitude and condescending eastern voice that begs for a punch in the mouth, the state attorney lectured me when I politely asked for an explanation.

Leroy, now mostly recovered from the injuries received three months earlier, openly wept as he watched Morgen strolling from the courthouse with a smirk on his face. The D.A. shook hands with the defense attorney and left without comment.

The jury in Naknek was a mixture of Alaskan Natives and whites, leading ordinary lives in the community. They couldn't find Morgen guilty. One juror approached me after court and explained how they wanted to convict him because of what he did to an innocent disabled veteran, but they couldn't, because nothing was *stolen* from the house.

The Morgen case did end on a happy note. In true "Church of the Woods" fashion, some locals got together and we helped Leroy rehabilitate from his injuries. A better ramp was built for his wheelchair and everyone chipped in a bought him a television and a new, high-tech gadget called a video player. Leroy had a passion for John Wayne movies, and we found six of them on videotape.

That prompted Leroy to quote from *The Man Who Shot Liberty Valance*: "Out here a man settles his own problems." Then he added, "I just wish I could still solve my own problems, I'd love to have had Morgen come at me before I took a bullet to my spine in Nam."

When John Wayne arrived in his battleship gray Lear 24 for a fishing trip, we took Leroy to the King Salmon Inn for a pre-arranged meeting with his movie hero. The Duke's warm treatment of Leroy drew tears and is something I'll never forget. He was a real American, not just an actor.

It gets even better: Pete, the pilot, approached me with a proposition that is only now being revealed. And, if I survive my current little setback, this may be erased from the tape.

Pete, along with a couple more pilots and a few mechanics, conceived a plan to deal with Morgen. He promised that the community would be relieved of the mean-spirited bully once and for all, assuring me that no one, including Morgen, would be injured.

"I can't be party to anything illegal or anything that is done to Morgen against his will." I added that I would be out of town the next day on a trip to Cold Bay.

Nodding with a smile, Pete said he understood. Pete and his crew chipped in and bought Crazy Mark a one-way ticket on Wien to Anchorage. Equipped with the proper tools of encouragement, including baseball bats, they hunted Morgen down like a wounded grizzly. After dragging the menace from his hiding spot on the tundra, they escorted Morgen to the Wien jet.

"You got your perverted 'justice' in that sorry excuse for a court. If you ever set foot in King Salmon again, your next justice will be from a bullet," Pete reportedly said. Crazy Mark took their advice.

CHAPTER 14

Trooper, come quick! Ellie and Frank Manning have gone missing!" The man calling from the village of Ekwok's radiotelephone was excited. By this time I'd flown enough winter searches that I knew the drill—fly to the last known spot of the missing party and follow their tracks. If wind drifts or fresh snow hadn't covered their trail, we usually found them. If not, ground searchers on snowmachines would be called in to help.

"You won't need one." It was a strange reply when I asked if there was a snowmachine in Ekwok I could borrow for the search. How did he know what I would need to search for the villagers? That question kept my mind occupied as I bounced along on the fifty mile icy scud-run to Ekwok in the little Cub, wondering if it was a good thing that I'd become a state pilot.

By the time the Morgen case was wrapped up, I had passed the six-month probationary period for the troopers and was told to report to the department aircraft section in Anchorage. The checkride in the Super Cub started out badly when the checkpilot—a civilian wearing a severely stretched out burgundy sweater vest—started by yelling at me for the way I entered the cockpit. I would learn that Larry Lasso was a very proficient pilot, but had the manners of Archie Bunker chewing out Meathead.

After demonstrating spins, spot landings, simulating canyon escape maneuvers, landing the tundra-tire equipped plane on the beach in the McKenzie Mud Flats, and a few more fun exercises, Lasso ordered me to draw the schematic for a Cessna

185 electrical system on his office chalkboard. Since he seemed a bit hoarse after two hours of screaming at me in the cockpit, and the checkride wasn't even for a Cessna, I thought this was Lasso's way of busting me. Not only had I not read the manual for a 185, I'd never even ridden in one. In a moment of frustration, I drew a smiley face stick figure standing next to a Cessna pointing at a battery. I don't know why, but Lasso signed me off, even offering, "nice flying, Blake."

Suitable for a rookie pilot, I was assigned an old Super Cub that had seen better days. This specimen was mostly orange, evidence it had been transferred to the troopers from the Department of Fish and Game. Somewhere between the transfer and a few dings, numerous blue parts, including one aileron, the horizontal stabilizer, and one complete wing had replaced the orange. Leaving from the Lake Hood airport for King Salmon, the tower cleared the "multi-colored Cub" for takeoff. It was ugly, but most state pilots had to start with a Cub, and at least I finally had a plane. I put it to good use.

Taking off from King Salmon, it was immediately clear that it wasn't a good day for an aerial search—winds gusting to forty-two knots, with light snow turning to sleet and moderate turbulence. The windsock at the Ekwok airstrip was straight out, with a direct crosswind.

I made a low pass over the runway. A layer of hard crust and crud covered the surface. Braking action would be zero, so I pumped the landing gear handle to change from wheels to skis. The landing kept me busy. I used the fifty feet of width to land diagonally across the runway, then scooted across the entire tie-down area. Cranking in full right rudder, and adding a blast of power to lift the tail, I was able to make a hard sliding turn, stopping just short of a solid snow bank.

"Trooper, I take you to Manning house." The Native man wasn't wasting time with introductions, he just pointed to the sled attached to his snowmachine. Standing on the runners reminded me of dog mushing in Talkeetna. Only instead of watching dog tails, I watched the snowmachine spew smelly blue smoke as we rode the trail to the village. Passing mostly government-built frame houses with frozen moose meat and fish hung on racks, we stopped at an attractive log house at the end of town. A pickup truck, the only road vehicle I'd seen so far, was snuggled in the deep snow in front of the residence.

About fifteen villagers were standing around, all stopping their conversations to stare at me. A lone teenage boy stood away from the crowd. I began walking toward the cabin, but the red contrasted with the white halted my crunching footsteps.

Blood—drips of blood, streaks of blood, then pools of blood, then pools of blood containing human hair, surrounded me. Far too much blood for this search to have a happy ending.

The crowd, apparently satisfied that I didn't miss the plentiful evidence, stepped back, mumbling in their native language. Some disappeared into a neighboring house, some walked back toward the main village. The teenager stared at me as he moved fifty yards away to lean against a birch tree.

"Trooper, I go now, you can follow the trail, I don't want to see." My driver left before I could ask more. After picking up four spent 30-06 cartridges, I started on the blood trail.

Two distinct pools of blood—of such quantity that the bright white snow had melted around the deep red—framed the end of the driveway. Some of the blood had frozen into the snow, forming dark red stalagmites deep into the frozen matter. A woman's pink lacy slipper lay on the ice next to one pool. Following tracks and photographing along the way, I made out two deep lines in the snow on either side of boot prints. I could tell that the victims were in a sled, being pulled by manpower.

The sled-puller's boots dug in deeply and led down the trail toward the Nushagak River. A wooden shed, about the size of an outhouse, sat on the bank overlooking the river. The sled tracks, the human tracks, and the blood trail all stopped at the shed door. Blood ran from the shed and froze in a pool in front. A bloodstained dogsled sat next to the shed. Red boot tracks led away from the scene.

After photographing the shed from all angles, I finally had to take the next step. It was dreaded, but necessary.

By all the blood, I knew it was unlikely, but I was still hoping to find the Mannings alive.

Slowly opening the creaking door, two life forms appeared in the darkness. Then my flashlight exposed a horrific site. Frank Manning was on top of, and wrapped around, his wife Ellie. Both were dressed in sleepwear.

Hypostasis—the gravitation of blood to the lowest parts of the body, creating an appearance of severe bruising, had already set in with both bodies. The homicide investigation course at the Trooper academy taught us it takes six to eight hours after death for the effect to commence and up to twelve hours for it to be fully pronounced, so I deducted that the murders must have happened the night before.

After taking more photos and collecting a bubble gum wrapper from in front of the shed as evidence, I took a minute to reflect. If it wasn't for all the blood and trauma to the couples' faces, they could have passed for lovers just cuddling to keep warm. They looked so peaceful, if you ignored their faces. My thoughts were interrupted. Footsteps crunched behind me in the snow. Before I could turn, the intruder spoke.

"Hey, Trooper, you come here often?" Turning, I recognized the voice, then the warm face—sudden beauty amidst the terrible tragedy.

"Jet! It's been too long." Returning her hug, I felt humanized again.

"It sure has, Jack. It looks like you could use a hand here."

Jet and I did another search of the crime scene, finding two more cartridges, another gum wrapper, and a wad of chewed gum. After the unpleasant task of pulling the bodies from the shed and placing them in body bags, Jet excused herself to talk to a man standing on the trail.

Speaking to the Native in Yupik while gesturing in my direction, I could sense Jet was making progress. Shortly she returned with a snowmachine towing a sled.

"Nice work." I said. "How did you learn Yupik?"

As we loaded the bodies onto the sled, Jet explained that she grew up in South Naknek. Her ancestors were Norwegian Laplanders, herding reindeer for a living. Her great-grandmother was Aleut. She learned Native languages growing up in her village and while traveling to surrounding villages with her father, who supplied remote stores with his Cessna Skymaster. He delivered groceries, hardware, fishing nets, and other essentials.

I had one more unpleasant task. The Mannings had three children—four, six and nine. It's always tough notifying family members of death of a loved one, especially when it's a homicide. Telling those wide-eyed little kids was heart wrenching.

Jet and I towed the bodies to the airport with the snow-machine and loaded them into the Cessna 206 she was flying. Jet put her knowledge of the Yupik language to work again, asking the village leader to immediately call a meeting of the village elders. Twenty minutes later, five Native men sat with us at a table in the council hall. One of the elders, who lived next to the Mannings, said that a village kid name Billy wanted to take the victim's truck for a spin. When Frank Manning showed him that the truck was buried in the snow and offered to take him for a ride in the spring when it thawed, the boy threw a tantrum.

He opened fire with a 30-06 rifle. Two bullets to the chest killed Frank instantly. Hearing the shots, Ellie Manning rushed outside of the cabin. Billy shot her twice in the face and once in the stomach.

Jet thanked the men and asked the village leader for directions to the home of the fourteen year-old suspect.

Billy Kayo opened the door. Standing about five feet, six inches tall, and sturdily built, he looked like most other teenagers in the village—except for darting marbles for eyes. Jet spoke Yupik to the boy's mother and then told Billy that I needed to speak to him.

Switching on my tape recorder, I got right to the point: "Why did you kill the Mannings?" Looking at the floor, then moving his marble-eyes from his mother, to Jet, then to me, he responded with a chilling smile.

"They wouldn't let me drive their truck."

Tears ran down Mrs. Kayo's face. She knew what her son was capable of and she knew where he was headed. She told us her husband drowned two years ago running his subsistence fishing net. She would be alone in her small cabin in the cold village.

After reading Billy his rights, taking his statement, searching him—finding 30-06 cartridges and bubble gum in his pocket—I took the rifle from his room. Then I spent a few minutes hauling wood from a pile beside the house and onto the porch. It wasn't much, but at least Mrs. Kayo could keep warm until she got more help.

"I'll take the bodies to Dillingham. Can you transport Billy?" Jet asked, as she secured the body bags to the airplane's floor tie-down rings. Smiling, she added, "I still owe you that dinner, Jack. You need to drop by Dillingham one day soon."

"No problem, and thanks very much for your help, Jet. This has been a sad day, but you made it brighter. I think I owe *you* dinner now." The shackled Billy Kayo stood next to me, his marble eyes watching Jet.

Still smiling, Jet climbed into the Cessna, now serving as a hearse. "You're on, we just have to find the time."

I nodded, trying to calculate when that would ever be. We always seemed to be going in opposite directions with no time to spare.

"Wow, Trooper, getting a plane ride is even better than driving a car!" The cheerful words from Billy Kayo were distressing—he acted as if he was on a field trip instead of going to jail, and seemed pleased that his plan worked out better than he had even hoped. After handcuffing him to the back seat of the Cub, we took off for King Salmon.

Turning to check on the juvenile murderer during the flight, I couldn't believe his demeanor. There no sign of remorse for what he had done. With the darting, evil eyes, he scanned the tundra with a constant smile on his face, looking much older than his fourteen years.

My back seat passenger made me reflect on what my uncle once told me about ultimate evil in one of our Church of the Woods sessions: *"Like a roaring lion, looking for some victim to devour."*

The Dillingham district attorney struck again. Electing not to try Billy Kayo as an adult for the two murders, he was sent to a juvenile detention center in Anchorage. Escaping two years later, Kayo robbed a store in the city and killed the clerk with a knife. At eighteen, he was released and returned to his village where he began an adult life of crime—assaults, attempted rape and other violent offenses, culminating in the murders of three upriver villagers when he was twenty-one. Billy disappeared before the troopers could find him. He was never found. The best guess is that Bush justice took care of Billy Kayo.

CHAPTER 15

You could tell summer was coming. Nasty little "white-socks" were bouncing off the underside of the Cub wings, occasionally dive-bombing in to take a bite of my neck, leaving welts on my skin. Removing the winter cowling covers, I next changed the oil and filter, completing the job just as the Wien jet landed. After picking up tools, loading the truck and swatting more bugs, I drove back to the office to tidy up a bit. I was surprised to find someone sitting at my desk.

"Sit down, Blake. I'm First Sergeant Lutz." His pudgy hand presented a limp grip. It reminded me of picking up a day-old silver salmon from a riverbank.

"Where's your tie?"

I was cut off when starting to explain the ludicrous aspect of wearing a tie while working on a plane. In fact, I found it highly impracticable for anything but court and funerals. However, I thought it wise not to share that line of reasoning with the First Sergeant.

"You have to respect the uniform, then the public will respect you."

I studied Lutz's face to see if he was joking. He wasn't. Then I examined the rest of him. His stained tie sat on top of his very prominent gut. The tie rested about halfway between the fat overhanging his belt buckle and his second chin. He lacked a neck, so his flushed, pasty, round face sat right on his collar.

His shiny shoes moved pigeon-toed as he waddled around the small office, expounding the virtues of keeping a sharp appearance.

Since this was the first post visit by a supervisor, I was taking my chewing out with great interest. It didn't anger me. What could they do as punishment, transfer me to *King Salmon?*

My rookie tenure in King Salmon was successful overall. I busted my tail all year, taking only a total of eight days off, without putting in for overtime. *Donate to the cause,* was my thought, as I was learning on the job. I filed more than sixty cases. Only six required a trial, and all but the Morgen case ended in convictions, so what I heard next was a surprise. The first sergeant had an award for my dedication.

"The colonel wants your talents elsewhere. Pipeline construction is going full bore and the oil workers—from Texas, Oklahoma and who knows where else—are raising hell. Fighting, bringing in whores, gambling, that sort of thing. So you're being transferred to Glennallen—right in the middle of the action. You will be on the SERT team and you will fly a 185. Pack your stuff, you're leaving next week."

First Sergeant Lutz waddled out of my office before I could ask where Glennallen was. And what was SERT?

Trooper Torsen. May I help you?" Jet's voice sounded official when I called the Dillingham post.

"Yes, Trooper, you can *help* me. You can join me for lunch, but it will have to be in Glennallen."

"Jack! It's good to hear from you, but why lunch in *Glennallen* of all places? We have a decent restaurant here in Dillingham."

"Jet, I'm being transferred to Glennallen, I'm packing right now."

"Says *who,* Jack? And *why?*"

"First Sergeant Lutz delivered the news and he seemed to enjoy it. He says the colonel wants me there."

"Lutz? excuse me, but what an ass! Let me share my feelings about him with you some time. I'll tell you what, Jack, how about I fly over there tonight? I'll make that dinner I promised you and I'll tell some great Lutz stories."

"Sure, Jet, if it's not too much trouble." Like I was going to turn that down!

Jet surprised me at the King Salmon airport. Instead of her usual trooper plane, she piloted a shiny bronze and white single-engine Piper Comanche.

"Hop in, Jack, you probably need a break from packing. Let's go for a little ride."

Banking the low-wing Piper to the south, Jet smiled and offered, "this was my dad's favorite plane, he left it to me in his will."

"I'm sorry Jet, I didn't know you had lost your father."

"Plane crash. He was flying low in the scud from Clarks Point to South Naknek and went down in Kvichak Bay, probably icing."

We could talk later about the coincidence of our fathers' deaths in airplane crashes. Right then I was intrigued by Jet's narrative as we flew along the Bering Sea beach.

She dipped the right wing. "That's a walrus carcass and the ivory is still on the head. Some lucky pilot in a Cub will land and get the tusks and oosik. A brown bear will be on it within a day."

Next we flew over the fishing village of Egegik, continuing down the beach to Pilot Point, counting six whales along the way. Suddenly Jet made a quick turn. "Jack, look there, crossing the Ugashik River."

About a hundred caribou were swimming across the broad river. Then I saw the rest. A line of the elk-like animals stretched across the tundra, as far as I could see.

Even though we were in a fast plane, it seemed we would never reach the end of the migrating herd.

"How many are down there, Jet?" I asked.

"The herd estimate is about ten thousand and I think they all showed up for us today." Finally finding the end of the caribou parade, the plane banked to the east and we popped over the mountains to another coast.

We're now on the Pacific side," Jet explained as we followed the rugged coastline north.   Every couple of miles or so we would see a brown bear roaming the beach for food. "The big game guides will be after that one in a couple of weeks," she said, nodding to an especially large boar feeding on a whale carcass.

Cutting back to the west, we came across a sow grizzly with four cubs. Three of the cubs were similar in size, but one was much smaller. "That little guy was probably adopted," noted Jet.

Then I saw the smoke.

"Jet, do you see that?" Jet nodded and while increasing the plane's power, turned toward smoke rising about ten miles to the southwest.

"That's Becharof Lake and the smoke is coming from the southern shoreline," Jet said.

There was simply no reason for smoke of this magnitude on the Alaska Peninsula at that time of the year. It was much too big for a campfire, and the hunting season hadn't started yet.

The only logical explanation was a plane crash. As we got closer, the smoke changed to steam and Jet made the connection.

"Volcano! It must be a volcano. But it's at ground level, not on a mountain."

Jet handed me her camera and I began snapping photos of the steam coming from the ground. Then all hell broke loose.

The Comanche blew straight up into the air—not nose first like in a climb, but like an elevator. It was much stronger than any updraft I'd ever flown through—so violent that it felt as though the blood was draining from my head.

Dark smoke surrounded us, accompanied by the clamor of a freight train. Smoking pellets blasted the underside of the wings. We were helpless. The controls had no effect on the airplane.

We just hung on for the ride as it rapidly lifted us a couple thousand feet skyward.

Finally, Jet regained control and banked the plane to see a yellowish-orange pool of molten lava. Car-size boulders were being expelled hundreds of feet into the air.

"Wow! That was a rush," laughed Jet. She reported the sighting to the FAA in King Salmon and then asked, "Is that enough sightseeing for today, Jack?"

After the eruption, which continued for the next ten days, a crater lake was formed on the site, big enough for a Cub on floats. I thought the lake should be named "Jet," since she discovered it. The geologists decided on "Ukinrek Maars Crater."

Landing back at King Salmon, we loaded grocery bags from the Comanche into the Jeep and drove back to my embarrassing little trailer.

"No expense spared for our troopers, eh Jack?" Jet said as she surveyed my sad home. "But no offense. You certainly tidied it up nicely and I like your bookcase. Did you build that, and have you read all of those books?"

I'd scrubbed the mildew from all the walls and floors and cleaned the place thoroughly. Using burls from Talkeetna birch trees for both ends, I'd built a bookcase. The job had kept me so busy that I wasn't home enough to make too much of a mess.

"Thanks Jet, welcome to my 'Royal Court.' That's the name of this beauty. And, yes, I've read those books. I guess that speaks for my social life."

Jet's dinner was spectacular, better than any meal I could remember. Freshly grilled salmon stuffed with succulent crab, tender baby vegetables from her garden, the best homemade carrot cake and a perfect Oregon Pinot Noir.

Dinner conversation started with the transfer.

"Jack, I checked with a friend in the Anchorage headquarters. She tells me the colonel is retiring next year and really could care less who goes where, since he is a 'short-timer.' The word is a guy named Fred Roderick requested your transfer. He is the head guy at DPS, not the Department of Public Safety you and I work for, but Denali Pipeline Security. Cute take off, isn't it? They're the cops for the pipeline and, get this, they hire retired troopers, mostly higher-ups like the colonel, for their administrative staff. I don't think the colonel has anything against you, but I guess if his future boss has a suggestion, or even a demand for a trooper to be transferred to a pipeline hotspot, it's going to happen.

"Do you know this Roderick guy? Could be he thinks highly of you, or it could be he wants you in the line of fire. Glennallen is pretty crazy now, with all the pipeliners."

I didn't know Roderick and I didn't like the process. Maybe it was just politics. Or had I somehow crossed this Roderick guy? Racking my brain, I couldn't place the name. I would give it more thought later. Right now, it was just Jet and me. Finally.

"Oh well, Jet, I guess there's a reason for everything. I'll make the best of it." I was trying to sound optimistic, but I was already missing her. Jet's stories about First Sergeant Lutz made me laugh more than I had in years.

We were really getting to know each other when the phone rang. I didn't want to answer it, but interruptions came with the job.

"Jack, come over here quick, we need you!" Big Red's voice sounded more distressed than usual.

"I'm sorry Jet, but it looks like another bar fight at Eddie's. Shouldn't take long."

"I'm coming with you Jack. There's a police force in Dillingham, so I don't get to have this kind of fun at home."

There was no use arguing and maybe with two of us we could wrap the disturbance up quickly and get back to our evening.

Walking into the bar, I knew something wasn't right. It was too quiet and there were only a couple of customers. Then the action started. People came from everywhere, screaming their heads off. The only word I made out was: "Surprise!"

Turns out Big Red, Leroy, Pete the Pilot, the Naknek magistrate, and the local chapter of the Church of the Woods were throwing me a "Get out of King Salmon" party, instigated by one Jet Torsen.

The governor even called and, along with wishing me his best, offered to "see what I could do to keep you in King Salmon." The governor certainly had the power to quash my transfer orders, but at what cost? There would be repercussions if I stayed, so I thanked him, but declined his generosity.

The party wrapped up pretty late. Jet and I indulged in a few draft beers. So after handshakes and a hug from Big Red, I led my date through the starry night for the short walk back to my mildewed haven.

The log cabin quilt from my room on the Idaho ranch now covered the torn couch, making it suitable for Jet to join me on the only piece of living room furniture. Jet told me about her sadness in leaving South Naknek when she flew away to attend the University of Alaska in Fairbanks, and her good fortune of eventually winning a transfer back to Bristol Bay. I even learned how she became Jet.

"Jessi Emma Torsen is my full name. Jessi was for my Dad, Jesse. Emma is Norwegian and my grandmother's name. As a little kid, my parents said I ran around like a jet, so the nickname stuck."

I finally got my kiss. Then Jet made a confession.

"Jack, I have been hiding something from you. Since our first meeting, I've had this overwhelming feeling that you are the one I was meant to be with. I don't want you to leave, but it has to be."

I told Jet that I felt the same, that she dazzled me the first day and had ever since. We kissed again. Then, it occurred to me: it was dark and Jet had been drinking, so she wouldn't be flying home that night.

"Jet, you can have my bedroom if you like. I can sleep on the couch," I said, knowing it was proper, but wanting to kick myself at the same time.

"That's okay, Jack, I'll just cozy up here." Cuddled up in my lap, Jet looked up with those bottomless blue-green eyes. I grabbed a pillow and blanket, tucked her in and said goodnight, but she was already asleep.

It took more than an hour for sleep to overtake me. I thought of the day with Jet. She showed me more wildlife than I'd ever seen and we discovered a volcano! What could top this? I thought of how lucky I was, but at the same time, I wondered where we went from here. How could we make it work? There would be more than six hundred miles of tundra and the Alaska Range between us. Sure, if she is willing, she could jump in her Comanche and be in Glennallen in less than three hours, but would either of us ever get a few days off in a row to spend time together?

I also realized that we would have to keep our relationship secret for now. There were probably more Lutz-types in the department who would make life miserable for both of us if they knew.

I had the best dream of my life that night. Visions of Jet, wearing nothing but her beautiful smile, snuggling into bed with me, her warm breasts against my back. We made love then fell asleep—cuddling like spoons in restful slumber.

Sunlight crept through the window at 5 a.m. I tried to force myself back to sleep, but something was different. I wasn't alone. A sweet scent, not the usual mildew, filled the room and gentle breath caressed my neck. Jet's arm was wrapped around my chest.

CHAPTER 16

I'm tending to my wounds now. I have one heck of a headache. A self-assessment of my injuries: bad cut on forehead, broken ribs, right arm and left ankle fractured, and a concussion of unknown severity. I'm trying to find something to make a splint and I'm looking for the first aid kit. Lots of pain, which maybe is good. At least I know where my injuries are. That's productive. I'm analyzing the situation and taking action.

I've named the Gray Jay "J.R.," short for jay robber. He? Or is it a she? It is keeping me company, although more than wanting to be a comfort, I think it wants my flesh. I dragged my hurting body around the perimeter of this crash site. I'd hoped to find a spruce tree to make tea from the needles. Or a birch tree to make a meal of the inner bark. But, I found something even better. My survival pack had been ejected about two hundred stumbling and painful paces from the wreckage. Now I have a supply of food bars. Like my uncle told me in a story about Teddy Roosevelt giving a pep talk to the Rough Riders before storming San Juan Hill: "Do what you can, with what you have, where you are."

Back to my humor therapy, I remember a story Jet told me about First Sergeant Lutz. Jet, I'm sorry if I'm not telling this right. I'm sure you can tell it better. I love you Jessi.

First Sergeant Lutz on patrol

Jet says Lutz is famous for his impromptu visits, always trying to catch a trooper doing something wrong. One summer he made a surprise visit at Jet's post, only it wasn't much of a surprise. Jet's friend at Anchorage headquarters phoned the Dillingham post as soon as Lutz waddled out of the office. This gave her time to organize the piles of paperwork, find her tie, and arrange a little patrol for her boss.

Acting shocked when Lutz barged into her office, she immediately told him she was sorry, but he would have to inspect her files later. Jet said she needed to take the post riverboat up the Wood River to investigate an illegal fishing net. Lutz didn't much care for fieldwork, but a quick once over didn't show anything off beam in Jet's office and, after all, she was wearing a tie. Most certainly hoping to find her marine operation improper or some other imagined violation of department policy, he plopped down on the front seat of the boat.

To get to the Wood River, the Nushagak first had to be navigated, and the high winds that day meant rough water. Insisting on wearing his proper Stetson while Jet opted for the more practical trooper stocking cap, he held on to the brim as the little skiff crashed through the waves. Every time they hit a big crest, twenty gallons of silty water was dumped on Lutz, just as if a barrel had been poured over his head. Each time, the sergeant quickly removed his hat, shook off the water, and then clamped it back on his enormous head. Then another wave hit. The process was repeated, over and over. After an hour of this, Jet was nearly busting her gut from restraining her laughter.

They beached next to the net on the Wood River. Jet went to investigate, but Lutz had other needs. "I have to go to the bathroom, I'll be right back," the sergeant moaned.

After wrapping up her net investigation, Jet heard something crashing through the brush. It was her fearless leader, swatting bugs with one hand and carrying his revolver on a stick in the other. "Trooper Torsen, do you have any toilet paper?" The gun was covered in feces! Seems that while First Sergeant Gene Lutz was squatting, his duty weapon fell out of the holster. Jet couldn't constrain herself and, probably forever earning a strike against her, burst out laughing.

CHAPTER 17

The mammoth fuselage of the C-119 Flying Boxcar hummed with vibrations from the roaring radial engines, lulling me in and out of sleep. My only function as a temporary crew-member on the Alaska Cargo Carriers freight plane was to help load and unload my personal belongings. The Alaska Department of Public Safety was saving money on my transfer from King Salmon to Glennallen. Instead of buying a ticket for me to fly to Anchorage on Wien, then driving me on the Glenn Highway to my new post, I was ordered to sit in what once was the radio operator's seat in the old beast. This budget-saving trip was fine with me, as an up-close view from the deck on this old bird was a real treat.

Focusing back through the oblong entryway to the worn army-green flight deck, I envisioned the sixty-two troops packed into the cargo hold, off to fight a war in some faraway place. My drop-off at the Gulkana airport was just the first stop on this cargo flight, so we were heavily loaded. Maybe loaded a little over the gross legal maximum, judging by the length of runway used on takeoff, and the struggle to gain altitude as the floor rattled under my boots.

My Jeep was strapped down in the back, next to the tons of freight, including boats, motors, boxes, and a diverse mixture of equipment. Even more importantly, my Cub was sitting on its wheels in the womb of the much larger plane. Gently swaying with the turbulence, the Cub's wings hung in slings from the walls of the C-119.

The Chugach Mountains passed beneath us while, with each inhalation, I searched for fresh air sneaking in my side window. In vain, I was trying to escape the nauseating cigar smoke being spewed by the captain. Through the haze I could see the signs of wear and tear on his face, complementing the war wounds on the Boxcar he was piloting. Through the side window of the cockpit, I studied the crevasses and canyons, and considered the chance of surviving a crash in this rugged environment where a plane could be lost forever. Senator Nick Begich's plane disappeared near this area a couple years before, prompting Congress to pass the law requiring emergency locator transmitters.

"What did you do to piss off the bosses *this* time, Trooper?" The captain threw the question back to me while rolling his cigar stub to the side of his mouth. "King Salmon was bad enough, but do you know what kind of crap you're getting into in Glennallen with that friggin' pipeline construction mess?" My response was unnecessary.

Without warning, the right engine coughed, sputtered and belched smoke. Then the prop stood at attention and the plane yawed in the air.

"What the *hell*?" The captain yelled as he cranked his neck, glaring out the window as if he would somehow will the old engine back to life.

Rapidly pushing and pulling levers and throwing switches, all the while cussing up a storm, the pilot and co-pilot first pleaded with the old bird to cooperate. That failing to work, the captain next issued threats of violence as he ordered it to restart. Refusing, the old bird began a gradual descent. The ice fields seemed to be waving us in for a crash landing, but the closer we got, the more rugged they looked. I imagined the searchers who would find the mess. The carnage—a big plane surrounded by a Cub, a Jeep, boats, and all the cargo, would certainly puzzle an unknowing search crew.

Low enough to see the aqua-blue depths of a crag, I braced for impact. But the engine decided it had screwed with us enough for one day.

Puffing a big cloud of smoke, as if mocking the captain's cigar, the big radial flung the prop around once, stopped, then started for real.

"Well, that's better. There's no way we would have made it over these man-eating mountains with one engine," the captain barked with a puff of cigar smoke.

"Now where were we, trooper? Oh yeah, how did you manage to get transferred out of one hell hole to a *worse* hell hole and be forced to ride in this P.O.S. to get there?"

There wasn't a good answer for the captain. I was just glad both props once again were spinning and we were gaining altitude.

I decided it wasn't going to help the old radial engine run any better by me staring at it. I picked up the front page of the *Anchorage Daily Times,* which was stuck in the back pocket of the co-pilot's seat, focusing on the article, "Murder Case Dismissed." My head just about exploded as I read how an Anchorage drug dealer shot a police investigator in the face during a search warrant raid. The defense attorney argued that his client was denied his rights because the police didn't knock before entering his apartment, and that he responded as any homeowner would. No matter that five police officers testified they yelled "POLICE" before, and after they entered the defendant's residence. No matter that he was a convicted felon without the right to possess a firearm. No matter the pistol he used was stolen. No matter the place was loaded with illegal drugs. No matter the search warrant was valid. No matter the police officer had a wife and three little children.

Has the court system in our country gone insane? Or was it just Alaska? Where is the justice? Who protects the *good* guys?

The promised state trooper truck wasn't on the ramp at the Gulkana airport. After tossing out my boxes, rolling the Jeep down the ramps, then carefully unloading the Cub, the crew got the beast started and left me standing among my belongings.

I grabbed the portable radio tucked away inside my Jeep and called Glennallen trooper dispatch. The dispatcher's reply was abrupt. "All troopers are on calls. Estimated time of arrival for assistance at your location is two hours."

In other words, "don't screw with me, don't you know we are busy? Who the hell are you, anyway?"

Since the Boxcar captain insisted on the gas being drained from the Jeep before loading it in his plane, it was of no use. There were aviation gas pumps just two hundred yards away, but pushing the heavy Jeep up the slight grade wasn't a solo project and no one was in sight. Surveying the freight on the ramp, I made a decision.

I stacked the boxes about six feet high and ten feet apart. Pulling the wing tip first on one end of the boxes, then the heavy end, I next dragged the Cub alongside. Sliding the wing spar against the fuselage, I attached the front and rear bolts with a socket wrench. Cables were next, and then the wing strut was bolted in place. I swung the Cub around and repeated the process on the opposite wing. In less than an hour the Cub was ready. Although I had drained all fuel from the tanks, there was just enough av-gas in the header tanks in the cockpit to start and taxi to the self-service pumps.

Ready for a test flight, I taxied back to the Jeep to secure valuables. Inside the Jeep, I locked my duty weapon, shotgun, and the Colt Model 1911 forty-five caliber my uncle had willed me. Just before leaving King Salmon, I traded a spare rifle for a new Beretta 92 pistol and I decided to slip that into my shoulder holster. I started packing more valuables into the Jeep, but the police radio cut me short.

"All units, H-24 requests back-up for the stop of a suspicious subject at Mile 170 on the Glenn Highway."

The dispatcher paused, but there was no response. She loudly repeated the message twice more, earning only silence. Flying in on the Boxcar, I had followed our progress on the chart and noted the long, straight Glenn Highway, the east-west road through town, so I had an idea where the trooper was.

"Glennallen dispatch, this is Trooper Blake, I'll respond."

"Thank you, Trooper Blake. H-24 received a motorist's report that he dropped off a hitchhiker who he says has a weapon and acts disturbed. H-24 did you copy? *H-24!*"

The dispatcher now sounded frantic and repeated the message, but there was no response.

The Cub's engine jumped to life. After a quick run up and check of the controls, I slammed the throttle forward. Wasting no time by taxiing to the runway, I took off in front of the gas pumps on the parking ramp and pointed the nose west with maximum RPM. Ten minutes later, I circled over the trooper's car.

The trooper leaned over the trunk, weapon drawn. On the side of the road a man was in a combat stance, holding a pistol with both hands. I made a quick pre-landing check of the area, noting road signs, power lines, and the rows of black spruce lining the pavement. The only road traffic was at least a mile away, and I figured I could land and get off the highway before the car was a factor.

Sliding the throttle back, I silently glided to a landing on the wide roadway. Hitting the heel brakes, the Cub was forced into a hard left turn, stopping on the centerline of the Glenn Highway. Jumping out the door, I pulled the plane tail-first into the ditch, cautiously edging toward the patrol car.

The trooper nodded at me and pointed toward the armed man. He slowly moved toward the passenger side of his vehicle, pleading, "Take it easy sir, it isn't worth it. Just drop your weapon and it will be okay." The low-profile Plymouth offered little protection for the trooper's tall frame. The suspect answered with two puffs of smoke from his gun.

WHAP, WHAP! Two bullets punched the trooper in the chest. Grunting and expelling wind from deep within, the trooper fell forward into the ditch.

My weapon already drawn, I leveled the Beretta at the still-firing shooter. My first two shots hit his left arm and the next two penetrated his stomach. My pistol was now sighted in.

He kept firing and so did I.

The academy trained us to keep shooting until the threat was neutralized, so I fired until I thought he was down for good.

But, as I approached, he pulled another pistol from his waist and pointed. I countered with two quick shots to his chest and one to his forehead.

Out of ammo, but satisfied the threat had finally ended, I quickly moved back to the trooper.

"Jack, you son of a gun, nice of you to drop in," he whispered as his eyes slowly closed. The mustache made Trooper David Daniels easily recognizable.

"Sorry I broke your rule about shooting," I offered. As he lapsed into unconsciousness, I checked his vitals. Steady breathing and a strong pulse. Opening his shirt, I found the two .44 caliber slugs had barely penetrated the ballistic vest. He would have a heck of a bruise, but he would survive. I called dispatch for an ambulance just as another squad car screeched to a stop.

A trooper with single gold bars on his lapels quickly slid from the driver's seat.

"Trooper Blake, I'm Lieutenant Emery. What do we have here?"

"Dave took two to his vest, but should be okay. The guy who shot him is dead, lieutenant."

"I'll need your weapon, Trooper Blake. We'll get statements and you can do the report tomorrow."

I was happy to turn the nine-millimeter pistol over to the lieutenant. It was a standard part of a shooting investigation to seize all weapons, and that was enough ballistics experimentation for me.

"You can keep it if you want, Lieutenant. I'll stick with my .45 from now on."

The supervisor carefully looked at me. Then he glanced down the road to my Cub. Next he studied the empty magazine and counted the fifteen shell casings on the ground between the road and the body.

"One question, Trooper Blake. Why did you shoot *fifteen* times?"

"Because that's all I had, Lieutenant."

"You'll fit in just fine here Blake, just fine."

CHAPTER 18

I said a little prayer for Daniels as he was loaded into the ambulance. Then I said another one for the soul of the man I'd just shot. Waiting on the side of the road, per the lieutenant's orders, I watched his examination of the body. First he secured the pistol, and then he removed a piece of paper from the dead man's shirt pocket.

"Seems like this guy was looking for you, Jack. These are directions to the trooper-housing unit, which has been assigned to you. Your name is scratched on the top of the page. Do you know him?"

"Can't say I do, but I haven't had a close look at him yet."

The lieutenant lifted a wallet from the man's bloodstained jeans and read his driver's license. "Name is Mark Morgen."

A chill ran up my vertebrae. I wondered how Morgen, aka "Crazy Mark," could hold a grudge that serious from our King Salmon encounter.

The lieutenant pulled his white Dodge onto the middle of the Glenn Highway and activated the overhead emergency lights while I back-taxied the Cub. I made a quick takeoff and popped off the road, well short of the patrol car, and buzzed back to the Gulkana airport.

The mess I left on the airport ramp looked like a garage sale, but now there was a pickup truck parked next to my Jeep.

As I shut down the Cub, a trooper quickly, but in an uncoordinated fashion, shuttled his round frame toward the cockpit.

Bong! The trooper's temple firmly bounced off the wing strut.

"Greetings, fellow Trooper. Welcome to Glennallen! I'm Ronnie Torgy," the trooper exclaimed with enthusiasm as he rubbed his bald, and now red, forehead. Stumbling into the Cub's tundra tire, he stretched out his hand. I returned the handshake and introduced myself.

"I brought the trooper truck and I'm going to help you move. Been here for about an hour. Did you do some flight-seeing of the area?"

I told Ronnie—I still find it hard to say "Trooper Torgy"—why I was late, and I assured him that David Daniels would be okay.

"Darn! I wish I could have responded, but the radio on this old truck is busted," Ronnie explained. He seemed to be lost in deep thought, silently staring at the white Ford pickup, while blocking my exit from the cockpit.

I took a short intermission from Ronnie's animated, mostly one-way conversation, to study the trooper. His round face was clean-shaven, except for pork chop sideburns. Most of his brown hair would never return to his head, which featured numerous scars—most likely from encounters with inanimate objects. Maybe five feet nine inches tall, the buttons popping on the belly of his uniform shirt looked like he was concealing a beach ball. His muscular arms indicated he pumped iron.

Ronnie and I moved all of my belongings in two trips. The only loss was when he dropped the box with my dishes. He showed me the trail from the trooper housing compound down to a little airstrip where a state Super Cub was parked. Tripping on a pebble while coming back up the trail, Ronnie's chin suffered a minor scrape.

An "in your face" talker, he didn't miss a beat. He continued a lengthy description of his love for the Glennallen post, his wife and kids, and his passion for his "other life" as a Judo sensei to elementary school children. It was right then that I realized he looked like a Buddha. It was also then that I realized that he would be a good friend.

I'm really looking forward to working with you and it was great talking to you. I will see you tomorrow at the annual picnic," Ronnie said, attacking the door of the truck.

As he wrestled with the door, I finally had an opening to speak. "Thank you for all the help, Ronnie. What's this about a *picnic?*"

CHAPTER 19

My new trailer was a big improvement from the King Salmon shanty. The trailer park was exclusively for troopers and rather than a bar being around the corner, tall birch trees grew between each unit and horses grazed at the end of the grass airstrip.

After unpacking, I followed a routine my uncle taught me on the ranch. He didn't believe in wasting time worrying about or over-thinking a problem. If there was an issue requiring a big decision, he would first write down all the alternatives on a piece of paper. Then he would choose one and be done, and he would live with his decision. If something bothered him, he allowed thirty minutes to the issue, then settled it. He said to take any bad thoughts and put them in a paper bag. Then he said to burn the bag.

I gave thirty minutes to the shooting. I thought about what led to the events. Did Morgen have a tough childhood? Maybe abusive parents? There must have been something that put him on a path to destruction, but it wasn't me. Killing an individual, when you can see his face, is not like returning fire on unseen enemies in war. But sometimes it's necessary. On the ranch when meat was needed, we harvested an elk, a deer, or fished. There was no joy in the kill itself; it was just an act necessary for survival. Killing Morgen was the same—if someone is trying to kill you, you kill him first.

In the final analysis, I care about the victim, not the criminal. I burned the full bag and resolved not to let my act of survival haunt me.

My thoughts turned to more pleasant things. I fell asleep thinking of Jet and those thoughts merged into a dream. Our float-equipped Beaver was moored offshore from a little cove on the island of Antigua. We swam to the beach in the tepid turquoise waters, with bright yellow fish escorting us. We spent the sunny day running around in the sand without the encumbrance of clothes. We drank Wadadli beer and dined on mahi-mahi and mangos. The red-orange sunset sank right into the ocean, turning the dark sky into a display of endless brilliant stars. Jet made a grass skirt and we danced in front of a fire. I don't think she would appreciate me providing all the details, so I'll just say it was a romantic night in the Caribbean.

Ronnie banged on my door at 7:45 a.m. He promised the day before to give me a lift when I reminded him I didn't know where the post was and that I didn't have a patrol rig. "Hope I didn't wake you up, Jack." I had been up for two hours, completing a nice run and the exercise routine prescribed by my uncle.

The trooper office in Glennallen looked more like a large one-level old house than an official building. Jill, the cheery blonde dispatcher, greeted Ronnie when we came in the back door. "Hey Ronnie, good morning, did you break anything yet today?"

"Not yet, Sweetie, but the day's young," laughed Ronnie. "This is the new kid on the block, Jack Blake."

Good to meet you Jack. Welcome to Glennallen."

The building housed offices for eight troopers, the lieutenant, and a grandmotherly-looking clerk who issued drivers' licenses. Ronnie led me down the hall, stopping at the door of each vacant room, telling which trooper sat at what desk, until we came to the last office on the left.

"That's yours," nodding to one of the four gray metal military-style desks. Ronnie clanged his shin on another of the desks, then fell into a chair.

"Ronnie, is that you?" I recognized the lieutenant's voice from the office across the hall.

"Good morning, Lieutenant," Ronnie responded, "Jack Blake is with me."

"Come on in, Jack, if you have a minute."

The lieutenant motioned me to sit in one of the three hardback gray leatherette chairs in his office.

"I see Ronnie got you here in one piece. Hope he didn't destroy too many of your belongings in the move yesterday." I smiled, but thought it best not to seed the rain cloud that seemed to hover over Ronnie's head.

Lieutenant Rich Emery is what military types call "squared away." His uniform was impeccable. The perfectly pressed creases on his dark-blue pants made the gold and red stripes seem even brighter. The brass buttons on his shirt reflected the overhead lights and the leather on his Sam Browne gun belt matched the high gloss polish of his black boots. His black hair, peppered with gray, was perfectly cut and combed. On the wall behind him hung a master's degree from the University of Washington, next to a certificate of graduation from a leadership school at the FBI academy. At about forty years old, he was destined for higher places with the troopers.

"Jack, first all, let me tell you how glad I am to have you on our team. You have a lot of skills that will be assets to the Glennallen post. I must admit that I'm surprised you were transferred here, due to your lack of seniority, but someone wanted you for a reason and that's good for us.

"Ronnie is a great guy and knows the job. Sometimes his enthusiasm gets in the way, but he means well and will do anything to help his fellow troopers—that's why he serves as the one and only trooper on my office staff. He is much better with auxiliary functions than working the road. He will make a good sergeant some day. He will get you a car and whatever else you need.

"Jack, before we get into your job description, let me bring you up to speed on the shooting."

The lieutenant slid on a pair of silver-rimmed glasses. He reached for a document from the papers stacked in perfect order on his desk.

"Here's the initial report on yesterday's incident. Since a trooper was injured and the suspect was killed, this is a high-priority investigation. The body was flown to the Anchorage crime lab and the autopsy was expedited. We have to deal with the media with accuracy and compassion. Before that, the brass needs to know all the facts quickly and in total. The autopsy report here shows Morgen had twelve bullet wounds. Off the record Jack, that was a nice shooting, especially under stressful conditions.

"Morgen had enough PCP in his system to stone a horse, and a blood-alcohol level three times the legal limit. Nothing else of interest, but I'll read what the coroner says: 'Identifying marks include a mole on his right thigh, six scars averaging 1.2 centimeters on left forearm, previous trauma to both knees, and a tattoo of a flag of unknown origin on his right wrist.' Before you do anything else this morning, you need to sit down and write a statement of what happened yesterday, so I can attach it to my report and send it off to headquarters."

The lieutenant shifted gears.

"The eight-billion dollar pipeline construction project is just peaking. The state government, along with the oil companies, is going to be rich as long as the oil flows. So, it's in the interest of both big oil, and the State of Alaska, that the pipeline gets built and is not sabotaged. That's where we come in."

Now standing, the boss pointed at a map.

"There are around twenty-eight thousand workers building this thing. Most of them are making more money than they ever had, or probably ever will have again. Maybe it's welding at seventy degrees below zero. Maybe it's just that the kitchen ran out of lobster and had to serve Alaskan king crab instead, but some of these guys will do anything to cause a ruckus.

"Alyeska Pipeline Company built fourteen airstrips by the camps. We can land on any of them, on the highway, or anywhere else we need to do business in the camps.

We try to settle disputes on the spot and keep the workers on the job. But, if necessary, we make arrests and book them into the Glennallen jail.

"Jack, here is where I see you fitting in. We have an airplane, but no pilot, so you're it. Your file says you have some martial arts training. That could come in handy when breaking up fights in the camps, but I suggest 'verbal karate' when possible to settle a dispute. If there is a sabotage attempt on the pipeline, you respond as soon as possible. There are continual investigations, some not at all related to the pipeline, and you will be assigned to those as needed. We might use you for some undercover work until your face is known.

"Most importantly, you are now part of S.E.R.T., short for 'Special Emergency Response Team.' You respond to emergencies, anywhere in the state. You will get some very intensive training with the team. But before that, we need to get you through a quick and dirty Field Training Program as required by state code. All that means is, you ride along with three other troopers for a couple of weeks, cross the T's and dot the I's and you'll officially pass the certification program that you *should* have done during your rookie year.

"Follow the rules, do your job and all will be well. Things are a little crazy here now, but, with the crew we have, it's manageable. Do you have any questions, Jack?" The lieutenant sat back in his chair and smiled.

Lieutenant Emery seemed fair and by the book and that's all I needed to know.

CHAPTER 20

Until Glennallen, I drove only pickup trucks or Jeeps. Ronnie introduced me to my first car.

"This thing's a beast. A Grand Fury with a 440 Magnum engine. The mechanic added special headers and a tuned exhaust. Not many bad guys will be able to run away from you."

Ronnie swung open the driver's door and started to sit in the wide plastic front seat, but his Stetson got caught on the door jam. Like it was standard procedure, Ronnie twisted his hat straight and planted himself on the seat with a second try.

"Listen to this baby, Jack." The exhaust rumbled, and as Ronnie revved the engine, the whole car swayed. He showed me the concealed release for the shotgun, which was mounted in a rack on the middle of the floorboard. Another button popped the trunk, which housed—among blankets, flares, a shovel, and other safety gear—a rifle.

"That's an M-16, Jack. It shoots .223 rounds."

I didn't tell Ronnie that I knew M-16s from Laos. It felt nice in my hands. I liked the folding stock and the quickly detachable scope mount system. It was compact, yet the thirty round clips offered plenty of chances to hit a target.

"Thanks, Ronnie, looks like I have everything I need."

"Okay, follow me to the picnic then."

It was a sunny spring day, with temperatures topping in the low forties. Buds on the birch trees were threatening to sprout and the mosquitoes weren't biting yet—a perfect day for a picnic.

Ronnie drove as if he was responding to a crisis. I lost his truck in the dust as he raced down a dirt road near the office. It was good I slowed, for just as I came around a corner, Ronnie's truck slid sideways in the gravel and drifted off the roadway into the ditch. A gate blocked the road where several other trooper vehicles were parked.

"Trooper Torgy has *arrived!*" One trooper shouted and two others laughed at Ronnie's mishap.

"You okay, Ronnie?" I asked.

"Yep, fine. Thanks, Jack. I guess I was going a bit too fast."

One of the troopers hooked a chain to Ronnie's pickup, pulling him from the ditch. Ronnie introduced me to the troopers from the Northway Post, located about two hundred road miles from Glennallen. Then he told us the details of the picnic.

"Okay, guys, here's the drill. First we shoot, then we eat." Ronnie held up a portable radio and continued. "This is a new course. When I get a call, one of you goes through the gate. Once you get to the shooting range, you will go through three courses. The first is a shotgun course. The scenario is, you are being fired upon, so you will exit your vehicle in the safest manner, using it for cover. Then you will shoot at four targets. The score is based on time and accuracy. Then you draw your sidearm and move to the pistol targets, again with a score based on accuracy and time. The time for both begins when you get to the range, so you don't need to race from here and maybe end up in a ditch-dive, like me. Finally, those of you with rifles will proceed to a course with targets set at various distances. That is scored for accuracy only, and you have two minutes to complete it. Any questions?"

One trooper joked about Ronnie crashing into the firing range, but no one had questions.

"Jack, you are up first." Ronnie motioned me to drive to the closed gate. The radio crackled and Ronnie yelled, "GO!"

I drove around one short bend and came to the range. Just as I parked the Plymouth, the loudspeaker ordered: "Trooper Blake, you are under fire on the driver's side of your car, time has begun!"

While pushing the shotgun rack release button, I slid across the front seat of the car, pushed the passenger door open, and dove into the dirt. Rising over the hood, I blasted the first target with the twelve gauge. Rolling on the ground, I popped up behind a bench and hit the second target. Standing, I next fired from the hip on the third and fourth targets.

"Shotgun phase complete, Blake. Proceed to the pistol course," the loudspeaker commanded. Standing behind a post, I fired at metal targets as they popped up on the range, reloading my .357 four times. The rifle course was like shooting on the ranch airstrip with my uncle. I fired at eight silhouettes, which were set from thirty yards to three hundred yards from kneeling and prone positions. I then fired and connected with something metal past the last target. "Secure weapons!" The loudspeaker cracked and I was done.

"Jack, come over and have a seat." Lt. Emery motioned for me to sit next to him in a lawn chair. "Nice work, Jack. Welcome to one of our little picnics. Sit back and relax and watch the fun."

The two Northway Post troopers were next. Neither shot the rifle course, but both punched plenty of holes in the paper targets with their shotguns and pistols.

The next guy was flat out impressive.

The white squad car braked hard. A trooper bailed out the right side and quickly fired his shotgun at the targets. He moved fast and deliberately. Something was different about this trooper—different than the other troopers—but in some way familiar. The bright sun reflected off his left hand. He hit the targets with accuracy and speed, and then stood at attention with his rifle when done.

"That's Ted Herlihy. Some of the guys call him 'Titanium Ted.' Not to his face, because he probably wouldn't appreciate it. His left hand was blown off in 'Nam but, as you can see, it doesn't slow him down a bit. He's black and white in enforcing the law. He doesn't care much for department rules and procedure, so he can be a handful for me as a supervisor, but he's the guy you want for backup in a tight situation—although he might also be the one who gets you *into* that tight situation. He is one of your training officers, so you will ride with him for a week.

Fourteen more troopers from Glennallen and surrounding posts shot the courses. Then came Ronnie. He didn't crash into the range as one of the Northway troopers joked. He only knocked over one metal trashcan as he parked. He did have a little problem when exiting from his truck. There was a loud "zing," then Ronnie was jerked back into the cab. It took him at least thirty seconds to untangle his shirt from the long rubber cord attached to the microphone. Once unhooked, Ronnie fell out of the truck, dropping his shotgun. I felt for him and cringed as he struggled through the remainder of the qualifications.

"Jack, I hate to tell you this, but Ronnie is your other field training officer. He is the only other trooper besides Ted and Dave Daniels who has taken the training officer course. You only have to ride with him for a week, so please bear with it."

"No problem, Lieutenant, I get along fine with Ronnie," I said, hoping for the best.

After the shooting ceased, the lieutenant, standing behind a massive, smoking barbeque grill, delivered a short speech to the eighteen assembled troopers.

"Men, first of all I know you heard about Dave Daniels. I spoke to the doctor this morning and he predicts Dave will be back on duty in two weeks. Your enthusiasm in today's qualification is appreciated and I realize the course was a bit different this time. I wanted to set up something that is more realistic than just standing and shooting at paper targets. I have been involved in two shootings in my ten-year career with the troopers, so I know a real shooting isn't like practicing on the range."

Emery then added, "Trooper Blake's very recent experience attests to the rest of my sermon. Persons loaded with drugs or alcohol, or who are mentally ill, may take multiple hits, suffering wounds, which should be fatal, but still not go down immediately. So don't shoot, then pause and assess the damage like some of us were taught. Also, don't count on having cover, since most shootings take place in close quarters and in the open.

Shoot with speed, shoot with accuracy and shoot to kill. Train with the mindset 'I will react decisively and I will survive.'"

All of the troopers applauded.

"Now for today's winners in the bi-annual Glennallen picnic and shoot out. Shotgun: first place with a time of forty-two seconds and a score of one hundred, Ted Herlihy. Second place with a time of forty-four seconds and a score of one hundred, Jack Blake. First place in the pistol course, with a time of twenty-two seconds and a score of one hundred, Jack Blake. Second place, with a time of twenty-five seconds and a score of one hundred, Ted Herlihy. Blake and Herlihy both had dead-center hits in all targets in the rifle course. But I have to give the edge to Blake, because he took out a tin can that wasn't part of the course, but is about five hundred yards out. Great work, gentlemen, now let's dig into these grizzly ribs and caribou steaks."

I was embarrassed by the attention. I didn't want the other troopers to think I was some sort of gun nut. I wanted to tell them that, when I was on the ranch, shooting and flying were my two favorite pastimes. Otherwise, I was as normal as the next trooper.

CHAPTER 21

"**Y**ou're driving." No "Good evening." No introduction. This was my first day on the job in Glennallen and Titanium Ted was assigned as my field-training officer for the swing shift, which began at 4 p.m. He didn't smile. He didn't offer his hand. There was to be no small talk. I have been accused of being too quiet, but this was uncomfortably silent. Sitting next to me with a clipboard holding a form to rate my every move, the stoic trooper sat rigid. His profile was familiar, but I couldn't place it and I didn't see our conversation taking us anywhere but the present. "Take a right. We are going to a call," T-Ted grunted.

I made the turn, and then he barked, "When are you going to tell dispatch you are on the road?"

I'd heard enough chatter between dispatch and troopers to know a little radio procedure, although I'd had no training yet. I had yet to use my newly-assigned radio call sign, "H-22." "H" stood for H Detachment, of which Glennallen was headquarters. Twenty-two was a random number assigned to a road trooper within the detachment.

"Glennallen dispatch, H-22 10-8." "10-8" meant "on duty." Forcing only enough words to get us to the nearby settlement of Copper Center, T-Ted motioned for me to stop in front of a compact hovel of weather-beaten timbers with purple trim.

"Watch and take notes," Herlihy ordered, as he pulled black leather gloves over his hands.

An Athabaskan man, about fifty, flung the door open as we walked up the steps.

"Mr. Hills?" T-Ted asked, and got a nod in return.

"I'm Trooper Herlihy. You called the office about some-one stealing your fishwheel on the Copper River. Tell me about it."

"That's right. I go down to the river this morning to check my wheel and it was gone. You going to find it? I need it for fishing next week when red salmon run."

"Okay, describe your wheel," T-Ted directed.

"Number one-five-four and 'Hills' on a sign on side of wheel."

"Anything else?" T-Ted asked.

"You white guys don't know much, do you? Fish wheels all look alike—big wooden baskets turn in the river, scoop fish up and throw them in box."

T-Ted didn't like the complainant's tone. His frame became even more rigid and his gray eyes zoomed in on the man, but the interview continued. "How do you know it didn't just drift down the river in the high water?"

"Rope cut from tree. You probably won't get out of your fancy car to look at it, but it was cut. Probably couldn't find my wheel if it fell on you."

I could almost see steam rising from the back of the trooper's neck as he adjusted his tight blue collar. He could be restrained no longer.

"Mr. Hills, there are only two people in this world who give a damn about finding your stinking fishwheel, and one of them is quickly losing interest. If you have any more information, give it to me now. Otherwise, shut up before I drag your lazy ass down to the river and throw it in. Then, maybe you can swim the river and look for your big wooden baskets."

Hills looked like a spaceship had landed in his yard and T-Ted was the head alien. "Okay Trooper Hell-ray. I don't want no trouble, I just worried about fishing season."

"That's *Her-lihee*. Now here's what we are going to do, Mr. Hills. Trooper Blake and I will fly the river and see if we spot your wheel. I will let you know what I find. Have a nice day, sir."

With that T-Ted closed his notebook and marched back to the patrol car with a quick tempo.

I offered my hand to Mr. Hills, but he just slammed the door and peered out the window as I returned to the car. I needed to learn more about dealing with the local Native population and right then, T-Ted was my only source.

"He seems a little hostile." I gambled, daring to speak.

"Do ya *think?*" It wasn't the tone as much as the way he emphasized "think." There was definitely something familiar about the way T-Ted formed his words. My mind began rolling through faces, names and places, like a Rolodex, searching for T-Ted. He spoke before anything clicked.

"Hills is one of the Natives who is going through some sort of revolution. You'd think maybe they have a beef, because of the pipeline, but that's not it. They are set to get very rich from the oil. Some, like Hills, just think it's time to challenge white man's authority. But it's not like in the Lower 48 where the white man stole their land. They have always had it their way up here. Now Hills just wants to sit on his butt and watch television all day. He gives other Ahtna tribal members a bad name. I have Indian friends I hunt and fish with and they are all good guys. Jerks like Hills hunt and fish anytime they want, regardless of seasons or limits. They get drunk, break the law, and then get off with a warning from the judge. That doesn't sit well with me."

Before we got out of Mr. Hill's driveway, the radio cracked: "H-22, fight in progress at Pump Station Twelve, can you respond?"

T-Ted acknowledged the radio call, then ordered: "Step on it." The Fury began to accelerate. Then like an afterburner kicking in, the big engine let out a howl, the automatic transmission shifted to the passing gear, and we were pressed against the hard bench seat.

"Faster, I want to see how you handle a cruiser. And throw on the damned overheads."

I flipped the switch for the red lights and watched the trees fly by as cars pulled onto the shoulder.

"Faster, keep the throttle all the way down," T-Ted ordered.

The Richardson Highway straightened as the big car accelerated. As the speedometer passed one hundred, I thought about the moose standing right on the centerline that I'd seen on the way to work that morning. Hitting one of those big animals would be like slamming into a thousand pounds of bricks.

At one hundred twenty, the big car seemed very light, feeling like it wanted to take off. Now four lanes, the highway was clear and we floated over the permafrost-created dips. I glanced at the speedometer: one hundred forty-two miles an hour. We should have been in an airplane at that speed, not challenging moose for the right of way.

"Slow down, turn left up there." T-Ted finally spoke and pointed to a road. A guard at the pump station waved our patrol car through the gate. "Go up there, to the mess hall." Ted nodded toward a long white building.

Fighting words and the sounds of flying furniture greeted us as we walked up the short steps to the mess hall. The smell of good food drifted from the double metal doors. Inside, it was chaos under the fluorescent lights. Ted went into action, moving to the end of a long dining table.

CLANG! CLANG! CLANG! The titanium hand banged on a tabletop. The fracas stopped and the room went silent, as if the fighters were familiar with the sound. "What are you idiots skirmishing about today? Didn't you get breakfast in bed?"

A few of the silent diners laughed, giving hopes to a peaceful ending. But then one of the fighters yelled, "somebody shut that Smokey up and get him the hell out of here." Wearing a "Chicago Bridge and Iron" t-shirt, a muscled worker advanced toward Ted. He got too close. A load of titanium caught the aggressor in his gut. As he buckled forward, Ted's right hand smashed into the big man's cheek. He was down and out.

Movement came from my left. I turned just in time to see a particularly tall man running at me. Instinctively, I threw a straight punch to stop the attack. The blow caught him dead center in his throat. Choking and retching, he went down on one knee, no longer a threat. Another man went for Ted. A couple of inches shorter and about twenty pounds lighter than me, Ted was a good street fighter. He simply backhanded the guy with his prosthesis. The attack ended quickly as the attacker's nose gushed with blood.

Three more of the rowdies charged me. Now set up in a fighting stance, I blocked, kicked and punched until they were all down. Even though I was sorely out of practice, it was reassuring that my training, and luck, came back when needed.

A flying coffee cup struck Ted in the side of his head, drawing blood. He shook it off, but it made him madder. Spewing obscenities, he slammed the glass-thrower face-first into the dining room wall.

There was a pile of guys on the floor after our little battle, but no serious injuries. This was the most fun I'd had in martial arts since sparring with my uncle at the ranch. It was just like a bunch of guys horsing around on a playground.

Catching his breath while wiping blood from his head, Ted addressed the group: "Okay, if you clowns have had enough fun for the day, we need to get back on the road. Don't make us come back, 'cause I don't want to screw with hauling any of you bums to jail. Enjoy the prime rib."

The cook came from the kitchen and shook Ted's hand, thanking him for restoring order. He handed Ted two bags.

I began recording the events in my notebook, but Ted interrupted me. "No need to write a report, just drive." I pointed the cruiser back towards the Glennallen post while Ted toweled the blood from his face. He handed me one of the bags saying, simply, "eat." I drove while munching on a prime rib sandwich, wondering how those workers could complain, with such good grub.

Dark was creeping up on us as we turned from the Richardson Highway onto the Glenn Highway.

It looked like a jet airliner was landing on the Glenn Highway in the distance. Bright lights illuminated the road, blinding my forward vision. Pulling the cruiser to the side of the road, I flashed my high beams then turned on the overhead emergency reds. The light show raced towards us, then abruptly peeled off the road in the distance.

"Pull into that joint." T-Ted motioned for me to park in front of "The Glennallen Cracker Barrel Qwik Shop and Eatery."

"Son of a bitch!" Ted wasn't pleased. A jacked-up Z-28 Camaro, decked out with bright mag wheels and racing stripes, squatted in front of the Cracker Barrel's door like a chained pit bull. This wasn't the type of transportation most people living in a remote part of Alaska choose, as snow covers the road a good chunk of the year. Four bulging driving lights were mounted on the bumpers and two were bolted to the roof. Ted touched a light with his non-titanium hand, muttering, "still hot."

T-Ted threw open the Cracker Barrel door and twisted his head toward the lunch counter. He quickly saw the light-brandishing subject.

A tall, thin teenager was leaning against the counter, sucking on a cigarette. His yellow and gray spotted silk disco shirt was tucked into baby blue tight bell-bottom denim pants, accessorized by a wide white belt with large silver metal rings. Slip-on platform shoes made him look taller and even skinnier than his already too–thin frame. Turning his feather–cut black hair towards the door, he announced our presence: "the Fuzz have arrived. Everybody stay cool. It's the trooper from hell."

T-Ted wasn't amused and motioned the kid to the candy bar aisle, away from the diners. "What you want, man? Just come in here to hassle me?" He was toying with Ted. Even though I had known Ted for a very short time, I knew that wasn't going to work well for the young man.

Ted was already a notch hotter than I'd seen him earlier in the day. "I've warned you before about those lights. You could cause someone to crash by not dimming them."

"Cool it man, your photophobia is showing. Those lights are gnarly. What are you going to do, give me a ticket? My ol' man will just spit on it." The punk blew smoke into Ted's face. It was like watching a bull fight, with a carefree matador taunting an enraged bull for the crowd.

"This is your last warning, you little scum bag, and I don't give a crap about your father." Ted was now boring his stern gray eyes into the young face and whispering.

"I'll mention that to him. See you on the flip flop." Pulling on his orange leather jacket, the teenager slammed the front door behind him. Ted moved to the window to watch him spin out in the parking lot, throwing gravel on my patrol car.

"That's enough. Let's go. I'll drive." I threw the keys to Ted and jumped into the right seat. Taillights were just going over the western horizon on the highway out of town. Ted punched the gas and within a mile, we passed the Camaro. All six running lights were on, generating thousands of candlepower into our rearview mirror. A late season snow shower had left a skim of ice on the road surface, and Ted used that to his advantage.

About a half-mile past the Camaro, Ted slammed his left foot on the emergency brake pedal, whipping the steering wheel to the left simultaneously. The big Plymouth spun into a one hundred-eighty degree turn and we now were headed back toward the Camaro. Ted flashed his lights, then the overheads, but the landing lights kept heading toward us. Squinting, Ted pulled to the side and let the Camaro pass in the opposite direction. The kid stuck out his middle finger, honked his horn, then stomped on the gas.

Cranking the cruiser around, Ted floored the V-8, catching up with the Camaro quickly. He flipped on the siren, which complemented the emergency lights. The Camaro pulled over.

Figuring this was my training segment for traffic work, something that I hoped I'd never have to do, I offered to help. "Do you want me to get his license and registration?" I asked Ted.

"Nope, not necessary." Ted pulled the glove off his prosthetic as he strode to the car.

Breaking glass, crashing onto asphalt, disturbed the otherwise quiet roadway. The titanium hand flashed in the bright lights—one, two, three, four, five, six times. Then Ted stood still, with only the Camaro's headlights illuminating his face, revealing a slight smile.

"What the hell? You crazy pig. I'll have your ass." The driver screamed as he stood in front of his car, which now met legal equipment standards.

Quickly, Ted threw the kid onto the hood and handcuffed him. "You threatening a police officer?" Before a response was possible, Ted added, "now I have to search you, to make sure you don't have any weapons."

Ted made a quick pat down then reached into the kid's front pocket. "What do we have here?" Ted waved a plastic bag of grass. The kid burst into tears.

"Don't tell my dad, *please*. He will take my car away, maybe even ground me. *Please*, Trooper Herlihy, I won't give you any more trouble, please don't arrest me or tell my father about my stash."

"Here's what we are going to do. First, you can use your pretty jacket to clean this glass from the highway. Then you get your tail home. I'll hang onto this evidence and see how it goes. You follow the rules, show a little respect, and I may not file charges. And, I *may* not tell your father."

"Yes sir, thank you, Trooper, thank you, *sir*." As we drove away, the sobbing kid was sweeping the glass with his orange jacket.

Ted was his usual quiet self on the drive back to the office. "His father is a big shot with the pipeline company. He's a jerk, with a jerk for a son," Ted proclaimed, as he emptied the plastic bag through the car's open window into the cold night air.

Chapter 22

I met a new friend on the next morning's run. Jogging down a steep trail, I surprised a sleeping juvenile black bear. My forward momentum prevented me from stopping, so I yelled. The bear awakened, just as I piled into him. I don't know who was more scared, but fortunately for me, he let out a squeal and ran the other way.

That run got my heart rate up a little higher than usual, so to cool down, I examined the backyard airstrip. It was plenty long for the aircraft I'd be flying. A road crossed the strip, separating it from the plot of land occupied by trooper housing and a small ranch and a country store. One end of the road terminated at the Richardson Highway, and the other ended at a housing development on the Copper River. I walked off four hundred forty feet on the trooper end. That left twelve hundred sixty feet on the long side, but the constantly grazing horses added another challenge. I'd use the short side whenever possible.

After checking the tie-down ropes for the blue state Super Cub, sitting neglected in the tall grass, I jogged up the trail to my trailer. I spent the day organizing my new accommodations and unpacking my books, including *The Spirit of St. Louis* by Charles Lindbergh, which Jet gave me the morning I left King Salmon. A smile came to my face as I placed a framed photo of Jet, standing next to her Comanche, on the top shelf of the burl wood bookcase. I'd been busy since arriving in Glennallen, but still found plenty of time to miss her.

I pulled up to the post fifteen minutes before my shift. "Good afternoon, Jack. The lieutenant wants to see you." Jill, the pretty dispatcher, smiled and motioned towards Lieutenant Emery's office. As my boots clunked down the wooden hall, I considered the possibility of the pipeline big-shot learning of last night's encounter with his son, and having already conferred with the lieutenant. Emery waved me to sit in his office as he hung up is phone.

"Jack, we have a situation. I need to launch you and Ted on a search. A young lady is missing, overdue from a horse trip in the mountains south of the Chitina River. Take the Cub and start combing the mountains. Ronnie will haul fuel and supplies to the Chitina airport, so you can base down there. Ted knows the area well and will make a good spotter. Good luck. Oh yeah, by the way, Ted gave you top ratings on your training patrol yesterday. Keep up the good work." He obviously didn't know about our little traffic stop.

I parked the patrol car at the trooper trailer, grabbed my flying gear, and hurried down the trail to the Cub. Ted was waiting for me. "I did a pre-flight, checked the gas and oil. I'm ready when you are." I did a quick once over, not wanting to look as if I was questioning Ted's ability to inspect an airplane, but just to confirm everything was going to hang on. Not knowing how long it had been sitting, it was worth the effort to spend a little more time. Surprised to find both gas caps loose, I guessed I was being tested.

"So, I see you noticed the caps. Around here, we loosen the caps just a bit after securing a plane. Then on pre-flight, if they are tight, we know someone has screwed with the gas. Maybe added some sugar, dirt, or something else. If they are still loose, you are probably okay."

"Good idea, I'll use that trick," I said as I tightened the caps.

Like a weed-whacker, the propeller chopped the tall grass as I taxied the Cub as far back as I dared. After a run-up, I pointed the nose into the slight south wind. The big tundra tires popped off the sod with about a hundred feet to spare.

We quickly gained enough altitude to clear any vehicles that might surprise us coming down the road.

The Cub seemed eager to show me my new surroundings. Climbing, I made a series of turns to establish my bearings, and to get an aerial view of my new post. At about forty-five degrees with clear and sunny skies, it was a great day for flying. The Wrangell and Saint Elias mountain ranges, with glaciers pouring from their centers, loomed over the eastern skyline. Mount St. Elias, at 18,008 feet, is second only in height to Mt. McKinley, which is the highest peak in the United States. Cutting through the Chugach Mountains to the south, the wide and silty Copper River meandered as far as I could see. Running fast with the spring runoff, the river had spit out trees and other debris on its gravel bars.

"Let's check out the river," Ted's voice crackled over the intercom.

Dropping low to get a good view of the glacier-fed waterway, something appeared out of place on a sandbar just below the old village of Tazlina. Bringing the power back and pulling on a notch of flaps, we circled the object. Then I saw the sign: "Hills, Permit # 154." Twisted from banging down the river at the mercy of the swift water, it was the fishwheel belonging to Trooper Hell-ray's fan in Copper Center. Ted drew a little map of the location in his notebook. He nodded and we continued following the meandering riverbed to the south.

The day was starting out well. Only a few minutes into the flight and we'd found the fishwheel. I hoped we would have the same kind of luck in finding the missing woman. I asked Ted if he wanted to head directly to Chitina to meet with Ronnie.

"Nope. It's too early in the day to deal with 'Crash and Burn.' Turn a bit to the left and we will come onto the Chitina River. Let's search for a while, then we can go to Chitina and refuel."

Smaller and faster than the Copper River, the headwaters of the Chitina led to the east and mountains on both sides soon surrounded us. I pointed the Cub wherever Ted directed, still not knowing exactly what, or for whom we were looking. He only spoke when necessary to direct me up canyons, along tributaries, and occasionally to drop low to check out something on a gravel bar. After four hours of banging around in the hills seeing four grizzlies, twenty-five moose, and one wolf, but no humans, he directed me to turn towards the Chitina airport.

Standing alongside his white state pickup truck, Trooper Ronnie Torgy looked concerned as I taxied the Cub from the gravel Chitina airstrip to the parking ramp.

"I was worried about you guys. Everything okay?"

"We're okay. Didn't find her. Anything new?" Straight to the point, Ted didn't want to spend time explaining our afternoon recon.

Torgy turned to Ted, excitingly telling all he knew. "I've been down here for three hours and haven't heard anything. But, before I left, the lieutenant told me that this search and rescue might turn into more of a criminal investigation. Turns out the guy she was with has an interesting background. Two other women in his past turned up dead. One died when his cabin burned. The other fell out of his truck while going down the road at sixty miles per hour. Nothing could be proven, but the odds are he killed both of them. This gal signed up with the guy to drive horses from a big game guide's winter camp. The guy says she rode off by herself and may have fallen in a stream. Call me suspicious, but I think there is more to this one. The lieutenant wants us to go all out."

"We've got about two more hours before dark. Let's gas up and do all the mountain flying we can while we still have light. Maybe we'll get lucky and see a campfire at night. Any problem with that, Blake?"

Ted's plan sounded reasonable. The only concern I had was landing back at the unlighted Chitina airport at dark. The runway was plenty long, but tall spruce trees surrounded the hole it laid in. "Ronnie, can you get a couple of lanterns? I'd like you to put them at the end of runway for our night landing." I asked.

"No problem, I'll make a run to the Chitina trading post." Ronnie eagerly replied, as he pumped gas from the drums in the bed of his truck into the plane, spilling a good amount on his uniform.

After pacing the distance from the approach end of the runway, to a point where a descent would give a wide berth from the tall spruce trees, I marked two big Xs in the dirt with my boot heels.

"Please put the lanterns right here, Ronnie. I'll set up to flare between them to give us a good landing."

"Roger on that, Jack, the lights will be there."

I wanted to have faith in Ronnie, but it was getting tough.

We searched every stream that flowed into the south side of the Chitina River, between where it merged with the Copper River and the old mining town of McCarthy. We explored more canyons and revisited some from our earlier search. We saw two loose horses on one trail, but no riders.

Dark snuck upon us as the sun dropped behind the mountains. Our flight then concentrated on the Chitina and Copper River flats where we hoped to see a campfire. There was just enough light reflecting from the quarter moon onto the river to give some guidance—guidance we needed to keep away from the mountains and over the lower terrain. Finally, with the fuel sight-gauge balls sinking out of sight, it was time to return to the Chitina airport.

It was pretty much how I envisioned it. The airport was dark and hidden in the trees. However, not only had Ronnie placed the lanterns on the approach end of the strip, but he had waited for us—now with the lights of his truck illuminating the far end of the strip. I was ashamed to have doubted Ronnie. This would be easy. So I thought.

I had memorized the proper altitudes for the approach when we took off in the evening light. I used those numbers to set up the approach and descended at five hundred feet per minute from three miles out. It was a little eerie flying over the hidden trees, but the calm air and lanterns welcomed us.

We glided silently through the dark forest for a long, straight-in descent. I focused on the lanterns, with an occasional scan to the instrument panel.

Finally, only the lanterns filled the windshield. Just when a glow of light filled each side window, I chopped the power. The

Cub began to sink. I waited for the familiar scuff of tundra tires touching dirt. I waited more, but still no dirt—this was taking too long. The truck lights were coming up too fast, so I didn't want to add power and overshoot the runway. Straining, creaking, trying to keep flying, the plane warned that it couldn't hold on to the air much longer. I considered a go-around, but I didn't know if we could clear the tall spruce in the unknown depths at the runway's end. The right wing dropped. We hit hard, and then bounced back into the air. Pushing the stick forward, I added just a burst of power, concentrating on the truck lights in the distance. We hit again, this time not as firm, but still the big tires bounced. When I next felt dirt, I slammed hard on the heel brakes, pulling the stick into my lap and hitting the left rudder, forcing the plane into a minor ground loop.

We slid to stop just short of the truck lights. I switched off the electrical and climbed from the Cub, trying to figure out how I blew the landing.

"What was *that* all about, Blake?" I had forgotten about my silent passenger. He had the right to question my sloppy piloting.

"Hey, you guys okay? That was a pretty nasty landing, Jack. Guess you are a little rusty at night flying, huh?" Ronnie was out of breath after running to the Cub.

I walked on the dark gravel towards the approach end of the runway, with Ronnie at my side. Then I noticed the lanterns. They seemed to be floating high in the darkness. Both lanterns were mounted on the top of two poles—reaching about fifteen feet into the night sky—accounting for my landing flare being much too high. That's what can happen when pilots depend on others for their safety.

Ronnie bragged, "I had plenty of time, Jack, so I got a couple of skinny Black Spruce logs and tied the lanterns on them. I dug holes and stuck the logs into the ground. Figured having the lights higher in the air would make them easier to see. You can thank me by buying me dinner in Chitina."

I sprang for greasy dog salmon cheeseburgers at the Chitina Bar to properly thank Ronnie, and as a poor attempt to make up to Ted for the scary landing. Ted and I decided to camp for the night at the airstrip, to get an early morning jump on the search.

It was the glow of the campfire at the airstrip. The yellow-red beam hit Trooper Ted Herlihy's face as he reached with a stick to move the embers. The Rolodex popped open in my brain and I remembered who he was.

CHAPTER 23

It's funny how the mind works. Thinking of that campfire at Chitina makes me remember how wonderful fire can be. It can change one's total attitude when stuck out in the cold. I think it's been dipping to the minus thirties, maybe colder, during the night. My sleeping bag cuts the chill, but a fire would make my survival odds much better. Then I recalled! An old federal Fish and Wildlife pilot told me to always carry waterproof matches, along with a 35mm film can with cotton balls soaked in Vaseline. I reached into my vest pocket and there they were. I'll keep talking while I try to scrounge up some willow branches over by the crash.

J.R. and I have become friends. I shared some crumbs from my food bar with him and now he has moved closer, even perching on my shoulder for a few seconds this morning. I covered the body with snow, which has kept J.R. away. We are friends for the moment, but I still know he will feed on me if I don't make it.

Laying under the Cub's wing that night in Chitina, I didn't get much sleep. Waiting until I knew Herlihy's snores were for real, I allowed myself to doze occasionally, but I kept waking—in part because I was trying to figure the odds. How was it possible the special services guy I picked up with the Helio Courier, that eventful day in Laos, is sleeping on the other side of a campfire from me in Alaska? Did he have it in for me? Did he hold me accountable for his buddy's death? Even more importantly, how would I approach him on the subject? Or maybe he didn't even remember me.

During one of my short spurts of sleep, I had a dream. Herlihy and I were in Laos. Bombs were exploding and bullets were flying. Then Herlihy ran up to me with only a blood-pumping stump at the end of his left arm. Waking up in sweat, I confirmed he was still sleeping. I stayed awake until daylight.

Trooper Ronnie Torgy drove up as I was pre-flighting the Cub, delivering coffee and freshly baked blueberry muffins from his wife.

"Did you break anything with that atrocious landing last night, Jack?" Ronnie was rubbing it in. I wanted to explain the lantern placement, but would wait until Herlihy or another witness wasn't present. They would be unmerciful to Ronnie. I just laughed and shook my head. I had been surprised to find that the gear was intact. The only discrepancy I found was that the tailwheel didn't caster freely from side to side. That could have been old damage from normal rough duty of the job. I decided it wasn't a significant threat. That was a bad decision.

"Hang on, gentlemen, I hear my radio." Ronnie quickly turned around and banged into his truck door. He forced the door open and grabbed the radio microphone, talking for a minute before running back to the Cub.

"That was the lieutenant. He wants you guys to get in the air right now. An air taxi pilot just reported seeing a body lying on a gravel bar on the Chitina River. He wasn't clear if it is a live or a dead body. Here, I wrote down the coordinates."

"Blake, let's hit it, I'll get a fix on the map while you fly."

We climbed in the Cub and I did a quick run-up. We were soon flying above the Chitina River. It occurred to me in my haste that I didn't give the tailwheel a good shake down while taxiing, but it seemed okay in the little bit of ground turning we had done.

"There will be a creek coming up on our right. The coordinates show the gravel bar should be just past that."

As Herlihy's words broke over the headset, I saw two bald eagles soaring over the river. Then I saw another one on a gravel bar. I learned from flying in the wilderness that a group of birds of prey can mean there is a kill nearby. I reduced the throttle and slowed the Cub down to sixty with half flaps.

"There, by the eagle on the gravel bar! Get lower, Blake, there's something down there!"

The body was laying parallel to the long part of the gravel bar, on the right side near the rapidly flowing river.

"Can you get us down there, Blake? Is it long enough?

The gravel bar was about six hundred by forty feet—plenty of space for a Cub, but the uneven surface had chunks of driftwood, big rocks, and the body, as obstacles. The wind was light, so I had my choice of landing direction. I circled twice, selecting a course that, with two minor turns on rollout, would allow a touchdown without bumping into anything larger than a softball-size stone. I planned to land on the main tires to allow for best control and the most efficient braking.

The Cub thumped onto the gravel bar just where I wanted it. Keeping the nose forward until we cleared the first obstacle—a piece of driftwood the size of a black bear—I let the tail drop as the sand began to feel soft. That's when the tailwheel decided to go its own way. The plane jerked violently to the left, pointing us toward big rocks and another piece of driftwood. A nudge of right rudder straightened the erratic track, but now the body was smack dab on course.

A go-around at this point wasn't an option—a big cottonwood was lying across the end of the gravel bar. Gingerly using power and lightly tapping the brakes, the Cub gear nicely straddled the body. We stopped in the wet sand just past her.

"You better hope she wasn't alive, 'cause that landing would have given her a heart attack. What the hell was that all about?"

I explained the tailwheel failure to Herlihy as we walked back to the body. He shook his head.

Her face was gone. The eagles had completely eaten the eyes and flesh off what was probably a pretty face, exposing tissue, bone, blood and maggots. She was not a small woman, but the bloating made her naked body appear huge. As we turned her to inspect for wounds on her back, tiny bugs wiggled from every orifice. The nauseating stench was overwhelming. No worry about the landing killing her. She had obviously been there for a while.

"We need to take her back to Chitina. Get the bodybag that Torgy brought yesterday." Herlihy didn't like what I found in the plane: "What the hell? That idiot must have grabbed the only body bag that is ripped. That should have been trashed a long time ago!"

After photographing the body, we checked for more wounds. But it was too far gone for anything but a coroner at this point. The body was stiff, but with a lot of maneuvering, we shoved and pushed it into the compact back seat of the Cub. She was too large and too rigid for a seatbelt, but passenger safety was not a concern. After wiring the tailwheel in a more or less straight position, we turned the Cub around to make use of all the remaining gravel. Herlihy said he would stay put while I flew to Chitina to drop off the body and make proper repairs.

Just as I was about to start the Cub, Herlihy yelled, "At least you won't get shot at during this rescue."

Climbing out from the river, I thought briefly about Herlihy's words and realized he knew who I was. I'd think more about that later, right now, my thoughts turned to my passenger. She was too young to die, especially if it was murder. And if it was murder, who is the killer? Did she have family? Would someone miss her?

A cold hand touched the back of my head, just after climbing to a thousand feet above the river. Slowly turning around, I saw the grayish fingers sticking out of the rip in the body bag. I pushed the body back, but she kept slipping forward into my seat.

Releasing my shoulder harness and leaning forward into the panel was the only way to avoid contact. With the belt loose, my nose reached the side vent, giving some relief from the horrible odor. I circled the Chitina airport, but no Ronnie. Now I'd have to continue the especially unpleasant flight all the way to Glennallen.

The stench, the continual shoving of the body back into the rear seat, and the maggots, made the flight seem much longer than thirty minutes. As I recall that flight today, the odor is still fresh. To wash my brain then, and now, here is a story Jill the dispatcher had told me about a Ronnie adventure. It still makes me smile.

Jill showed me a plaque in the Glennallen post, which read: "So the next one won't get away." Surrounding the edges of the plaque was a miniature lasso and in the center was a photo of a smiling Ronnie in front of his trooper truck.

Laughing as she told the story, Jill said it was a cold winter day when she took a call from the operators of Eureka Lodge—located on the summit between Anchorage and Glennallen. The owners were strong supporters of the Glennallen troopers, and would warn the post whenever the brass stopped in for lunch, en route for a surprise inspection. That day, the lodge owner reported that the infamous First Sergeant Lutz and a captain were, at that very moment, eating Eureka burgers. The lodge owner had overheard Lutz boasting: "I'm going to shake up those Glennallen slugs today."

The only one in the office was Ronnie, so Jill warned him. Ronnie rushed through the next hour washing his patrol truck, polishing his shoes and brass, and checking himself in the mirror. When he felt all was perfect, he pulled out on the Glenn Highway and headed west toward Eureka. His plan was well thought out: he'd be patrolling the Glenn Highway, looking sharp and working hard, and he would be "surprised" by the bosses. He would surely impress them enough to get first dibs on the next departmental promotion. Great plan!

The car carrying the inspectors met Ronnie's truck about half way between Glennallen and Eureka. Ronnie pulled over on the north side of the road and Lutz stopped on the south side. Making an unusually flawless exit from the truck with his Stetson in place, Ronnie snapped a salute and quickly paced toward the supervisors. "Well, what a surprise! It's an honor to see you gentlemen visit our little post."

Neither the captain nor the first sergeant returned the greeting. Instead, they both ran past Ronnie at top speed. "What the hey…?" Ronnie began to say. But then he turned and saw why.

Ronnie's shiny patrol truck was headed back to Glennallen—on its own. He had made only one mistake. Instead of putting the truck in park, he had selected reverse. The captain almost caught up with the truck—just before its rear tire bumped a chunk of ice in the road, causing a slight backward turn into the ditch filled with deep snow. While the three men awaited the wrecker, Ronnie received a serious ass chewing. The good news is that the rescue took so long that the bosses decided to forget the post inspection on that trip, earning Ronnie a few points with the post troopers. But, not enough points to forget the event at the annual post awards banquet, when Ronnie received his plaque.

Ronnie's smiling face greeted me at the trooper airstrip. His smile turned to a grimace as we struggled to pull the body between the Piper's clamshell door. Without warning, he jerked his head and vomited all over his shoes. "Whew, how did you guys rip up the body bag? You're sure hard on equipment!" The guy cracked me up, even at the worst times.

As I replaced the broken tailwheel, Ronnie laid out the new plan. "You and Ted need to head to McCarthy. The guy who was with the girl last was seen there yesterday. Name is Butch Saint. Far as I can tell, he's not a saint at all—quite the opposite. The lieutenant wants him interviewed, but don't force the issue about the girl's death. Don't say *anything* about the other dead girls. Just get his story on the horse trip. When did he last see the girl? Did they fight? Were they lovers? The homicide investigators from Anchorage will follow up on this later, once they put the pieces together. Try to find out where he plans on being for the next couple of months. Get a photo of him if you can."

Ronnie handed me an envelope with Saint's rap sheet and a pack that Ted had left at Chitina. "His clothes and sleeping bag are in there." After a quick shower, I put on a fresh uniform and threw some gear into my backpack. I taxied the Cub to the horse-grazing end of the airstrip to grab some groceries at the general store. Then I was again airborne.

The gravel bar landing was much easier with a good working tailwheel. After briefing Herlihy on the plan, we lifted off for McCarthy.

I was looking forward to our visit with Butch Saint.

CHAPTER 24

We're not ghosts." An old timer reminded me that although McCarthy was considered a ghost town in the travel brochures, the current residents didn't much like that term. Once home to more than six hundred, complete with hotels, trading posts, bars, brothels, and one of the world's biggest copper mines, only about thirty resided there now. It's hard to believe McCarthy was once the largest town in Alaska. Now it seems to be just the right size.

Instead of making their living from copper, the locals now subsisted on income generated from summer tourists who climbed the mountains, explored the barn-red deserted buildings, and bought trinkets. A couple of big game guides worked from town during the hunting season. One guy operated an air taxi, flying mail, passengers and freight.

Until 1938, J.P. Morgan pumped money into the local economy for the mining operation. A railroad hauled workers and ore from the mines to Cordova. Now, the town was isolated from the real world. The only way to get there was by small plane, or by driving three hours on the rutted dirt road from Chitina, then using the hand-pulled trolley to cross the raging Kennicott River. It seemed like a peaceful little haven in the wilderness.

We parked the Cub just off the McCarthy runway, down the trail from the combination general store/post office and walked up the path under the nimbostratus-filled skies. Frank and Franny Huber met us at the door. The smell of freshly baked bread wafted from the kitchen. Franny gave Herlihy a big hug and

Frank shook his hand. Surprisingly, Herlihy responded with kind words. Probably the most words, and certainly the nicest, I'd heard from his mouth at one time: "It's great to see you both again." I was introduced as Trooper Blake, but the Hubers quickly knew me as Jack.

"Come on in, boys, we're just about to have lunch and there's plenty for everyone." Franny was happy to have the company. With her blonde-gray hair tied in a bun and her blue checkered apron, the sixty-year old looked liked an advertisement for Grandma's Cookies. Frank's round body, red cheeks and white hair made him a dead-ringer for an off-duty Santa Claus.

Franny proudly showed me around their rustic log cabin. The front room served as their informal post office. Mail was neatly stuck in little cubbyholes in Frank's oak roll-top desk. Adjacent to the office, was the kitchen—the source of the fresh bread, now cooling on top of a black and white wood cook stove. Pots boiled away on the stove and coffee perked on a back burner. Open shelves displayed canned goods of all sorts, most likely berries from the local hills and vegetables from the Huber garden.

A fire blazed in the cozy living room's woodstove. The old Golden Retriever, warming himself by the fire, wagged his tail as we entered, too comfortable to get up and welcome us formally. Overstuffed chairs and a couch, covered with Fanny's brightly crocheted afghans, complemented the glossy wooden floor. Through the large windows, the inspiring Wrangell Mountains hovered over the Kennicott River. Happy oil paintings of downtown McCarthy, spring flowers, and mountains, decorated the walls. Franny Huber had signed them all. This was the kind of home I wanted to share with Jet someday.

Franny's delicious lunch featured bison stew and bread fresh from the oven. Rhubarb pie with homemade ice cream was dessert. During the lighthearted dinner conversation, I heard Herlihy laugh for the first time. He seemed human, especially when pitching in with me to clean the table and take the dishes to the sink. He now was Ted to me, not Trooper Herlihy, not Herlihy, not T-Ted, but *Ted*.

Just after lunch, three people came in for their mail and to visit with Franny. Helen Jackson had crossed the river on the hand trolley. Tall and attractive, Helen wore a black cap with "Cat" in yellow, and grease-stained brown insulated Carhartt overalls. She was full of energy and laughter. She grabbed her mail with her rough hands, expressing delight over the latest *Gourmet* magazine. Helen smiled and waved at Ted and said she was pleased to meet me. She offered that she and her husband were homesteaders and that I was welcome to drop in on them anytime.

Tom and Suzi Brix walked down from their house in the old mining district. The newly–married, professional-looking couple in their thirties drank coffee at the Hubers' table. Suzi quietly entered the table conversation, while Tom glanced through the Alaska Bush Outfitters' catalog that came with his mail.

Ted took the opportunity to ask the locals about Butch Saint. The general consensus was that Saint was a loner. No one knew him well and no one seemed to want to know him any better. Franny offered that he only occasionally got mail and never had time to visit. Then a man walked in by himself.

"Ted, this is Gordon Tate, he lives by Butch," announced Franny. Tate was a scruffy-looking guy, maybe thirty-five. Long unwashed brown hair stuck out of his worn cap and thick glasses slid up and down his nose.

"Mr. Tate, can you tell me if Saint is around?" Ted asked.

"He came in two days ago on the mail plane." Tate studied his boots as he spoke.

"Do you know where we can find him?" Ted pursued.

"His cabin is above the Mill Building. He was there this morning. Uh, you should know, something is not right with that guy."

Ted got directions from Tate, thanked the Hubers for lunch, and told them we would be on our way.

"Watch out for the storm that's coming, it's a big one. One last hit by Old Man Winter." Frank Huber was standing by the weather radio he maintained for reports to the National Weather Service. The broadcast was issuing a winter storm warning, predicting heavy snow. It seemed much too late in the spring for a blizzard, but this *was* Alaska.

"Taxi to the end of the airport. A guide I know keeps an old pickup there we can use. I want to get up the hill to Butch Saint's cabin before he gets the word we are looking for him." Herlihy's voice had lost the tenseness with which I'd become familiar. The short visit with the friendly locals seemed to soften him somehow.

"I forgot that this ol' pickup lost its muffler years ago," Ted said as exhaust fumes seeped into the cab. "Saint has to be deaf not to hear us." We had driven almost five miles and now Ted pulled the truck between two old buildings. "Let's walk from here."

"That's the old Mill Building, the tallest wooden structure in Alaska, maybe even in the whole U.S." The massive structure of weathered red-painted wood cascaded down a hill, ending at the street front. "Let's hike up and see if Saint will talk to us." We walked on the old boardwalk between the company buildings. Unlike the title of "Sin City" McCarthy once earned, Kennicott housed mine employees and company offices. I glanced in one of the windows and saw magazines from the 1930s, an old steel beer can, a pair of spectacles missing one lens, and a Cole's woodstove that looked like it could still keep the old building warm on a winter day. It was apparent that when the mines were closed in 1938, the miners left much behind. It remained just as it had been.

Avoiding the rickety steps, we climbed the dirt hill to be as quiet as possible.

Halfway up the hill, I saw movement on the porch of the cabin perched on a cliff above the Mill Building. Ted saw it too. "That must be him. Let's pick up the pace." We heard a door squeak open. Then footsteps.

"Up at the cabin. State troopers, we need to talk to you!" Ted bellowed.

The footsteps quickened, then scuffled on the top level of the Mill Building. "Let's go, Jack, he's rabbiting."

We scrambled up the hill, pulling ourselves up by the stalks of weeds, deciding to try and cut Saint off by entering the mill on the fourth level from the top. The cold structure smelled of mildew and diesel, and old light bulbs hung limp on long cords from the ceiling. Ted went in first.

"Damn!" The pain–filled yell echoed off the walls.

Rotted planks in the floor had broken underfoot causing Ted to fall through to his waist—stuck between building levels. The timbers were creaking and it appeared as if the whole floor could collapse in the old building. Ted didn't dare move and I couldn't go in after him without adding to the problem. I glanced down the hill to see a man running down the main street of Kennicott, through blowing snowflakes. No doubt it was Butch Saint.

Grabbing a length of rope from amongst the abandoned supplies, I quickly threw it over a beam and lowered an end to Ted, hoping it would hold his weight. He drew the line around him and I pulled him out. Simple and fast. At least something was going right. "Thanks, partner, I owe you one," Ted said as he shook himself off and carefully limped to the door. He had a nasty scrape on his shin, but was otherwise okay. Being called "partner" was real progress, but we didn't have time for niceties. A storm was brewing.

We checked a couple of shacks on the way back to the airport and made a swing over Kennicott in the Cub, but didn't catch sight of Saint. We would have to talk to him another day. The Anchorage homicide investigators would be picking up the case anyway.

Since making the connection between Ted Herlihy and Laos, I hoped for the opportunity to clear the air. Was that the reason for his unfriendliness during our first few days together, or was it just a front he thought appropriate for a field-training officer? Now that he was being more civil, the hour flight back to Glennallen in the Cub would be a good opportunity to talk. The weather changed that plan.

Snow was now falling heavily. I pushed the nose of the Cub over and began snaking over the dirt road to Chitina. Soon we were down to two hundred feet and snow was building on the wings. I dropped to one hundred feet. When forward visibility dropped to almost zero, I slid open the window on the left. Squinting out the side was the only way to see, with the pelting snow totally blinding the windscreen.

I'd hoped we could fly through the storm system, but it only got worse. Now carrying a lot of extra weight with the heavy ice, the little plane began the feel sluggish and it was snowing so hard that I was losing sight of the road. The blizzard had closed us in on all sides. We had to get down before we turned into a lump of ice.

"There's an airstrip up here somewhere. It's called Long Lake." Ted, who had remained silent in the storm, finally spoke.

I tried to make a lake out of the white. I just hoped we could stay airborne long enough to find it. Then a group of small green cabins popped into sight through the side window.

"Ted, look out the left side, do you recognize those cabins?"

"That's Buddy Cole's place, the airstrip should be on the right," Ted replied, with stress in his voice.

I flung open the clamshell door on the right. Seventy mile per hour winds filled the cockpit, but the limited view offered my only chance to see the airstrip in the blinding snowstorm.

The lake showed itself first, then the airstrip. The landing would be with a tailwind, but I didn't care. I just wanted out of that mess, and cranked the Cub into a steep bank, slipping toward the surface. We touched down on the snow-covered field with the tundra tires. Now I just had to maintain enough power and enough backpressure to keep the plane from flipping in the snow, which had already accumulated on the strip. We used most of the runway, but we were down.

The wind was blowing about forty knots, so we used extra rope to secure the Cub. Then we grabbed our packs and trudged through the snow to the cabins. Only one cabin had smoke coming from the stovepipe, so we knocked on that door.

The surprised occupant greeted us. "What the heck! Where did you boys come from?"

Ted explained our dropping in unannounced, and re-minded Buddy Cole that they had met before.

"Sure, sure, Trooper, I remember you. Come on in out of that mess."

Like an early morning fog on a fall day, blue smoke swirled in the cabin from about a foot above the wood floor all the way to the ceiling. My nose told me it wasn't from the woodstove.

As obvious as it was that Buddy was a smoker, it was equally obvious that he was a hunter and trapper. Heads of caribou, Dahl sheep, goat, moose, bison and a musk ox hung from the walls. A dark brown grizzly bear hide graced one wall, next to a blond grizzly. Pelts from lynx, wolverine, wolves and other furbearers took up the rest of the wall space.

Buddy Cole was one of those guys that you liked right away. With an infectious laugh and sincere desire to accommodate his guests, he made a person feel welcome in his home. His tall, lanky frame required him to duck under the exposed beams of his stick-framed cabin. I guessed his age at sixty, but he spoke as lively as a twenty-year old.

"Joy, we have company," Buddy said as he lit a cigarette to replace the one he had put down to shake our hands.

Buddy's wife, Joy, was ten years younger and a foot shorter than him. Her jet-black hair was perfectly kept and the bright red sweater and black dress slacks she wore were much nicer than the Bush conditions required.

"Welcome, fellas, I didn't hear you drive in. That's some blizzard out there. How about a cup of coffee?" Joy coughed, smiled, then coughed again. She took a drag on a lady-like skinny cigarette while reaching for the coffee percolator on the potbelly woodstove.

The Coles were surprised to find we'd been flying in the storm. "Well you won't be going anywhere tonight. I'll fix up a cabin." But the Coles wanted to visit first. I'm sure they didn't get winter guests very often and they were starved for conversation from outsiders.

"So Ted, where did you guys fly in from?" Can't we talk outside? I thought to myself.

Ted explained our mission and how we got caught in the storm, trying to get back to Glennallen.

"You sure are sneezing a lot, Ted. Not allergic to cats, are you?" Buddy asked. Ted glanced toward the two felines, peacefully sleeping in front of the fireplace.

"Nope, must be getting a cold, I guess." I knew Ted was suffering as badly from the smoke as I was.

"Can't say I've heard of that Saint fellow. You say he was running horses for Max Smithers? You know, I've been a big game guide for thirty-seven years, hunted right next to Smithers for most of that time, and I still can't figure him out. I do know he got busted a few years back for wasting meat, but that's about it. He's never has been friendly enough to get to know. What kind of plane are ya flying today?"`

"Super Cub? That's great! I have twenty thousand or so flying hours, all in a Cub. Sure, I've had the chance to fly all sorts of planes—185s, Beavers and all the rest. But I've always thought that I should stick with one plane to be the best pilot I can be. And, like a wise man once said: 'A Cub is the safest plane you can fly—it will only barely kill you.'"

Buddy held a photograph in his nicotine-stained hand. In the black and white snapshot, he smiled, standing in the snow next to a ski–equipped Super Cub. Two bloody wolves hung from the wing struts.

For the next two hours, Buddy entertained us with stories about flying and hunting. Ted dozed off several times, coming alive when the conversation highlighted hunting rather than airplanes. I learned then that Ted had a passion for hunting and that he ran a trapline in the winter.

I had a heck of a headache from the bad air and needed to get out of the cabin to get some oxygen. Finally, I realized my escape. "Excuse me Buddy, but I need to see how the Cub is doing." I knew a fellow pilot would understand the need to check an airplane in a storm, especially when snow was accumulating on the wings.

Like a sleeping dog hearing his master saying he was going for a walk, Ted jumped up.

"I better help you, Jack. There's bound to be a lot of snow on the wings by now." Buddy was saying something about loaning us a broom for sweeping snow, but we bolted for the door without hearing the details.

Fresh air, even in the blowing snow, never tasted so good. Tinged with the scent of spruce and heavy with frozen moisture, I forced deep breaths of the wonderful winter oxygen into my lungs.

We strapped on snowshoes and tromped a quarter mile to the airstrip. The tracks we had laid two hours ago were barely visible. The poor wings sagged under the heavy snow. I took a rope from the Cub and threw it over a wing. Ted grabbed one end and I grabbed the other. We walked along, pulling snow off by sliding the rope. Snow was coming down so hard that by the time we finished one wing, the other one needed to be cleaned again.

Joy treated us to a hearty meal of moose steaks and potatoes. I escaped twice during an after-dinner Scrabble game, excusing myself to go to the outhouse. I really just needed more fresh air. Ted caught on to my trick and did the same.

Finally, at 10 p.m., Buddy showed us to our cabin and checked us out on the wood stove operation. By 10:30, we had the little cabin up to about fifty degrees and with an oil lantern providing light, we settled in. Finally, I could approach Ted. I could get some answers. I'd take a relief run outside, and then we could talk. After only a minute in the still-snowing dark skies, I went back in the cabin to snoring echoing off the wooden walls.

The man with all the answers was asleep.

CHAPTER 25

Awake, I was waiting for Ted's snoring to stop when Buddy beat on the cabin at six o'clock. "Breakfast is on, boys."

The snow hadn't let up all night. Ted and I followed Buddy's tracks to the main cabin where we devoured Joy's abundant breakfast. After the meal, Ted and I cleaned snow off the Cub wings, then returned to the cabin for colorful conversation and a lunch of moose burgers. We later snowshoed to the Cub for more snow cleaning, then back to the cabin for talk, dinner, and Scrabble, with a few fresh air escapes in between. This scene was repeated for four days—resulting in at least six feet of snow accumulating outside and a lifetime of smoke ingested inside.

On the second night, Ted and I finally answered all the questions we had about each other. The conversation changed everything.

"I didn't know if I could trust you." Crackling from the woodstove and howling from the continual blizzard emphasized Ted's intense stare.

What Ted said next was almost unbelievable—until he made it believable. Then it all came together and made sense.

"I thought for a while that you were one of F-Rod's boys. Until McCarthy, I didn't know." I remember hearing the name in Laos, but I never knew who F-Rod was. He continued before I could ask a question. "I finally got a look at your wrist at the Hubers'."

"My wrist?"

"Yeah, I was relieved to see you don't have a tattoo. When we did the dishes for Franny and you rolled up your sleeves, I saw—you don't have one of F-Rod's tattoos."

Ted had my attention.

"F-Rod was with the CIA in Laos. But he wasn't happy just working for the government. Right after the war, he bought all the surplus weaponry he could get his hands on. His old man in Cuba is loaded, so he had unlimited funds. At a huge profit, he sold arms to whatever country or private terrorist group would buy them. When he bailed from the CIA, he took the millions he made and moved back to the U.S.

"F-Rod's real name is Felix Rodriguez, but he wanted to break the connection to his past, so he changed that. He now goes by Fred Roderick to make him sound more like an Anglo. Living the life of luxury bored him. His family made its fortunes in oil, so, with that background, he came to Alaska to get in on the oil rush.

"He started Denali Security, providing protection services to the oil companies. He brought some of the men who worked under his command in Laos. The functionally sane ones work with his company at his Prudhoe Bay headquarters. Some he weeded out and he uses them elsewhere—I don't know exactly in what capacity, but I aim to find out. Here's the kicker—he hires retiring troopers and sometimes troopers still on the job, paying them very well. That gives him a lot of influence on the department. Don't get his operation confused with Alyeska Security. They are our friends and do a lot to support us here. Roderick does his own thing, and I'm not sure exactly all that entails. It's almost like he set this whole company up to have something to play with."

I was mesmerized, and had lots of questions.

"Can you tell me what the tattoo looks like," I asked.

"Better yet, here's a photo."

Ted slid a tattered photograph from his wallet. It was of a tattoo on a dead man's wrist. I recognized it immediately. It was the same tattoo as Mark Morgen's. It was same tattoo I had seen on a young Mexican boy in Dallas a lifetime ago.

"I wouldn't join F-Rod's little group, like that guy with us in the plane who got shot. I wouldn't wear the tattoo. I wouldn't do his dirty work. So, F-Rod's boys made it simple. No tattoo, no need for a left wrist, or a left hand."

"How did it happen, Ted?"

"One of his bomb guys set up a little explosive, on the toilet handle in my room, of all places. I reached over, pushed the lever and my hand gets blown into the bathtub. He made his point, I guess."

"So how did you get on with the troopers?" I needed more.

"Well, you're not the only Air America pilot who came to Alaska. Several guys are flying out of Merrill Field. Ace Jackson and I were good buds in Laos. When he got the flying gig in Anchorage, he tracked me down. Alaska sounded good, so I flew up. I heard the troopers were hiring and applied. I passed all the tests and they said if I could do the job just like any other trooper, without any limitation from my fake hand, I was in. That's pretty much it."

"So what's your plan with F-Rod, now?" I asked.

"Jack, I don't give a crap about that son of a bitch. I just want to do my twenty years, get my retirement, and live out in the Bush somewhere."

Ted Herlihy didn't convince me that he could forget what was done to him in Laos. That metal hand reminded him every day.

It was sunny and windy on the morning of the fifth day. Joy made us one last breakfast and Buddy helped us sweep snow from the wings of the Cub and shovel snow from in front of the wheels. Then he ran his snomachine up and down the airstrip to pack down the runway.

The Coles had become great friends and I was sincere when I told Buddy that I hoped our paths would cross again.

They did, but not as any of us had hoped.

CHAPTER 26

Snow was blowing off the hills by Chitina. I whipped the stick back and forth—as if I was churning homemade ice cream—trying to counter the wind forces. Glancing down at the Copper River, I could tell our ground speed was very slow, but until we finally made radio contact with Gulkana Flight Service, I didn't know we were bucking fifty mile an hour headwinds. Turbulence picked up to severe about ten miles south of the Gulkana airport.

We had no way to check the weather in Glennallen, before taking off from Long Lake, but after a four-day blizzard, the blue skies were inviting. Once we were level at one thousand feet, Ted and I began a nice discussion, even chuckling a bit when he told stories about Ronnie. But then… *Bang!* Ted's head smashed into the overhead cross bar in the Cub and he let out a profanity. I told him to cinch down on his harness belts and I did the same. We were in for a hard ride home.

There was too much crosswind to land at the trooper airstrip, so I radioed flight service that we would land at Gulkana. The long, wide runway would give us a lot more room for maneuvering. Flight Service reported the winds were gusting to fifty-six knots with twenty degrees of crosswind, and that the ice-covered runway offered no braking action.

The landing was a fight all the way to the ground and we bounced back in the air a couple of times before we settled onto the icy surface. A little power was needed to keep us from sliding backwards on the slick runway, and I realized that we couldn't taxi to the tie downs on our own without flipping over in the wind. A call to flight service resulted in two airport trucks rolling out to the runway. One guy in the bed of each truck held onto the wing ropes and we were safely escorted to the parking ramp where Lt. Emery was waiting.

"That's fine, Ted, you men did all you could." Lieutenant Emery had listened intently to Ted's briefing.

"Anchorage Investigations will handle the Saint investigation from here. I'm glad you guys made it through that storm. We really got dumped on here," the lieutenant continued.

We hadn't changed clothes or showered for five days, so I was relieved when Ted asked if we could head home and get cleaned up.

"No problem. In fact, I *insist!* You guys smell like you have been hanging around a smoky bar. Take a couple days off.

"By the way, Jack, there is a slight change of plans for your field training, now that Ted is done with you. Dave is still on light duty, stuck in the office for a couple of weeks. Ronnie is working down in Valdez on a special project. So, to keep you on the schedule, a training officer from another post, who is also a check pilot, is coming out to spend the week with you. You'll not only get a week of certified field training, but you will get checked out in a Cessna 185. The Cub will go back with the training officer and we'll keep the 185, which is better for our use anyway."

Oh *joy!* My thoughts went to the aircraft supervisor who had made my first flight in a state plane so miserable last year. I dreaded working with another strict, humorless, unfriendly, pain in the tail checkpilot, riding me from the right seat. This was going to be another miserable experience. The only difference was that it was to be much longer than just one check flight.

CHAPTER 27

The early June day was perfect and I should have been happy. Sun was beating down on the airfield, there was little wind, and the bugs weren't buzzing around my head. Today I'd get to fly a Cessna 185, and with six seats and three hundred horsepower, the performance would be close to Air America's Helio Couriers. I'm usually a positive thinker and I should have been excited, but I wasn't. I pictured the check pilot, who was scheduled to land in a few minutes, to be just like Larry Lasso, however, this time wearing a trooper uniform, and now judging me on my job performance as well as my flying. This one would probably be even worse than Lasso. And the lieutenant had told me to pack for a week, so it would be long and painful. I'd get through the training, but I wouldn't *enjoy* it.

The blue, white, and gold Cessna's propeller screamed like an angry lynx as it flew over Gulkana airport. Oh great, exactly on time. This guy is going to be a real stickler for detail—probably more into paperwork procedures than Bush flying. I caught myself scowling as the plane taxied from the runway to the parking ramp.

The 185 made a quick turn and pulled between the tie-down ropes perfectly. Well, I thought, at least he knows how to park. I considered that this was probably his best ability—other than chewing out troopers in the left seat.

The Cessna's door snapped opened. I could hear the gyros spinning down. Then the pilot spoke.

"What's a nice guy like you doing in a place like this?" I knew the voice, I knew the smile. I was wrong to have pre-judged the checkpilot. I was never so glad to be so wrong.

"Jet!" We embraced and her soft lips made the world right again.

"I'm your check pilot and your field training officer for the next week, Jack. I hope you can put up with me. After two seasons working here, I know your lieutenant pretty well. He asked if I could possibly break away from my post to help him out with training. I just couldn't turn him down. He is the only one in the department who knows about us. Now get your gear Jack, we're headed to the hills."

The Cessna leaped off the field and, on Jet's instruction, I turned towards Mount Drum. I couldn't stop grinning while dividing my attention between flying and gazing at Jet. She noticed.

"Okay Trooper Blake, I will be rating you on all your actions, as both a pilot and trooper, during the next five days, so shape up!" Jet directed me to fly low up a river that poured from the nearby mountains. Snow covered the ragged peaks and caribou scattered beneath our plane. Glaciers were everywhere, with silty waters cascading from the melting ice.

"You're flying the 'Rice Rocket.' It was forfeited in an illegal guiding case. Performs well, and lives up to its name," Jet explained.

"See that lodge?" Jet pointed at a big green building with a few cabins circling it. "That's a base for Ross Payne's corrupt guiding operation. We've been investigating him for years. His day will come."

We navigated around Mount Drum and soon the headwaters of the Copper River appeared below us. The lush greenery draped across the landscape like golf courses. "That's Tanada Peak off to the right and Tanada Lake above and to the left. The department owns that little cabin on the lake. Game wardens base out of there during sheep season."

A long dirt road emerged over the next ridge, leading to the Nabesna airstrip, where we did a few touch and goes. After two full-stall and three wheel-landings, Jet had me fly down the runway, touching on one wheel, then the other, repeating it over and over until we were near the end of the runway. Then we popped off and did it again and again.

Apparently satisfied I wasn't going to wreck the airplane, Jet directed me through Cooper Pass for practice on another gravel airstrip at the old mining town of Chisana. We popped over Chitistone Canyon and the White River for my next assignment.

"Okay, Jack, you're ready, now let's have some fun." Jet handed me a chart and pointed to the closest X. "Take me there."

Solo Creek lay in a valley framed by mountains covered halfway up from their bases with winter snow. The brushy airstrip paralleled the river at an elevation of thirty-six hundred feet. After an easy landing, we got out and stretched. Jet checked on an outfitter's grazing horses.

For the rest of the day we reconnoitered the Wrangells. We hiked at Iceberg Lake, passed over Pyramid Peak and Wolverine Mountain, flew up and down canyons and glaciers, and explored an old mine. We saw grizzlies, Dahl sheep, mountain goats, moose and caribou.

"Okay, find this and we're home for the night." Jet pointed to another X and I turned towards Nugget Creek, zooming down the Kuskalana Glacier with sixteen thousand-foot Mount Blackburn hovering over it. Nugget Creek airstrip was tucked in a small forest of spruce and a little log cabin, just a short hike from the airstrip, welcomed us.

"Do you hear that Jack?"

I stopped walking and listened. We had crossed a river with clear water pleasantly cascading over stones and an eagle had screeched in the distance,. but now I heard nothing.

"Hear what?" I asked.

"Nothing, that's what is so perfect," Jet answered with that dazzling smile.

"Ordinarily, we'd catch dinner in the creek, but it's late. So what are you bringing to the table, Jack?"

"I have some freeze-dried dinners. 'El Rancho Soft Tacos' or 'Leonardo's Lasagna.'" I emptied my bag of survival rations on the table.

"Well, well. Let me get my recruit–rating form, Jack. That's pretty bad grub. How about you building the fire? And, instead of that cardboard-tasting junk, I guess we could grill these moose steaks I marinated in a balsamic rosemary sauce. And, I guess instead of your powdered milk, we could have this bottle of Washington Syrah." Jet never failed to amaze me.

As we sat by the campfire in front of the cabin, a black wolf trotted by. Most likely part of his normal route, the predator apparently wasn't used to seeing humans here at this time of year. He stopped dead in his tracks, sniffed in our direction, and then bolted away just as a half moon rose over the mountains.

We talked about how much we missed each other. I told her of my visit to McCarthy and how I could see us living like that someday. We saved work talk for another time. Jet shared her oversized sleeping bag with me in the cold night.

The sun blasted through the cabin window the next morning, promising another perfect day. After breakfast, we hiked up the glacier, seeing a dark brown grizzly with a startling blond chest. A herd of sheep, with four big rams, ten ewes and four tiny lambs, casually crossed the trail in front of us. Back at the cabin, Jet tossed out a challenge.

"Jack, I'm going to give you a special assignment today. If you somehow figure out how to do what has eluded game wardens for years, I promise you a surprise." Any surprise Jet could offer would be worth my best effort. I readily agreed.

It was a little sad to see the tiny cabin on Nugget Creek disappear under our wing, but this day would be even better than yesterday.

We flew back to the trooper airstrip, took showers at my trailer, and then hopped over to the Gulkana airport. After loading twenty square metal five-gallon cans of aviation gas in the 185, we took off to the south. "Go to this X next, please, Jack."

During the forty-minutes of dead reckoning to the headwaters of the Chitina River, I told Jet all I'd learned about Fred Roderick, tattoos, and all the rest. She offered to find out what she could from her sources at headquarters.

Passing over Long Lake, I waved the wings at the Coles, who stopped working in their garden long enough to search the sky for the noisy 185. I told Jet about Ted and my extended stay at their cabin. "Buddy and Joy are great people and they are always willing to help us," Jet said.

The X this time took me to a barren airstrip where the Nizana Glacier splits into braided waters. The landing area was marked on both ends by small orange-painted boulders. With the extra weight of canned gas, we approached the strip with a little more speed, but stopped well within the confines of the gravel bar. The rugged area was void of any trees. Just gravel and flat ground everywhere. A brown frame cabin, riddled with bullet holes, sat on the side of the airstrip. A sign over the door identified it as State of Alaska property.

"Here's your challenge, Trooper. Find a place to hide those twenty cans of fuel. Every year troopers haul av gas in here for hunting season patrols, and it gets stolen. We have a pretty good idea that a local big game guide makes off with it, but we can't prove it. I'm going over to McCarthy to say 'hi' to the Hubers and see if any bear hunters are still there. I'll be back in an hour."

After the Rice Rocket faded into the eastern horizon, I took another look over the flat lands. Then I opened the cabin. The appointments were sparse: two bunk beds, a compact woodstove, a cobbled together table with stools made from Chevron wooden gas boxes, a Coleman stove and two cans of orange spray paint. There were no shovels or other tools for digging. I looked for a trap door in the floor and outside for access to get underneath the cabin, but nothing.

Back outside, I again surveyed the landscape. No trees, no brush, nothing to conceal the gas cans. I walked to the ends of the seven hundred foot airstrip—both ends terminated in water. I really wanted Jet's surprise, but maybe it wasn't to be. Then I looked at the painted boulders and it hit me.

Taking the orange paint from the cabin, I sprayed each gas can. I placed two cans on each end of the airstrip and spaced the other eighteen evenly along both sides. The airstrip was now properly marked and the cans were "hidden."

Jet killed the 185's engine, climbed out and laughed. "Jack, that's a crazy idea, but it might just work. I'll give you partial credit now and full credit if they are there through the hunting season. So, you get part of the surprise today."

On the way to the next X, we flew up a raging stream, which dumped into the Chitina River. "That's where the girl on the horse supposedly fell in." I told Jet about the body we had recovered and our search for the guide's horse wrangler.

"I know that guide. He is a shaky operator. I don't think he would kill anyone, although he would hire Charles Manson if he'd work cheap enough. It sounds like you may be on the trail of the right guy."

The X led us to an open meadow at the end of a lake-covered valley. Glaciers and rugged mountains hung over the landing area. After climbing out of the plane onto the soft grassy runway, Jet gave me the much-anticipated surprise. She pulled a fly rod from the Cessna's baggage compartment and pointed me to a creek. We quickly set up camp and changed into civilian clothing, Jet opting for shorts, even though it was only in the 50s.

"Let's see if you can catch dinner," she challenged. Leading the way to the creek, Jet's bronze, athletic legs were easy to follow.

Every cast rewarded me with a rainbow trout hitting the fly I tossed into the water. After twenty minutes of playing with the red-sided fish, and keeping one, we hiked to another little creek that was boiling with huge steelheads. The big trout snapped at the red streamers Jet had hand-tied. I caught and released the trophies for an hour.

"The steelhead only come here in the spring and the fall," Jet explained. We found a little waterfall on the way back to camp and we bathed in the cool water.

Rainbow trout, cooked over a campfire in front of our tent, was the main course for dinner. As the skies darkened, we heard splashing in the steelhead creek—no doubt a bear was getting *his* dinner.

"Lights out, recruit," Jet ordered after a couple of hours discussing our future. In a few years we would both have enough seniority to bid for a transfer to a post where we could be together. Figuring out how to wait that long was the unresolved question.

Jet was beautiful in the tent's candlelight. Her golden hair had grown a little longer since I left King Salmon. Now it was cascading over her tank top, which sported a trooper emblem on the front. Now that's dedication! For the moment, I didn't care about the job, murderers, F-Rod or even the nearby bear. It was our night.

CHAPTER 28

For me, one of the greatest feelings is waking up in the same wilderness tent with someone you love. But there was work to be done. I certainly didn't want to disappoint my trainer and risk a poor rating, so I made the fire and perked coffee over the flames. I fried caribou sausage and eggs and surprised Jet with breakfast in bed. Then we got unexpected company.

"Trooper, I need help, *quick!*" The man seemed to appear from nowhere. His face was draped with fear and he spoke with urgency.

Struggling to get a breath, the stranger identified himself as Gary Van Sickle. He hurriedly explained that he was on his honeymoon with his new bride, Judy. A pilot friend had dropped them off at the Bremner Mine a week ago and they began the forty-five mile hike to Tebay Lakes. They carried no firearms.

The Van Sickles spotted a large grizzly bear on the third day. On the fourth day they realized it was following their trail. They were careful to cache their food in trees, but when Gary was awakened in the night by the bear looming over their plastic lean-to, he became worried. The bear left that night, but Gary knew it wouldn't be the last of him.

The morning of the fifth day, they came upon an old trapper's cabin with a small landing area on a nearby ridge. It's a custom among Alaskans to leave their cabins unlocked so they can be used in an emergency, often posting a note asking users to replace firewood and whatever else they use. The couple thought they were safe once they got into the cabin. They decided to wait out the bear, hoping it would eventually leave.

The bride heard it first. Then she saw it. Judy dropped a pan and screamed—the bear was staring in the cabin window. Gary jumped from his cot and slammed cooking pots together. Startled, the bear dropped from the window and darted into the brush.

Fifteen minutes later, it was back. This time, its giant claw crashed through the window with the force of a bowling ball. A shard of glass flew across the room, impaling itself in Judy's thigh like a dagger. The man acted quickly. Grabbing a kitchen knife, he stabbed the bear's arm. Bellowing, it retreated again. But the couple knew it would be back.

Gary pulled the glass from Judy's thigh and made a compress from a towel, tying it in place with his belt so the wound would clot. He then made a calculated and difficult decision. He helped his wife—now too injured to walk—to the roof of the cabin. Reassuring her, he promised to run as fast as he could to Tebay Lakes. His pilot friend told him that there was a cabin with a radio that could be used in an emergency. Judy pleaded with him not to leave, as she was afraid the bear would maul him. But he believed it was their only chance.

"I know the cabin, but that airstrip is rough and very short. Sir, you will have to wait here. We need to go in as light as possible." Jet touched Gary's forearm as she spoke. He reluctantly stayed at our camp while we taxied to the end of the strip and quickly took off. In a few minutes we were over the cabin. It didn't appear promising.

Judy Van Sickle wasn't on the roof. A pink jacket, along with other clothing and gear, was spread on the ground and in the bushes around the cabin.

Circling the cabin at a low altitude, we saw it. The large grizzly draped itself over something on the ground. I made a lower pass and the beast stood up, clawing at the air, as if trying to snag our airplane in his grasp.

"This doesn't look good, Jack. Let's get down there." The strip was short and the end fell off a ledge into a rocky creek.

One side dropped fifty feet to a meadow and the other was littered with big rocks.

"Do you want to take this one, Jet?" I wasn't sure if she was confident enough of my 185 flying ability to handle the scant excuse for an airstrip. I wasn't sure if I was, either. There was zero room for error.

"It's all yours, Jack."

I lucked out and planted the big tires close to the end of the landing strip. We popped up and back down a couple of times on the rough surface, but the Cleveland brakes did their job. We stopped with twenty feet to spare.   Jet slung a twelve-gauge shotgun over her shoulder and I carried her .358 Winchester rifle.

Bear scat dotted the trail on the short hike to the cabin. In the thick brush, we would have little chance to get a shot off if we startled a bear that refused to give up its kill. We stopped to examine our surroundings before approaching the cabin. The air was heavy with the scent of death.

Gouge marks defaced the blue-painted walls of the cabin. Pieces of clothing lay by the front door. Jet silently nodded her head to the tundra past the cabin. Carefully, we eased back to the trail to get into the opening for a better view.

"Wuf, *wuf.*" It sounded almost like a big dog. Not threatening, more of an inquisition. We got a quick glance of the giant bear as it rose to its hind legs. It sniffed the air and searched with its limited eyesight as blood dripped from its jaws.

The monster dropped to all fours and we lost sight of him. Had he failed to detect our scent or had he decided to just go on with his business? We listened and watched. It was quiet for what seemed the longest time, then…

The willow bushes came alive. A blur of dark fur—no more than fifty feet away—burst onto the trail and charged.

Jet leveled her shotgun, but I had the angle and my rifle had the range. The .358 recoiled and the big bear slammed onto the trail. As I lowered my scoped weapon to get a better look, it dragged itself up and charged again. It was incredibly fast, closing the space between us in a flash. But Jet was ready. She fired two quick blasts from her shotgun.

The first was a Brenneke slug, followed by double-ought buckshot. All I could see were bloody teeth as the bear lunged at us. It was now too close. We couldn't get a shot off in time.

In a crash of fur and a final growl, the bear dropped at our feet. I thought one more .358 bullet into its head would end it. But it wouldn't give up. It stirred once again, so I put two more into its skull. The huge bear let out one last gasp and it was over.

Judy had obediently stayed on the roof like her husband instructed, but, tragically, learned that bears can climb. By the claw marks on the wall, it was apparent the bear had scaled the cabin and dragged her to the tundra. The chips of red-painted fingernails on the roof were stark evidence that the doomed woman had fought hard. She didn't have a chance. It must have been a horrible death—she would have realized she couldn't win a battle with a six-hundred pound grizzly. Did she scream for help, and if so, what were her pleas? Did she die immediately, or did the beast toy with her, maybe taking her apart slowly? I prayed it was over quickly.

We located pieces of a shirt and of pants. The only remains of Judy was a foot—still in a Chippewa boot.

After photographing the scene and collecting the couple's personal belongings, Jet secured the boot with the foot into her pack. Next she examined the huge bear carcass.

"Look at this Jack. This bear has been shot before."

One wound on its forehead was partially healed. The one on his back had festered. Jet guessed it had been shot a couple of weeks before. "Looks like a .223. Not much of a bear gun," Jet said, after she removed the slug from the back wound with her pocket knife.

The husband collapsed when we delivered the horrible news. "I shouldn't have left her. Why did I insist on this hike for our honeymoon? Why didn't I take a gun?" Those were questions which would haunt him for a lifetime. Jet hugged him, letting him cry onto her uniform shirt.

We quickly broke camp and flew the widower and the remains of his bride to Glennallen.

Chapter 29

We found Mr. Van Sickle a room in the Glennallen Motel and helped him contact relatives. I called Pastor Tuttle at the Community Church to make sure he would get whatever help he needed while Jet secured the remains of Judy in the post freezer.

Lieutenant Emery was waiting for us.

"Troopers Torsen and Blake, could I speak to you for a minute?" The lieutenant discussed the bear mauling for a short time, then gave us a new assignment.

"Jet, do you remember that character from Delta Junction who was running the illegal subsistence fishing operation last year? You may recall he got busted for that, plus selling a little dope?"

"Bart Seltice. What's he up to now?" Jet inquired.

"Same old thing, according to an informant in Chitina. He's netting salmon in the river and selling them, as if he had a legitimate commercial business. But here's the kicker: he teamed up with Butch Saint this year. This may be our chance to question Saint. Jet, maybe you can talk to Seltice separately from Saint and offer him a deal—we don't bust him for the misdemeanor fishing violation if he has some good information on Saint."

"By the way, Jack, I got a call a few days back from the homicide investigators about the girl you and Ted picked up on the Chitina River. Funny thing, Saint told his boss that she fell from a horse into the stream. That may be, but she may have had a little help. And, did he just ride on, leaving her there? The guide recovered her saddle by the stream that flows into the Chitina. He knows Dave Daniels, so called him to say he should take a look at it. Dave dug a .223 bullet from that saddle. If she was being fired upon while on horseback, I could see her heading for the stream."

The town of Chitina had character. Established in 1908 as a stop on the Copper River & Northwestern Railway, it had served as a supply town for the Kennicott mines at McCarthy. When the Kennicott operation closed in 1938, Chitina was abandoned. "Mudhole" Smith, a famous Bush pilot, bought most of the townsite and quickly sold it to investors and others just wanting to get away. Now a general store, a couple of eateries, three bars, and a gas station with one of those old glass gas pumps, was all there was available for locals and summer fishermen—besides the majestic mountains and the river full of salmon.

Fishing was allowed in the Copper River when spawning salmon migrated on their way from the ocean to the upper streambeds. State residents could use nets attached to long poles or fishwheels to catch fish in the fast, muddy waters. Commercial use of the salmon was not legal, but Jet said that didn't stop the bandits.

Bart Seltice was one of those bandits. He dragged his long history of criminal activity to Chitina two summers ago, setting up camp a mile up the river. Seltice hired men who didn't mind driving his flat-bottomed riverboat in the treacherous waters. The payoff was big—the fresh catch could be run up the highway to Fairbanks and illegally sold in restaurants for a tidy profit. Even bigger profits were made in selling drugs to locals and tourists.

Jet and I coerced my patrol car as far as we dared on the muddy one lane road, then parked and walked to the Seltice camp. The campsite was cluttered. An old travel trailer, sitting on wooden blocks, was parked next to an even older twelve-man military surplus tent. Fish drying racks were strung around the camp, holding the remains of red salmon hanging like burned and soundless wind chimes. Blue fifty-five gallon gas drums lay near the slough leading to the Copper River.

A beat up crew cab Chevy truck, with fishing nets in the bed, sat near the trailer. The remains of a campfire smoldered beneath the dripping skies.

"Get the hell out of here, someone's coming!" The voice rang through the trees.

A spinning electric starter was trying hard to crank an outboard motor. It succeeded on the third try. Just as we got to the slough, the flat-bottom riverboat made a quick turn from the bank and swung toward the Copper River, with a man draped in a green rain slicker at the controls. He didn't look back, so we didn't see his face as he turned the corner to the main river channel.

Bart Seltice's unshaven mug and oily long hair almost hid the four-inch scar on his right jaw. His missing lateral incisor drew attention to the rest of his yellow-green teeth, which gripped a thin cigar. The sleeves of the ragged red and white checked shirt didn't reach to his unwashed wrists. His green hip boots were covered in the blood and scales of salmon. He smelled like he hadn't bathed yet this season.

"Hello, Mister Seltice. How are you today? It looks like you have set up a good camp and are ready for the salmon run. How's the fishing?" Jet greeted the man with a smile.

"Well, if it isn't the prettiest darn trooper in Alaska! How ya doing sweetie? Did ya come for a social call? 'Cause I got plenty of Olie beer. Or did ya come down here to bust me, like last year?"

"Neither, actually. I know what you've been up to, but let's forget that for a minute. Trooper Blake would like to speak to you about a different subject." Jet avoided Seltice's attempt to close in for a hug by moving to the side and pointing at me, as if to formalize the introduction.

Seltice stuck out a rough hand punctuated with long, dirty fingernails. "Good to meet ya, Trooper Blake. Any friend of this cutie is a friend of mine." Seltice winked a bloodshot eye at Jet.

"Nice to meet you, sir. Sorry we missed Butch, I need to check with him on something." I gambled that if I threw out Butch's name, Seltice would think we knew for certain that he was there.

"Yeah, too bad…" Seltice started to say more, but his face revealed he was considering he was being bluffed.

"I mean, uh, Butch? Butch *who?*"

Jet jumped in. "Mister Seltice, like I said, I know what you've been up to this year, just like before. And we also know Butch Saint is working for you. Now cut the nonsense and answer Trooper Blake's questions. You know the alternative."

"Okay, okay, I was just kidding around. I don't know much about Saint. He came down here last week looking for work. I hired him to run fishermen down the river in my boat. To tell you the truth, he kind of creeps me out. He stays in the tent, I stay in the trailer. We've had a couple of beers together, but he isn't exactly an easy guy to get to know. He doesn't say much."

Did he talk about wrangling horses this spring?" I pursued.

"Yep, said he was hired to move some horses for some prick, but he didn't go into detail. Like I said, he doesn't talk much."

"Anything about a girl helping him move the horses?" I asked.

"Now that you mention it, he did say some little bitch was with him for a while. Says she whined about the cold weather and split before the job was done. *Women!*"

His other bloodshot eye winked at Jet.

"When do you expect him back?" I asked.

"He said he was headed down to the rapids, then maybe going hunting for Russian trading beads in the old trapper cabins, so who knows? Could be hours, could be days with that one. We don't have any customers lined up until the weekend, and it's only Wednesday. Fishing season doesn't open until Friday night and, as you know, I have strict rules about obeying the law. So, there isn't much reason for him to come back until then."The stained teeth grinned at Jet.

"Mister Seltice, I know you will follow the rules this year and I wish you a good season. I'd be careful with Butch Saint."

Jet returned his smile and said goodbye.

As we walked back to the car, I complimented Jet on her professionalism. I told her I would have to try to be more like that, even to characters like Seltice.

"Jack, I feel that we should leave even the worst dirt bags with what little dignity they have. It cuts down on the physical confrontations and makes life a lot easier, especially if we have to arrest them later. Or in the case of Seltice, maybe we need to pump him for information and *still* arrest him."

That's Jet—smart *and* pretty.

Jet can feel good about leaving Bart Seltice with his dignity. But she need not have worried about arresting him in the future. His future was very short.

CHAPTER 30

Magistrate Addison Pemberton gave us cursory approval to move the body, but warned, "It won't be needed. I've been on the bench in Glennallen for twenty years. Thirty-three bodies that we know have gone into the Copper River during that time. None have been found. The Copper swallows people and doesn't spit them out. I fly the river in my old Stearman at least once a month when I go to Cordova to sit on the bench. The speed of that silty glacier water is awe-inspiring, and the rapids below Chitina chew logs up and turn them into sawdust. So, good luck on your search, troopers."

Jet had returned to her post two days ago, taking the Cub and leaving me the 185. It was lonely without her, but there was too much work for me to have time to feel sorry for myself. I had passed Jet's field training and was now the worry of Dave Daniels.

By now I had every turn in the road and every homestead between Glennallen and Chitina memorized, but Dave, in his quiet and well thought-out manner, pointed out the hidden details. I now knew which homesteads welcomed us, which grew pot, which harbored criminals, and which ones were occupied by people who had no relationship with the law, good or bad—just average Alaskans.

We towed a twenty-two foot deep-welled riverboat behind Dave's Bronco. This Chitina trip was in response to a citizen's call reporting a boat floating down the Copper River, with no one in it. Dave and I did a recon with the 185 and found a boat matching the description stuck on the riverbank five miles below Chitina.

The Department of Fish and Game maintained an office in Chitina during the summer, staffed by two college students. Their mission was to keep tabs on the salmon harvest, feeding the statistics to a biologist in Glennallen, who adjusted the season openings accordingly. One of the students had called the troopers early that morning.

The student reported that late the night before, a gruff man stormed in, reporting his boat had just overturned in the middle of the wide part of the Copper River. The man said that the other person on the boat had drowned, but that he swam to shore and this was the first place he came to after dragging himself from the river.

"Not likely. The water is too fast, too cold, and too full of sand to swim any distance." Dave told me. He added that just last year a man had waded from the shoreline to rescue his Labrador retriever that dove in to grab a stick. The man went under in a matter of seconds. His partner jumped in to save him. Both men drowned and their bodies were never recovered. The lab swam back to the beach, stick in mouth.

"And that was five feet from shore," Dave added, and then turned his attention to the female college student who appeared to be in charge.

"Did you get the guy's name?" Dave asked.

"No, not at the time. Honestly, the man startled me the way he burst in here after hours. And, well, just his appearance and the way he acted was frightening. But, I know the man he was working with, so I should be able to look up his fishing permit, if you want. When they fill out the form for the permit, they have to show an Alaska driver's license," the employee offered. Dave nodded.

"Here it is, the boat owner is Bart Seltice and this guy got the permit numbered just after his. His name is B. Saint."

"One more thing," Dave pursued. "What was Saint wearing?"

"Camouflage military pants, shirt and hip boots."

"Was his clothing wet?"

"No, not that I noticed," the employee answered.

We thanked the college students and pulled our boat to the ramp.

All the reports I'd heard about the Copper River were quickly proven true. As soon as we started the outboard motor on our boat and pushed from shore, the hydrodynamic force slapped us around into the current. Quick on the wheel, Dave steered us downstream. I scooped a handful of the frigid water, finding it to be full of sediment. It was clear that even with our flotation vests, if we went in the river, we wouldn't be coming out.

Our first stop was the Seltice camp. Seltice's truck was still there, as were the trailer and the tent. Ashes in the fire pit were cold. After beating on the door, we peered in the trailer windows and pulled open the tent flap. As suspected, no one was home. We were about to leave when something fluttering in the slight breeze caught my attention. Just across the small slough, attached to the trunk of a Cottonwood, was a piece of paper. We walked in a direct line towards the tree, coming to a small hill in the sand. Dave saw them first—.223 spent cartridges. While he gathered the brass, I waded across the slough in my hip boots. The flapping paper was a crudely drawn target, which I carefully pulled free. Then digging into one of the exposed holes in the cottonwood trunk, I removed a .223 slug.

Have you ever stood under a trestle when a train was passing on top? Well that's the sound of the Copper River canyon below Chitina. Like the magistrate said, the rapids were scary. More like a whirlpool, or a giant blender, than rapids.

It took fifteen minutes to get to Seltice's boat and to turn it over. It took an hour and a half to tow it back in the unrelenting current.

"Let's go visit an old buddy of mine." Dave pointed the Bronco toward Chitina.

The Chitina Café was a greasy spoon stuck against the base of a mountain in town. Two booths, two tables, and a counter were enough to handle the lunch crowds dining on the popular salmon burgers.

Owned by an Anchorage investor, the messy eatery was run by a nervous little man named Harold Winston. He looked stunned when Dave opened the door decorated by the sign, "No Gun, No Service."

"Morning, Harold, how are you today?" Dave smiled at the skinny man who was bent over, cleaning the counter. His haggard face looked as if he'd dedicated a good portion of his life to the consumption of hard liquor.

"Well, I'm... I'm just fine, I guess, Trooper. Is there anything I can get you?"

"Just some information, please. Have you had occasion to meet Butch Saint?"

"Well... well, uh... yes, I have met him. Harold rubbed his head as if he was trying to push information from his brain, then he knocked a glass off the counter.

"He came in a couple times with Bart for lunch." I wasn't sure whether Harold was holding back, or if he was always that jumpy, but Dave persisted.

"Harold, we need to know the last time you saw Saint."

"Well, sir, let me think." He rubbed his head some more.

"It was last night, he came in for dinner. Yeah, that's it."

"Okay, Harold, that's good. Did he seem okay? Were his clothes wet? Did he act differently than usual?"

"Well, wait a minute. He didn't eat. He just swallowed a couple of beers. Then he had a few more. Went outside a couple times, probably smoking pot. Probably selling it, too. No, I don't recollect his clothes being wet. He had his sleeves rolled up, so you could see that dang tattoo on his wrist. I asked him where Bart was, you know, just to be friendly, and he 'bout bit my head off. He said it was none of my frickin' business. He told me to put the beers on Seltice's tab and stormed out. You know, I don't much care for that man," Harold said, as he gazed out the café window toward the mountain.

"Do you know where we can find him?" Dave asked.

"Don't know. He and Bart was always fighting, so maybe he took to the hills or headed back to Kennicott, no telling. I'd be glad if he never came back in here. Makes me nervous."

I asked Harold about that tattoo and yes, it was the same as the ones worn by F-Rod and his men—the flag of Cuba.

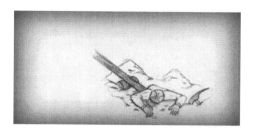

CHAPTER 31

Seltice was number thirty-four on Magistrate Pemberton's list of missing bodies in the Copper River. Neither Seltice nor his remains ever showed up. Dave and I did a couple of aerial searches of the river, but it was hopeless. Nearly as hopeless was the search for Butch Saint. He seemed to have disappeared. No one in Chitina admitted seeing him—same in McCarthy. We saw no evidence that he had returned to the fish camp when we accompanied Seltice's family to claim his belongings.

The next time Saint's name surfaced was when the Chitina café went up in flames. Harold Winston said it was arson, but had no proof, except that the café owner was tired of being in the red and had a big insurance policy. His guess was that Butch Saint was behind the burning, but other than his seeing Saint and the owner whispering in the corner of the café recently, once again, there was no proof.

"Oh yeah, I guess I was supposed to call you guys if Saint came back. Sorry. I forgot," Winston mumbled.

I'd like to say that we pulled out all the stops to find Butch Saint, but we just flat out didn't have the time. Other cases raced in, along with the continual pipeline disturbances. The force was depleted with all the troopers quitting to get rich on the pipeline construction, while crime doubled statewide. We ran from one call to another all summer and through the fall. Twelve-hour days were common, but that wasn't enough to keep up, much less dedicate any time to finding Butch Saint. He was just a suspect in cases that couldn't be proved with what we had, and there were too many hot cases to handle. The Anchorage homicide investigators had their hands full as well, although their interest in Saint increased when ballistic tests showed a match of the .223 bullets in the saddle, the bear, and the tree.

The golden leaves of birch trees put on a flashy display, but fall was much too short and winter came quickly. After I'd passed all the required field training, the lieutenant put my face to good use in the pipeline town of Valdez, where it was unknown.

I was a cab driver in Valdez for a week, buying cocaine from drug dealers and setting up dates with prostitutes. It was great training, but the life of an undercover officer wasn't for me. I did learn one thing from a hooker with a sense of humor. She asked if me if I knew what was the world's oldest profession. I'd always heard it was prostitution, but she said that was too obvious. She corrected me, "Nope, *gardener.*"

The best case of my short tenure working narcotics was when I bought the last of a Ukrainian drug dealer's cocaine for five thousand dollars. He had sold a quarter million dollars' worth of the white powder in a week and thought he was home free. We made the transaction in my cab at the Valdez airport then, as a signal to waiting troopers, I put my cap on the dashboard. Law enforcement officers swarmed on the cab and the little guy was shocked. Big Dave Daniels was kind enough to carry him over his arm like a duffle bag, as the diminutive drug dealer was fretting about his dress loafers filling with mud. That was the least of his problems once he appeared before Magistrate Addison Pemberton. My week in that wild little town, living the night life in smoky bars packed with shady characters, made me yearn to get back to my post and the Wrangell Mountains.

Winter hit hard. It seemed like we couldn't get out of the sixty below zero and colder temperatures. The pipeliners didn't give us a break, and the fights seemed to get more frequent and nastier as the winter dragged on in the last year of pipeline construction.

The cold weather didn't slow the flying activity. Super Cub pilots chased wolves and Cessnas carried passengers to the villages and flew hunters out to harvest their winter meat.

That meant searches and rescues for our post.

One search was for a Cessna 180 carrying a pilot and two passengers. The pilot's wife called when the plane didn't return from dropping off the hunters for a winter goat hunt in the Wrangells.

We quickly used up all the short daylight hours, flying and looking for any sign of the hunters and the missing plane. We flew into the night, looking for campfires. Two weeks of searching, hundreds of hours flown between the troopers, the Civil Air Patrol, and volunteers, didn't bring us any closer to finding the men. Then we got a call from the FAA.

A flight service operator had just returned from vacation and was briefed about the missing plane. His memory was jogged—he recalled a pilot radioing him reporting he was ten miles south of the airport for landing. Gulkana is an uncontrolled airport, so there was no requirement of the airport or the pilot to communicate further. The flight service employee went off duty a few minutes after the radio conversation and didn't think any more about it until his return from vacation. The flight service chief checked the logs for that day and the tail number from the radio call matched the missing plane.

It had snowed two feet, followed by a hard freeze of minus fifty degrees, but now we had a much smaller search area. Dave and I found the wing of the 180 after an hour of snowshoeing near the airport. We recovered two bodies from the airplane just as darkness fell. Returning to the crash site the next morning, Ronnie Torgy, who had recently been promoted to corporal, came along to help, dragging a portable heater fired by propane.

With the aid of the heater and a Pulaski, we found the third victim's cap. Under the cap was his head. The rest of his body was frozen into the swamp, covered by two weeks of snow and ice.

Recovering the body was a slow process—after several hours of heating and digging, the top half of the poor guy was exposed. We now had to act quickly to finish the unpleasant job before dark.

Ronnie dragged a log to the excavation site. Considering Ronnie's history with logs, I should have known better, but we were cold and night was almost upon us. Ronnie stuck the log under the man's frozen outstretched arms. Then he fastened a rope to secure the hunched-over body to the log. He put a smaller log under the big log to make a fulcrum. Corporal Torgy ordered Dave, by far the biggest and strongest of us, to push down on the log with all his might. Ronnie's theory was the log would pop the victim's body from the frozen ground. Ronnie was half right.

Ted Herlihy strode up as only the top half of the poor guy came free. The torso broke cleanly in two, like an icicle, in the extreme cold. "So, Corporal, shall I call the magistrate and get approval to move half a body?" Ted mused in his usual deadpan manner.

It wasn't at all funny, but cops sometimes have a weird way of dealing with the more horrible aspects of the job. There would be more searches and rescues that year. Some in planes, some on snowmachines, some in avalanches. Most were found alive, but it was a tough winter.

Well, I guess I've fared better than those poor guys in the Cessna 180. The little fire I have going makes a big difference and takes the chill off. I'd hoped someone would be looking for me by now, but maybe the weather is keeping them grounded. I'm reminded of a saying my uncle told me: "Never expect anything from anyone and you will never be disappointed."

The cold seemed to drag on forever that winter. The only hope for warmer temperatures rode on the weather report of a big winter storm coming in from the west. That's how it goes in Alaska—about the only thing to break a cold spell is a warm front loaded with snow. It's a toss–up sometimes—which is better, cold or snow. It usually depends on what needs to be done outside.

Jet's voice warmed one especially cold night, even if it was only over the phone. We spoke about how long and dark the winter was without each other. We planned for our much-anticipated vacation together in Anchorage. I bragged that the full gas cans were still on the Nizana Glacier airstrip. She promised to make good on the rest of her surprise.

Then she told me the real reason for her call.

"Jack, sorry it took so long, but I finally got to do some checking on Fred Roderick. I talked to my friend at headquarters who put me in touch with a retired trooper who worked for Roderick up in Prudhoe. He said the money was great, but it just wasn't worth it. He still had enough integrity left to get out when he did. The short story is that Roderick is one sick son of a gun. But there's more, a lot more.

"Everything Ted told you is true—the Cuban background, the CIA and the weapons sales. And yes, some of the Special Forces guys work in his security company. What Ted didn't know is what Roderick does with the crazies—the ones too demented to work even for him. He basically sets them loose throughout Alaska. He may give them a cabin in the woods, like Butch Saint. Or he might get one a job with a guide—does that sound familiar? Or he might throw them out in the wilderness to see how they will survive, and to see what kind of havoc they can generate. It's just a big, sick chess game to him, Jack."

"So what am I to Roderick, Jet, a pawn?"

"Maybe a knight, but on the opposing side of the board. He wants to see you up against his knights, his rooks, and the rest of the players." "What does he have against me, Jet?"

"I don't know, but it must go back to Dallas."

Both of our days were to start early, as they always did, so we said goodnight.

I went to bed that night knowing someone wanted to kill me. I knew whom, but not how, when, or where.

CHAPTER 32

Pulling the control wheel into my gut, the ski-equipped Rice Rocket Cessna 185 leaped from the Duffy's Tavern airstrip into the spitting snow. The skies were mostly clear when I had landed to investigate a report of cabins near the old village of Slana being vandalized. But winter weather can change quickly in the North, as it was doing that afternoon.

Level at five hundred feet, the snowflakes were getting bigger, zooming at the windscreen like asteroids in a Star Wars movie. But it looked like I'd be able to beat the snowstorm back to Glennallen before it got really bad. I called dispatch to let them know I was headed home.

"H-22, *H-22!*" Dispatch returned my call with urgency. I lowered the nose of the 185 to get under a layer of clouds and answered. My plans were to be changed.

"H-22, this is H-1. Can you get to McCarthy?" Lieutenant Emery had taken the radio over from the dispatcher.

Raising the left wing of the Cessna, I looked to the south and east. The leading edge of storm left just enough room to sneak around the Wrangell Mountains.

"Roger, H-1, if it's critical, I can get there. But, I may be there for a while with the storm coming in."

"Roger, H-22. We have a report of multiple shootings in McCarthy. One victim is in transport to the Glennallen hospital. There is at least one other injured person at the airstrip. Suspect

Butch Saint may be at the airport, armed with an assault rifle and possibly handguns. We're unable to launch from the Gulkana airport due to the weather, so can't provide backup at this time. We'll get there as soon as we can."

Maybe I'd finally get to meet Butch Saint.

Pushing the power to the maximum, I turned towards McCarthy. The storm was on my tail, providing fast ground speed in the deteriorating weather. The air was getting bumpy, adding to the tension. My focus was to get to McCarthy as fast as possible, aid the injured, and stop Butch Saint before he did any more damage. Just as the base of Mount Blackburn came into view, I passed over Nugget Creek—making me think of the night Jet and I spent there—happily breaking the stress for a few pleasant moments.

Keeping the hills on my left and the Chitina-McCarthy Road on the right—now barely visible in the driving snow—Long Lake came into focus as I planned my approach to McCarthy. The high-pitched scream of the 185 would certainly announce my arrival to Saint, so using all eight hundred feet of ceiling the sky gave, I made a wide swing over the airport. If Saint was still waiting on the airstrip, I didn't want to provide an easy target for his rifle.

An overturned yellow Ski-Doo lay in a snowbank close to the runway. Next to the snowmachine, someone was prone in the snow. I was too high to see whether it was Saint, and it wasn't worth taking on the risk of gunfire to find out.

The snowstorm had caught up with me and, like it or not, I had to land right then. Making a long downwind over the river, I landed short on the runway, stopping before the turnoff to the parking ramp. Pushing open the right door, away from the line of fire, I crawled from the Cessna, grabbing my daypack of survival gear and the M-16.

Using the brush line for cover and keeping a low profile, I half-jogged towards the overturned snowmachine. I was a hundred yards away, and there was no movement from the person lying next to it. Now fifty yards and still nothing, but I still didn't have a clear sight through the bushes. Had he not seen me?

Certainly I couldn't have landed the noisy 185 without being heard. Twenty-five yards away and I could clearly see the body. I took cover and using the four-power riflescope, I could now see—the body wasn't moving—it was face down in the snow. Now running, maybe I could help. Maybe there was still some life left. Kneeling alongside the man, something looked familiar. The fingers—the yellow nicotine-stained fingers.

Blood from the man's face had frozen in the snow, sticking his head to the ground. He had no pulse, no life, and with the massive head wounds, it wasn't surprising. I grabbed an ice pick from the trailer behind the snowmachine and carefully chipped around the face. Finally, I could pull his cheek from the ice and turn the man over. It hit me—shock, rage—whatever you want to call it. I was sickened by the face of a friend—one of the kindest persons I'd ever met. Buddy Cole, a man with no enemies, had been murdered. And the murderer was Butch Saint.

I threw a tarp from the sled over Buddy. I needed to get composure—Butch Saint was probably still nearby. Taking a deep breath and saying a quiet prayer, I surveyed the airstrip. A blood trail led from Buddy. I followed it.

Thrown behind a snowberm were the bodies of Tom and Suzi Brix. Each had been shot in the head.

The Hubers! Would, could, Saint possibly hurt them? Maybe he had a beef with the young couple on the airstrip and Buddy got in the way, but not Frank and Franny—they were too sweet for anyone to harm.

My boots left blood tracks in the fresh snow as I plowed up to the Huber's house. The snowmachine I'd seen from the air flashed into my mind—maybe that meant someone was at the post office when the shooting began at the airstrip. Maybe they protected the Hubers. Maybe they'd done my job for me.

I thought I heard something, up the trail, in a distance. I stopped my boots from echoing in the snow and listened.

Have you ever had the feeling, when you are deep in the darkest woods, that you're not alone? Every sense in your body intensifies. You try to not even swallow. You do nothing to give up your location. You can feel it. You know there's something, or someone, around. You feel it in your spine and you feel it in your jaw, like an arctic hare must feel just before a fox springs onto his back and bites into his neck, quickly ending its life. My rifle felt like it weighed a hundred pounds and I dared only to turn my head, not my body, to search the woods between the post office and me. Then that same sense told me to get down—down immediately onto the frozen ground.

A rifle report cracked into the bitter cold and through the trees, shaking powdery-snow from the limbs. A branch broke behind where I had stood. The bullet would have pierced my chest if I hadn't obeyed what that unknown voice ordered me to do.

I dove off the trail into the brush, swinging my rifle towards the trail. Another shot. Then another. Saint must have had a line on me, but I couldn't see him. At least his line was not a good one, or he would have nailed me by now. I could only guess by the rifle reports that he was near the post office. I said a prayer for the Hubers and waited for the next shot.

The unmistakable whine of a snowmachine engine cracked through the cold air. I waited, anticipating it would come down the path towards me. I dug into the snow, focusing my rifle on the trail. But, instead, the whine got weaker—the machine was leaving. Now running up the trail, I hoped I could see Saint. Maybe I'd get a shot at him.

The black snowmachine dropped over a hill, just as I got to the top of the trail. It had to be Saint, but there was someone on the back of the machine. At that point, I didn't know if the passenger was a willing accomplice to the massacre, or another potential victim.

Seven huskies stood in the snow attached to a sled. They paid little attention to me. Their focus was on the departing snowmachine. They tugged on their lines, whimpering to follow.

The post office door at the Huber's hung by one hinge. Smoke—not from the woodstove or from a tobacco user—but the distinct odor of gunsmoke, filled the cabin.

Blood was splattered over Frank's desk and the day's mail. I swung my rifle towards the kitchen, calling out for the Hubers—

or for anyone. But the only voice was Paul Harvey speaking softly over the radio. Blood and matter dripped from Franny's kitchen, flowing over her jars of preserves and onto the pot of fresh coffee. Several of Franny's happy oil paintings had toppled to the floor in the wake of deadly violence. The couch, with the colorful crochet, was slammed into the corner. But wait—something moved in that corner, behind the couch. My rifle pointed towards it and I slowly peered over the couch. The old Golden Retriever's tail swayed as it looked up to me, head planted firmly on the floor. I moved the couch to free him and kept searching.

Bloodscuffs on the shiny wood floor led into the bedroom. I followed the trail, fearing how it would end.

The blood-saturated quilt on the floor covered something. Reluctantly, I lifted the quilt. Franny and Frank bled from the backs of their heads. So did Helen Jackson. Butch Saint had murdered all three.

I hurried to get back outside. Something stuck under the runner of the dogsled caught my eye—a bloodstained piece of paper. The note read: "I'M RUNNING FROM BUTCH SAINT, HE SHOT ME IN MY LEG. IF HE FINDS ME, HE IS GOING TO KILL ME, LIKE HE DID THE OTHERS. PLEASE HELP, GOD, PLEASE HELP AND PLEASE TAKE CARE OF MY DOGTEAM. LINDA DOTY."

Linda Doty was the unwilling passenger on Saint's snow-machine. The machine's engine still whined in the snow-filled winter air. The sled dogs looked at me with their sorrowful eyes, pleading to be unhitched, so they could be free to chase after their master.

Instead, I grabbed the ice hook from the snow and yelled "mush!"

The chase was on.

CHAPTER 33

The snowmachine track broke towards the Nizana River. My first thought was that Saint was going to hole up in his cabin at Kennicott, but he was on the move. I knew of old mining camps and cabins in the area and guessed that's where Saint was headed. His machine was faster than seven dogs pulling a sled, but I knew he would eventually run out of gas. I prayed he didn't kill the girl before I caught up to him.

Linda Doty had a good team. They were fast and got us within earshot of the snowmachine several times. That's one reason I always liked sled dogs over snowmachines—you didn't forfeit your sense of hearing.

It was snowing hard now. I could hardly see past the lead dog, but he seemed to know where he was going in the approaching darkness. I stopped every twenty minutes to make certain we were following the fresh snowmachine tracks, but the team didn't fail me. We would keep running all night if necessary. However long it took.

The dogs stopped just after dark. Almost in sequence, the huskies turned their heads toward me and yawned. The blue-eyed lead dog stared at the tarp-covered sled, then looked at my face, as if to say "dinner time." I grabbed the bag of dried fish I'd found earlier on the sled and fed the team before they started howling. After cramming the ice hook into the snow, I walked about a hundred feet in front of the team and listened. Nothing. Maybe the snowmachine was out of range, or maybe it had stopped. I kept walking until I came to a rise in the trail. A light came from a cabin, just before where I figured Young Creek airstrip should be. The black snowmachine was parked in front.

I circled the team around the sled, set up camp, and munched on a food bar from my pack. I didn't have much—just a tarp to wrap around me in the sled and the warm clothes I was wearing. I would have liked to build a fire, but that would have given away my position.

The snow had stopped and the skies were clear enough that the blue and green Northern Lights crackled above me in the dark sky. I snowshoed, as quietly as I could in the crunchy snow, towards the cabin. Digging in a snowbank, which gave me a view of the small window, I formed a support for my rifle with my elbow in the ice. All I needed at the hundred-yard range was just a glimpse of Saint and I would take the shot. I'd worked with my M-16 enough on the range that I was confident of my accuracy. Looking through the scope, a body came into focus.

Saint was playing the game like a pro. Linda Doty was bound with rope in a chair, duct tape covering her mouth, as she was forced to sit in front of the window. I watched for hours, but Saint never appeared in the cabin. Then the clear skies once again turned to snow.

Pulling the tarp around me in the dogsled, I slept off and on for a couple of hours, counting on the dogs to howl if an intruder came near. I wished I'd had a sleeping bag, but my heavy trooper parka, insulated flight pants, military-surplus "bunny boots" and fur hat would have to do.

Just before sunrise, I awoke to a cold and snowy morning. Snow had completely covered the tarp, providing extra insulation during the night, but the clothes next to my body were wet, creating a chill deep within. I'd hoped the brief break in the weather last night had allowed for backup to arrive in McCarty, but I later learned that the storm had not let up in Glennallen.

The two-cycle snow machine engine broke the silence of the morning. I pulled my rifle from under the tarp, hoping Saint was coming in my direction, but the yammering engine faded to the southeast.

Eager to resume the chase, the dogs tugged at their harnesses as I secured my gear in the sled. A hot cup of coffee would hit the spot, but there was no time to build a fire. Another food bar from my pack for me, more dried fish for the team, and we were back on the trail. Huge snowflakes swirled in the unrelenting wind. I pulled the wolf ruff of my parka hood close around my face, exposing only my eyes, and my arctic mittens gripped the dogsled. The dogs worked hard and I ran behind the sled, pushing up the hills in the deep snow.

A full blizzard of eye-stinging snow was raging, but the dogs mushed fearlessly, bending into the wind. The noise of the storm prevented hearing even the high-pitched cry of the snowmachine, so I just had to hope we didn't come upon Saint in the blindness—and have faith we wouldn't miss a turn-off on the trail. He would not make much better time than the dogs, for the limited visibility was now the factor, not horsepower. We kept up the pace for hours.

"Whoa!" I yelled to the team to stop, quickly feeding them before they could howl for the anticipated meal, as day turned into night. I walked up the trail to ascertain whether we were still following the snomachine tracks, and to listen. There was a distant whine, then an erratic light high on a ridge. Saint had maybe a mile lead and was climbing towards Dan Creek Camp. Maybe he could get fuel there. We had to keep up the chase.

The team was willing, so we pressed on. The dogs worked their hearts out and I jogged behind them to do my part. We were making good time and maybe could catch up with Saint soon. As the night wore on, I was losing the battle with fatigue as the trees closed around us, but I couldn't stop. I took short breaks from running in the heavy boots, stealing a few minutes of sleep while standing on the runners, putting my trust in the team. To keep from falling from the sled and being left on the trail, I lashed my left hand to the sled. I dozed off to the panting of the dogs and the music of the sled runners sliding across the snow.

The sudden halt rattled me awake. I grabbed a handful of snow and rubbed it on my face to shock the system. Then I saw why the team had stopped.

A black shadow stood on the trail in front of the team. The dogs whined as I reached for my rifle, but it was too late.

The shadow came fast. It smashed through the team then crashed into my sled, knocking it over with me under it. My gear tumbled with my rifle into the snow.

Nostrils flaring, the thousand pound moose pummeled the sled with its sharp hooves. It was all I could do to hold the sled over my body, hoping the moose wouldn't thrash through the sturdy oak. Suddenly, the right wheel dog broke from the gang line and sank its teeth into the huge animal's lower leg. Reeling from the sled, the moose came down hard on the dog's hindquarter, striking his front hoof through the dog's thick fur. Then, as quickly as he had charged, the moose trotted past the sled, fading back into the darkness behind us on the trail.

The brave wheel dog lay bleeding in the snow, with a gaping gash in his right hip. He only slightly whimpered as I carefully lifted him into the sled. I packed snow into his wound and used my parka sleeve to apply direct pressure and stop the bleeding. I would sew the wound closed in the morning with fish line and a needle from the small survival box in my pack.

The rest of the dogs were uninjured. I rearranged the team so the dogs ran in pairs, now six strong. It would be harder for the team and I would have to run more, but it would work. I no longer would nap while behind the team.

The Nizana River broke to the left and Dan Creek branched to the right. The old mining camp sat at the base of ragged mountains, overlooking the valley. Saint would have to make a decision—either hole-up at Dan Creek Camp—or forge ahead up the mountain creek towards Pyramid Peak and Hawkins Glacier. He would not get past me to return to the lowlands on the only trail.

There was no luxury of a viewpoint like the night before. The wind-blown snow's icy surface loudly announced each of my steps. My surveillance was limited to viewing the light reflected from the cabin onto the snow-encrusted cliffs. There was no opportunity to approach the cabin without being detected, and that detection would certainly mean death for Linda Doty. The dark skies cleared enough during the night to see half way up Pyramid Peak in the full moon, to what I guessed was the six thousand foot level. Maybe backup would come in the morning.

I slept in spurts with my rifle in my arms. I would be awakened quickly by the dogs if Saint made his move—if he came to the realization that he wouldn't be able to cross the glacier field above him—that his only way out was past me. It had snowed again in the early morning, dumping another six inches. I climbed to an observation point and saw the snowmachine was gone—Saint had left during the night. I ran back to the team and we quickly returned to the chase.

Flying over Hawkins Glacier the previous summer with Jet, I had marveled at the deep blue crevasses that seemed to have no bottoms. Certain death would greet anyone foolish enough to recklessly challenge these glaciers. But, either not considering the outcome, or ignoring the threat, Saint had begun scaling the trail with the snowmachine. I followed with the team, but soon the trail split into a Y. The snow had covered the snowmachine tracks, preventing me from determining whether Saint went to the left or the right. I had a decision to make. Listening in the still air, I could only hear the dogs breathing. Should I yell "gee" for right, or "haw" for left?

The whine broke the silence. I knew the snowmachine was above us, but which direction? As ridiculous as it sounds, I talked to the team, telling the side-by-side leaders to find their master. The dogs lunged at their harnesses and broke to the left.

Only a half-mile past the Y, the trail narrowed and became steeper. The hill on my left threatened an avalanche. On the right, it dropped into a deep gorge. Even leaning into the side of the hill, the heels of the dogsled runners slipped towards the gorge. I stopped.

After anchoring the sled, I gave each dog half of a whitefish and water. I strapped on the big wooden snowshoes. I pulled on my pack, slung my rifle over my shoulder, and began snowshoeing up the canyon. Fog dominated the early morning, allowing visibility of no more than a hundred feet. Eerie shadows played tricks on me. What looked like a man standing on the side of the trail became just a tree as I got closer. The ceiling was lifting, and the sun, looking more like the moon as the fuzzy clouds screened it, gave hope for a better day. Something was different. The constant shrilling of the snow machine had stopped. Saint must be at the glacier.

Snowshoeing through the deep snow was like mucking through swamp mud in hip boots. Each step was a struggle. Every lift of a snow-laden birchwood snowshoe was like lifting a heavy weight strapped to my ankle. Maybe it was from running behind the dogsled, or maybe it was the cold, but my legs began cramping and were failing to do their job. Straining in protest, my thighs refused to lift the snowshoes any longer. Remembering a tip from Buddy Cole, I pulled a wrap of parachute cord from my pack, cutting two pieces of cord and tying a piece to the tip of each snowshoe. Now, as I walked, I could use my arm strength to help lift the snowshoes.

Each stride shot pain up through my leg muscles, but I was making steady progress up the mountain. My physical strength was waning, but my motivation to stop Saint was stronger than ever.

The sun blasted through the clouds and the new snow glistened like millions of little flashbulbs. As I slipped on my sunglasses to keep the sun bouncing off the snow from blinding me, I saw a reflection on the ridge.

Breaking off the trail, I took a direct line toward the snowmachine windshield.

The tracks of Saint and his hostage revealed their struggle to walk in the deep snow. I finally had the advantage. They lacked snowshoes and I would soon overtake them—a fate Saint must have realized.

The scream from Linda Doty announced her position—as well as her captor's. The back of Saint's head was clearly visible in my riflescope. At seventy-five yards, it would be an easy shot. The .223 bullet would pierce his skull causing the pistol in his right hand, which he was holding to the woman's head, to fall harmlessly into the snow. But I hesitated, wanting to make sure I had a clean shot to avoid injury or death to Linda.

I pulled myself up to a little outcropping of rocks to get a better vantage. It was a blessing that I didn't fire at Saint. My heart sank and my pulse increased when I saw the hostage.

Linda Doty was swaying in her caribou skin mukluks on the ledge. Below her was one of the bottomless, turquoise crevasses that Jet had showed me from the air. Falling into one would mean certain death. The best outcome would be smashing your head on the first ledge, causing immediate unconsciousness. The second best outcome would be death by the impact at the bottom of the crevasse. Death from being trapped in the dark confines of the cold, silent, pit would be the worst.

Without turning, Saint yelled, "Welcome, Trooper Blake, go ahead and shoot!" He either was guessing, or he somehow knew I had him in my sights.

"How about letting her go, Saint? This isn't her battle!"

I knew reasoning with a madman was fruitless, but I talked on, feeling I had to give it a try. I was trying to buy time, not knowing what I'd do with it if I got it.

"That ain't gonna happen. Now either throw your rifle into the snow, or she's going in."

Rubbing the fog from the glass with my finger, I peered through the scope again, calculating an angle for the shot. Taking Saint out without endangering Linda was risky, but maybe the only chance I could give her. My finger tightened on the trigger and I said a little prayer—I needed help.

A Pratt & Whitney R985 radial engine rumbles with a perfect tone that is pure music to airplane lovers' ears. Was I hallucinating due to lack of sleep and overexertion? The rumbling echoed off the faces of the steep mountains. I scanned the skies. A wonderful vision came from the sun, skimming the surface of the stark white glacier. Immaculately painted in the original Air Force scheme of battleship gray, yellow, red, white and blue, with a gleaming propeller hub, Magistrate Addison Pemberton's Stearman was highly modified and restored to perfection. Pemberton took the Boeing 75, replaced the engine with a four-hundred fifty horsepower Pratt, and installed part of an AT-6 canopy over the rear cockpit to make it more appropriate for Alaska flying.

Abruptly, the Stearman broke into a steep diving turn towards Saint, like an eagle plunging for a salmon. The radial engine's growling was deafening and the huge Hamilton Standard spinning propeller threatened to decapitate the killer. Saint jerked his rifle toward the bi–plane, turning his attention from his captive. Linda Doty took the opportunity—leaping away from Saint, and the crevasse, into the snow.

My shot missed Saint's head. He was turning to fire on the plane just as I squeezed the trigger. Instead, the .223 hit his right shoulder. Spinning him from the impact, Saint's boots slipped on the icy ledge. He pulled one erratic shot into the air and screamed. With his rifle flung awkwardly over his head, Saint fell backwards into the deep hole to nowhere. Even over the roars of the circling Stearman, his screams echoed for an eternity as he bounced off the walls of the icy cavern.

Ted Herlihy's titanium hand had never looked so good as it flashed from the open front cockpit, dropping a trooper note-book into the air. Struggling in the deep snow, Linda Doty grabbed the blue pad that had landed between us. Half running, half falling, she fell into me with a hug, refusing to let go until I promised it was over.

The notebook cover read: "JUSTICE SERVED. NO SIGHT OF SAINT IN THE ICEBOX. MEET YOU IN MCCARTHY. TED."

Linda Doty had suffered only a flesh wound during Saint's shooting spree in McCarthy. The bleeding had stopped, but she was in no condition to mush back to McCarthy, so she drove the snowmachine and I followed with her team. With good weather and a broken trail, we pulled into McCarthy late that day.

Buddy Cole had broken trail from Long Lake the day he and Linda were surprised by gunfire in McCarthy. When the firing started, Buddy called out to the shooter, sacrificing his life so Linda could escape.

After thanking Ted and the magistrate, they told me the rest of their story. The two-day blizzard had prevented airplanes from taking off from Glennallen. Pemberton got weathered in at Chitina, stuck in the snowstorm while returning from court in Cordova. He jumped at the chance to help and was airborne with Ted as soon as the weather broke.

Soon the Anchorage investigative team landed in chartered twin-engine airplane, spending the next two days transporting bodies and recovering evidence.

Saint was now dead. His body was never recovered.

Maybe now, my life would be normal. So I'd hoped.

CHAPTER 34

*T*his little cluster of willow bushes looks like the inside of a freezer in dire need of defrosting. Hoarfrost covers the branches of these scrubby little excuses for trees. I found the temperature gauge from the wreck yesterday. Now it even seems colder as I read minus fifty-two through the cracked glass. Dragging my bum leg around in the deep snow to scan the area provides no clue to my location. I see nothing but white. Fog hangs low in the frigid sky, stealing the horizon.

The fog in my brain cleared a little last night. I remember flying over the Kuskokwim River, then, just before dropping over the frozen swamps, seeing big trees out the right side of the plane. The first village above where the Kuskokwin drains into the Bering Sea boasting any significant trees is Lower Kalskag. Since I don't remember crossing the biggest river in Alaska, the Yukon, I must be between Kalskag and Russian Mission. If I can somehow get to the river, maybe I can get some help.

Duct tape is now wrapped around my fractured ribs, but it still hurts to take more than a shallow breath. I taped my broken right arm to my chest and immobilized my ankle with even more duct tape. I probably look like an old bush plane after a hard hunting season, but the self-administered first aid helps. I can chew the food bars from the survival bag with only the left side of my mouth, as the right side of my face is swollen and bruised. I melted water from the snow for drinking, and have been able to keep a little fire going with willow branches. I don't have much, but I keep singing the few words I can remember from a Rolling Stones song: "You can't always get what you want. But, if you try sometimes, you just might find, you get what you need."

J.R. twisted his head to the sky this morning. He was right—there was something up there. An airplane was flying just above the fog. A harsh cry from J.R. alerted me to something else. There were snowmachines in the distance. Maybe, hopefully, they are headed this way.

Anger and sadness will always be deep within me for what Butch Saint did to those innocent victims. Memories—to be opened, when least expected, and when least wanted—from the pictures permanently floating in the recesses of my brain. But, a few years later, another shooting spree, by another demented killer, was just as horrible.

Life had changed in the six years since I transferred to Glennallen. My flying mentor, Don Sheldon, had passed away— much too young—from cancer. The pipeline was pretty much complete, prompting Ted Herlihy's observation: "Joy is seeing a Texan leaving on a plane from Anchorage International Airport with an Okie under each arm."

Once the State of Alaska tapped into the pipeline revenue, the troopers' budget improved significantly. One of the best investments made with the new money was to upgrade the old .357 revolvers to Smith and Wesson 40-06 semi-automatics for duty weapons. New aircraft were added to the aging fleet, and the department began an aggressive recruiting campaign to replace all the men who had abandoned the force for lucrative pipeline jobs.

H-detachment was dissolved, leaving only four troopers at the Glennallen post. G-detachment, based in Palmer, a small town forty miles east of Anchorage, absorbed what was left of the Glennallen troopers. Pipeline activity moved north and the most northern detachment, based in Fairbanks, became the new hotspot. Rich Emery was justly promoted to captain and was sent to Fairbanks as the detachment commander. Jill, the Glennallen dispatcher, became Emery's administrative assistant. The captain took his "right hand man," Ronnie Torgy, with him. Ronnie now proudly wore sergeant stripes.

Ted Herlihy was chosen to lead the northern detachment's Special Emergency Response Team. Ted encouraged me to join him, with the words: "Get your butt up here and help me on SERT. Not much action compared to Glennallen, but we have some good times."

I like to keep busy, and the fast pace at Glennallen made the time go by quickly, but it would be nice to actually have regular days off like the normal working population. Certainly I wouldn't have to jump in a plane, or race down the highway, to break up fights at the pipeline camps. Maybe I'd finally be able to explore the Brooks Range in my Cub on my days off. It didn't take much convincing from Ted or the captain. Two trips with my little plane and I had moved all of my worldly belongings to Fairbanks.

Dave Daniels was the first to welcome me. He had been promoted to investigator and transferred to major crimes unit in Fairbanks. One of Dave's first tasks was closing the Butch Saint investigation. He learned that a man and his girlfriend from Chitina who, according to an informant, knew about the café arson, were missing. Dave suspected that Saint had also killed them, but their bodies were never found.

Dave also reviewed the airplane crash he and I had found near Gulkana. He interviewed a witness who swore he heard shooting just before the plane crashed. On a hunch, he had the pilot's body exhumed and a new autopsy performed. Dave's hunch was right—a .223 bullet was lodged in the pilot's back. That means the potential body count from Butch Saint could be as high as fourteen. Dave confirmed Jet's findings that Roderick was tied to both Morgen and Saint. But, since there was no firm evidence to prove the connection to their criminal actions, F-Rod would walk free. For now.

Captain Emery knew how to best use the strengths of each of his men. He also realized that getting the job done was far more important than *how* the job was done. As long as Emery was our leader, Fairbanks was a great place to work.

Dave Daniels found me a desk in the investigative section, taking me under his wing for training as an investigator. Soon, my job was providing aerial support and investigative assistance for the remote posts of Tanana, Manley Hot Springs, Bettles, Fort

Yukon, Circle and Coldfoot. Along with being on the Special Emergency Response Team, I had plenty of work.

I piloted a trooper-blue Cessna 207, along with the fish and wildlife troopers' Super Cub and their factory-new Cessna 185. The 185 was purchased with a federal highway safety grant but, in a bit of Bush irony, it was used mostly in the Brooks Range, where there are no roads. A Bell Jet Ranger complemented the fleet, and I was trained to operate its "FLIR," or "forward looking infrared radar," camera system.

Captain Emery did all he could to help Jet and me coordinate our days off and vacation time so we could meet somewhere between our distant posts. Jet finally made good on the rest of her surprise for my successful hiding of the gas cans on the glacier strip. It was what every guy could want. She treated me to a fishing trip on south-central Alaska's Talachulitna River for king salmon—complete with hand-tied flies and a cabin right on the water. We had a secluded section of the clear stream, loaded with huge fish, all to ourselves. It was a romantic get-away with dandy fishing and time to plan more strategy for our future together. Hopefully, we would soon be able to serve in the same post. In the meantime, we would use our vacation breaks to spend as much time together as possible. That is, if we ever got another vacation, with our crazy schedules.

CHAPTER 35

Thud! Interrupted from my morning of settling into my desk at the Fairbanks office, I looked up to see a familiar face. Ronnie Torgy, rubbing his shinbone, had just smashed into the desk next to mine.

"Ronnie, I mean *Sergeant Torgy*, it's good to see you again." I got up to shake his hand.

"Ah, Jack, you can always call me Ronnie, even if I make colonel. Sorry I don't have time to show you around the place right now, but we have a situation. You need to grab your gear. The emergency response team is going to a fishcamp by Unalakleet."

"Fishcamp" is usually a peaceful place. Native Alaskans leave their villages to spend part of the summer pulling in net loads of salmon. The subsistence way of life is a tradition and continues today in the fishcamps dotted along Alaska's rivers. The men run the gear and the women, dressed in thin summer parkas called kuspucks and colorful headscarves, skin and preserve the catch. Red strips of salmon hang from drying racks to preserve food for the winter and for dogteams. But as Ronnie reported when he rushed into my office, a fishcamp on a tributary to the Unalakleet River was anything but peaceful.

After a long night of chugging home brew, the Inupiat fisherman grabbed his .300 Winchester hunting rifle from his tent and began shooting at anything that moved.

Reporting by the camp radio, a distressed woman said that she was nearly hit, and that some kids playing on the riverbank were in danger.

"This should be easy for you guys, Jack. It's just one drunk with one rifle and there are six of you. Plus, you have a boat to use in Unalakleet. You should be back by lunch. This is a piece of cake." Ronnie spoke with his usual enthusiasm as he stumbled out of the office.

A twin-engine Piper Navajo was chartered for the trip. The plan was to fly to Unalakleet, then borrow a Department of Fish and Game boat to run the ten miles up the river to the fishcamp. Dressed in our black tactical gear, we loaded our assault rifles and filled all seats in the six-passenger plane.

The trip went well—until we had to land at Unalakleet. The airport was below landing minimums with the normal early-summer scud hanging over the village. The closest airport open for an instrument approach was Nome, a hundred twenty-seven miles away. Ted Herlihy came up with a plan. The charter would divert to Nome where I would team up with the local fish and wildlife trooper pilot and fly to Unalakleet in his plane. Meanwhile, after refueling the Navajo, the rest of the SERT troopers would return to Unalakleet, flying over the airport until conditions lifted for the airplane's approach. We would then all meet and head upriver to the camp.

The first snag with the revised plan revealed itself just after landing in Nome with the Navajo. Calling from flight service, we learned from the Nome trooper's office that the fish and wildlife trooper was grounded with his Super Cub in the village of Shaktoolik. The good news was, the department's Cessna 185 floatplane was anchored in the city port, just off the Snake River. However, no one knew where the Cessna's keys were hidden.

Nome Trooper Dan Bell offered to drive me to the aircraft maintenance hangar on the Nome airport, where he hoped to find a spare set of keys. It was only 4:30 in the afternoon, but the secretary said Sammy Thomas, the sole mechanic, was gone for the day.

"Jump in," Trooper Bell said, "I think I know where to find him."

Bell turned the trooper truck onto Seppala Drive, named for one of the sled dog drivers who delivered serum for treating victims of the 1925 diphtheria epidemic. The mushers' marathon run across frozen Alaska set the course for the Iditarod Trail Sled Dog Race, which finishes in Nome. Bell pointed to a red and white Cessna 185 floatplane bobbing in the salty water as we passed the city docks.

Distressed buildings on Front Street were huddled up to each other to join forces against frigid winds from the Bering Sea. I wondered out loud if downtown Nome had changed much since the gold rush days. Trooper Bell pointed out that during the early 1900s, Nome was the largest city in Alaska. He added that the name "Nome" was a fluke. The story goes that a British officer, on a ship off the coast of Alaska, noted a point of land that was not identified. He wrote "Name?" next to the point. When the map was copied, the draftsman thought "Name" was "Nome," and so it became. Fires and floods redrew the map of Nome's face, and its fate, many times over the years.

Trooper Bell knew the mechanic liked to partake of an afternoon beverage at one of Nome's waterfront bars, and that that beverage often turned into a full evening of hell–raising. "Wyatt Earp, the famous wild west lawman, ran a saloon here in 1900," Bell, said, while nodding at the row of bars.

The Polar Café was our first stop. Appearing more like a warehouse than a restaurant, the brown metal-sided building was decorated with white bear tracks. The proprietor said that Sammy came in about 4:45, quickly devoured a burger, then went to the bar to wash it down with a few beers before leaving.

Our next stop was the Breakers Bar, a bright blue wooden structure with a neon "Miller Light" sign dangling from chains in the front window. The bartender hadn't seen Sammy but suggested the nearby Anchor Tavern. Sammy had just left the Anchor after downing two beers, according to the Eskimo waitress.

"Alaska's Oldest Saloon, Since 1900." The sign alone made me want to check inside the Board of Trade, even if Sammy wasn't there. Overheated air and smoke, scented with a combination of beer, sweat and fish, blasted out when we pulled open the heavy door. Faces of Alaska Natives and gruff-looking white men, hunched over their booze, were reflected in the gilt mirrors behind the long, hand-carved wooden bar in the dark and dank room. Over the mumbled arguments, a band ground away on "North to Alaska."

"Vern, have you seen Sammy?" Trooper Bell called to a man who was fumbling with a money clip behind the bar while negotiating with a drunken Eskimo holding a piece of hand-carved ivory.

Vern grabbed the ivory piece and announced his payment: "half a bottle of Yukon Jack." He looked up at Bell and nodded towards the end of the bar. Maneuvering around a couple on the floor who were engaged in leg wrestling, we came to a dark-skinned man having a conversation with his beer bottle. "Nome Air-Repair" was embroidered on the back of the man's blue overalls in gold cursive lettering.

"Sammy, how's it going?" Bell tapped on the mechanic's shoulder and asked him if he had a key for the 185.

Sammy was drunk, but with the skill of a quick-draw cowboy, he yanked a key ring from his belt and twirled it on his finger. He turned to Bell and slurred, "here ya go, Trooper, it's one of them." There were about thirty keys on the ring, but we got lucky—only one key had the initials "AST."

Bell offered to accompany me to the fishcamp, but since I was planning on meeting the rest of the SERT troopers in Unalakleet, there didn't seem to be a need. I would just as soon go with the guys who were equipped and trained for the situation.

Whitecaps were rolling off Norton Sound, so I taxied the Cessna floatplane up the wind-protected Snake River. Three hundred horsepower quickly brought the lightly loaded plane onto the "step" position, allowing take–off in the river instead of having to battle the sizeable waves.

The direct route to Unalakleet led over Bering Sea ice floes, limiting the chance for a safe emergency landing in the rough seas.

I could follow the shoreline instead, but that would take much longer, and too much time already had been wasted.

Icebergs appeared like ghosts from the sea while the 185 slipped under the lowering clouds as I dialed the Loran to lock in on Unalakleet. Now just above the water, there were only two options.

If the visibility and ceiling dropped any lower, I'd either follow the navigation radio beam and head to Unalakleet or, if lucky, I'd pick up the shoreline near the village.

"Trooper Cessna, this is Nome Flight Service." Transmitting on Unalakleet's remote radio, the FAA radio operator broke my concentration to pass on a message from the Navajo. Still unable to land due to poor weather, the SERT plane would continue to circle over the airport and wait for a break in the weather. Nome was now below landing minimums, so if it didn't break before they ran low on fuel, they would return to Fairbanks. For now, I was on my own.

I smeared condensation around on the side window with my shirtsleeve and peered out the little opening at the fuzzy grayness. As a chunk of unfamiliar topography appeared, I'd try to match clues from my chart. After half an hour searching near Unalakleet, a big inlet came through the fog. It matched the chart's depiction of the entrance to the Unalakleet River from Norton Sound, so I banked to the left, following the braided waterway upstream. As the caller had reported, a smaller river broke off the Unalakleet, ten miles up from the Sound. Large white tents dotted the hill above the slow-moving stream. Boats were beached in front of the camp.

Reducing the power and pulling the flaps, I approached the camp at seventy knots and scanned the slough for the best landing area, while also searching for the shooter. The camp appeared empty, which was unusual during summer daylight hours.

Tonk, TONK! The noise from the back right side of the plane was disturbing, but, the controls worked fine and the gauges read normal. Maybe the nylon line attached to the right float was slapping in the wind as the airspeed slowed.

I'd have to accept that for now.

Taking advantage of the protection offered by the steep bank of the slough, I landed downstream from the camp and fast-taxied onto the soft beach. Swiftly exiting the 185, I jogged to the edge of the cliff. Laying on the edge of the bank, I cased the area. Like a parking lot, the naked bluff lacked foliage and terrain definition.

Twelve identical tents sat neatly in a line, spaced about fifty yards apart. Pulling myself to the top of the bank, I jogged to the first tent. With my rifle at the ready, I announced: "State Troopers."

An Inupiat woman pulled open the tent flap. "Trooper, Peter Nowark is shooting his big rifle, he live in second to last tent." She said that all of the other fishing families had agreed amongst themselves to stay in their tents until the shooting was over. She added that no one has been injured yet, but that Nowark had pulled off two shots as I was landing. I thanked her, and using one tent after another to conceal my approach, I continued along the row.

The first shot came at the eighth tent, striking the dirt a few feet from me. Yelling toward the shooter, I identified myself and ordered him to stop firing. His answer was two more shots blasted into the dirt, a little nearer to me this time. To keep the people in the row of tents from further danger, I bolted for the slough. Three bullets hit near my boots as I jumped off the bank. I now had the protection of the overhang, but I had lost my view of the tents.

Maybe Nowark would pass out and I could approach his tent, or maybe Ted and the rest of the team would show up soon. But what if my visit had agitated Nowark to take more desperate measures?

Voices came from around the muddy shoreline. Cautiously approaching, I found two young Eskimo boys huddled under the bank. One, wearing a muddy Chicago Bulls number twenty-three jersey, asked, "Hey trooper, you come to kill Peter?" I assured the pre-teenager that I was just trying to get Peter to stop shooting and asked them to stay put. The boy continued, "Peter got mad because somebody drank some of his homebrew, so he got in his boat and ran around in the slough for a while. Then he come back and start shooting. He went crazy!"

Number twenty-three gave me an idea. An old Alaskan Bush rat told me once that Natives cherish their "kickers," or outboard motors, more than anything during fishing season. I asked the boy to point out which one was Peter's.

"That white Evinrude 70 on the Lund over there," the boy pointed to the second to last boat on the muddy beach. The red skiff was pulled onto the bank with the outboard engine tilted up. I thanked the boys and told them to stay put. Bending at the waist to keep under the bank and out of Nowark's view, I walked to within fifty yards of the Lund, then yelled at the tent.

"Peter, it's Trooper Blake. Come on out now, and drop your gun!"

Two quick shots hit the bank just above me, so I moved to Plan B. I took a quick peek over the bank. Peter Nowark, a young Eskimo wearing a dark blue sweatshirt, baggy jeans, and a white cap, was standing in front of his tent. His rifle was being held in the ready position.

"Okay Peter, I hate to do this, but you give me no choice."

The target came into focus through the riflescope of my M-16. I had a clear shot of the head-concealing cover. I carefully studied it for the best-shot placement.

Through my scope, I read "Johnson" and "70." My shooting eye moved from the bottom of the white corner, across the red and black stripe, up to the top right edge, which was pointing toward the sky. My finger eased behind the trigger guard and I took a deep breath. I exhaled as I squeezed the trigger.

A small chunk of white fiberglass flung into the air as the .223 bullet hit the outboard engine cowling. Almost before the debris hit the water, Peter Nowark screamed. He then began jumping up and down and threw his cap to the tundra.

"What the hell are you doing, Trooper, are you *crazy?* That's my kicker you just shot!"

"I *know* it is, Peter, and the next shot is going to be dead center, right in the cylinder head," I yelled back.

"Okay, *okay*, please don't shoot my motor any more, I give up." With that, I peeked over the slough bank to see Peter Nowark walking with his hands over his head. After he was satisfied his cowling was not beyond duct tape repair, he put his wrists out for cuffing.

Peter's rifle was in his tent, next to a white plastic five-gallon bucket. The homebrew, made of rubbing alcohol, fruit cocktail, and other secret ingredients, had at least a hundred dead mosquitoes floating on the surface. Nowark was cooperative as he walked in front of me to the floatplane waiting in the slough. As we passed the tents, families stared silently, anxious to get back to fishing.

Something didn't look right with the floatplane—it was severely listing to the right side. I helped Nowark slide down to the muddy beach and inspected the right pontoon.

The aluminum EDO 3430 float had two gaping exit wounds on the inside of the bulkheads, one just aft of the step and one just before the step. The entrance wounds were on the opposite side of the bulkheads, just below the waterline. I glanced at Nowark. His eyes searched the mud. He finally spoke. "Sorry, Trooper."

I dug through the plane's baggage area, but found no tools to patch the floats, just a hand pump. I pumped all the water I could from the compartments. That would have to do.

The two boys ran down the shoreline and watched as I handcuffed Nowark and assisted him into the 185, yelling that it was just like watching a television cop show. After the prisoner promised to behave, we fast-taxied down the slough, making a quick turning takeoff to get airborne quickly. We were over Unalakleet in a few minutes.

The challenge would be in the landing. I wasn't sure whether the takeoff had increased the size of the floats' wound. If so, and the gaping hole was snagged in the water on landing, it could result in a rough ride, maybe enough to capsize us.

The chartered plane had finally made in through the weather to Unalakleet, and Ted Herlihy and the rest of crew were waiting for me on the riverbank near the airport. With the on-board police radio, I called Ted on his portable, asking him to check on the float as I made a low pass.

"It looks like I punched my fist through the float." The assessment was bad news, especially considering Ted's unique fist. The gash had peeled back and opened. I asked Ted to try and find a trailer in Unalakleet, while I burned fuel from the right tank.

Thirty minutes later, Ted came back on the radio.

"You're in luck, Jack, I found a guy with a flatbed. Where do you want me?" I directed Ted to back the trailer down the boat ramp into the Unalakleet River.

Fortunately, daylight lasted almost twenty hours in June, and the ceiling now was a high overcast. I flew for an hour and half, until the electric fuel gauge showed empty on the right tank. That gave Ted and me plenty of time to go over our plan.

After a long downwind over Norton Sound, a left one-eighty set up a long approach to the Unalakleet River. With power and flaps set for landing, we dropped low over the cloudy river, slowing to sixty knots. The left float touched.

The landing turned into a one-float step-taxi. By cross-controlling the floatplane and jockeying the power, I was able to keep the float with the jagged holes in the air. With the winter trail on the left, the nose of the 185 was lined up with the trailer, now partially submerged in the river. Turning the control wheel hard to the left, simultaneously stepping on the right rudder, I hung the damaged float out of the water as long as possible. Letting the power drop at the last minute, the right float joined the left on the water and we glided onto the trailer.

Ted had placed the trailer perfectly in the water and the 185 did its job. It was a lucky day.

"Showoff," Ted said, as he took custody of the prisoner and his rifle. "We were just about to leave in a skiff to help you at the fishcamp, but it looks like you didn't need any."

"Peter here decided to cooperate. Good job with the trailer, Ted. That was a lifesaver," I said, shaking Ted's hand.

"Trooper, the next time I have to fly from fishcamp, I think I go with someone else. That was pretty scary." Nowark's words were his first since we had taken off.

I started to explain that our landing was not standard procedure. But, then I saw the twinkle in the Eskimo's eye and his slight smile, realizing he had a sense of humor, even after a rough twenty-four hours at fishcamp.

We arranged for an air taxi service in Unalakleet to trailer the 185 to its hangar for repair. Then we all piled into the Navajo. After being booked into the Anvil Mountain Correctional Center, Nowark said, "sorry about shooting your plane, Trooper." I could have said I was sorry about shooting his kicker, but it was better than shooting *him*.

I wish that all SERT call-outs ended so well.

CHAPTER 36

O'Reilly's Air Taxi had flown two moose hunters into Silver Lake, southwest of the Yukon River and the village of Tanana. The men had planned to hike from the base camp until they shot a big moose and then pack the meat back to the lake. O'Reily's would then haul the men and their bounty back to Fairbanks.

The hunters were three days overdue on returning to Silver Lake for their pickup. The air taxi pilot had searched the area, but couldn't find his customers.

In the fall, the Alaska Range Mountains are topped with fresh snow and the valleys' deciduous trees break into a show of red, yellow and lime-green. Animals are on the move and hunters head out to get winter meat or trophies. Dropped off in the right place by an air taxi service, they have a good chance of success. But elements unique to Alaska create challenges, and hunters sometimes get into trouble.

"Good to meet you, *sir.*" The baby-faced rookie trooper shook my hand and crawled into the back of the Piper Super Cub floatplane. He was only a couple of years my junior, so his politeness had to be in respect for my seniority with the troopers. It was a nice gesture, but certainly uncalled for.

"Just call me Jack."

Recruit Trooper Toby Clay was about to make his first flight in a small plane, so I was extra careful to brief him on safety procedures. He laughed when I asked him to please not decorate the side of the Cub, like others had done when overcome with airsickness. The common practice, rather than using a bag, was for sick passengers to stick their heads out the window and let it go. The draft splashed the mess on the fuselage and the pilot usually had to clean it up.

Every time I looked back at Toby, he was smiling as he intently scanned the ground. Talking through the headsets as we searched, I learned that Toby had completed his military service just last year. He hoped to switch to the fish and wildlife trooper division some day, saying he loved the outdoors.

The days were getting shorter so, by early evening, after four and a half hours on the hard Cub seats, we were considering heading back to Fairbanks and resuming the search the next morning. We refueled from the air taxi's cache at Silver Lake and decided to make one more sweep of the Tanana flats. Toby had great vision, picking out every moose on every pond, so I wasn't surprised when he yelled over the headset, "smoke, smoke, on the left." The blue haze drifting above the tall spruce trees led us to a campfire.

Two men waved frantically as we flew over. The four trooper decals on the Cub must have been a welcome sight. Meat hung in white bags in the trees, but there was no tent. We made a timed pass over the lake at sixty miles per hour. Quick math showed the water landing and takeoff area was very short, even for a Cub. The almost perfectly round pond was in a hole surrounded by tall trees.

Cutting the power of the one hundred and sixty horse engine, I dropped over the spruce, but the lake was too short for a straight in landing over the obstacles. I cranked the Cub into a tight turn, circling down amongst the trees in the hole. We splashed onto the water surface. Since we were still scooting along at a quick pace, I nudged the stick forward, stubbing the nose of the floats into the water to stop about twenty feet short of the lakeshore.

It had been raining during the day and freezing at night. The hunters were cold, wet, and near hypothermia. Except for fresh meat, they were out of food. One hunter had twisted his ankle, causing such swelling that he couldn't walk. Added to their woes were a grizzly sow and her two yearling cubs skulking around the camp. The bears raided the hunters' meat cache the past two nights and, having found a good source of grub to fatten up for the winter, would certainly be back for another feeding at dark. All factors considered, these guys needed to be flown out right away. Toby was in top shape, so without effort, he slung the one hundred and seventy pound injured hunter over his shoulder, carrying him onto the right float of the Cub and helping him into the rear seat.

As we taxied around the small body of water, I sized up the obstacles. There was nothing in the Piper flight manual that provided take-off distance from a short lake surrounded by sixty-foot trees. Since a straight-out departure was not possible over the obstacles, I added full power until the floatplane jumped onto the step, turning it into a speedboat, then reduced it to nineteen hundred RPM. We made a series of tight turns in a circumference as wide as the lake allowed. The turning motion turned the glassy water into a choppy surface, allowing the floats to break free of the surface tension as I again slammed in full throttle.

I wasn't sure we were going to get airborne but, coming around on the third turn, the Cub hit the wakes. Rolling onto the right float and pulling the flaps to full, we popped off the water. Easing the flaps to the half position and pushing the stick hard left, we made a tight turn within the trees, gaining altitude.

We cleared the trees with a few feet to spare. After a twenty minute round trip to Silver Lake, I was back over the pond, setting up for another, tight circling landing.

Toby had added brush to the fire. It now reflected onto the lake's surface, providing guidance as the daylight became dusk. With the second hunter in the back, we repeated the takeoff process, clearing the trees just as dusk gelled into darkness. The moon was only a quarter full and the few stars weren't much help.

The trip back into the lake to pick up Toby was a little more tricky. The campfire now shone across the lake on the glassy water, but the trees were invisible in the black skies.

I had memorized the altitudes, so I circled over the center of the water several times, losing altitude while focusing on the firelight.

Chuckling to myself, I realized the lighting wasn't much, but maybe it was a little better than lanterns hanging from poles, like Ronnie set up for me in Chitina.

Cutting the power and adding flaps, I was able to glide in a tight left turn into the darkness. Using the firelight as a guide, I flared just above the water. The left float splashed hard. I jerked the control stick to the right, causing both floats to plop firmly onto the black surface. Next, I eased the stick forward and wagged the rudders hard to help in slowing the plane, thumping onto the beach.

Toby pointed to a big spruce tree where the bags of game meat dangled from large branches.

"I was able to get most of the meat hung up there. It's higher than the hunters had it. Should make it a little harder for the bears. I'd hate to see the meat go to waste. If it's okay with you, sir, I'd like to throw this back strap in the plane, so the hunters can have fresh meat for dinner tonight."

The fifty pounds of extra weight would make the takeoff even more of a challenge, but Toby had gone to too much work to deny him.

Before throwing water on the fire, I offered to camp and wait until daylight.

"If it's all the same to you, sir, I'll take my chances in flying out, rather than spend the night here with fresh meat and hungry bears."

Taxiing onto the lake, we used the Cub's landing light to reflect off the water and the trees, repeating the step turn take off. Focusing on the plane's instruments to clear the tree line, I became blind to the outside environment once off the water. Struggling to climb into the black skies, the landing light shone on one of the tall spruce as the airspeed indicator read forty-five. I popped the flaps back to full and we flew over the tree with a resounding snap.

We learned the source of the snap after landing at Silver Lake and inspecting the plane with a flashlight. A three-foot section of a spruce tree was lodged on the walk-across cable between the front of the floats.

Back in Fairbanks, we used the instrument approach to runway one-left, then stepped over to the water runway for a glassy water night landing. It was a real luxury to have both guidance and no obstructions for the last landing of the day.

"Great working with you," Toby said, as he shook my hand.

I returned the compliment to the still-smiling trooper. Rookie or not, Toby Clay was a good guy to have along, and I hoped we could work together again someday. We would, but for his sake, I wish we wouldn't have.

CHAPTER 37

"**B**lake, I need you to handle this investigation." Captain William Tower didn't look healthy as he leaned forward onto his desk. His doughy complexion cried for a little sun. He rarely wore a uniform, instead preferring a blue blazer and gray slacks, with a state trooper logo tie complementing a starched white shirt. With his slicked-back hair, the five foot, six inches tall, two hundred and thirty pound playboy wanna-be looked more like he should be selling Buicks than working in law enforcement.

Rich Emery was promoted to the rank of major on a Friday and reported to his new job at Anchorage headquarters the following Monday. All of the hard-working troopers hated to see him leave. The entire staff, even the ones he had to push to do their jobs, hated his replacement.

Tower should have been a politician. He was a real "glad-hander" toward department brass, the media, and anyone he thought could make a difference in his future advancement with the Department of Public Safety. He wasn't always that way, once being known as a dedicated trooper and a tenacious investigator. His desire for power changed his priorities as he lobbied hard to become the next commissioner of the Department of Public Safety, a position appointed by the governor.

During the governor's race, Tower campaigned for the "shoo-in" candidate. When the shoo-in's opponent wanted the standard customary tour of the Public Safety Building, Tower denied him. Alaskan elections can be surprising, as was that one.

Tower's choice didn't get elected. The new governor finally got his building tour. It was during that tour that he congratulated Tower on his new assignment. No, he wasn't to be commissioner, but captain of the Fairbanks detachment, replacing Rich Emery. It was a forced transfer, not a promotion. Tower wasn't happy. The troopers under his new command weren't either.

Tower more or less went on strike when he moved to Fairbanks, becoming more of a skirt-chaser than a cop or a leader. He went so far as having the civilian helicopter pilot fly him weekly to a female trooper's post for a rendezvous, which he called "beyond the call of duty."

Like he did with most of his subordinates, Tower pretty much ignored me, which was fine. Then one day he summoned me into his office.

The captain tossed a case card—a long skinny form with a brief case summary—at me. The title of the case was "Moose Poaching." That was a surprise.

"Captain, shouldn't this go to the fish and wildlife troopers?" I was sincere and not trying to get out of the work.

"I want *you* to handle this one, Blake. Let me know what you find." Tower reached with one hand to answer his phone and motioned me to exit his office with the other. Before I cleared the door, he cupped his hand over the phone mouthpiece.

"Oh and, Blake, Fred Roderick sends his best." Well, I thought, at least F-Rod wasn't throwing to a psychopath this time. Just a poacher.

Jill, who once confided to me that her main chore was ducking from Tower's lewd advances, reported the captain's new career plans. Upon his retirement, just a few months away, he would immediately start at a high-paying administrative position with F-Rod's Denali Pipeline Security. That wasn't comforting.

The captain may have thought assigning me a poaching case was demeaning, but I looked forward to the variety. Working with Jet, I'd come to appreciate the job game wardens did and found the outdoor work appealing.

When I called Jet for tips on investigating a moose poaching, she replied, "it's pretty much like investigating a homicide, but you don't have the luxury of interviewing the moose's family and friends."

Chena Ridge is a little community on a hillside west of Fairbanks. Home sites, surrounded by tall spruce, overlook the Tanana River, the Alaska Range, and the city of Fairbanks. The complainant, Charlotte Wickham, owned four small log cabins. She rented them without the commitment of long-term leases, enticing a range of renters. Two college professors, who had just accepted positions at the nearby University of Alaska, wisely decided to try a winter in the north before buying a home, and each had a cabin. A newly-divorced mother of two rented another.

Ike Rayon occupied the fourth. Wickham didn't know much about the bearded Rayon with the long hair who kept to himself—that was, until his recent confrontation with a neighbor. Calvin Sims, the neighbor, hadn't been seen since the incident.

Wickham said that several moose winter on her five acres, feeding on the willow brush. She added that the moose are no bother and that she enjoys watching them. Wickham heard gunshots the night of the beef between Rayon and Sims. The shots came from the direction of Rayon's cabin, so she figured the men may have made up and conspired on a moose poaching.

Stinky smoke drifted low from the log cabin. The two front windows were glazed over with ice in the twenty below zero temperature. A ten-year old brown Dodge sedan, topped with a wooden box, sat next to the cabin. An orange electrical cord connected the car to an outlet on the side of the cabin, so a heater could keep the engine warm enough to start.

In the frozen front yard, an axe, used to split birch into firewood, was stuck in a chopping block. Specs of bright red blood decorated the snow, from the truck to the cabin door.

There was no response when I banged on Rayon's sturdy door, so I looked around the yard. Using a stick, I dug into a mound of snow behind the cabin. The digging uncovered a moose hide. I found another piece hanging from a tree branch.

Prodding around with my boots in the foot-deep snow covering the front yard exposed more blood. Even though I knew nothing about investigating a poaching, something made me want to take some of the frozen red snow for evidence. I scooped some into a baggie and stuck it in my pocket.

Something squeaked behind me.

I slowly turned as the cabin door opened a crack. A bearded man, looking like a disheveled, younger, and stronger version of John Lennon, complete with the gold circular glasses, peeped out the opening.

"Mr. Rayon? I'm Jack Blake, Alaska State Trooper."

"Are you alone?" Strange question. One that caused me to open the slit in my parka to assure my pistol was ready.

Walking closer, I studied Rayon. Half of his body was now showing. Only one of his hands was visible.

"Yes, I'm alone. I just need to talk to you about the moose hide."

"Oh, that." Rayon sounded relieved, and he cracked the door wider. But one hand was still hidden. I noticed something that I'd missed the first time I'd approached the cabin—a small pool of blood just in front of the door.

"Mr. Rayon, I need you to come outside for a minute." I wanted to see his other hand and I wanted him in the open.

"Just a second," Rayon said, as he again closed the door.

I didn't trust the guy, but at that point, I had no particular reason. A check with dispatch on my way to Chena Ridge revealed no criminal history on Rayon, but there was just something about him that raised the hairs on the back of my neck. I moved over to his sedan, so I'd have some cover if he came out shooting.

Swinging the door open, Rayon stepped into the snow. He wore white military bunny boots and green army pants. He kept both hands in the matching green parka. I kept one hand on my pistol.

"Do you have any weapons?" Not necessarily expecting to get the truth, I asked anyway.

"Just an old Remington Rolling Block."

I knew the rifle. My uncle had a Norway-Swedish Remington Rolling Block he used for target practice on the ranch. Designed over a hundred years ago, the rifle's twelve-millimeter rounds could be fired with great accuracy in the right hands. The single shot action, heavy weight and long length, made it more a collector's item than a hunting weapon. I asked to see it.

The old rifle was well taken care of, but the smell of gunpowder on the muzzle told me it hadn't been cleaned since its last firing. There was no bullet in the chamber.

"I was target practicing the other night." Rayon had noticed my close inspection. He slid his gloved hands back into his coat.

"Tell me about the moose hide. And would you mind removing your hands from your pockets?"

Rayon slowly drew his hands into the cold air. His gaze focused on the axe. "The hide came from Calvin Sims. He lives up the trail. He gave me a chunk of hide so I could try to tan it."

After a few more minutes of conversation, with a few leading questions thrown in, it was clear Rayon wasn't going to admit to poaching a moose. I wasn't even sure he had. But there was still the question about Calvin Sims.

Rayon's line of vision jerked from the axe when I asked him where I could find Sims.

"Don't know. Haven't seen him today." Rayon again stared at the axe. I left just before dark.

Once back at the post, my first call was to the tech at the crime lab. The lab tech said he could turn around a blood sample test within a week. My second call was to Jet.

"That sounds like a lot of blood for one piece of moose hide," Jet said when I described the scene. We agreed that I should return and look around for more evidence.

CHAPTER 38

Blood samples from Ike Rayon's yard were sent to the lab and I had to wait until the test results were available to pursue the case any further. Meanwhile, there was work to do. After serving court papers in Bettles and spending the night in Coldfoot, I was routed by dispatch to Fort Yukon. The Gwitchin Indian village of about five hundred sits on the banks of the Yukon River. It's about a hundred twenty miles from Fairbanks and eight miles north of the Arctic Circle. Alex Clark, the local police chief, had reported a local was drunk and "shooting up the village."

Chief Clark met the 185 at the Fort Yukon airstrip. "Jump in. Jimmy Bayo is running around town with his rifle. He's already shot one dog and two cars. Fired a shot at me, too." We bumped over the rough road into the village in Clark's pick up.

Bayo stumbled down the icy, one-lane road. He didn't notice us until the truck was just behind him.

"State troopers!" I yelled at Bayo as he looked over his shoulder, running faster than I've ever seen a drunk move. I almost caught him as he jumped onto the steps of his cabin, but I paused when he swung around with his rifle. Banging the front door open with his butt, he fell into the shack and locked himself in.

Clark banged on the door. Bayo responded by breaking a glass pane from the cabin's front window and firing a shot at nothing in particular. Looking through the scope of my rifle, I watched Bayo's expressionless face searching the area for something to shoot at, then finding nothing, shooting anyway. His gaze reflected the hopelessness of the villagers who have given in to booze and drugs, sacrificing their proud, traditional way of life in the process.

Clark grabbed a dog chain from the side of the cabin. He slung the chain around a hook ring that was mounted on the old wood plank door. Like in a tug of war, Clark and I dug in and pulled on the chain, yanking the door right off the frame. Bayo was sitting on the floor, with his 30-06 in his arms and forty rounds of brass lying around him. I grabbed the rifle and Clark threw the shooter out into the snow.

As we were driving Bayo to Clark's office, we turned to look back at the cabin. Smoke was pouring out the door and windows. By the time the relic of a fire truck could respond, the cabin was in flames. Bayo and his assorted friends and relatives claimed "the cops" had set the cabin on fire as punishment. Chief Clark, knowing the local politics, wisely suggested calling an investigator from the Fairbanks fire Marshall's office. Bayo was booked into the Fort Yukon jail, while the volunteer fire department soaked what was left of his little cabin. I bunked on the police department couch for the night.

State Fire Marshall Bernie Short spent an hour digging through the ashes and taking photos the next day. Short determined, through his investigation and interviews, that Jimmy and some of his drunken buddies had dropped cigarette butts on a mattress. The mattress smoldered all day, erupting later into a fire. The arrest of Jimmie Bayo most likely saved his life.

We loaded Bayo into the 185 for a flight to the Fairbanks jail. He had calmed down a little since his alcohol-fueled frenzy the night before, but he was still cussing and fighting at the restraints. After helping him into the backseat, I handcuffed his wrist cuffs to shackles attached to the floor of the 185. The fire marshal sat in front of him, next to me in the cockpit. Both of us told Bayo a couple of times to settle down so I could concentrate on the takeoff. He kept being a nuisance, at one point even trying to head-butt Short.

The fire marshal had had enough. Short pulled a .38 revolver from inside his jacket, pointing at Bayo's face with the words: "If you try anything, and I mean *anything* at all during this flight, I will consider it a hijacking attempt. As an officer of the law, I will stop the hijacking attempt. The only way I can accomplish that safely is by putting a bullet between your eyes and I will do just that."

Bayo behaved all the way to Fairbanks, and I had learned a new technique for hauling disruptive prisoners in airplanes.

First thing Thursday morning, I called the Anchorage lab to check on the test results for the blood sample from the moose poaching and found that nothing would be available until Monday. Checking with dispatch, I was assured that no new information had come in on the Ike Rayon case, so I took my two regularly scheduled days off—Thursday and Friday.

Toby Clay had asked me to call him if I ever wanted company when I went flying in my own plane. I usually liked exploring the backcountry on my own, but Toby was so enthusiastic that it was selfish of me not to make the offer. We warmed my Cub with a propane heater, threw our winter survival gear in the back, and headed towards the Brooks Range. As I turned around to hand Toby a chart so he could follow our course, I caught him smiling at the wonder of the stark white terrain in the largely undeveloped land north of Fairbanks

We picked up a line of tracks just past the Tolovana River and followed them to the source—a pack of wolves. The eight grays and three blacks were on their morning hunt. They would certainly take down a moose from the herd we soon came upon. The moose wagged their ears in an attempt to detect the source of the offending airplane racket. The horse–plus sized animals struggled to survive the harsh Alaska winter, only to be fed on by the wolf pack. But that's how nature works.

Following the ridgeline of the White Mountains, we came upon a wolverine — pound for pound, the nastiest critter in Alaska — as it scrounged for its breakfast. Dropping down onto the Yukon Flats, a small herd of caribou was digging for lichens in the snow. Turning west, we followed Hess Creek until it dropped into the Yukon River, and then turned back towards Fairbanks.

"How about trying a little ice fishing, Toby?"

The Cub silently glided onto the frozen surface of Minto Lake. We chopped holes in the ice and, in an hour, we had pulled out two big northern pike, eight grayling, and three burbot—called "Poor Man's Lobster" by Alaska anglers. We dragged our catch toward the airplane, then decided it was time to head home for the day. But the lake had other ideas.

"Overflow," a condition in which water becomes trapped between a layer of snow and ice, had swallowed the airplane's skis. The Cub had sunk to its axles in the slush. This wouldn't be an easy fix, for as soon as the water-laden metal skis hit the twenty-five degree temperature, they would freeze. We cut willow branches and by lifting a wing, stuck the limbs under the skis. This got the plane back onto the snow, but now we had to find good ice.

We tried pulling the Cub with lines attached to the wings and the tail, but it wouldn't budge. We must have looked like frosted-over snowmen as we slopped in and out of the icy bath. Toby's heavy wool pants shed the ice, reminding me of what an old timer once told me: "Wool keeps you warm and dry, even when you are cold and wet."

It was looking like the Cub might become frozen into the lake. It's funny how help comes in the most unexpected times, and from the most unexpected sources.

"Hike!" A woman's voice echoed across the frozen lake. Then we saw the team. Fourteen huskies were racing toward us with their tongues hanging. "Whoa!" The musher stopped the team next to us. She introduced herself, but I'm sorry to admit that, right now, I can't remember her name. I can blame it on the cold, the lack of sleep, and the lack of food, but I should remember someone who got us out of a tough bind.

The friendly lady with the big smile and big, braided pigtails, hitched her team to the Cub's tail ski. Toby and I pushed on the wing struts and with the added dog power, the plane was towed to the hard ice.

"If that works for you boys, I'm going to hit the trail. I'm training for next year's Iditarod and got to get my miles in."

We thanked our savior, and promised to root for her in the race next March. Ice and snow, about eight inches deep and two feet long, was frozen to each airplane ski. The extra weight and very irregular surface would prevent a takeoff that day. We lifted the Cub onto branches and fired up the portable heater to melt the mess, but we soon realized we would be there for the night. Fortunately, there was a little cabin on the shore. Toby got a fire going in the woodstove, while I drained the oil from the Cub's engine into a pot to it keep warm overnight in the cabin.

That night Toby and I discussed life, family, and our plans after retirement. Recently married, Toby had dreams to follow, and I suspected a good life ahead of him.

"Are you kidding? This is one of the best days I ever had!" Toby's response to my apologizing for the tough day was refreshing. If I could have chosen a little brother, Toby would have been him.

CHAPTER 39

It wasn't *moose* blood, but human. I had called the crime lab at 8 a.m. on Monday, speaking to a lab tech who seemed flustered. He briefed me on his findings on the blood samples I'd sent to the lab from Ike Rayon's yard.

I drove back to Chena Ridge as fast as I could. The tires of my truck slopped through the snow, made mushy by above-normal temperatures. Spring had arrived.

Ike Rayon's yard had changed. The white snow had turned red. The cabin window was no longer covered with ice and I could see in. It was vacant and the brown sedan was gone. I grabbed a shovel from my truck and dug into the thin layer of ice. Flour and peat moss had been mixed into the snow to cover the evidence. The crime lab had proven the blood, which Rayon claimed was from the moose hide, was human. And now there was more of it. A lot more of it.

Dave Daniels and two more investigators responded to my call. Interviews of all the neighbors turned up one interesting witness — the girlfriend and roommate of Calvin Sims. The girlfriend said that Sims had not returned on the day he had been fighting with Rayon. She said she was afraid to make a complaint, thinking Rayon would try to harm her if she did. Smart thinking, in retrospect.

The search for Ike Rayon began. A locate order was entered in the FBI's National Crime Information Center system and photos were given to troopers. It didn't take long for Rayon to make his presence known. Dispatch took the call from Manley Hot Springs, a community of one hundred on the bank of the

Tanana River, seventy-two air miles northwest of Fairbanks. The caller was concerned about friends and neighbors who had begun disappearing from the town's boat launch on the Tanana River three days ago. The ice had just gone out and the river was open for boat travel.

Two buddies had not been seen since launching their boat. Another guy had driven down the river with a load of brush and never returned home. A trapper, who lived a little distance upriver from Manley, had boated to town to repair his truck and was missing. A pregnant woman, her baby, and her husband had ridden to the river on their ATV, and they were simply gone.

The complainant said that a strange man had been hanging around the boat landing lately. The man had been showing off his shooting skills—he could keep a tin can bouncing down the dirt road by reloading his single-shot rifle from cartridges held in his mouth.

The caller added that the stranger's car was still parked at the river, but that he was gone, along with the canoe that was tied on top of the car. She gave dispatch the number from his license plate.

It was a brown Dodge, registered to Ike Rayon.

The wheels of the 185 touched down on the grass airstrip in Manley less than an hour after dispatch had radioed me. It was a short walk to the boat launch where the scene looked like a battle zone. Amongst shell casings, blood splatters covered the ground. Bloody drag marks in the gravel led to the river, indicating that bodies had been dumped into the fast current.

As I began collecting evidence, the trooper helicopter landed at the nearby airstrip.

Ted Herlihy had assembled his team well. He would sit in the left seat, next to the pilot. Behind him, with the door removed, Toby Clay was strapped in, smiling as usual. Although a fairly new trooper, Toby was uniquely qualified to join SERT. Before joining the troopers, he had been a Marine Corps sniper. Sitting next to Clay was another top marksman, but that was to change.

The fish and wildlife trooper Super Cub landed and taxied to the helicopter. Captain Tower, dressed in slacks and a golf shirt, climbed out of the back.

"Hold it, don't start that thing!" Tower yelled at the helicopter pilot. Herlihy, get one of your men out of there, I'm taking command."

"Captain, I need my men on this. You don't have the training or the weapon if this gets nasty. And, you don't even have a flak vest."

Ignoring Ted's plea, the captain motioned for the SERT trooper next to Clay to get out. He pulled himself in, plopping in the seat.

"Jack, he's going to get us all killed. Do you think you can find Rayon's boat with the 185?"

"Better yet, we'll take the Cub—it's better for spotting. Can I borrow a rifle?"

The ejected trooper reluctantly handed me his M-16. I hopped in the Cub, piloted by a fish and wildlife trooper, and we were quickly airborne. Fifteen minutes later, we were over the Zitziana River, a tributary of the Tanana. About ten miles upriver, a boat—matching the description of one missing from Manley Hot Springs—slowly maneuvered up a slough, towing a canoe.

Popping the side door open, I asked the pilot to make a low pass and to fly as slowly as possible. Through the scope of the M-16, I could clearly see Ike Rayon, cradling the Rolling Block rifle in his arms. Rayon slid the hull onto a sandbar, sprang from the boat, and swung the rifle at the Cub.

Smoke puffed from the rifle's barrel, prompting me to yell at the pilot to pull up. We came around once more at about seven hundred feet, and I leveled the M-16 at Rayon. Compensating for the light chop in the air and our moving shooting platform, I had Rayon in my sights. We hit rough air, my rifle bounced, and Rayon disappeared from the scope.

Slap! Fabric from the Rolling Block's bullet ripped just behind my head. I refocused. Once again, Rayon came into view through my sights. The turbulence settled and I could take the shot, but…without warning, something blue filled the scope.

"What the hell?" The pilot screamed as he slammed the stick back, pushed the power to full, and cranked us in to a hard left turn as the wake from the intruder hit. I swung my head out the open door to see the helicopter.

"Ted, hold on, *hold* on! Don't get too low! There's a clearing where you can land and approach him with the protection of the row of trees. There's no hurry, let's get some altitude and map this out." I yelled at Ted to break off the chopper's approach.

"Roger, Jack, that sounds like a…"

A screaming voice interrupted Ted: "Screw that, we're going to take him out, NOW!"

The helicopter dove awkwardly toward the slough. "What's he *doing?*" My pilot yelled. Neither of us could believe it. The Jet Ranger contorted sideways and seemed to stop in mid-air. Hovering, it turned with the doors facing the killer.

Two more puffs of smoke came from the ground.

Red tracers zoomed from the helicopter.

"We got the bastard, we *got* him!" The captain yelled over the radio.

But then Ted broke in.

"Toby has been *hit.* Toby's *down.* Jack, meet us in Manley. You need to get Toby to the Fairbanks hospital in the 185. It's bad!" Ted screamed over the radio.

We landed at Manley just before the helicopter. I quickly pulled the front passenger seat and the rear jump seat out of the 185, making it ready for patient transport. I ran over to the helo as it touched down.

Except for a bullet hole two inches from the transmission, the helicopter looked intact, gleaming in the afternoon sun. But as I rounded the tail, I saw the blood. Blood glazed the helicopter's Plexiglas. It flowed along the outside of the craft, smearing the "State Troopers" decal.

My heart rushed and my guts sank as I moved to the passenger compartment. Toby was laying back in his seat with his eyes wide open. He had a gaping wound in his neck.

The smile was gone.

The baby face was gone.

Ted ran over. He cried while holding Toby's hand.

Captain Tower got out of the helicopter, wiping blood from the side of his neck with a white handkerchief. He looked at Ted and Toby, then threw up. "Trooper Herlihy, I'm sorry, I didn't mean for it to work out that way," the captain mumbled as he shuffled to the TV news van.

Ted fell to his knee. It was minutes before he could speak. "Toby didn't need to die, we had that bastard trapped. We could easily have taken him."

Ted told me of the chaos inside the helicopter, once Tower barked orders to the pilot. Before Ted could yell an objection, the helicopter swerved violently, presenting the whole side of the fuselage to the killer. "Toby was trying to rip his headset off, so he could get his rifle up, when he was hit. He didn't have a chance.

"I took him out after that, but it was too late, Toby is still dead. There was absolutely no damn reason for this. That idiot captain….." Ted slipped into tears again, unable to continue.

"Jack, I need you to take me to the scene. I've been as-signed the investigation." Dave Daniels had walked up behind me. We piled into the bloody helicopter and returned to the slough.

"I don't understand, he was stuck on this dead end little creek, there was no place to go. What was the *rush?*" Dave spoke as we hovered over the scene.

As the Jet Ranger settled onto the sand, Dave and I scrambled out. The boat was loaded with the victims' gear, stolen after they were killed in Manley. The Rolling Block rifle lay in the sand. Rayon was on his back in the dirt. The top of his skull was separated from his head—we found it a few minutes later in the shallow water. Grayling were biting away at it.

"Look at this, Jack." Dave pulled back Rayon's army jacket. An F-Rod tattoo was inked onto his wrist.

CHAPTER 40

"**A**mazing Grace" and "Scotland the Brave" were played on bagpipes at Toby's funeral. Beyond words, Ted and I served as color guards. Ike Rayon had murdered nine innocent people. But, since he had served in Viet Nam, he received the honors of a government-funded burial in the Sitka National Cemetery. The graveyard is adjacent to the Alaska State Trooper academy.

Ted was selected to be the commander of the trooper academy. He said he took the job only so he could lead each graduation class to the cemetery to urinate on Rayon's grave. But, we all knew he would do a superb job in training the recruits.

I wasn't as lucky as Ted.

Ronnie Torgy, who had transferred to Bethel just before the Manley shooting, called Bethel the "armpit of Alaska." Some call it worse. The only good thing about the transfer is that Jet and I would be much closer, as Bethel was only a hundred miles from Jet's post in Dillingham. And, at least Ronnie would be there to lighten things up a bit.

All I knew about the Yukon-Kuskokwin Delta—which had Bethel right in the middle—was what I'd recently read in the newspaper. Much of the Native population was digging in on the sovereignty issue. One trooper, investigating a case in which a minor was sexually abused, was taken hostage in one of the tundra villages. More than a hundred angry villagers in the community center had surrounded another.

Troopers had to respond en masse with a chartered aircraft both times to get their men out safely.

Fifty-four villages were served by the Bethel trooper post and at least forty of those were doing all they could to keep "white man's law enforcement" away. It was no wonder troopers were transferring out of Bethel as fast as they could, and no one volunteered to replace them.

"Blake, you and Herlihy did right in your testimony to the shooting board. I screwed up and it's something I have to live with. Your transfer is not my doing. They need help in Bethel. These orders came from the top. I'm leaving myself, going to take that job with Denali Security a little earlier than I'd planned. You are to report to Bethel in two weeks." Tower's change in attitude was surprising. It almost made me want to warn him about F-Rod, but maybe he already knew. Maybe this was just some sort of sick ploy.

Some of the guys signed a going away card for me. It depicted one of Custer's scouts returning to the Cavalry's base camp, his chest full of arrows. The card read: "Maybe the tribes really don't want us here, General."

Perhaps if I'd transferred directly from King Salmon to Bethel, way back at the beginning of my career—just after Laos, or just after guiding in the Bush—it wouldn't have been such a cultural shock.

Some told me that Bethel and the surrounding "tundra villages," were the closest comparisons to Third World countries we have in the United States. Not only are living conditions tough, but also a trooper could feel, and almost taste, the hostility from many of the villagers.

CHAPTER 41

I've made do in this little spot, and it hasn't been all that bad. But, I ran out of food bars two days ago and I'm now weaker. J.R. leaves for a while each day—most likely to pick at the remains of a wolf kill, or some other piece of carrion—but he comes back every afternoon. I've thought a lot about the rugby team that crashed in the Andes and resorted to cannibalism. But so far, I haven't seriously considered cutting a steak off the body lying next to the plane. Last night's wind blew the snow blanket from him. He again stares at nothing. The snow is too deep for me to get to the Yukon in my condition. I tried again this morning, but that only stole what little strength I have left. I'm lying back in the snow; maybe I'll take a little nap. As I lay here, I'm looking at a photo of Jet from my wallet. I have dedicated too much time to the job and not enough to the woman I love. If I ever get out of here, no—when I get out of here—I'm going to ask her if she will honor me by marrying me. It's little things like this adventure that helps a guy get his priorities in order.

Wait! I think I again hear a snowmachine. Yes, and I think it's coming closer. Maybe today I will be rescued.

"Kren, kren, kren, jaayy!" J.R. curses like I've never heard him before. It's like he is trying to warn me. He doesn't know that the snowmachine means rescue. Frantically, he flies from the branch, winging up into the low ceiling. The gray bird merges with the gray skies, then metamorphoses into a much larger bird. I must be hallucinating. No, wait, the bird is really a blue airplane. I can see the badges. It's a Super Cub on wheel-skis.

The black snowmachine stops its whining, halting just out of the brush line, fifty feet away. I struggle to my feet. "Hello friend, am I glad to see you," finding my voice, and with my body rejuvenated, I limp towards the snowmachine. But the rider isn't returning my greeting. Maybe he speaks only Yupik. No wait, he is a white man. What's he doing? What is he grabbing? Hang on, it's a rifle, what? Where's my pistol?

Crack! Flop! Jesus! I've been shot! My right shoulder. The pain—it feels I've been kicked by a moose. The breath has been knocked out of me. And now it burns like a hot probe being stuck into an open wound. Now blood—I feel warm blood running down my chest and down my back.

Why? What's going on? My right hand tries to move for my pistol, but my arm won't help it. I'm sitting up now.

The man is walking toward me. That looks like a .22 in his hand.

He's a white male, about thirty-five, brown hair, brown eyes, maybe six foot three, with a skimpy mustache and a scar on his right cheek.

I'll get what I can from him on the tape. I hope somebody finds it. I love you, Jet. He says "it's over."

"Okay, I know it's over, but before you kill me, just tell me why. And, who you are. Why are you after me?"

"It doesn't matter who I am. F-Rod gave you every chance to die a hero, but you somehow beat the odds. He's grown tired of this match. Game over."

POP.

Light is breaking through the clouds. Something is coming through the overcast now.

It's so quiet.

CHAPTER 42

Are you sure it's this way? Trooper Jack Blake found himself in a familiar position—flying a single engine plane in the Alaska Bush in lousy weather. Asking his non-pilot front seat passenger for directions was just plain reckless. Should have never let it happen, but things like this go with the job.

Over the years with the state troopers, Blake often found himself pushed into situations that no reasonable man would intentionally pursue. His meticulous nature as a pilot and flight instructor was in direct opposition to the emergency operations he often had to deal with in his job. Operating like this, without a plan, was crazy.

Jack Blake had planned to stay in Fairbanks until he retired. He and Jet dreamed of buying a roadhouse and air service in Talkeetna, and living out their lives together in that little town between Anchorage and Fairbanks.

Jack's dream of being an Alaska State Trooper included goals of high adventure, flying airplanes, and equal justice for all.

High expectations. But, except for the last goal, his career so far had pretty much worked out that way. He loved being a trooper, but couldn't believe the way the justice system had so far often failed.

A combination of liberal legislators and judges made for weak laws and inept courts. Throw in overcrowded jails, understaffed posts, too few prosecuting attorneys, and Alaska was in the same situation as most of the Lower 48 states. All the rights seem to be on the side of the guilty, not the victims of crimes.

Jack had transferred to the mostly Eskimo town of Bethel just two days ago. His first impression was when flying over the river on approach to the Bethel airport. Trash, wrecked vehicles—and whatever else someone wanted to get rid of and were too lazy to haul to the city dump—had been tossed on the beach, for who knows how many years, right in front of town. The town itself wasn't much prettier than the beach.

Jack was used to the pristine Brooks Range and the wild rivers of the Talkeetna Mountains, and he wasn't especially looking forward to being assigned in the vast, treeless, and sometimes hostile Kuskokwin Delta. But, he was determined to make the best of the situation, as he always did.

He was lucky to find a cramped, dark, one-bedroom modular house to rent for the bargain price of eighteen hundred dollars per month, plus utilities. Blake had spent the last two days unpacking, repairing broken windows, and trying to settle in. He hadn't even looked at the airplane he would be assigned, much less reviewed the flying charts. He felt fortunate to have his two scheduled days off, plus an extra leave day to adjust to his new environment. One more day and he would be on duty in his new post.

Oh, I'm sorry. I should have introduced myself earlier. I'm Dave Daniels. I'm an investigator with the Alaska State Troopers. Major Rich Emery told me to compile this report. Jack Blake was a good friend. The kind of friend anyone would want. Jack was also a great trooper. Dedicated to the job more than anyone I knew, Jack had some unique skills. He could shoot the proboscis off a mosquito at fifty yards. He could take a Cub off in a hundred feet, then come back around and land in the same hundred feet. And, even though he would avoid a battle whenever possible, he never came out of a fight a loser. But, more than that, he enforced the law fairly to all and truly believed in justice. And most importantly, he was a fine human being.

I found a pile of tapes and a box of notebooks in Jack's house. He kept very detailed records of each day on the job, as well as much of his personal life, making my job of continuing his story easy. Also, Jack's friends and co-workers gave me plenty of input. I will do the best I can to honor my friend with this biography.

CHAPTER 43

Jack worked all night building shelves to house his collection of books. He carefully placed "Wager with the Wind," the story of Don Sheldon, on the top shelf. Jack's head hit the pillow at 2 a.m. and he quickly fell asleep.

The waters transitioned from cobalt to powder blue to turquoise as the Widgeon skimmed the surface. Coming in from a day of island hopping along the Napali Coast of Kauai, Jack was having his favorite dream. A smiling bikini-clad blond named Jet was the co-pilot. Soon they would pull the flying boat onto the golden beach, settling in for the night under a coconut tree. Even during the day, Jack dreamed about someday owning a Grumman Widgeon. The twin-engine amphibian was used as a patrol and anti-submarine craft in World War II, but Jack thought it as the perfect airplane for exploring the world in his retirement days.

What's that racket? The stall warning horn? Jack pushed the controls forward to regain flying speed and tried to identify the loud, annoying ringing. Awake now, he realized it was just his telephone.

"Jack, this is Brock Sheets."

"*Who?*" Blake demanded to know who was ruining his dream.

"Sorry to wake you Jack, this is Sheets, Investigator Sheets. I need you for a flight." Blake squinted at the clock radio: 5:17 a.m. It seemed like he'd just fallen asleep.

Trying to make sense of where he was and why he was being rousted, Jack sat on the side of the bed.

It was late in the Alaskan summer and daylight was just beginning to filter through the torn orange drapes of his bedroom. Oh yeah, Bethel, a.k.a. "the Banana Belt of Alaska," Jack must have thought, as his mind began working again.

Brock Sheets, in his early thirties, looked like he stepped out of a feature article in *GQ* magazine on physically-fit professionals. The frames on his low correction glasses matched his meticulously-kept dark hair, complementing his olive complexion and toothpaste-ad quality teeth. Sheets was promoted to sergeant just four years out of the academy. Jack had met him during a field training officer class in Anchorage last year. He remembered that Sheets dressed very stylishly for a trooper, and that he volunteered more answers than anyone else in the course. During the class breaks, Sheets made it a point to introduce himself to all of the guys—sort of like he was running for political office—Jack noted at the time.

Sheets became an excellent training officer and, with his outgoing personality and attention to detail, he caught the eye of the bosses. When his lieutenant suggested he do his time in the Bush to increase his chances of getting a promotion, Sheets eagerly agreed to transfer into the Bethel investigator slot. Jack was glad others wanted the sergeant jobs. He had avoided promotions throughout his career. He knew being a trooper was where the action was—not sitting behind a desk.

"Oh yeah, Brock Sheets. Brock, I haven't even checked in at the office yet. Haven't checked out the bird here yet. Don't know the country and haven't looked at the charts. I'm not trying to get out of the mission, but what about Oscar? Wouldn't he be the safest bet?"

Oscar Samuels was the only fixed-wing civilian Bush pilot the troopers had on the payroll. An Eskimo, born and reared in Bethel, Oscar knew the country like no other pilot. His territorial knowledge, excellent pilot skills, and ability to speak Yupik, the language of the local Eskimo, earned him the job.

Jack had hoped to pick Oscar's brain before taking on any flying assignments in this treeless post, which rarely featured decent flying weather.

"Oscar's at his fish camp and won't be back for weeks. You're *it*, Jack. Don't worry, I know the way, and the weather is *good* for a change. You just have to fly. Billy Coffee shot his brother and is running around Kalskag with the rifle. We've got to run up there, do the scene, snatch the body, and arrest Billy. The village public safety officer supervisor says Billy is in the house, probably passed out, but you never know. He could go on a spree and shoot up the rest of the village. Shouldn't take more than a couple of hours. Got to go *now*. I'll pick you up in ten minutes, bring your shotgun."

This couldn't be happening. Jack preferred a more orderly way of flying. Planning, checking weather, filing a flight plan with trooper dispatch, plotting the route, and learning about the airstrip where he would be landing.

He fell out of bed, found the bathroom, then the closet. Pulling on his uniform and flight suit, Jack realized something was missing. His bullet-resistant vest, enclosed in what was supposed to look like an ordinary down-type hiking vest, but containing layers of Kevlar, pockets for survival gear and a miniature tape recorder, wasn't with his uniform. He slid hangars across the one-rod closet that smelled of mothballs and dampness, but the vest wasn't there. Still trying to shake the sleep from his head, Jack found the box marked "uniform stuff" on the closet shelf. Grabbing the knife from the sheath of his duty belt, he sliced open the box. The vest was on top. Jack pulled the vest over his head, closed the Velcro sides, and snapped on his gun belt.

Shotgun, where's my shotgun? Jack thought to himself, just as the horn honked in front of his house. That's right, he no longer had a shotgun. He was required to turn his in to the Fairbanks post when he transferred and had not yet been issued a replacement. His Smith and Wesson 40-06 pistol would have to do.

A gust of wind hit Jack's face as he slammed the door of his shanty. He looked up at the sky and quickly estimated the ceiling at a thousand feet, with visibility at three-to-five miles. Not too bad. A little windy perhaps, but not too bad.

He pulled the door open to Sheet's white four-wheel drive Chevy Blazer, marked with state trooper badges on both doors. "Morning, Jack, jump in, we're outta here. Wife made us some muffins and coffee. Where's your shotgun?"

"Had to leave it in Fairbanks."

"I've got an extra assault rifle in the back, you still qualified? Oh *damn*, I don't care if you're qualified. You won't have to use it anyway, but we'll take it just in case. I know you can handle one."

Jack must have wondered, "What the hell is this kid getting me into?" He knew that everyone in the department was well aware that he could handle a rifle. Young bucks, like Brock Sheets, were given a discourse on the famous "McCarthy Murders," as well as some of Jack's other cases, during their academy training. He grabbed the AR-15 semi-automatic rifle and checked that the magazine was full of ammo and that the chamber was empty.

Handling the rifle caused the Manley incident to pop into his brain. He didn't want to think about it anymore. He just recently stopped having the bad dreams, and just wanted to forget the whole thing. It was a senseless waste of a good trooper's life and a botched mission by an over–zealous administrator who shouldn't have been in the helicopter.

At the annual department awards banquet, hero awards were presented to the captain and the helicopter pilot for the Manley screw up. No posthumous award was given in the honor of Trooper Toby Clay—despite the request of Jack and twenty-four other troopers who submitted a signed petition. To Jack, it made the awards that he had received during his career seem meaningless.

Jack's *award* for his part in the Manley incident came when he was called into the captain's office in Fairbanks and given his transfer orders to Bethel. Yeah, maybe the department needed his talents out in that God-forsaken place, but his seniority and years of dedication should have allowed him his choice of posts.

"Hi, Jill, understand you have a vacation package for me." The attractive and always witty clerk had a smile for Jack.

"I'm sorry Jack. It isn't fair. You're a good trooper and this shouldn't be happening to you. And Bethel! Why couldn't he have just put you in front of a *firing squad?*"

Jill was doing her usual routine of mixing a little humor with always being supportive.

"Maybe this will cheer you up a little. We made the news in Bethel today. Looks like the natives are restless."

Jill handed Jack a paper from her printer. It was from the Community Information Office of the troopers in Anchorage and had not made the newspapers yet.

"Thanks, Jill, see you later," Jack said as he saw the captain watching them from his office.

Still dazed from the order that was turning his life upside down, Jack walked to the squad room and read the news article. "Bethel State Troopers responded today to the village of Quinhagak and clashed with armed villagers. The suspects allegedly took a state trooper hostage at gunpoint last night when he attempted to arrest a local suspect in a case involving the sexual abuse of a six-year-old girl. First Sergeant Gene Lutz of the Bethel post gave this statement: 'This was apparently an attempt by the villagers to assert sovereignty rights and not follow white man's law. We will continue our work with Native leaders to resolve this difficult issue.' One trooper received minor injuries and four villagers were arrested. The investigation continues."

"Oh great, now we're getting touchy-feelie with armed suspects who threaten our guys at gunpoint," Jack mumbled to himself. He was being thrown into a real hotbed. Not only was it one the most desolate places in Alaska, but lately hostility had been brewing in some of villages. The Yupik Eskimo, by nature friendly and quiet, were undergoing a political change. Outside influences, including Indian activists from the Lower 48 had incited some Alaskan Natives to take on a cause that didn't really apply to their situation.

"You got a lot of hours in a 206?" Sheets asked Jack like he was hoping the answer would be in the thousands.

"A *206?* I thought the post had a *207.*" Jack replied. The 206 was a real workhorse in the North Country. It seated six people and had a generous cabin. Jack had plenty of time in the bigger Cessna 207, but had never flown a 206.

"Nope, but it *looks* a lot like the 207."

"Guess we are a little short on time to stop at the Flight Service office and check weather?" Jack asked, but knew the answer.

"Trooper pilots and Oscar have a saying here Jack—'why check the weather, you're going *anyway.*'" Brock chuckled.

That was a down to basics way of saying what all trooper pilots, all troopers, for that matter knew: you often have to risk your life if you hope to save another. Not smart flying, not the kind of flying that anyone *should* do, but sometimes that was just the way it was. Normal patrol flights gave trooper pilots the luxury of exercising normal safe piloting procedures. Responses to save a life were like going to war. Civilians had come up to Jack at airports and chided him about having such a great job—just flying around in a pretty airplane for pay. If they only knew the *rest* of the story.

"We've got to hurry, don't want anyone else to get shot," Sheets said as Jack was doing a quick pre-flight. The unmarked plane was white with blue trim and brown highlights. Not paint highlights, but mud from the runways of the Kuskokwim Delta.

"Okay get in," Jack said, after completing the brief safety check. Jack climbed in through the pilot's door and was adjusting the seat when a confused–looking Sheets tapped on his window.

"Jack, you've got to let me in first, there is no front passenger door on the 206." He glanced at the passenger side, then at Sheets. Somewhat embarrassed and feeling even more unqualified to be on this mission, he opened the door, got out, and let Sheets in. It was an effort for Sheets to curve and strain his muscled, two hundred thirty pound frame into the cockpit and across the pilot seat.

"Don't worry about driving this thing Jack, there's a manual in the glove box. You can read it on the way."

Jack grabbed the checklist and started the engine. This wasn't the way Jack liked to get to know an airplane. Studying the airplane manual and getting a checkout by another flight instructor is the proper way. But in his job, strange situations sometimes required unorthodox responses. Jack knew the numbers on the 206 were close enough to the 207 that they would be safe enough.

The Continental engine responded with a reassuring hum when Jack ran the power up for a systems check as they taxied toward Bethel's main runway.

"Which way do we go after takeoff?" Jack asked Sheets.

"Use that big runway over there and take a left turn and head up the river. It's about an eighty mile run upriver to Kals-kag."

During the taxiing, Jack did his best to become familiar with the 206. No big deal, it feels a lot like the 207. Referring again to the airplane checklist, Jack did the published pre-takeoff check and lined the plane on the runway. Pushing the throttle to full power goosed the three hundred horses to life.

They quickly became airborne in the thirty-knot headwind. The sun was just beginning to rise above the horizon, brightening the gray sky. Jack had seen the Kuskokwim River when flying in as a passenger on the Alaska Airlines jet two days ago. He banked the airplane to follow it.

After ten minutes, the ceiling began to lower. Shoving the nose of the Cessna down to get under the seven hundred-foot layer of clouds, Jack squinted to see up the river.

"Don't worry Jack, the river is plenty wide and easy to follow. The highest river banks are about a hundred feet, so we can get down low if we need to."

"Want some java?" Sheets said, as he was pouring coffee into the thermos cup.

"Yeah I'll have a cup, thanks. I'd just as soon be awake when we land." Jack replied with a half-hearted chuckle.

"Here you are Jack. Hope you like Vanilla Kona Blend." Jack took a sip, thinking about the absurdness of flying in the Alaska Bush while drinking a cup of gourmet coffee. But he needed the caffeine.

The weather deteriorated. Clouds now hung at four hundred feet. The visibility was down to three miles with fog patches and a light mist. Jack lowered the Cessna to two hundred feet. The treeless tundra was now giving way to spruce and cottonwoods.

Jack had done a lot of "scud running" in his years of flying, but if he didn't know the terrain he usually at least had charts for reference. None were handy in the plane.

"Oscar knows every bush and swamp in the Kuskokwim, so I guess he doesn't use charts much," Sheets offered.

The river braided, branching off in several directions. Visibility deteriorated more and the clouds forced them to just fifty feet above the river. Heavy fog draped over the riverbanks like muslin drapes on a window.

"Which way, which channel do we follow?" Jack asked Sheets, who was staring wide-eyed at the river.

"Right. Take a right turn, follow the narrow part of the river." Jack banked to the right, slowing to eighty knots and adding a notch of flaps. He was now ready for serious low-level maneuvering. He found the GPS navigation system and tuned "KSG" for the village of Kalskag.

"Jack, *Jack*, look *out!*" Sheets screamed.

The rock cliff filled the Cessna's windshield.

Quickly throwing the plane into a steep right turn, Jack began to follow what now had become a trickle of a stream instead of the wide Kuskokwim River. His coffee spilled on the floor.

Barely clearing the ridge, the plane was now being swallowed by low fog rising from the ground—all the way to the cloud layer. They were now in the thick soup. Was there another cliff in the fog? Jack didn't have time to consider that any further.

"Hang on, were climbing through it." Jack yelled.

Prop in, full power. The Cessna was abruptly pulled into a steep climb. Quickly finding the panel and focusing on the primary instruments, Jack took a deep breath as the plane banged through the turbulence. Every nerve in his body must have vibrated.

Seventy knots, hold seventy, center the ball. The basic instrument training from his uncle, stuck way back in Jack's mind, was paying off. Moments of silence seemed much longer as the plane ascended through the dense, gray moisture. The engine and wind sounded different than in cruise flight and Jack quickly considered whether he'd made the right decision—would they hit a mountain, another plane, or would the wings be encased in ice, causing them to fall out of the sky?

It was at times like this that Jack imagined his uncle next to him. Instead of a frightened passenger's frets, there were J.D.'s encouraging words: "This is nothing Jack, you have plenty of air beneath you. The plane is doing its part. You just have to fly. Inhale a breath of good air, now exhale the bad. Keep *calm*."

Light! Where's the light coming from in these clouds? Jack tensed his grip on the control wheel. The light became brighter. Then it happened—the Cessna popped through the fog layer. The bright morning sun filled the cockpit through the back window.

Jack and Brock glanced and exchanged half-smiles, simultaneously exhaling. Leveling out at two thousand feet, Jack checked the GPS. Kalskag was twenty degrees to the left of the nose and eighteen miles away. The edge of the fog revealed a hill in the distance.

"Kalskag is at the bottom of that hill, the river runs to the right of the airstrip," Brock sighed with relief.

"I'll trust you on that one," Jack said as he checked the GPS reading. He sized up the strip as he flew over the village. Good gravel and plenty long enough. He'd heard a lot about the muddy, short, narrow, and crosswind-plagued airstrips in the Kuskokwim Delta. He was glad this wasn't one of them.

Ramshackle cabins, empty blue fifty-five gallon fuel drums, broken boats lying on their sides in the dirt, trash, trash, and more trash, guided the plane on final to the airstrip.

Pulling the control wheel until the stall warning horn buzzed, Jack flared for landing. Gravel bouncing off the belly of the Cessna never sounded so good. It was wonderful to be back on the ground.

CHAPTER 44

"**N**ice landing. Pull over to that little building, Jack," directed Sheets. Next to the twelve by twelve unpainted frame building that served as the airport terminal, freight warehouse, and sometimes party house for the village teenagers, stood an unshaven, robust Native man. At his side was a faded red three-wheeled all terrain vehicle. His stocky build, big brown eyes, wide grin, and tan jacket gave him the appearance of a giant teddy bear.

Is that our man?" Jack asked.

Laughing, Brock replied, "That's the village public safety officer. He's on our side."

Jack climbed out of the Cessna then held the door for Sheets. He pulled the rifle from behind the pilot seat, slinging it over his shoulder.

"How's it going, Josh?" Sheets said as he vigorously shook the officer's hand.

"Not so good. I had Billy for a while, but he decided to leave. He ran off in the woods with his rifle," a sad-looking Josh answered.

"Guess it would be a little easier if they would give you a gun, huh, Josh?" Sheets spoke with sympathy.

Village Public Safety Officers, or VPSOs, were trained to be first responders in emergency situations, but most weren't commissioned to carry weapons. That made their job especially hazardous when booze or drugs were mixed with guns in the villages.

"Let's see the scene, Josh. By the way, this is the new guy, Jack Blake. Jack, meet Josh Luko."

Josh and Jack exchanged greetings as the three began walking into the village. Jack kept the AR-15 rifle at his side, while scanning each building lining the dusty path. Josh, an Eskimo, lived in the downriver village of Kwethluk. He spoke fluent Yupik, the most common language of the Kuskokwim Delta. Inland villages from Kalskag and north were mostly Indian, speaking the Athabaskan language.

Josh seemed to like everyone. He didn't care about the pedigree of those he served or arrested but he was not always treated kindly when working upriver. However, since he was the supervisor of the VPSOs in the region, he had to go where the work took him.

This was a critical weekend, as the "government checks" had arrived. They included funds for aid to dependent children, unemployment compensation, and a variety of other monies funneled to the villagers. That meant lots of cash for the bootleggers who smuggled cheap booze into the villages and sold it for fifty dollars a bottle. Josh calculated that with all the government freebies, free housing, and medical care, that the average Native family of five could make about forty-thousand dollars a year without working.

Josh looked at these handouts as a disgrace to his people. The son of the first Eskimo chief of police in Bethel, he was a dedicated lawman. His father had been killed by a drunk in Bethel twenty years ago and Josh did all he could to honor his memory.

"Jack, you and I do a TV approach on the cabin. Josh you wait in the back, behind that wrecked pickup truck and let us know if you see anything," Sheets instructed.

"Before we go in, could you tell me what a TV approach is?" Jack had to ask Sheets.

"Most cops get their real training from television shows, not the academy. "Let's cover it like on a cop show. I'll go in the front, you cover me—guns drawn—the TV approach," Sheets replied.

Jack hoped that didn't mean that Sheets would be waving his gun straight out in front of him like a fire torch—finger on the trigger—in the fashion of Hollywood cops.

Too much chance of shooting your partner.

Jack relied on his SERT training and in the tight quarters, he shouldered his rifle, holding his duty pistol in his right hand.

"*Billy*. You in there, Billy?" There was no answer. The dimly lit cabin had few windows. It smelled of wood smoke, whiskey, sewage, and vomit. The blaring television showed only static.

"Jack, I'll check the bedroom, you check the kitchen to the right. Be careful," Sheets directed.

Jack approached the kitchen cautiously. Unable to find the light switch, he was trying to identify anything in the dim and gloomy space. His right boot smashed into something mushy on the kitchen floor, knocking him off balance. Jack stuck his non-gun hand out to brace his fall. Slipping to the floor, his hand slid along the wet, slick, vinyl. He came to rest on his elbow, stopping abruptly on the dirty floor. The liquid was warm and sticky.

Rising to his right knee, Jack pulled the miniature flashlight from his gun belt. Next to him, in a pool of blood, lay the body of Ned Coffee. The victim was wearing an old t–shirt, soggy with deep red blood leaking from a small hole. He rolled the body over to check for life signs and saw the large exit hole in the front of Coffee's shirt.

The high–powered rifle had blown Coffee's heart apart.

"Jack, you okay?" Brock Sheets had heard Jack's fall. He pulled the kitchen light cord and took in the scene.

"Good, you found Ned. Billy split. Jack, why don't you and Josh go find Billy, I'll do the scene. I need all the experience I can get on homicides. You want some breakfast first?" Sheets nodded toward the cold moose stew that had been left on the greasy stove.

Jack wasn't sure if Sheets was trying to be funny, or actually was planning on preparing breakfast in the stinky, gore–covered kitchen. "No thanks, I'd better get going," Jack said as he reached for the kitchen faucet to wash blood from his hands.

"Trooper Blake, over here. See the tracks? Billy went this way, into the woods," Josh motioned. "This trail heads to the river bank, where the boats are beached."

After a fierce battle with mosquitoes and the tangled willow bushes, the men broke out at the riverbank.

Six flat–bottom riverboats were tied to pieces of driftwood. Josh checked each boat then stopped just past a yellow skiff. "Stole a boat," he declared.

"How do you know that?" Jack asked.

"Those are Billy's boot tracks and those lines are from the skegs on the bottom of a boat that was pushed into the river. My guess is Billy boated upriver to the first fish camp. It's about a mile. If we go by boat, he will hear us. Then he will either keep running or start shooting again. We better sneak in by foot, Trooper Blake."

"Whatever you say Josh. You know the country and the people. I'm the greenhorn here."

Jack had missed his morning workout and the thought of a little hike didn't sound so bad.

"Josh, how 'bout you call me Jack?"

"Good for me," Josh responded. The two men spent the next hour sloshing along the banks of the Kuskokwim River and thrashing through heavy underbrush.

Soon they were covered with mud. Swarms of mosquitoes hovered around their heads, occasionally being inhaled into their mouths and nostrils. The metal skiff with a white outboard motor had skidded onto the gravel riverbank. An empty bottle of Gold Leaf Extra 18 Year Old sat upright on a seat in the boat. Tracks led from the boat along the wide bank to another skiff.

"That's Otis' boat. He's the postmaster, his camp is just up there," Josh said. A cloud of blue haze, scented with smoked salmon, hung over the tall spruce trees.

"How many people in Otis' family and what do they look like?" Jack wanted to know who the good guys were.

"It won't be hard to pick out Otis. He's big—about six four, and he's the only black man upriver from Bethel. His wife is Indian and they have two little daughters. Billy doesn't look like any of them."

Jack laughed to himself and appreciated Josh's gentle humor in a tense situation. "Okay Josh, how about if you take cover behind the trees. I'll see who's home."

The layout was simple: a smokehouse near the steep riverbank, an outhouse in the woods, two large, green military-style tents in the middle of the clearing, a piece of clear plastic tied between two log poles protecting camp gear from the elements. Jack listened for sounds of people and heard nothing. He considered the worst and hoped for the best.

Jack's rifle was pointed in front of him. Both tents had the window and door flaps open, so peeking in would be easy. Reaching the tent wall, he waited for the pounding of his heart to subside. He flashed back to the bullet wound in Ned Coffee. Brother Billy's rifle could be sighted in on me right now, Jack must have thought. He listened for sounds of life. Light breathing. Not the breathing of an adult man and his wife, but of children.

Two little girls were peacefully sleeping in the tent. Relieved that at least the children were safe, Jack crawled to the other tent. Not like the city, Jack thought. In the city, backup was not far away. And, unlike Josh, backup carried guns.

Jack studied the tent while crawling on the tundra. The tent door was unzipped at the bottom. His best chance would be to make a quick entry through the door. But how quick is "quick" when you're unzipping a tent door? The zipper could, as tent zippers usually do, hang up. Then what? Jack imagined himself yanking on the zipper while the drunken murderer inside blasted away with his rifle.

No, the better way would be to slowly unzip the door, making as little noise as possible. With the constant swarming of mosquitoes, maybe the sound of the zipper will blend in. Jack kept his crawl—left knee, right elbow, right knee, left elbow, until he was within an arm's length of the door. Snoring rumbled from the canvass. Maybe the shooter, maybe the postmaster. No, Jack reasoned, neither scenario was likely.

If Billy Coffee was awake and holding the couple hostage, the postmaster and his wife wouldn't be sleeping. If the postmaster was awake, then certainly the drunk and armed Billy Coffee would not be invited to sleep in his tent. A third possibility occurred to Jack—what if Billy Coffee had surprised the couple, shot both of them, then passed out? Jack reached for the zipper pull with his left hand, with his right hand on the trigger of his pistol. He pushed the flap into the tent. Although a little darker than the outside, Jack could see well enough to make out two sleeping bags with bodies inside. No movement from either bag, just snoring.

Clothes, a couple of boxes, a lantern—the usual camping gear. There was no one else but the two people in the sleeping bags.

"State Troopers!"

The snoring stopped.

"What the hell? What's going on?"

"*State Troopers*, are you the postmaster?"

"Yeah, yeah, that's me, what time is it?" The groggy, puzzled postmaster identified himself.

"About 7 a.m. have you seen Billy Coffee?"

Kitty Jenkins was awake now.

"What's going on Otis, is Billy back?" she asked.

"I'm sorry to barge in on you folks. I was concerned that Mr. Coffee might be in here and that you were in danger."

"That's okay, Trooper, we're just glad it's not Billy again. He's all drunked up and acting crazy," Otis Jenkins spoke while pulling a sweatshirt over his head.

"What time did he leave?" Jack asked.

Otis focused on the Big Ben alarm clock on the tent floor and did some quick math. "Been about an hour. Billy came in here waving his rifle around and cussing. Said something about his boat running out of gas and he was going to take ours."

"What did you do?" Jack asked.

"Well, after I slugged him in the mouth, I unloaded his rifle and threw it out of the tent. I told Billy to get his drunk ass out of my fishcamp before I beat the crap out of him."

Jack guessed that by Otis' linebacker type-build and his facial expression that he had the desired impact of deterring Billy Coffee from taking his boat and further threatening his family.

"I suppose Billy left after that, but can you tell me anymore, did he say anything else?"

"Yeah, he started crying, mumbled something about hurting his brother, said he was sorry to bother us, then left."

"Did you see which way he went?"

"He stumbled off on the trail, down river toward Kalskag."

While Otis spoke, Jack picked up three 30:30 rifle cartridges from the tent floor. He thanked the Jenkins and apologized for waking them.

"Always glad to help the law, Trooper, what did Billy do this time?"

Standing outside now, Jack held the tent door open again. "Billy's brother was shot last night, Billy is a suspect."

"Well, I guess we're up for the day, sorry to hear about Ned, both of the Coffee boys were Kitty's students."

The muffled cries of Kitty filtered through the canvas tent as Jack turned away.

Jack froze in his tracks when he saw movement from behind the trees. He quickly brought his rifle up and pointed in that direction. A figure moved from behind the tree and into the clearing. Something was in his arms. Jack's finger moved to the trigger of his rifle. Then the figure calmly spoke.

"The rifle is gone, Jack."

"Josh, you surprised me. What do you have there?"

"Sorry, Jack. I grabbed this club fishermen use for knocking salmon over the head, in case Billy tried to come back and sneak up on you in the tent."

Pretty good backup, Jack thought, but these are not details to share with the bosses. Both he and Josh could get in trouble for bending the rules against armed village police officers, even if the weapon was only a stick. "Thanks, Josh, now let's get back to the village."

The trail back was mostly downgrade and unlike the river trail, didn't meander along the water's edge, allowing for faster travel. About 7:30 a.m., the men arrived at Coffee's cabin, where Brock Sheets was sitting on the steps, writing in his trooper notebook. "You guys been on an expedition or what?" Sheets asked, as he looked the two men up and down. Both were spotted with mud and welts from mosquito bites.

"Billy is probably somewhere in the village," Josh quickly offered.

"I'll grab a couple more photos and finish these notes. Then we'll go find him. Jack would you grab the other end of this tape so I can get some measurements?"

Jack was a little confused over Sheet's sense of priority. After all, there was an armed murderer somewhere in the village. Jack realized he knew nothing yet about law enforcement in this part of Alaska, but his face must have relayed his concern as he took the metal tape measure.

"Trust me Jack, by now he's either shot himself or he's passed out somewhere. This will only take a few minutes."

Jack and Sheets took measurements from the body to a shell casing in the living room. Then they measured from the first blood spatter to the body. They bagged evidence, including a box of Gold Leaf Extra 18 Year Old Scotch. They put Ned Coffee's bloody body in a bright yellow body bag and carried it to the front porch. Sheets took several photos of the cabin, then stored his investigative tools in his red knapsack.

"Let's go hunt for Billy. Ned will be fine here. The village won't be up for another couple of hours." Sheets said.

"Which way?" Jack asked.

Before Sheets could answer, Josh appeared.

"I found Billy over in the meat house, he's passed out. Here's his rifle. We should go now."

Josh carried the rifle by the leather sling, being careful not to ruin any fingerprints. The two troopers followed Josh to the meat shed.

When they were within several feet, Josh yelled, "Billy, let's go. Get up now, the Troopers are here."

Both troopers had their rifles pointed at the shed when Billy came staggering out.

"I'm sorry, I'm *so* sorry, I didn't mean to shoot him. We got into a fight over which movie to watch. I loved my brother.

I'm sorry, *so* sorry." Billy's voice trailed off in tears as he slowly sat down, with his back against the front of the meat shed.

Jack's tape recorder was in the front pocket of his shirt and had been activated when they began approaching the shed. He reached for his handcuffs but Sheets shook his head.

"We won't need those, he'll go with us. Josh, you take Billy to the plane and we'll meet you there," Sheets ordered.

Josh touched Billy Coffee on the shoulder and asked him to get up. Coffee struggled to his feet and Josh helped him down the trail toward the airport. Jack and Brock returned to the cabin, loaded the body in the trailer that was attached to the ATV and returned to the airplane.

Billy turned his stare to the ground when he saw the yellow body bag in the trailer. Jack opened the large cargo door of the Cessna. The second row of seats was removed from its tracks and stacked in the back of the plane. The two troopers lifted the body into the plane and wedged it next to the remaining rear passenger seat, lengthwise in the generous cabin.

"Okay, Billy, get in the back," Sheets ordered. Billy obeyed and sat in the rear seat. He slowly turned his head and looked at the bloody body bag. He let out a deep sigh, then looked at the floor. Sheets crawled into his seat.

Jack began closing the cargo door when he noticed that Billy was still not handcuffed. Here was the murderer, with the victim laying next to him, soon to be flying in a small plane with plenty of time to think about what he had done. Jack has known prisoners to do crazy things, even without provocation. This guy had plenty of reason to get wild. Jack took his handcuffs out of the gun belt case and started to cuff Billy.

Brock Sheets turned to the distinctive ratcheting of handcuffs. "Whoa, Jack, what are you doing? We don't handcuff prisoners in the airplanes. It makes them even *more* scared of flying."

Jack was surprised. This *couldn't* be a policy. Anyway, it wouldn't be *his* policy, as long as he was the pilot in command.

"Sorry, Brock, but flying violent prisoners that are not handcuffed makes *me* scared of flying."

"Have it your way, Jack. Guess someday, when I'm a pilot, I can make in-flight policies. Right now, it's your call." Brock answered with a shake of his head.

Billy, still looking at the floor, held up his hands. Jack handcuffed him, latched his seat belt, then secured those handcuffs to a second pair that he attached to the bottom of the front passenger seat.

Jack thanked Josh and offered to buy him lunch the next time he came to the Bethel post. "Nice working with you, Jack. Welcome to Bethel," Josh said while shaking Jack's hand and grinning.

The fog had burned off and the clouds had lifted, allowing a direct course to Bethel. The starkness of the vast, brown tundra looked like another planet to Jack. No, not just stark, but plain ugly. It made him miss the mountains, trees, and clear streams of the Brooks Range.

"Trooper Aircraft November 39 Zulu, Bethel Radio." Jack answered the radio call from Bethel Flight Service.

"Three–nine Zulu, Bethel Troopers request you expedite to Bethel, you are needed for an emergency flight in the trooper floatplane."

"Roger." Jack answered, then turned to Sheets. "Brock, do we *have* a float plane in Bethel?" A floatplane was an unexpected bonus to Jack's otherwise depressing new post.

"Sure do, Jack, it's a real nice Cessna 185. It's kept out on Hangar Lake. You better pour on the coals. Sounds like something important." Jack increased the power and picked up speed. They were on the ground in Bethel in twenty-five minutes.

CHAPTER 45

Taxiing from the Bethel runway, Jack aimed for the dilapidated Quonset hangar and parked the Cessna next to a white Ford pickup with a stocky trooper standing next to it. The face, the build, and the sideburns were familiar.

"There's 'Crash and Burn,'" Sheets chuckled. "Sergeant Torgy is well-intentioned. He just breaks things. Squad cars, boats, and, oh yeah, his bones. Some of the VPSOs started calling him 'Ninja,' because every time one of them comes into the Bethel office, Ronnie sneaks up and puts some nasty headlock or big-time wrestler move on them."

Jack was glad to hear that Ronnie fit in so well at the Bethel post. Ronnie excitedly ran to the pilot's door just as it was being opened. The door banged into his head, knocking his Stetson onto the tarmac. Landing on its brim, the hat began rolling on its edge, like a Frisbee, blowing toward the hangar. It spun through the open hangar doors with Torgy in pursuit, his sideburns now in stark contrast to his balding head.

Sheets laughed out loud. Jack restrained himself—he would have felt bad if Torgy saw him laughing at this minor misfortune, remembering his own hat sailing out of control once or twice. It was a silly hat for Alaska, especially in wind or cold. Jack preferred the trooper cap, approved for pilots and much more practical.

After locking the parking brake, Jack got out of the plane and walked around the tail to open the cargo door. Billy Coffee was still studying the aircraft floor, as if intently reading a book.

Jack removed the bottom handcuffs from those attached to Billy's cuffs and helped him out of the plane.

Ronnie was back, his hat now in place. He spoke quickly and with a lot of animation, waving his hands constantly.

"Jack, it's great to see you. Welcome to the beautiful Kuskokwim Delta, you are now part of 'Delta Force.' We'll visit later and I'll show you around, but right now, we have a crisis in the village of Platinum.

"Here's the situation, gentlemen. The storeowner went berserk, shot two people. Now he has his wife and two kids as hostages. He has at least twelve guns in the store. We can't use the airstrip. That would give him a clear shot at the plane. We will have to use the floatplane and land in the bay. Gotta get there before he kills someone."

"Okay, Ronnie. How about if you guys help me get the body into the pickup and you can take the Blazer. Billy and I will put the plane away," Sheets directed.

The three troopers loaded the body into the truck. The murderer lowered the tailgate for them, then shuffled to the airplane, ready to help push it into the hangar.

Sheets handed Jack the assault rifle along with two extra loaded magazines. "Hope you don't need these. Good luck."

Torgy jammed the accelerator of the Blazer to the floor, racing onto Chief Eddie Hoffman Highway. Named for the former village leader, the asphalt road had long since succumbed to the tundra's permafrost, with frost heaves providing a roller coaster ride. When the Blazer re-connected with the ground after each short flight on the frost heave, Ronnie's hat would hit the ceiling, crushing it lower and lower on his head. Jack again contained his laughter, held on tightly, and tried to keep up with Ronnie's non-stop conversation.

"Like I said, he's got hostages. We gotta be very careful. There are windows on two sides of the store. It will be hard to get up on him without being seen. If we fly in low over the bay and keep it quiet, we can sneak in."

Before Jack could ask where Platinum was, Torgy slid the Blazer to the edge of Hangar Lake.

The lake didn't have a beach. Instead, a rickety pathway of waterlogged boards led through a swamp of floating muskeg to the plane. The lake's namesake, a World War II airplane hanger, was long gone. Fortunately, Jack had been able to interrupt Ronnie's monolog and divert him to stop by his shack to pick up a pair of hip boots. Torgy sloshed through in his black uniform boots, getting his gold and red striped blue trooper pants wet to the knees.

"When's the last time that this plane was flown?" Jack asked after sizing up the dust-covered 185.

"Probably a month or more," Ronnie answered.

After his second too quick pre-flight of the day and a cursory pumping of the floats, Jack loaded his rifle in the float-plane. Torgy was already buckled in and anxious to go, with water from his boots pooling on the floor in front of him.

Jack quickly went through the checklist and asked Ronnie which way he needed to take off for the flight to Platinum. "Hang a right over the river, follow along those hills to the east."

Jack turned the Cessna key. Nothing. Dead battery.

"I'll need your help, Ronnie We will have to hand prop this thing."

"What do you want me to do, Jack?"

"I'm going out on the float and pull the prop through, but first let me check you out on the procedure."

Guiding Ronnie's hand, Jack showed him how to pull the throttle knob back to reduce the engine to idle. He had Torgy repeat the procedure five times, each time repeating "pull back for off." Jack also showed Ronnie the red knob, emphasizing that if something went wrong, it could be yanked back to cut the fuel to the engine.

"No sweat. I got it, Jack." Ronnie confidently said.

After pulling the propeller through several cycles, Jack set the throttle to the start position, and switched the key on.

"Remember, *back* for off." Jack reminded Ronnie.

Standing on the float behind the prop, Jack pulled hard on the metal blade. Surprisingly, the engine came to life on the first pull and the plane inched forward in the water.

Suddenly, the engine roared. Jack was thrown back into the wing strut as the plane jumped into the plow position, like a speedboat starting a drag race. The wind from the prop wash blew the door closed. Fighting to keep from being thrown into the cold lake water, now spraying all over his flight suit, Jack swung under the strut.

Now on the step, the floatplane began a gradual left turn. The north bank of the small lake was coming up very quickly as Jack struggled to hold on against the wind force. The screaming from the three-bladed propeller and high performance engine was unnerving.

On his knees, hanging onto the strut with his left hand, Jack grabbed the door handle. Barely able to force the Cessna door open against the wind, he reached over Ronnie.

Finding the throttle pushed all the way in, Jack jerked it back. The engine dropped to idle and the plane fell off the step then bumped gently onto the lake bank. Jack, dripping from the lake water, looked at Torgy for an explanation, although he knew what had happened.

"Sorry Jack, I know you said to pull it *back* for off. But when it started, I grabbed it and my instincts told me to push it in. I don't know what happened. Man, I'm sorry. Are you *okay?*"

"I'm fine, Ronnie. Don't worry about it. These things happen sometimes when car drivers try to drive airplanes. No harm done. We'd better get going."

Jack got his bearings on the lake and set the GPS for Platinum. He didn't like what he heard of the non-stop radio traffic between the Bethel tower and the countless small planes either on the ground, or in the air, trying to access the local airspace. The ceiling was below weather minimums for a non-instrument flight and the tower was advising pilots that they would have at least a twenty-minute wait before entering the Bethel control area. Enough time had been wasted.

"Bethel tower, Trooper Cessna November 9252 November, special request," Jack broke in over the aircraft radio.

"Cessna November 9252 November," a somber voice replied to Jack's query.

"Tower, November 9252 November is responding to an emergency, and we are requesting you expedite our request for a special departure to the south."

"Five two November, cleared for an immediate departure to the south, stay below four hundred feet, report clear of the control zone to the south. Good luck."

After circling in the water for a quick run up to check the airplane's systems, Jack smoothly applied maximum takeoff power to the 185. At an indicated fifty-five knots, he rolled onto the right float and they were airborne.

Steady at three hundred feet, visibility was about three miles under the cloud layer, no challenge for this flight over mostly flat land. Ordinarily, Jack would ask a trooper passenger to take the controls and hold the flight steady. It was a simple task, once the aircraft was in trim, and it gave Jack time to catch up on his notebook entry or other paperwork. He would have liked to do that then, as he hadn't had a chance to make notes about his morning activities. He looked over at Ronnie, now yammering something about department politics. Jack decided not to push his luck. The Kilbuck Mountains became visible to the east as they passed the village of Eek. Ronnie offered, "Eek is a funny name for a town, but Yupik is a tough language to learn. Of course, many people say English is a tough language to learn, but I had no problem," Ronnie chuckled.

Jack tuned in Ronnie's conversation when he pointed at something out of the airplane. "Follow along those hills on the left and we'll come out at Goodnews Bay," Ronnie chattered. Jack confirmed the directions with the sectional chart and the GPS.

"Take a look at that Ronnie." Jack said as he dipped the right wing to see a grizzly sow and two cubs, half swimming and half wading, as they crossed the fast waters of the Kanetok River.

"Beautiful, but I'm glad I'm up here and not down there with them," Ronnie joked.

Fifteen minutes later, Goodnews Bay came into view.

"Is that Platinum over there?" Jack asked, pointing to the right of the windscreen.

"That's it all right. Just on the other side of the outlet of the bay there is an old boat. You can tie up next to it."

Goodnews Bay is in a large bowl, with hills on three sides. On the fourth side was a rock spit, which lay between the bay and the sea. The village of Platinum was on the spit, made up of just a row of multi-colored frame houses, an airstrip, and the store.

Jack pushed the plane into a gentle dive, picking up airspeed and losing altitude. At ten feet above the silver water of Goodnews Bay he reduced the power. He pulled it back to idle as they crossed the outlet, providing a silent approach and a gentle splash onto the calm water next to the shoreline. He kept the plane on the step until thirty feet from the bank, killed the engine, and quietly glided towards the rocky shore.

The plane nosed up to the bank next to an old herring gill net skiff. When the prop came to a full stop, Jack jumped onto the muddy bank with the bow cleat rope in hand, tying the float to an old, rusting Mercury outboard motor on the beach.

Splash!

"Darn!" Ronnie had dropped his trooper notebook while crawling out the passenger side of the floatplane. Bending over to find it in the milky waters, his sunglasses fell out of his vest pocket.

"Oh well, those glasses were scratched anyway, Torgy said, fishing his dripping notebook out of the water.

"That green building over there is the store. We better walk along the shore and use the boats for cover."

Grabbing his assault rifle and eyeing Ronnie hopefully, Jack said, "I'm ready when you are, Ronnie."

With Ronnie's boots squishing loudly, the troopers kept a low profile as they quickly walked along the shore toward the store. They took cover behind the "Melanie Mae," a beached wooden fishing boat. Across the street a hand painted sign proclaimed "Platinum Store."

Ronnie excitingly spoke while pointing at the store's door. "That's the main entrance. I'll go around to the airstrip side, where the owner's living quarters are. I'll pull a ninja-style sneak and see what I can see. I'll be on the radio, channel one."

Jack pulled his portable radio from his gun belt and confirmed the channel. "Be careful, Ronnie."

"Always." Ronnie nodded, then dropped his radio.

Scurrying behind the small houses, Ronnie ran past the store, disappearing on the other side of the one lane street. Jack quickly spun to a movement behind the boat, with his hand reaching for his sidearm. He relaxed when he saw the young Eskimo woman.

"Trooper, trooper, please don't shoot him. Levi Tungolook, he's my husband. We run the store. My kids are in there with him. He's pretty drunk. Got some booze from some bootlegger, then got drunk and got mad at everybody. It's my son's birthday. We were having a party. Please don't shoot him, he's a good man." A tearful Melanie Tungolook pleaded for her husband.

"We will do our best to see that no one else gets hurt, ma'am." Jack then questioned Melanie to find out as much as he could as fast as he could.

"How many people are in the store?"

"Three: my husband, and our two boys."

"How many people are hurt?"

"Stella Bitluck has a broken arm, I think. Levi smashed his rifle over it. Jimmy Alexie got shot in the leg. Simon Fisher is the worst, Levi shot him in the stomach. They are all at the health clinic."

"Is there any way that I can talk to your husband?"

"Yes, here, I've been talking to him on this." Melanie handed Jack the handset of her cordless phone. Jack couldn't believe his luck.

"Thank you, Mrs....." Jack didn't want to botch her name.

"You can call me Mel, Trooper. Just push the intercom button and it will buzz inside."

"Ronnie, are you on the radio?"

"Ten–four Jack, I'm on the roof of the storage shed next to the store, haven't been able to see much so far. I'm going to move onto the store roof."

Jack told Ronnie about the phone and asked him to stand by while he assessed the situation.

"Okay, Jack. I'll hang tight. Tell Mel 'hi.'"

Mel smiled at Ronnie's voice. "He's a funny guy. He comes in the store and buys candy bars whenever he's in town. He eats a couple of the bars himself and passes the rest to the little kids that follow him around the village."

Jack pushed the intercom button.

"*Mel!* What do you want now? Leave me the hell alone!" Screaming blasted over the phone.

"Levi, this is Jack Blake, I'm from the Alaska State Troopers. How are you doing in there?"

"Jack what? Jack who? Who the hell are *you*? I don't know no Trooper Jack." The voice still screamed.

"My name is Jack and I'm new in Bethel. I just transferred here from Fairbanks. Sorry to have to meet you like this, Levi. Can I come in and talk to you now?"

"Another dumb-ass cussack! All they send out here are dumb ass cussacks. Get the hell out of my village, Cussack. Or I'll start blasting." Jack knew what cussack meant. Eskimo slang for a white person—particularly, a dumb-ass white man.

"Okay, you can call me cussack, or how about 'Gus' for short. Mind if I call you Levi?" Jack was doing his best to calm the situation.

"Very funny, white man. What the hell do you want?" Levi wasn't screaming anymore.

"I just want to talk to you Levi. What happened here?"

"Some son of a bitch gave me booze and got me drunk. Everybody knows I can't drink. I go crazy when I do. I haven't been in trouble for six years, since the last time I drank. Somehow, this bastard knew that. He came here in his black airplane, wearing camo, and handed me two bottles of scotch. I've never had such fancy booze before. Each bottle was even in its own pretty little box, with a gold label. He flew in, says 'drink up,' then he left."

"Levi, are your sons okay?"

"Of course they are okay. I wouldn't let anything happen to my kids," Levi slurred.

"Okay, Levi, why don't you come outside now and let's meet in person and talk this over."

"No way in hell. I'm drunk, not *stupid*. Maybe I'll just blow your ass away." Levi was screaming again.

"Levi, I've had bad days too. But let's not let this go any further. Melanie is here talking with me and she tells me you're a good guy. I want to believe that, Levi."

"I just want to kick that bootlegger's ass, that's all," Levi began to cry into the phone.

"Levi, no one is seriously hurt. You're not in all that much trouble yet." Jack hoped the first part was true. With his experience in the justice system, he knew the second part was true.

"You lying cussack. Just trying to get me out so you can shoot me down like a dog."

Jack decided it was time for a new approach.

"No, Levi. I *hate* bootleggers too. I want you to come out so you and I can go and find this guy. Then both of us will kick his ass."

There was a long pause on Levi's end of the phone.

"*Really?* Would *you* help me kick his ass?"

"Let's do it!" Jack yelled into the phone.

"Okay, Gus. Which gun do you want me to bring? I have four pistols and a dozen rifles in here. Pistol or rifle?"

"No Levi. How about I hold him and you just use your hands? I bet you could do a good job kicking his ass without a weapon."

"Damn straight, Trooper. That *would* be better. I could mess him up real good." Levi sounded sleepy now. "You put your guns away and meet me in the middle of the road. I will come out without a gun. Then we'll go kick some bootlegger ass."

Jack called Torgy on the radio. "Ronnie, are you there?"

"Right here on the roof, Jack. What do you have?"

"Levi is going to meet me in the road. Can you stay there, cover me, and keep hidden?"

"Okay Jack, got you covered. Watch out now."

Jack took his 40-06 semi-automatic pistol out of the holster and put it in the right leg pocket of his flightsuit. He walked out from the cover of the boat with the assault rifle in his arms, then slowly put it on the deck of the Melanie Mae. Then he removed his gun belt, laying it next to the rifle. Both actions were done with extra animation as he knew Levi was watching from the store.

Unarmed, Levi came out of the store and the two men began walking toward each other in the gravel.

"Hey, Gus, are you ready to kick some..." Levi stopped and spun around to see the source of the disturbance behind him.

Now leaning over the peak, Ronnie had shifted to get a better view. Stumbling over the ridge, he caused the old metal roof to groan and squeak.

Levi glanced up and saw Ronnie's Stetson.

"You're dead, cussack." Levi screamed over his shoulder to Jack as he ran up the four stairs into the store.

Jack acted quickly. If he tried to return to the safety of the boat, he was likely to be shot in the back. Although Levi had a head start, Jack knew his only chance was to go in after him.

"Don't shoot my husband!" Mel pleaded as Jack crashed through the screen door to the store.

Levi's back was to the door. He was bending over, grabbing something. Jack was five feet away when Levi swung around with a rifle, pointing it at the center of his flightsuit. Now two feet away, Jack stopped.

"Put it down, Levi, you don't want to shoot anyone."

"Oh yeah? Watch me, cussack!"

Gripping the .30-30 with his shaking hands, Levi thrust the rifle at Jack's chest. He glared at Jack through rage-filled eyes, red from crying.

There was no time to react. It was like a movie being played in slow motion. Jack looked at the rifle, now inches from his chest, and at the holder's eyes. "This is going to hurt," is all he remembered thinking.

CLICK. CLICK.

Jack's right hand went to the rifle's muzzle. His left went to the forestock. Quickly shoving the muzzle toward Levi, simultaneously pulling the stock toward him, he jammed the rifle toward the floor. Levi, hanging on with all his might, flipped with the rifle to the wooden planking. Jack's knee went to Levis' back and the rifle went crashing across the floor. He bent Levis' left wrist behind his back and slapped on a handcuff. Then he grabbed Levis' right wrist and the handcuffs were locked in place.

"You're lucky, Trooper," Levi moaned. "I grabbed the wrong rifle. That's the one I broke over Stella's arm. The receiver is busted."

Ronnie banged on the back door of the store. "Jack, you okay? *Jack*, the door is locked."

"Is everyone okay?" Mel asked, as she burst into the store and pulled her boys into her arms

"Yes, thank you, Mel, would you please let Sergeant Torgy in the back door? Jack asked, as he helped Levi to his feet.

Torgy stumbled into the room. "Jack, what the heck happened? Are you okay?"

"I'm fine, Ronnie. I think you know Levi."

"Oh yeah. Hi, Levi, how ya doing?"

"I've been better," Levi mumbled.

"Sounds like a Cessna," Jack said at the sound of a plane circling over the village.

"That's probably our backup in the 206," Ronnie offered. He then turned to Levi and began reading him his rights.

"I'll go meet the 206 and help load the victims," Jack said as he walked through the doorway, halting when he heard the voice.

"Hold it right there, don't move."

Jack froze in the entryway as the muzzle of a twelve-gauge shotgun came around the door.

Jack started to go for the pistol in his flight suit, but something made him stop. It was now late in the day and the sun was behind the hills that surrounded Goodnews Bay. He could make out an outline, but not a face. The figure was thin with hair cascading on the shoulders.

There was a bulge on the right hip—a sidearm on a gun belt.

"State Troopers."

"State Troopers!"

"Jet, is that *you?*"

"Jack, is that *you?*"

Jet laid the shotgun to her side and relaxed. Jack stepped down out of the dark entryway. They quickly embraced.

"We've got to stop meeting like this, Jack. Is everybody okay?" Jet asked with her cover–girl smile.

"There are three injured that should be here from the clinic any second and need to get to the Bethel hospital. Jet, I was hoping we would see each other as soon as I got to Bethel. I didn't know it would be so hectic. I should of known better."

"I know. I can't wait to spend some more time together. It's been too long. Now we are finally on the same side of the state again. What are your days off supposed to be?"

"The way it's going right now, I'm not sure I will ever get a day off," Jack laughed.

"Okay, let's take care of this. We'll talk later. Levi can be a handful. I cited him two years for illegal commercial fishing. He went crazy and pulled a .357 magnum. I had to arrest him."

"Assault on a police officer. That's a felony, shouldn't he still be in jail?"

"He should be, yes, but the judge gave him a suspended sentence. That's Alaska justice for you. If no one was seriously hurt this time, Levi will probably only get two months in jail. And, in case you haven't heard, the Bethel jail has cable TV in each cell and a chef who was hired directly from a major cruise ship line."

"One victim is pretty bad, but it sounds like the rest will be okay. I guess Levi's assaults on them, and his trying to shoot me, should earn him at least two months vacation," Jack said, shaking his head.

"How about Ronnie. Is he okay?" Jet asked.

"As okay as Ronnie gets." Jack took a quick look into the store to be sure no one was looking.

Then he turned to Jet and they kissed.

"Mmm, wow! I missed that. But, we had better watch it. Major Emery is still the only one in the department who knows about us and we better keep it that way for now. I should make the ambulance run. Oh, by the way Jack, this is supposed to be a dry village. Did you find out where Levi got the booze?"

"Levi says a guy brought it in a plane and gave it to him and others for free," Jack said.

"Huh, that's interesting, we need to talk more about that, Jack. It may tie in to something else I've heard."

Two red four-wheelers with trailers pulled in front of the store. The first was being driven by the village health aide with Stella Bitluck sitting behind her. Stella's left arm was wrapped in an elastic bandage and fastened to her chest. Sitting in the trailer was Jimmy Alexie. His leg, with bloody gauze showing out of the jeans cut back to his thigh, rested on the trailer side rail. He was too drunk to feel pain.

A Native man in his fifties was driving the second four-wheeler. Lying on his side in the trailer was Simon Fisher, a young Native man, moaning and holding his belly.

"I'll take it from here, Jack. You'd better get back inside and try to keep Ronnie out of trouble. See you soon." Jet winked at Jack as she walked to the group.

"So long, and thanks for the backup." Jack stopped at the top step to the store, turning to watch Jet. It was tough to be so close to her, yet so far away.

Ronnie twisted red evidence tags on the three rifles while eating a candy bar. "These are the only guns that were used, Jack. The broken one wasn't fired, the other two were. I picked up sixteen shell casings in the store. Oh yeah, I'm also bagging these empties—Gold Leaf Extra 18 Year Old Scotch. Levi must be doing okay to afford these. I bet a bootlegger gets two hundred a bottle for this stuff."

"I'm sorry. I didn't mean to hurt anyone," Levi sobbed to Mel and the boys as he was led out of the store.

"Boy, the wind sure picked up," Ronnie commented to Jack as they slowly bobbed along the shoreline in the rough water.

Jack nodded to Ronnie, estimating the wind to be about forty knots from the south. "The takeoff might be a little rough, but we'll have a good tailwind home."

Waves crashed onto the shore and the 185 rocked in the water. Holding the yoke all the way back, Jack eased the power in slowly, carefully working the plane onto the step in the rough water. The 185 became airborne twice before it had enough flying speed to make a takeoff, bouncing back on the water both times. On the third try, Jack lowered the nose into a wave, splashing through the breaker and gaining airspeed so the plane could climb.

Leveling at fifteen hundred feet, Jack turned northwest toward Bethel, trimming the airplane while tuning the GPS.

"That's the guy's plane, right down there. He's the one who is giving away the booze," Levi yelled. A black Piper Apache—an old twin-engine plane, was parked just off the Eek airstrip. Jack started to ask Levi more, but the prisoner had passed out by the time Jack turned around.

"I'll call the Eek VPSO about that plane when we get home. So how do you like your new post so far, Jack?" Ronnie asked.

"Well, there seems to be enough work to do here."

"You bet there is. That's what I like about it. Time goes fast, because there's always excitement. The Yupiks are great people when they're sober. Friendly, and as honest as the day is long. But when they drink, smoke dope, or sniff gas, they turn into a different character. Some can get really violent. Keeps us in business. Jack, anything I can do to help you get adjusted let me know. Oh, and I'm sure sorry about the way Manley turned out. Toby was a great trooper."

"Yes, he was. Thanks, Ronnie."

Twilight turned to darkness when they reached altitude, and the GPS read twenty miles from Bethel.

"There's a cabin on the road to the lake that Oscar uses as a marker to find the water." Torgy informed Jack.

"Okay Ronnie, how about you give me references as we approach Bethel and the lake. This is my first night flight into here."

Torgy pointed out the village of Napasiak, then Napakiak, then the lights of Bethel. Jack remembered from his departure earlier that day that the lake was about a half mile to the left of a big bend on the river in front of town.

After announcing his approach to the Bethel tower, Jack reduced the power over the river. Still unable to see the lake, he set the controls for landing. The wind would require a turn around the lake to head back to the south. Jack didn't want to wander around in the darkness in unfamiliar territory at low altitude. He would rely on the cabin's light glowing on the lake's surface for guidance.

"There's the cabin. The lake is about two hundred yards to the right of it." Ronnie pointed to a light out the left side of the airplane.

Jack set up the descent for five hundred feet per minute at sixty-five knots. They passed over the river, then tundra. Adjacent to the cabin, Jack reduced the power for the downwind part of his landing pattern and stabilized at sixty knots. After forty seconds, Jack turned the plane and headed back to the cabin, beginning a dive at two hundred feet per minute in the total darkness.

When the landing lights reflected water, Jack reduced the throttle and pulled the controls back to flare. Then, just a touch of power was added for a glassy-water type landing. The 185 gently contacted the lake surface. Jack raised the flaps and lowered the water rudders.

"Wow, are we on the water? That was smooth, Jack. I never even saw the lake. It sure got dark fast."

They woke up Levi Tungolook, helped him from the plane, and booked him into the Bethel jail.

"Jack, why don't you come over to the house with me? My wife will have dinner on."

"Thanks anyway, Ronnie. But I really need to just get home and get some sleep. I would appreciate the offer another time." Dinner sounded good. Jack was starving, but he needed sleep more than socializing.

After a cold moose meat sandwich and an apple, Jack grabbed a newspaper that he had snatched on the airline flight from Anchorage. Jack had loved reading everything from flying magazines to Hemingway since growing up on the ranch without a television.

The headline in the paper grabbed Jack's attention: "KILLER OF PRE-SCHOOLERS ACQUITTED." Jack scanned the article to find that a killer had walked into a school with a shotgun blasting. Two kids were dead and five were seriously injured. The suspect was arrested an hour later in a car that matched the description from the scene, carrying the gun matching the casings found in the classroom, and the bullets in the bodies. His fingerprints were on the gun, on the classroom door, the bullet casings, and the teacher's desk. A restraining order had just been issued the day before the shooting to keep him away from his kids, whom he liked to beat and now were dead, so the motive was clear. After his arrest, he had fully confessed. The slick attorney told the jury that his defendant was under a lot of stress and the evil cops coerced a confession. That was enough to allow him to walk.

Justice, Jack asked himself, where's the *justice?* The weary trooper fell asleep wondering how things got so screwed up in the system.

CHAPTER 46

Jack's dream was in a Mallard this time. The huge amphibian had been converted into a flying motor home, complete with a big leather couch, beds, galley, and a bathroom. Just like the last time they flew over a molten eruption, Jet was at the controls and Jack snapped photos as they roared over Kilauea volcano, however, this time Jet wore a flower-covered bikini instead of her uniform. They flew along the black sandy beaches to Hilo, where the big flying boat splashed into the blue waters and taxied to the shore. After restocking with fresh fruit from the farmers' market, they strolled to a little beachside restaurant for a dinner of Hawaiian Red Snapper in a macadamia nut crust and fresh asparagus. Just as a mango-colored sunset glowed into the seaport, they taxied to the ocean for takeoff. A piercing sound caused Jack to hesitate pushing in the throttle levers—the same grating sound that had interrupted his last dream, now almost twenty-four hours earlier.

Jack fumbled for the phone and tried to make sense of place and time. The receiver fell to the floor and he got out of bed to pick it up.

"Did I wake you?"

Jack was confused. Was he still dreaming or was there a woman's soft voice on the phone?

"No, no, I was just getting up." Jack lied. He looked at the clock. Almost 5 a.m.

"Good morning Jet," Jack mumbled into the handset.

"You recognized my voice. I'm impressed, after the day you had yesterday. That's pretty good for being in a dead sleep— must be your police training. I'm at your office. Ronnie didn't know how to find your place, nor did he have your number. I just now tracked down Brock Sheets—he is the only who knew how to find you."

"Sorry, Jet. Busted. I was in dreamland. Of course, *you* were in it. How did you get back from Dillingham so early?"

"I was in your *dream?* You will have to share more about that with me later. I never made it to Dillingham last night. After getting the folks to the hospital, it was pretty late. I didn't feel like climbing in the Cub and flying back to Dillingham in the dark. I stayed with the Torgys."

"Wish I'd known you were in town last night. It would have been nice to get together after so much time apart. Guess I shouldn't have turned down Ronnie's dinner invitation."

"I know, Jack, but as soon as we stomp out these brush fires, we will have time. I'm just glad our posts are so close now. Anyway, you and I now are the only two pilot troopers within five hundred miles and we have two missions."

"Duty calls. I haven't checked in yet, but I can be ready in five minutes," Jack replied optimistically.

"There was a serious assault last night in Emmonak. Someone needs to go there and take statements and make the arrest. Downriver from Emmonak on the Yukon, there's a moose poaching to check out. That's one mission."

"And the other?"

"There was a plane crash on a ridge top near the village of Nightmute on Nelson Island—a guide with a musk ox hunter. The mail plane spotted it late last night. Looks like no survivors, but no one knows for sure. I know the area—there are several ridges nearby where a Super Cub can land. The nearest helicopter is in Bristol Bay for the salmon fishery and they're on hold because of the weather. Your choice, Jack."

"If it's all the same to you, I'd better take the plane crash. I haven't worked a moose poaching since Fairbanks and that didn't turn out so well."

"You got it. The Cub is in the hangar next to the 206."

"See you at the airport, Jet."

Jack made coffee and filled his thermos, then grabbed a few food bars and headed into the windy morning air. He threw his survival gear in the back of his Jeep and drove to the airport.

Jet had already opened the hand-cranked hangar door and was pre-flighting the 206. She ran up and wrapped her arms around Jack. He thought she smelled of fresh peaches and papaya.

"Good morning, love," she whispered into his ear.

It was good that they were dedicated to their jobs—they kissed quickly, then focused on the emergencies.

"Jack, you are getting a fast introduction to the Kuskokwim Delta. How about you helping me push this pig out of the hangar and I'll help you with the Cub?"

"Sounds fair to me. Are there charts in your plane? I have no idea where I'm going. But then, I haven't known that since I got here."

Jet handed Jack an aeronautical chart with a line drawn from the Bethel airport toward the southwest. Latitude and longitude were written at the termination of the line. Jack leaned over, took in the chart and gave Jet a kiss on her neck.

"Looks like about ninety miles from the Bethel airport with a heading of 243 degrees. It should be the first geographic relief you come to. The tower is still picking up the emergency locator beacon, so you should be able to find the crash site. The Cub has about three hours of fuel left. I wouldn't top it off—you need to be light to get off the ridge."

"Thanks for the briefing. Who's going with you?" Jack was impressed with Jet's preparation for the mission, but was concerned about her going into what could be a potentially dangerous situation alone. He tried not to show it in his voice.

"No problem. There's a village police officer that I can count on in Emmonak. I know the suspect—it's about the fourth assault he's committed in the past year. He'll probably be passed out and won't remember what he did. Should be an easy arrest. You be careful with my Cub. Call me on the trooper radio if you need anything."

Jet climbed into the 206 and gave Jack the thumbs up sign then started the Cessna, beginning an immediate taxi.

It was almost like a married couple in the suburbs, leaving for work in separate vehicles.

He pulled himself into the tight cockpit of the Super Cub. The plane felt familiar and fit him well. It smelled of aviation gasoline and leather and was worn in all the right places for a working airplane. Jack had owned a Super Cub since he was kid but wasn't sure when he'd have the chance to fly his own plane, judging from the workload so far.

The Super Cub is the ideal Alaska Bush plane, as far as Jack was concerned. It's commonly equipped with huge balloon tires for landing in rough terrain, can take off in a very short distance and land in even less. Covered with fabric instead of metal, it is very light and seats just two people sitting in tandem, with the pilot in the front. The tradeoff is the cockpit is cramped and can get downright uncomfortable on long flights and the big tires and other Bush gear can slow it to a top airspeed of only eighty knots.

Jack turned the Super Cub into the wind, pushed the throttle forward, and after a few seconds pulled the stick back and was airborne. He made a climbing turn to the southwest.

The wind was still blowing from the south and Jack felt lucky to have decent weather, with a cloud base at five thousand feet. The Super Cub climbed to forty–five hundred feet where Jack leveled the plane and tuned the radio to emergency frequency 121.5 to listen for the wreck's emergency locator beacon. He entered the coordinates of the crash into the GPS and turned as it ordered.

Jack followed the progress of his flight on the chart that Jet had given him. Nothing but swamps, ponds, and lakes. Although he had never been there, Jack imagined what he saw was like the Everglades. Only here it was colder and there was a lot less foliage. Bear and musk oxen instead of alligators and snakes. The tundra was brown and the water was dark. No signs of civilization as far as you could see. But, who would want to live in this mosquito–infested mess?

Twenty minutes into the flight Jack was alerted by the unmistakable WHURP, WHURP, WHURP, of an ELT. The signal got stronger and Jack's anticipation grew. Anticipation in finding the crash and concern about what he would find when he got there.

Jack had responded to many crashes in his years as a trooper. He always hoped for the best, but experience taught him to expect the worst. The majority of plane wrecks involving hunting usually fell into two categories. The first included "fender benders," where a landing gear or propeller was damaged because a pilot landed where either he, the plane, or both, were incapable of landing. The pilot and passengers received minor—or no—injuries.

The second category consisted of serious crashes. The most common was when the pilot focused on an animal on the ground instead of flying the airplane. Forgetting to fly, the pilot got too slow and too low and stalled into the ground. Rarely did anyone survive that type of impact. Jack knew the odds were slim and he knew that the mail pilot said it looked liked no survivors. Still there was the anticipation. Maybe *this time* it will be different.

Jack arrived at the coordinates. Just as Jet had said, it was the only bump on this vast wasteland of water-saturated flatland. Circling over the ridge of an eight hundred foot hill, he listened to the ELT signal fade and become stronger as he scanned for the crash. While making his second 360-degree turn, something caught Jack's eye. Something in contrast to the bleak topography. It was the color. Rather than the browns and grays of the terrain, it was red and white. Jack turned toward the color.

The closer and lower he got, the more colors he saw—blues, greens, oranges, whites, blacks—spread all over the ridge and down the side of a cliff. Jack knew these colors. They were the colors of a plane crash. Camping gear, clothes, airplane fabric, metal, and tires. And the colors of all the rest of the things that people overload into small planes.

Turning into the wind, Jack reduced power, bouncing around in the turbulent air. He fought the wind to get closer to the crash scene.

The red and white two-seater airplane was lying on its belly. The wings were pitched forward, separated from the fuselage. Pieces of the airplane were strewn in all directions.

The impact had been severe.

Jack glimpsed what looked like an arm amongst the wreckage. He pushed in the throttle and climbed to a thousand feet while searching for a place to set down. Two musk oxen peacefully grazed down slope from the crash site. The stocky, quarter-ton animals looked prehistoric, with long hair and short horns that curved upward.

The probable cause of the crash was clear. The men were looking at the musk oxen from the plane, most likely thinking how nice one of the heads would look on the hunter's trophy room wall. The plane was turned tighter as the pilot/guide judged the trophy and the excited hunter urged him on.

Then it happened. The pilot would have heard a quick beep from the stall warning horn and felt the plane shudder. Suddenly the airplane's nose dropped. The plane had lost its lift and airspeed. No fault of a good airplane. Totally pilot error. The pilot instinctively pushed the controls forward to break the stall, but they were too low. It happened so quickly. The last thing the pilot saw was tundra filling the windshield.

Maybe he had time to yell, "Oh *shi…*," or something more significant, before impact.

A half-mile from the crash site Jack saw a narrow path on the ridge. He estimated the doglegged strip to be four hundred feet long.

Jack made a low pass over the landing site. The surface appeared to be free of big rocks, ditches, and the sort of things that can tear an airplane apart—even with the balloon tires on the Super Cub. Landing would be into a twenty knot quartering headwind, so Jack should be able to stop the Cub short of the cliff at the end of the strip.

"Trooper Cessna, this is Trooper Super Cub." Jack had climbed again and tuned the radio to the trooper frequency.

"Hello, Jack, how's your flight going?" Jet's voice was soothing over the radio.

"Fine so far. Just wanted to let you know that I will be landing on a ridge about a half mile north of the wreck."

"Roger on that, Jack. How does the crash look?"

"Not good."

"Sorry to hear that. How long do you want me to give you before we come looking?"

"Give me two hours."

"Roger, I'll be landing in Emmonak shortly. I'll be back on the radio myself in an hour or so. Check on you then. Good luck."

Jack appreciated Jet's concern, but he was more concerned about her mission than his. The people he would be contacting wouldn't be a threat. He couldn't say the same for Jet's mission.

Jack cut the plane's power and made a gradual descending turn toward the ridge. He went through the simple checklist for the Cub and set up for landing.

As the Cub approached the end of the ridge, the wind burbling over the hills pushed it around like a leaf. The strip was just wide enough for the landing gear. No margin for error. Jack concentrated on keeping the landing site framed in the plane's windshield and his airspeed at fifty miles an hour for now. His left hand pulled the flap handle to full on short approach.

Just before touchdown Jack turned the master power switch off to lessen the chance of fire—in case the landing ended in a disaster. Jack guided the control stick back and forth, side to side, trying to stabilize the flight path and line up with the narrow ridge as the light airplane was tossed around in the air.

A gust of wind slammed the Cub into the ridge top before Jack was ready. The big balloon tires bounced the plane back into the sky. The crosswind shoved it to the side and the edge of the ridge came into Jack's peripheral vision. He applied a short burst of power, then lowered the nose while turning back to the strip. The main gear again touched ground just as the dogleg filled the windshield. Keeping the tailwheel off the ground, Jack turned the Cub to the right, following the dogleg.

He hit the brakes–gently, but firmly. He dropped the flaps as the plane straightened out again. As the tailwheel slapped the ground, Jack used the rudders to maneuver around hummocks the size of basketballs. The plane thrashed around violently. Fighting to salvage the landing, he needed to stop short of the sudden drop–off at the end of the strip. To keep the Cub from turning over on its back, a delicate balancing act was required with braking and stick control.

The end of the strip was coming up fast, but Jack saw something that provided hope. The ridge widened to the size of a neighborhood cul-de-sac. Fifty feet from the end, he made a gradual left turn then hit the brakes hard. The Cub spun into the left crosswind, stopping in a skid.

Jack sat back in the seat and exhaled. Cheated death—or at least lots of paperwork to report the damage—once again, he mused. He thought of the old Bush pilot who once told him, "Any landing you can walk away from is a good landing." Jack never bought that philosophy and felt this one was just sloppy.

Jack lashed the Cub with ropes to big rocks at either side of the strip, then grabbed his survival pack from the baggage compartment. Everything he needed for about any situation was in the pack—food bars, water, first aid kit, camera, investigative kit, extra ammunition, bug dope, and tools.

He fished around in the far reaches of the Cub until he found two body bags—standard equipment in a state trooper aircraft. He tied the bags to the pack.

Jack looked forward to the hike, but he didn't look forward to reaching the crash site. He knew the possibility of survivors was remote. His thoughts jumped to the condition of the bodies. Jack had retrieved victims that had been fed on by bears, foxes, and birds. Insects had worked on some. Others were dismembered by the impact of the crash. Some had to be dismembered with a saw, by the trooper, to separate them from the crash. Retrieving bodies wasn't a pleasant task, especially when you were doing it alone.

Just a few minutes into the hike, Jack caught his first view of the crash site from the ground. Standing on a hill overlooking the scene, he took his compact binoculars from his pack.

First, he checked for bears—nothing moving but bugs—then something caught his eye.

A flash of red came from the plane. Jack zoomed in with the glasses to the pilot side of the airplane and there it was.

Something red was waving.

Adrenalin rushed through Jack as he hustled down the slope. Maybe a chance of getting someone out alive! Nearing the plane, he detected the familiar scent of aviation fuel, spilled over the tundra from the wing tanks. The path took him first around the port side of the plane. The windows were broken and the fabric was torn open. The pilot was hanging over the instrument panel. There was a big gash in the back of his head and his skull was open to the morning sky. No hope for this poor guy, Jack thought as he quickly made his way to the other side of the craft to get to whatever, whomever, was waving.

An arm, covered in a red shirt, was sticking out of the plane on the right side of the cockpit. The "waving" was from the torn fabric of the shirt, caused by the compound fracture of the pilot's radius bone.

Jack pulled the pilot's head away from the aircraft panel. He smelled of whiskey and his head was cracked from the top of his hairline to his nose. Jack made cursory checks of the carotid arteries of both men. Both had been killed on impact. They only had time to brace for the crash, and that didn't help.

Jack grabbed a small hacksaw from his pack. Cutting through the metal tubes of the airplane, he made openings on both sides of the fuselage. He reached into the aft compartment and turned off the ELT. The passenger came out fairly easily, even though Jack estimated him at about two hundred pounds. Jack thought it was strange that a rifle was in his arms, as if he was ready to shoot.

The pilot weighed about one-sixty, but Jack couldn't pull him from the cockpit. Both of the pilot's legs had multiple compound fractures. The bones protruded from his jeans, jamming his legs under the panel. Jack had to do a little more cutting before lifting the pilot free. Then he found something strange—pieces of broken glass were stuck into the pilot's leg.

Digging around on the floorboard, Jack found more broken glass. Pieces of the glass were attached to a label. Holding it to the sunlight, Jack could read Gold Leaf Extra 18 Year Old Scotch.

Jack tucked both men into body bags. Now the task would be to get them into the airplane. He looked around for a closer landing spot, but the terrain was too rough. About a hundred yards behind the crash, Jack saw an animal—not a bear, but just as big.

Musk ox. This was the first time Jack had actually seen a real one up close. They were introduced to this area years ago and had become quite a trophy for sport hunters. The animal had recently been shot.

Jack looked at the dead animal, then back to the wreck. It was evident—the hunter had shot the musk oxen from the plane while they were flying over it. In all the excitement, with no telling how much scotch mixed in, the pilot crashed.

Taking rope from his pack, Jack tied it to the handles on the foot end of the body bag. The tough fabric would hold up as Jack dragged the poor soul across the tundra. Dragging, pulling, lifting, Jack spent the next hour ascending the hill. He sat down to take a break, dreading the chore of going through this workout again with a heavier body.

WHOP....WHOP....WHOP. A helicopter was nearby. Jack pulled a roll of orange survey tape from his pack, ready to wave it to draw the attention of the chopper pilot. He would do his best to talk whoever this guy was into flying his "cargo" to Bethel. Jack jogged up to the Cub, and flipped on the master power switch and the radio. Before he could talk, a transmission blasted over his headset.

"Hey Jack, you out there?" He knew the unmistakable voice of the helicopter pilot—Hayden Bensen, the big Swede from Anchorage. Jack had flown with Hayden many times and appreciated his piloting skills and his attitude and knew the helo pilot had saved many lives with his heroics over the years. Hayden had been en route to Manley the day of the big shootout. If he would have been the pilot in the number one helicopter instead of number two, things would have turned out differently and Jack wouldn't have been standing on a wind-blown ridge in the middle of nowhere.

"Hello, Hayden, sounds like you're a couple of miles to the east of my position. What are you doing in the neighborhood?"

"We're headed to the numbers given on the crash. Heard you might want a hand."

Shortly, the blue, white, and gold state trooper helicopter hovered over the crash then headed to the Cub. After landing on the ridge, a passenger got out of the helicopter, bent to clear the moving blades and walked quickly to the Cub. Jack recognized the figure in the flight suit immediately. Jet spoke while Hayden was completing the shut down procedure.

"Hi Jack, looks like no survivors. Don't tell me you dragged that victim up this hill? It's good to see that your back is still working."

"Glad you and Hayden showed up. I wasn't looking forward to stuffing those poor guys into the Cub. How did you wrap up your assault and moose poaching cases so fast? And how did you snag the helo?"

"Well, it all worked out pretty slick today. The suspect was waiting for me in Emmonak. He was being mushy and wanted to go to Bethel and make things all better. He knows the routine, so he was okay. The moose poaching turned out to be the remains of a legal kill from the current hunting season, so no investigation was needed. When I got back to Bethel, Hayden was waiting for me at the airport. The weather picked up in Bristol Bay and he decided to come over and play with us for the day."

Hayden Bensen pulled his lanky frame out of the Bell 206 helicopter. His oversized blond handlebar mustache nicely complemented his bright blue flightsuit.

"Howdy, partner," Hayden said, as he greeted Jack heartily with his firm handshake.

"Hope you don't mind us dropping in on you unannounced, but it looks like you might appreciate a little backup. From what I hear, you been hopping since you got here. Looks like nothing has changed, huh, Jack? You always seem to find the action."

"I can easily do without *this* kind of action, Hayden. And how have you been surviving?"

"Great, Jack. I've been spending the last couple of weeks chasing illegal fishing boats over the bay. I heard you were over here, so decided this was a good chance to escape. Plus, I get to see Jet again. Ya gotta love that gal, ya know."

"Yeah, and what does your wife think about that?" Jack asked, knowing Hayden was a loving husband with a wonderful wife who supported his crazy emergency pilot lifestyle.

"Oh yeah. Guess I better behave myself then, I don't want to lose my bride of twenty years. You need to find a good woman yourself, Jack. It makes life so much better to have someone to share it with." Hayden's tundra philosophy must have sunk in as Jack's eyes tracked Jet.

While the old friends were catching up, Jet surveyed the crash site from the ridge, speaking as Jack and Hayden walked to her. "Jack, what's with the musk ox carcass?"

Jack explained his theory of the aerial shooting and crash to Jet.

"Makes sense to me. This isn't the first time I've seen this happen with overly zealous hunters who have no regard for the resource. And it's not the first time I've seen a guide who boozes while he flies. But these guys broke the law and paid the ultimate price. Guess you call it instant, albeit *extreme,* justice. No trial, no fancy lawyers, no wimp judges or jury. I'm sure sorry for their families, though."

Jet's curly hair was blowing in the wind. Her blue-green eyes focused on the valley beneath. Jack couldn't wait to be alone with her.

Jet climbed down the ridge to the wreck while Jack and Hayden loaded the first victim onto the helicopter's litter. The men then jumped in the chopper and made the quick hop to the crash site, setting down alongside the body bag holding the pilot.

Jet was sketching the scene in her trooper notebook when Jack approached.

Take a look at these, Jack." Jet showed two 300 Winchester cartridges that she had found in the wrecked plane. "Bet these are the same as in the musk ox." Jet said as she pointed toward the kill site.

Hayden excused himself to "mark my territory," behind a hill, giving Jet her chance. Stepping over the body bag, she took a quick look to make sure Hayden was out of sight, then she kissed Jack on the lips.

"Guess he won't mind," Jack said, nodding at the body.

"We've got to do better than this, soon. *Real* soon," he added.

Jet examined the musk ox carcass while Hayden and Jack secured the second body on the helicopter. "Here is what I was looking for. A bullet from the neck of the musk ox. No Sherlock needed to figure this one out. Jack, if you don't mind, I'll take the Cub and you go back to Bethel with Hayden. I would like to fly over to Nightmute and notify the family of the pilot. I'll offer the meat from the musk ox to the villagers."

"Sounds good to me, Jet. I'll just take a few photos, grab some of the gear, and we'll head back. Hey, when you're in Nightmute would you check to see if a guy in a black Apache happened to fly in, handing out free scotch? Sure you don't need any help?"

"Thanks, Jack. I'll be fine. I had the same thought on the scotch. See you soon." Jet laughed, said goodbye to Hayden, and hiked up the ridge to her plane.

"Great gal. You should get to know her better, Jack."

"That's the best idea I've heard all year," Jack replied, as he watched Jet cresting the ridge. The men loaded the gear taken from the wreck and climbed into the helicopter. From the bubble cockpit, they saw the Cub lift off the ridge and bank towards Nightmute.

"Trooper Cub, Helo One. Have a great flight, Jet. Hope to see you again shortly." Hayden transmitted over the radio as they swept over the tundra.

Jet wagged the wings of the Cub and responded, "Thanks, see ya."

CHAPTER 47

Sergeant Ronnie Torgy stood by his trooper pickup as the helicopter landed in front of the Bethel hangar. "Seems like he would have figured this out by now. Happens every time." Hayden chuckled as Ronnie's Stetson once again blew off his head, today by the wash from the helicopter blades.

The three men hefted the body bags into the truck. "We'll take these over to the fish and game cooler. They'll be fine there until tomorrow's flight to Anchorage for autopsies." Ronnie explained that the Department of Fish and Game had large walk-in refrigeration lockers for storing biological samples. The biologists didn't mind if the troopers occasionally stored a body along the rows of wildlife carcasses and fish, as long as it was only overnight.

"You gentlemen are coming to my house for a 'Yukon Kuskokwim Delta Force' dinner, so let's get this done," Ronnie ordered.

Ronnie's wife, Patty, made Jack and Hayden feel at home immediately. She was a homemaker with jet-black hair, highlighted by a brilliant silver streak centered in her bangs. She directed her hearty laugh mostly at her husband, who seemed to enjoy it.

"So Hayden, how far did Ronnie's hat fly today?" Hayden had once landed the helicopter behind the Torgy's house—built on stilts in the frozen tundra. Patty watched from her kitchen window as Ronnie ran down the stairs to greet the helicopter. That time his Stetson was blown almost a mile across the land. Ronnie's oldest son found it the next day after a search and rescue operation with the neighborhood kids.

"Jack, it's wonderful to meet you. Welcome to our home. That's our tribe." Patty pointed to the couch where Ronnie was sitting. Four children, ranging from age five to fourteen, were crawling all over him.

"Jack, whose bad side did you get on to earn a transfer to Bethel? All Ronnie did was crash his patrol vehicle through the garage door at the Fairbanks post."

"Well, in Ronnie's case, the people of Bethel are better for it," Jack said. "I guess someone must have thought it would be a good career move for me."

"Seems like we've all heard that one a few too many times, Jack. But it makes life interesting." Patty laughed.

"By the way, Jack, Ronnie says you're single. Have you met Jet? I think you too would be great together."

Jack smiled.

Everyone crowded around the dinner table for a home-cooked meal of silver salmon that Patty had netted in front of town on the Kuskokwin River. Ronnie did his best to fill Jack in on the villages that the troopers served out of Bethel, while Hayden laughed at Patty's stories about life in the Bush and Ronnie's exploits.

Jack, needing some well-deserved rest, said his thanks and excused himself around 9:30 p.m. Patty and Ronnie were still telling stories to a laughing Hayden, who had accepted their invitation to camp on their couch for the night.

After walking two blocks to his house, Jack sliced open his mail from the Fairbanks troopers. Jill had attached a hand written note to a pile of transfer documents in Fairbanks. It read: "Sundance, here is your final transfer paperwork. I hope you know you are the envy of all the Fairbanks troopers for finally getting your dream post. Captain 'pain in the ass' leaves next week for his new job. No one is upset. Have fun, Jill."

Jack hit the flashing light on his telephone message machine. "Love: made it home just before dark. Heard you and Hayden on the radio landing in Bethel, so know you did too. Didn't get a chance to thank you for the help today, so thanks. I hope we can see each other very, very, soon. You're hunch was right—the guy in the black twin-engine plane did land in Nightmute, gifting some of the locals with that fancy scotch. The guide who was flying the crashed plane was seen drinking just before they took off. His widow said he had been on the wagon for years until then. One of the village public safety officers told me last week that a new bootlegger had been flying in booze. I called the officer yesterday, and what do you know? He says the plane was black. Miss you already. Love, Jet."

The phone rang before he could check the rest of the messages.

"Trooper Blake, this is First Sergeant Lutz. Where the hell have you been? You were supposed to report to duty at 0800 this morning!"

"Good evening to *you*, First Sergeant. Sorry I haven't had the chance to report in, but I've been on calls since I got here. By the way, where *is* the office?"

"Damn! Nobody around here tells me anything. Just make sure you are in my office at 0800 tomorrow." The phone slammed in Jack's ear.

The tiny bedroom was cold. The only heat in this overpriced dump was a kerosene wall unit in the living room. His self-built bookshelves surrounded the head of his bed, covering the entire wall. Nothing fancy this time. Maybe someday he would stain the pine and plywood, but probably not. The shelves did the job of holding his books and that was good enough. Jack pulled the blankets up, turned on the high intensity light over his bed, and grabbed the latest addition to his library.

Guilty: The Collapse of Criminal Justice, had caught Jack's attention at the airport bookstore in Anchorage as he was waiting for his Bethel flight.

The cover photo of the judge appealed to Jack. He was a straightforward looking gentleman, with gray hair combed back, rather large, thick glasses, and wearing his judicial robe. Not flashy, but an honest, well-worn face.

Jack read the introduction and surmised that this judge, with twenty-five years of hearing lies from New York's worst, had something to say about our country's criminal justice system going down the toilet. The judge's quote on the book jacket was all the sell Jack had needed: "We have formalism and technicalities, but little common sense. It's about time America wakes up to the fact that we're in the fight of our lives." Jack read the first one hundred pages, then fell asleep.

Sitting in a courtroom with tall ceilings and rows of bleachers, Jack was watching a trial. The defendant was charged with cop killing. The victim was Trooper Jack Blake of the Bethel post. The jury foreman yelled the verdict: "Not Guilty!"

The twelve jurors walked to the defendant who looked much like a recent photo Jack had seen of F-Rod, each giving him a high five. The judge was the pilot of the plane wreck the day before, complete with the open, bleeding skull and bottle of Gold Leaf Scotch. Leaping from the bench, he joined the defendant and jurors.

They walked toward Jack, chanting, "Not Guilty, not guilty!" The judge swung a bell in his hand: "ring, ring, RING!"

Jack woke in a cold sweat. He knew it was a dream, but the ringing continued. He silenced it by grabbing the phone.

"Blake, this is Brock Sheets. Sorry to call this early, but I need you."

The green LED light on the clock radio glowed 4:51 a.m. This is getting old, and I've only been here three days, Jack thought.

"Let me guess, you need a pilot." Jack mumbled into the phone over the wind whistling through gaps in the window frames.

"You got it Jack, I'll be there in five minutes."

CHAPTER 48

Jack lay on his stomach on the cold, mildewy floor, stretching his spine until it made a cracking sound louder than the wind banging the screen door. The improvised chiropractic treatment made his back—sore from dragging the body yesterday and still littered with shrapnel from Laos—usable once again. He stumbled to the bathroom, pulled on his uniform and gun belt, and grabbed the assault rifle and ammo magazines. Then he noticed the shaking—the entire house was wobbling on its foundation. His hand grabbed the cold doorknob just as Sheets drove up but Jack could hardly get the door of his arctic entry open against the storm. The gale forced him to bend at the waist to get out the door and onto the street. Spitting cold sand, Jack pulled the truck door open with both hands to counter the gusts.

"Brock, what the heck do we have here, a *hurricane*?"

"No Jack, it's only gusting seventy knots from the west. Technically, that means it's a tropical depression. Winds must be at least seventy-four knots to be a hurricane. Some dude in a downriver village we call 'Tunt,' is shooting out from the window of a second story, which happens to be the tallest building in town. One guy has been hit in the arm, otherwise nothing else but a dog has been shot. Troopers Stevens and Jones are pinned down behind a house and the shooter seems to want to kill anything that moves."

The trooper truck occasionally rocked sideways on the roller coaster road in the fierce blasts of wind under the racing gray skies.

"Is he drunk?" Jack guessed.

"Yeah, which is strange. His wife says he hasn't had any booze for years, but somebody gave him some fancy whiskey in a box. He couldn't resist, I guess. I'm wondering if that's the same stuff you and Josh found in Tuluksak. He's been screaming that he wants to die and take a trooper with him."

Brock explained that "Tunt" was only about twenty miles south of Bethel. "Ronnie and Josh will meet us at the floatplane."

"*Floatplane?* Brock, why use the floatplane in this wind?"

"The airstrip runs north and south, so the crosswind is too strong. The helicopter would be perfect, but Hayden took off early before this wind storm hit."

Jack appreciated Sheet's planning, but another question came to mind. "So, Brock, does this mean we will be landing across the Kuskokwim River, rather than with the current?"

"That's right Jack, but at least it is getting daylight."

"Hope you don't mind a little turbulence," Jack answered.

By the time they got the floatplane loaded, the sun was peeking over the Kilbuck Mountains, illuminating waterspouts formed by the vortex of wind racing across the surface of Hangar Lake. Ronnie was in the backseat of the Cessna 185, dripping stinky water from Hangar Lake on the floor. Josh, sitting next to Ronnie, smiled and offered "camai," a Yupik greeting. Sheets was seated next to Jack, busy writing in his trooper notebook.

Fortunately, the strong wind was blowing directly on the nose of the airplane, so no taxiing turns on the water were needed. Jack had untied the ropes from the floats and all he had to do was call the tower and blast off.

"Bethel Tower, this is Cessna 9252 November, requesting takeoff to the North from Hangar Lake."

"Uh, roger, 52 November, uh, cleared for takeoff, no reported traffic, current winds 320 degrees at fifty-eight knots, gusting to seventy-one knots."

Jack pushed the throttle in on the powerful airplane, holding the control yoke all the way back. He carefully played the controls, keeping the floats from nosing over in the whitecaps. Although the strong wind would have allowed for a short takeoff, Jack kept it on the water long enough to build a safety factor. The violent gusts could throw the plane back in the water if the takeoff speed was too slow. The Cessna creaked and rocked. The cockpit sounded like an empty metal barrel being pounded in the surf.

Breaking from the lake's surface, the plane quickly gained airspeed, but one only had to look out at the ground to see that didn't translate to groundspeed. They hardly moved over the tundra as Jack fought with the controls in the severe turbulence. It was good to be free of the rough water, but the rough skies were much more threatening—it was as if they were insulted that the little plane would consider challenging the winds. Sheet's notebook flew to the ceiling as he grabbed the tubular support by the windscreen. The war between the plane and the air had begun.

Tunt was a small Eskimo village on the west bank of the Kuskokwim River. Troopers Stevens and Jones had responded by boat at 3:30 a.m. to a report of a distraught man with a gun. Fighting high winds and fierce waves, the troopers had suffered through the hour and a half wild boat ride to the village.

Scurrying from the patrol boat on the mud bar in front of town, the troopers had to dive for cover as shots rang out from the house. Darting from behind beached skiffs, Stevens and Jones had eventually worked their way to the only street in the village, settling in behind a shack.

For the next fifteen minutes, the shooter blasted at anything that moved, and a few things that didn't. A husky sled dog, barking from his short chain in the yard of a neighbor, was silenced by a fatal shot to his head. When the neighbor opened his door, awakened by his dog's final howl, he was shot in the left forearm.

Joe Stevens, a fresh-faced trooper with three years on the job, was pinned down behind a shack. He had a clear view of the shooter and watched as his bullets struck the targets.

Stevens grabbed his portable radio and called the Bethel Police Department, which had a twenty-four hour dispatcher on duty, broadcasting through a system of repeaters.

"Bethel PD, this is 1D8."

"Go ahead, eight."

"Bethel, call Investigator Sheets, tell him we are under fire in Tunt. One civilian shot. Need assistance." Stevens yelled into the radio.

"Roger, ID8."

Stevens looked at Dene Jones. It was the first time either had been called to a situation in which shots were being fired. Their hearts were racing.

"This guy is a whacko," Jones exclaimed.

"Whacko maybe, but a pretty good shot," Joe answered.

"Yeah, well you are too, Joe. Keep your scope on him."

Joe trained his .308 rifle with the ten-power scope on the open window. He could clearly see the shooter and watched him recoil as shot after shot was fired.

"Let's get closer, Dene."

Moving between the small black and gray structures, the troopers approached the shooter's house, now just a hundred yards away. Stevens used the houses on the east side of the dirt road as cover, Jones the west.

Ping, ping. Shots hit the metal roof of the house next to Jones. Stevens motioned to Jones to stay concealed. He continued the approach, taking cover behind an old snowmachine.

"Well, I'm in a good position and can watch him. Let's just stay put until Sheets gets here. As long as everyone stays home it will be okay. There's not much moving to shoot at now." Stevens called Dene on his radio.

"Good plan, Joe, let's wait him out. Maybe he will shoot up all his ammo. But if not, take him out if you have to."

The wind continued to howl. The shots could hardly be heard now. There was only a muffled thunk, then dirt and debris would be kicked up and swiftly blown away. Stevens strained to listen for a plane or a boat that meant backup was near, but it was hopeless in the wind. The trooper didn't want to shoot anyone.

But he knew if he had to, his years of hunting had honed his skills in rifle shooting.

If there had been an award for "Mr. Congeniality" at the academy, Joe would have won it easily. He's a nice guy and gentle person with a good word for everyone. Joe and his best friend, Dene, had transferred to Bethel because the pay was higher and the overtime was plentiful. Both men were starting families and needed the extra income.

Jack wiped his moist palms on his pants and looked down at the whitecaps on the muddy Kuskokwim River. The floatplane had to crab into the wind to stay on the downriver course. The battle with the severe updrafts, downdrafts, and side drafts, made him feel like he was in an alley fight. He knew he wouldn't be able to inspect his landing options. A fly-over would give the shooter notice and would make them easy targets. Plus, that was just that much longer they would be at the mercy of the wild air.

The wind would be coming from town toward the river at about ninety degrees to the river current. Jack would have his hands full as they descended into the mad whirlpool — the turbulence would only get worse—then the towering waves would slam the airplane's floats with a severe side force, making control on the water even tougher than flying.

No sane pilot would even try this without serious entice-ment. It was one of those silly questions a kid might ask another: "For a million dollars, would you take this little floatplane, land cross-current on a raging river in violent, seventy mile an hour winds?"

"No *way*," the other kid would answer.

But this was different. A fellow trooper was under fire and people could get hurt. Jack wiped his hands again and set up for the landing.

Bang! Simultaneously, all four men's heads smashed into the plane's ceiling in the severe downdraft.

The village appeared through the morning mist as the floatplane followed the east bank of the Kuskokwim. The plane turned toward the buildings, lining up with the fishing boats pulled onto the beach as the descent began.

It was like being in the center of an explosion as they dropped through two hundred feet. Jack slammed the throttle in as a severe downdraft threatened to smash the plane into a gravel bar, then quickly brought it back to arrest the climb. Sheets hung onto the crossbar, Josh grabbed the back of Jack's seat.

"Jesus, help us," Ronnie prayed out loud.

With the strong headwind causing the airplane to hover just above the river, Jack eased the throttle in to keep the plane flying, looking for just the right spot. Fifty feet above the water now, Jack strained to find good water. Landing too far out in the river could mean disaster, as the strong waves would certainly capsize the Cessna. Too close to the bank could cause a crash into the boats. Just past a gravel bar, Jack pulled the flaps and reduced power. He was committed now. A go-around was impossible as the village filled the windscreen.

The floatplane slapped down hard in the water—first on the left float, then on both. The men were slammed around in the confined cockpit in the violent rapids. Jack reduced the power more and, pushing the control yoke forward, aimed for a narrow small slice of beach between the skiffs.

Floats sliding across mud never sounded so good to Jack. With the force of a car hitting a tree at five miles an hour, the plane jerked to a stop on the beach as the throttle was pulled back. The rushed parking job allowed for about four inches on each float between boats.

"Good job, Jack," Sheets said as opened his door.

"Praise the Lord." Ronnie said as he exhaled.

"Eee," agreed Josh in Yupik.

Stevens hadn't heard the plane land. He was focused on the shooter through his scope. Jones saw something in his peripheral vision, turning his attention to a small house between him and the shooter's house. He guessed the little Native girl wearing a purple kuspuck to be about four. She had opened the front door and was now skipping toward the street. He yelled to the child, but it was useless. His voice died in the wind.

"Joe, *Joe*, are you on?" Stevens had a speaker microphone attached to his lapel and heard his name. "Joe, look out at the street, there's a kid," Jones yelled.

Joe Stevens saw the shooter move in the window and adjust his rifle. The trooper lowered his weapon and saw the girl standing in the street. Her kuspuck flapped in the wind. She was oblivious to the commotion and danger of the early morning.

Dirt exploded next to the girl—the shooter had found a new target. Stevens focused his scope in the second story window. The man was recoiling from more shots. He was firing on the little girl.

"No, *no*, don't make me do it!" Stevens yelled. He looked quickly toward the girl. She now was gazing up at the shooter's window and giggling. She must have thought it was play. Dirt exploded next to her again and was whisked away in the wind.

Stevens took the shooter in his scope. Just as he had concentrated when hunting big game, he placed his target in the cross hairs. The shooter had calculated where to place his next shot to end the play with the little girl. His finger increased pressure on the trigger when the .308 bullet from Steven's rifle penetrated his skill. The force flung him back into his bedroom.

Trooper Stevens hoped he had only wounded the shooter, but knew what kind of damage the .308 could do. His heart pounded as he rose slowly from his crouch behind the snowmachine. He looked at the window, wishing the suspect would raise his hands and give up. Jones ran to the little Eskimo girl and grabbed her in his arms, taking her to shelter behind her house.

"Uncy Billy gone bye-bye." The little girl said, pointing to the window.

"Jones, are you guys on the radio?" Sheets yelled over the wind into the radio. Jones had left his radio when he ran out to the girl, so Stevens answered.

"This is Stevens, we're in the middle of the village. We have a man down in the two-story house."

"Hold tight, we just landed on the river. We'll be there in a minute," Sheets yelled.

Stevens met them on the river trail where it joined the village road and, speaking softly, said, "I had no choice. I didn't want to shoot him." Jack knew the feeling—you knew it had to be done—but you wished you didn't have to be the one pulling the trigger. Stevens' eyes were tearing and his hand was shaking.

"Where is he, Joe?" Sheets asked.

"Up there, the open window."

"Killer, damn pig, murdering *cussack!*" The troopers had not heard the group of young Native men approaching them from behind in the wind.

"Jack, you and Ronnie check out the house. Josh and I will talk with these gentlemen." Sheets then turned to Stevens and spoke low so the villagers couldn't hear. "Get to the floatplane and stay there until these guys calm down. It will be okay. You did the right thing."

"*But,*" Stevens started to protest.

"Go. Go *now!*" Sheets nodded to the plane.

Dene Jones, with the little Native girl in his arms, diverted the group's attention when he walked up, allowing Stevens to leave unnoticed.

"Why are you carrying around Lucy?" One of the men shouted at Jones.

"Just trying to keep her *alive.*" Jones responded. He gently put the girl on her feet, but she hung tight onto his leg.

"That trooper shot her uncle for no reason," one of the villagers yelled.

Josh said something to the men in Yupik, then Sheets continued.

"I know everyone is upset, but there was nothing else the trooper could do. Someone in the village was going to get killed."

"He was shot for no reason, you bastard cussack!" Malcolm George, the shooter's brother, yelled.

"Shut up, Malcolm! Look, Billy shot me and he killed my dog. Something was wrong in his head." The village elder, with his arm wrapped in a bloody makeshift sling, was the voice of reason.

"Let me check the upstairs, you look down here," Jack said. Ronnie nodded, then removed his pistol from the holster and entered the living room, bumping his shin on the coffee table. With the exception of the overturned furniture, broken glass, and other evidence of an out-of-control temper, the little house was well kept and showed the owner's pride.

The steps creaked as Jack made his way to the upper level. Reaching the landing, Jack strained to listen for human noises against the wind racing through the open bedroom window. Approaching with his pistol drawn, Jack quickly poked his head into the room. His eyes first fell to a rifle in the middle of the floor, then to spent cartridges, numbering at least fifty, spread all over the carpet. Then boots—boots attached to legs on the floor. Jack eased into the blood-splattered room. Seven feet from the open window, next to the only bed in the room, lay Billy Paul. He had a severe facial wound and was motionless. Jack carefully approached the man and watched for breathing. Nothing. Jack checked for signs of life. There were none.

Billy Paul was not going to hurt anyone else. He got his wish. At least part of it.

"Brock, this is Blake." Jack called into his portable radio.

"Go ahead, Jack."

"We got one 10-79 up here." Jack used the radio code for deceased.

Joe Stevens heard the radio traffic and smashed his fist onto the float of the Cessna.

Sheets was able to calm the crowd, which had grown to about thirty-five villagers. He promised there would be a full investigation, explaining that a headquarters task force from Anchorage investigated all shootings by troopers, so there would be no favoritism. The angry men shuffled back to their cabins.

"Jack, how about if you and Stevens get the victim to the hospital? Ronnie, you can stay here with me and Jones, and help with the evidence collection," Sheets directed the three troopers.

Jones had returned the little girl to her house to find that she was under the care of her seven-year-old sister. Her parents had boated to a village upriver three days ago to party with her aunt—the shooter's wife.

"They are just about out of grub." Jones said.

"I'll unload the food from my pack for the kids on my way back to the plane. See you guys later." Jack said.

Jack knocked on the door of the cabin. The shy Native girls were excited as Jack gave them apples, food bars, and oatmeal cookies. One little boy had been chewing tobacco, saying that was all he could find in the house to eat.

Jack estimated the wind had lessened to about thirty-five knots, which now felt almost calm to him. Joe Stevens was sitting on the float of the Cessna, softly speaking to himself.

Placing his hand on Steven's shoulder, Jack offered, "Joe, sorry to meet you like this. You did what you had to do. It was a clean shot, he felt no pain." Jack knew the first part of his speech to be true, and guessed at the last.

Joe Stevens, eyes red and looking like hell, stood up and shook Jack's hand. "Thanks, Jack. Coming from a guy that's been there before, I appreciate it."

The flight back to Hangar Lake was much smoother than the flight to the village. Flying in half the wind velocity of the earlier flight was pure joy, and with only moderate turbulence, they made good time. The troopers delivered the injured man to the hospital, then drove to the post.

CHAPTER 49

The faded "State Trooper" sign over the old blue metal building reminded Jack of the one in King Salmon. He wondered if it would look better or worse in sunny skies. He also wondered if the skies in Bethel were *ever* sunny. Stevens swung the door open to a dark hallway leading to a small room with dark, imitation walnut paneling. The green sculptured carpet and orange counter top helped establish the building's vintage. Unlike the professional atmosphere of the Fairbanks post, this musty-smelling building looked more like it should have housed a used car dealership than a law enforcement agency—except for the wall hangings.

Stuck to the paneling was an eye chart for driver's license applicants, FBI wanted posters, warnings about the dangers of drinking while driving, and a two-year old calendar with photographs of commercial fishing sponsored by the Bumble Bee Cannery.

"Ronnette, this is Trooper Blake." Stevens introduced Jack to the trooper clerk.

"Good to meet you." Jack said, smiling at the young Native woman. She returned Jack's smile with a frown and a headshake.

"Uh huh, the first sergeant wants to see you, Blake," the clerk said without looking up from the papers on her desk.

"She's not too crazy about white men in general, although her father was white. She seems to think troopers just want to come here, harass her people, and leave in a couple of years. At least she has the last part right. If you're lucky, maybe she will even make eye contact someday." Stevens whispered as they walked past the counter and through a door into the squad room.

"And she's on *our* side?" Jack asked, thinking to himself how much he would miss the smiling face of Jill. If only he could con her into transferring here from Fairbanks, he mused.

"Stevens, is that you?" A voiced growled from the first office off the main room.

"Yes, First Sergeant," Stevens responded.

"Get in here and shut the door."

"This should be fun." Stevens whispered as he looked at Jack, raised his eyebrows, and shook his head. He entered the office with the brown plastic sign on the door warning, "1st Sergeant Gene Lutz."

Jack examined the main office. He estimated the dimensions to be forty feet by forty feet. He could see over the gray cubicles crowded into the middle of the room. Paperwork—which may never be completed—was piled on top of gray metal desks. The same green carpet as in the entryway was in this room—all of it heavily stained by foot traffic and littered with scraps of paper. The dark walls seemed to close in around Jack as he looked up to the low suspended ceiling marked by water leaks. About a quarter of the bulbs in the fluorescent light fixtures were burned out and others buzzed loudly. A half-full pot of coffee spewed the odor of what must have been at least two-day-old brew into the room. Three old donuts lay in state on a grimy paper towel next to the coffee. Three aeronautical charts were taped together to form a display on one wall. Color pins were scattered about the chart. A note card explained the colors. Red pins were for shootings and other violent assaults, yellow for murders, blue for drownings, orange for sexual assaults, green for accidental deaths and black for search and rescues. Jack noticed there were a lot of red and orange pins, followed closely by yellow. Green was no slouch either, numbering at least twenty pins.

Opposite the first sergeant's office was a room with a plaque stating, "Post Sergeant." Jack looked in to see pictures of Ronnie's family on the desk. A judogi with a brown belt attached hung on a coat rack next to a uniform jacket with sergeant stripes.

"Evidence" written with a black marker, identified the room behind the only other door. Jack found the desk with the least litter on it, sat down, and took out his paperwork. He looked at his watch, 11:43 a.m. Jack began making entries in his notebook.

"Blake, get in here!"

Jack stood just inside the first sergeant's office. He hadn't seen Lutz since King Salmon, when he delivered Jack's transfer orders to Glennallen. Lutz had put on a few pounds since then, now weighing in at about 265, Jack guessed. His ruddy complexion made him appear as if he had just completed an exhausting physical task, but Jack came to learn that was how he always looked. He wore close-cropped gray hair and silver rimmed glasses were perched on his bulbous nose crossed with broken blood vessels. The wall hangings on the dark paneling in Lutz's office reminded Jack of Captain Tower's office. Lots of certificates for courses he had taken and photos of him with various supervisors in the department. Jack had heard that Lutz aspired to be promoted to the ranks of those in the photographs. He had also heard that there was little chance of that ever happening.

Lutz's uniform, although he had grown at least one size since his last shirt was issued, was neat. His brass was flashy and his blue wool shirt and pants had been cleaned professionally, with crisp creases and those shiny places that the professional irons make. He obviously didn't get out of the office much.

Jack had already decided to make use of the wash and wear uniforms, since the only professional cleaners were in Anchorage. That meant uniforms had to be shipped in and out of Bethel by air. Waste of time and money.

Jack did a quick recon of his own outfit, while Lutz was intently studying a memo on his desk. His flight suit was a mess. Fresh bloodstains from today, along with bloodstains from the plane crash and the two shooting calls the day before. A rip in one breast pocket—probably from Levi. Mud blotches from the Kuskokwim River and Goodnews Bay.

Instead of polished black shoes, Jack wore hip boots. One was pulled up a little higher than the other, and both were caked with mud. Jack had planned on showing up for his first duty day at his new post in a fresh uniform. But plans changed again and there he was.

Lutz finally peered up from his desk. He looked at Jack from head to toe, intently studying, as if he was trying to make sense of a crossword puzzle written in Portuguese.

"I thought I told you to report at 0800 this morning, Blake. I don't allow insubordination at my post. And you look like crap! Did you track mud on my carpet?" Lutz opened his desk drawer, removed his notebook and recorded something.

Jack examined Lutz for signs of a muffled smile. This has to be a joke. Seeing no sign of hope, Jack responded. "I planned on reporting two days ago, First Sergeant, but my priorities got changed by a series of emergencies."

"Emergencies? The only one I know about is today. What the hell are you talking about? You haven't already *killed* someone here, have you, Trooper Blake?"

"No, I've just been flying where I've been sent and doing what I was told."

"*Flying*, you aren't supposed to *fly* until you check in at the post and you get a briefing on the rules from me. Why the hell hasn't Samuels been doing the flying?"

"Fishing, I hear." Jack couldn't believe Lutz was this much out of the loop. That's when he realized that Sheets actually ran the post—doing a good job from what Jack could see—in spite of Lutz.

"Wait a minute, let me look at the leave schedule," Lutz said as he rolled his chair to a chart on the wall.

"Okay, Samuels *is* on leave, but you still are required to check in at your new post before you do *anything*." Lutz again took his notebook from his desk, making more entries. His complexion was quickly getting redder than before, and it looked as if one of the blood vessels on his nose would rupture.

Jack was having trouble digesting this treatment. It was senseless and he didn't want to start out his new job with a misunderstanding, or worse yet, have some overzealous administrator, thinking that he had a new "boy" to push around. An inner calmness prevailed when he thought of someday spending time again with Jet. By the book, show fake respect to the egomaniac, Jack told himself.

"First Sergeant, I need some clarification here, so no further issues are created. Who is my supervisor?" Jack asked in a calm voice.

"Investigator Sheets. You report directly to Investigator *Sheets.*" Lutz almost yelled.

"Good, that's what I've done since my first day on the job here." Jack explained, happy that the man he'd come to quickly respect would be his direct supervisor, giving him a buffer from Lutz.

"Crap, no one tells me anything. Doesn't anyone in this department know the chain of command? Where the hell is Sheets, anyway?" Now Lutz was definitely yelling.

"Sir, Investigator Sheets is down in Tunt, on this morning's call. As far as I can tell, he has been on one call after another since I got here."

"I'll talk to Sheets later. The keys to your patrol truck are on your desk. Get cleaned up and come back here and get your new assignment paperwork completed." Lutz ordered, waving his fleshy paw at Jack to leave his cave.

"So what do you think of First Sergeant A-Hole?" Stevens looked up from the reports on his squadroom desk.

"Really makes a guy feel welcome." Jack replied with a smile.

"Joe, remember, you did everything right, you had no other choice." Jack added.

"Thanks, Jack. Good luck in Bet-hell."

Jack found the beat-up white Ford three-quarter ton pickup behind the trooper office. It was five years old and had led a hard life. The state trooper decals were slopped onto the doors at obtuse angles to avoid having to remove the mirror brackets for their installation. Small dents were on both sides and the tailgate had a deep V-bend directly in the center. The muddy and scratched truck bed housed a short loop of nylon rope, two dirty body bags, a shovel, a pair of panties with a red evidence tag attached, and a collection of pop cans.

Jack bounced in his newly-assigned beater truck to his beater of a house on stilts. He threw his flight suit and the rest of his clothes in the washer and turned on the cycle. He climbed into the shower, only to find there was not enough water to do laundry and bathe at the same. He opted for the shower.

Jack did his best thinking in the shower. He tried to make sense of Lutz and remembered the wisdom of an old trooper he respected: "Some people are just jerks." Jack reviewed the conversation with the sergeant and concluded that, so far, Lutz fell into that category.

Jack praised himself for keeping his cool. He decided that his new attitude with all the Lutzs and Ronnettes he would be subjected to in his new post will be the same—respond with a smile and kindness. That would make his uncle proud. Jack knew that this approach would drive *them* crazy and keep *him* sane. It was a similar technique Jack had used in violent confrontations—something he had been taught years before—"verbal karate."

Flipping the Rolodex in his mind back to Glennallen, Jack was driving his patrol car down a dusty road to an old homestead, looking for a suspect in a burglary case. He came across a character with long hair, tattoos, and wearing a Hell's Angels vest. In checking his I.D. with dispatch, Jack learned there was a traffic warrant on the man.

Suddenly, about forty other bikers came from the woods and the house. All wore the "colors" of the Angels. Jack had inadvertently dropped in on an encampment of a bunch of badass motorcycle gang members.

Knowing he wouldn't have a chance if the bikers wanted to prevent the arrest, or if they wanted to kill him on the spot for that matter, Jack thought about Jet's theory on leaving even the lowest of low-life characters with dignity. He quickly devised a plan to save face for the biker and get out alive.

"Tell you what, how about I give you ride to the court-house? You can pay this silly ticket and be back here in an hour. That will sure be better than getting stopped on the road, having that beautiful bike impounded, and being thrown in jail. Not all cops are bike lovers like me, you know."

The biker, who turned out to be the leader of the farthest north chapter of this organization of drug-dealing, killing-for-hire, motorcycle group, looked at the group of misfits and laughed.

"Let's go, Trooper, I wouldn't want to have any of the guys get hurt because of my resisting."

Jack would use the same technique on the first sergeant, and others like him. Even though, like most of us, he probably would have preferred to just punch them in the face.

CHAPTER 50

Navy blue pants with gold and red stripes, powder blue shirt with navy trim—Jack could finally wear his uniform, instead of his flightsuit. He thought he'd cleaned up pretty well for his first day in the Bethel office. His black boots, although not nearly as shiny as the first sergeant's, would do. As a final touch, Jack wore his Stetson—securing it tightly with the head strap in the strong wind.

Jack kept in top shape and looked younger than his birth certificate told. With his neatly trimmed mustache and plentiful blond hair, Jack looked almost as good as a young Robert Redford. At least that's what his Fairbanks friend, Jill, told him once. Jack immediately turned red in embarrassment, and suspected it was just a ploy to get him to start her car on that sixty below zero day. From that day on, Jill called Jack "Sundance." Especially if she needed a favor.

Jack pushed open the door to the trooper office. Ronnette raised her head, making a quick identification. She looked back at her typewriter, looked up once more, then returned to typing. Jack knew he had earned the double take for his clean uniform. In her late twenties, Ronnette could have been an attractive woman, if it wasn't for the constant scowl.

Ronnette's brown hair was pulled from her face. That gave a full appreciation of her expression—she looked liked she was sucking on a sour pickle, simultaneously smelling something very bad.

"Hello again, Ronnette, you look lovely today." Jack offered, still trying to break the ice.

Jack thinks he detected a slight blush, but the clerk responded curtly, "I put some paperwork on your desk."

Jack completed the forms required to indoctrinate a trooper to a new post. He signed for the beater, or "patrol vehicle" as the form claimed. It would get him the four miles to the floatplane, to the airport, and to his shack—that's about all the roads there were in Bethel. He signed for a shotgun and an AR–15 rifle with a sniper scope. He started on the second pile of paperwork when the first sergeant yelled, "Blake, you out there?"

"Afternoon, first sergeant," Jack said as he entered Lutz's office.

Lutz studied Jack's clean uniform, focusing on his gold pilot wings. Saying nothing, he opened his center desk door and removed his notebook. He looked again at Jack's wings, scribbled something in the book with his paw and put it back in his desk. He then took a bite from one of those plastic-enclosed burritos purchased from the cooler section of a grocery store.

"Your wings are crooked," Lutz mumbled with his mouth full. Jack looked down to the wings on the right side of his chest. The wings looked like they were in straight and level flight to him, but he wasn't going to argue.

"Yes sir, thank you for pointing that out, I will take care of it." Jack said, trying not to gag on his words, and wondering if his sarcasm was evident.

"There's your rifle." Lutz pointed to the AR-15 lying on a table behind Jack. The rifle was stainless steel with a black collapsible stock, a knock down scope and sling. It would do fine.

"Sign for that and try not to shoot anyone with it." Lutz took another bite from the burrito, belched, and spilled beans onto his tie.

"First sergeant," Ronnette screeched over the telephone intercom.

"Yes." Lutz pushed the speaker button on the phone and wiped burrito juice from his chin.

"Frank Altoe, president of the Kusko Native Corporation is holding on line one for you."

"Well hello, sir, how are *you* today?" Jack figured this guy must be important, because Lutz's demeanor changed quickly. He was full speed in the brown nose mode.

"In Hooper Bay? In *two* hours? Yes, *sir*, we will be there. Thank you *so* much for the invitation."

Lutz hung up the phone and glared at Blake.

"I need you to take me to Hooper Bay in the 206 for an important meeting. Be ready in twenty minutes." He spoke as if it was a major emergency.

Lutz picked up the phone again as Jack was leaving the office.

"Ronnette, where is Trooper Torsen? They want the fish and wildlife trooper to attend the meeting too."

"The fish cop is up on the Yukon, near Saint Marys, I think." Ronnette sounded bored, and her use of "fish cop" made Jack think she and Jet were not shopping sisters.

"Get Torsen on the radio and tell her to head to Hooper."

Lutz spent most of the hour flight lecturing Jack on the importance of maintaining good relations with the Native leadership, all the while expelling noxious burrito gases into the cabin. Jack opened the airplane's ventilation system.

"Senator Lofton is the half-brother of Altoe, the head of the Native association. The senator sits on the budget committee for public safety and is very close to the governor. We must do all we can to appease him. When we get to Hooper Bay, just shut up and learn. You will see how to deal with the Natives. We must be very careful to present only the most *professional* image."

Jack suspected Lutz's main motive was to impress the senator and his men in hopes it would help him someday get the promotion he wanted so badly.

Jack looked on the chart for Hooper Bay. The handwritten notation on the approach end of runway 31 caught his eye. "When the weather is down, cut power when you see the red building on your left." Jack wouldn't have to use that navigation aid that day, as the clouds were a thousand feet above the runway. It looked as if sand was hauled from the nearby beaches and dumped in the middle of the hundreds of square miles of tundra swamps to make the town of Hooper Bay. The residents, mostly Eskimos, eked out a living from the local salmon and halibut fishery, subsistence hunting, and welfare checks.

Jack smiled when he saw that Jet's Cub was already tied down on the parking ramp.

"Hooper Bay Community Center." The sign hung over the pale green weather-beaten building. Eskimo men from Hooper Bay and nearby villages of Scammon Bay, Chevak, and Tooksook Bay, sat on about half of the two hundred metal chairs. The cold room was scented with the blood from salmon, beluga whales and seals, all stained onto the occupants' overalls and wolf-ruff parkas. Sitting at a long table in the front of the room were well-groomed Native men dressed in suits and ties.

"Remember, Blake, we must appear dignified before the Natives, especially the important leaders. Take a seat in the back," Lutz said, as he quickly turned and punctuated the order with another very dignified gaseous explosion. Lutz strutted to the front of the room and shook the hands of each of the men. The man who seemed to be in charge pointed Lutz to a chair at the table.

"Thank you, sir, but I must excuse myself and use the little boy's room before the meeting starts. I'll be right back."

Lutz threw a quick glance at Jack, wagging his index finger and nodding his head, as if to say, "don't move, I've got it under control."

"Glad to see you were called to school as well." Jet whispered into Jack's ear and sat next to him, her wonderful scent an extreme contrast to the rest of the room. "The first sergeant likes to strut his stuff for these big cheeses and it's his chance to show off in front of the troops as well," she added.

Jack smiled. "Yes, I've been ordered to sit quietly and learn. Think there will be a pop quiz later?"

"I wouldn't be surprised. Where is our fearless leader, anyway?" Jet looked around the room.

"He excused himself to use the potty. Based on the level of air pollution he was emitting on our flight over here, I think that's a good plan."

"Well I hope he takes into consideration the sorry excuse for a sewage system they have on this permafrost swamp," Jet smiled with raised eyebrows.

Kaplush!

With all his might, Lutz tried to cram his waste back into the overflowing toilet with his nightstick. But it was no use. It was simply too large a donation for the limited capacity of the village sewage system. In a gusher, the commode threw up at the first sergeant. Brown water splashed on his uniform trousers. Throwing the door open, Lutz rapidly waddled down the hall. Like the Queen Mary, a giant poop ship was chasing him. With toilet paper stuck on his dress shoe, Lutz stumbled in front of the crowd.

"Does anyone know where I can find a plunger?" Lutz was trying to ignore the flood of wastewater spreading in front of the podium, providing a canal for the Queen Mary.

"Is that what he meant by the 'certain way to present yourself?'" Jack dryly asked Jet.

"He does seem to have his toilet issues, *doesn't* he?" Jet responded, while stifling a laugh.

Acting as if nothing was out of the ordinary, Lutz cleaned up his mess and continued the meeting. He promised the leaders that he would do all he could to see the troopers worked within their tribal justice system. The leaders seemed satisfied and the meeting was quickly adjourned—most likely to avoid the repeated outbursts from the crowd—which had increased with the arrival of a group of disorderly young Native men. One of the men tried to stop Lutz and the troopers from leaving the building, but Jack delicately defused the situation.

Placing his hand on the troublemaker's chest, Jack politely asked him to move back. When the man cussed and surged, Jack abruptly rotated the heel of his hand into his sternum with force. Gasping for air, the protestor quickly fell forward.

"Are you okay, sir?" Jack innocently acted as if the man was having an anxiety attack of some sort, rather than having the air smacked out of him. The crowd buzzed around their fallen comrade and the troopers quietly made their exit.

"Nice work, Jack," Jet smiled as they walked toward the airstrip.

"You better not have hurt him, Blake," Lutz growled, as he picked the last piece of toilet paper from his shoe.

"Trooper Torsen, I'm VPSO Wassie. I've been waiting for you." The young Eskimo village officer stood by his all-terrain vehicle. "When I was driving from town, I saw some white guy messing with your airplane. I couldn't see what he was doing and he flew off in his own plane before I could get to the airstrip."

"Did you get a good look at the guy?" Jet asked.

"No, sorry, but I saw his plane as it was taxiing back for takeoff. It was a black twin engine. Here are the tail numbers."

The VPSO handed Jet a piece of paper with an "N" followed by the registration numbers.

"Thank you very much, officer. I'll check out the Cub a little more thoroughly than usual," Jet said as she strode to her plane.

Jet tightened the gas caps that she had left slightly loose to detect tampering with the fuel.

"Look at this, Jack." An inspection panel beneath the left wing was out of place. Jet pulled a miniature flashlight from her gun belt, removed the panel and looked inside the wing.

"I don't see any damage. The plate could have just slipped back from vibration."

Lutz didn't speak on the trip back to Bethel, most likely figuring he had impressed Jack enough for one day.

Jet called the next morning with news of the registration check from the black twin in Hooper Bay. "It's registered to Denali Security. Jack, we're finally getting somewhere. If we can tie F-Rod's company to bootlegging, we have something. Maybe just a misdemeanor, but it's a way into the company records. Who knows what we'll find there?"

CHAPTER 51

Minus 103 degrees. The ticker scrolling across the bottom of the Bethel cable television screen showed the temperature, compensated for wind chill. It didn't note that a blizzard was also raging. Winter was the time to catch up on investigations and paperwork and that's what the Bethel troopers were doing, except for the first sergeant, who was concentrating on public relations work with the Native corporations and studying for promotional exams.

Jack was only allowed two days off in six months. And the weather was so horrible on those two days that he couldn't fly out to see Jet, nor could she fly in. Long days made up those six months. Some of the days ran into the next, without a break. Ronnie inadvertently broke up the tension one day when answering a phone call from the village of Tunt.

"Paul Billy is running around the village with a gun and he's drunk!" The distraught caller reported.

"That can't be sir, we already killed him," Ronnie responded.

"No, that was Billy Paul," this is Paul Billy."

Names in the villages *could* be confusing. Josh had told Jack that Natives once went by only one name, but the U.S. government made them take a last name for census reasons. Some went to the trading post and chose names from the shelves—like coffee, or Folger.

Others just took the name of someone else and added it to theirs. That call ended with Jack taking a gun away from an unconscious Paul Billy and hauling him to jail.

Shootings, deaths by everything from inhaling gas to gunshots, far too many cases of sexual abuse of minors, fights with the Natives over the rights to land on their airstrips and enforcing the laws, search and rescues, drug cases, bootleggers, and hundreds of other cases Jack either forgot or tried to forget, flowed into the office like the Yukon River flowed into the ocean—fast and non-stop.

Jack was pouring over an intelligence report on Denali Security sent to him by the Fairbanks investigations unit. Working on the information Trooper Torsen had forwarded on the black Piper Apache, investigators learned that there was only one pilot under the employ of F-Rod. He had worked on the CIA team in Laos as F-Rod's personal pilot and now, in addition to flying, did "special projects" for his boss. Before the Laos assignment, he had been with Special Forces. The good news was that the investigators were just getting a break in the case. A top official within Denali Security had come forward, offering to be a "confidential informant," abbreviated as "C.I." in the investigative report.

The C.I. was Bill Tower, the former trooper captain in Fairbanks. As an old trooper once said, "I don't *understand* all I *know* about that," and that's how it was with Tower. He left the troopers after a career that was distinguished until his power struggle got in the way. His downward spiral cumulated in the loss of a good man, Toby Clay. It was like Tower got religion after he overheard his new boss, Fred Roderick, aka Rodriguez, bragging about how he was going to take out Blake. Tower then snooped further into Denali Pipeline Security and became a cop again— with almost daily confidential reports, funneled through Jill in the Fairbanks office. He gave us the break we needed.

Here's a section of the investigative report: *CI advises that he has personal knowledge, directly from Fred Roderick, that he wants Jack Blake dead, but not in an obvious manner. The CI further advises that Roderick told him the following: (1) through his influence with state trooper officials, he has arranged to have Blake transferred to what he considers dangerous assignments; (2) that he has "unleashed" Special Forces renegades around Alaska, specifically to challenge Blake; (3) that his pilot, identified as Olin Black, has been supplying booze in some of the Kuskokwim villages to take advantage of some of the Natives' low tolerance for alcohol, thereby inducing chaos; (4) that he finds it "sport" to see if Blake survives; (5) that his motive goes back to when he and Blake were schoolmates in Dallas; (6) that Roderick sees this as giving Blake the chance to die a hero; but if he beats the odds, he will "figure something else out." The C.I. added that Roderick is mentally unstable and that he is planning on staying under his employment only long enough to fully see our investigation through.*

We were close to arresting Roderick and shutting his operation down when it happened.

"Blake, get in here." Jack's intense focus on the incredulous report was broken by Lutz's yelling across the squadroom.

The first sergeant looked Blake up and down, then took the notebook from the top right drawer of his desk and scribbled.

"Your tie bar is crooked." Jack had become accustomed to Lutz's nonsense and it didn't bother him. Plus, the investigative report now gave Jack bigger concerns.

"Tomorrow there is going to be a big conference in Saint Marys to discuss oil development on the Yukon-Kuskokwim Delta. All the major players from the native corporations will attend. Important officials from some big companies will be there. The colonel will make an appearance, as will the state senator from this district. Most importantly, United States Senator Abraham Galt is flying in from Washington, D.C. I'm going up there today in the Native corporation plane. Tomorrow morning, you will fly a very important board member from a North Slope company to the Saint Marys airport. Don't be late, look sharp, and don't screw this up."

The first sergeant dismissed Jack with a backhand wave of his burrito-stained hand.

CHAPTER 52

Jack was at the airport at 0800 for the 0900 flight. He did a thorough inspection of the wheel-ski equipped white and red Cessna 185, loaded his survival pack and snowshoes, and pushed the plane out of the hangar into a blast of cold air. The temperature was hanging around twenty below zero with light ice fog and blowing snow in the forecast. It was an acceptable day for flying, but the conditions were worsening.

The man drove up quickly in a black Suburban, parking on the side of the hangar. Jack at first thought he was an Eskimo. Through the ruff of the man's wolf skin parka, Jack could see dark skin, a Satan-like goatee, and intense, dark eyes. He was about five foot eight, 220 pounds and he moved like a bull towards the airplane.

"Good morning, I'm Jack Blake."

The man in the wolf skin parka ignored Jack's hand, saying nothing as he opened the Cessna's passenger door and threw his black gym bag into the backseat.

Jack assumed the man didn't hear him in the wind funneling between the hangars. He tried again, once inside the airplane.

"Jack Blake, I'll be your pilot today."

"Yeah, I figured. Let's go, I don't want to be late." The man stared out the bubble side window of the cockpit.

Jack went through the run up checklist, then, after radio clearance from the Bethel tower, taxied to the main runway and turned north on takeoff for the Yukon River.

Stable at two thousand feet, Jack again tried to engage his passenger in conversation. "I didn't catch your name, sir."

"I didn't *offer* my name. How long a flight did you plan?"

"Forty-five minutes." Jack knew that would be a long and wordless three-quarters of an hour. A quick study of the man's face and Jack realized he definitely wasn't an Alaska Native. And in the few words he spoke, Jack detected an accent of Spanish descent. The hard lines of his face and his close-set eyes were familiar, but why?

Flight across the silent tundra seems even quieter when the only other occupant in the airplane is ignoring you, so Jack focused on the radios and navigation duties.

The man bumped Jack's shoulder when he swung his gym bag from the backseat onto his lap. Jack watched him slide the zipper and pull out a chart and a pen. His passenger checked his Glycine Airman wristwatch every few minutes, then wrote numbers on the chart. A sudden bump of turbulence caused the pen to fly from his hand and drop onto the floor. That's when Jack saw the tattoo on his wrist. That's when he knew the face — the same face of Smith — the man who recruited him so many years ago for a flying job in Laos.

Jack was wearing a shoulder holster that day—the standard issue gun belt interfered with the flap handle on the 185. It would be awkward to draw his pistol in the close quarters of the cockpit, but no matter. Jack didn't get the chance. The man drew first, pulling a Glock from his briefcase and sticking it in Jack's right ribcage.

"Keep both hands on the control wheel and look straight ahead." The dark eyes glared at Jack.

"You wanted to chat, well here it goes. Name is Miguel Rodriguez. I think you know my younger brother, Felix. You and him go way back. Do you have any idea how you ruined his life back in Dallas? Our father worked for Fidel Castro in the 60s. He came to hate your president, JFK. First it was forcing our country to get rid of our missiles—the only protection we had for our little island. Then it was the Bay of Pigs. But mostly importantly, it was the coup, in which he'd planned to overthrow our country in

December of '63. My father was in charge of President Castro's security force and was honored to be chosen to stop Kennedy. Most certainly, Felix got a little carried away back on that schoolyard and wanted to kill those boys, the sons of big Kennedy supporters. If it wasn't for you, he would have taken both of them out and gotten away with it. Just as my father would have been the one to kill Kennedy, with our help. Because of you, too much publicity came to our father and he was under watch by your police and the Secret Service. So that fool Oswald got the honor."

"That was a long time ago. What do I have to do with that now?" Jack was watching him intently, waiting for a chance to make a move.

"Today you are going to help us make things right. Senator Abraham Galt will address the conference in Saint Marys this morning. As a young senator, Galt was a major supporter of Kennedy and his plan to overthrow Cuba. He will be dead in an hour and you are going to help."

Rodriguez moved clothes around in the duffle, uncovering his tool of choice for the day's mission. The folding-stock SIG–550 scoped assault rifle fit nicely in the bag.

"Anchorage Center, Guard Flight zero zero one on the localizer approach to runway one-seven, Saint Marys." The radio transmission broke over the radio in the trooper plane.

"That will be the National Guard plane with the senator on board," Rodriguez said knowingly.

Jack studied his passenger intently. Jack knew he couldn't land in Saint Marys, giving Rodriguez the chance to carry out his plan.

Flashing to when his uncle introduced him to aerobatic maneuvers, Jack yanked the airplane's nose up to thirty degrees above the horizon, then neutralized the elevator.

"What the hell are you doi…."

In the middle of Rodriguez's yelling, Jack violently deflected the control wheel fully to the right, throwing the 185 into a roll. Scrambling frantically for something to hold on to, Rodriguez was slammed onto the door.

Forcing the plane inverted, Jack began a gradual turn back towards Bethel as the Yukon River passed in the distance. Smashing his fist into Rodriguez' gun hand, Jack knocked the Glock down between the seats. Next, Jack's knuckles slammed towards his passenger's face, but Rodriquez blocked the blow.

Rodriguez grabbed onto the passenger side control wheel with both hands, jerking it in an attempt to rotate the plane to straight and level flight. With both men fighting with their own set of rudders and control wheels, the plane contorted into a cross-controlled dive.

Jack thrust his elbow into Rodriguez's face, knocking him senseless. Jack again had sole control of the airplane as the passenger slumped to the side of the airplane. Now, just a hundred feet above the snow-covered tundra, he fought to break the rapid descent.

He almost made it.

"Get this thing flying and turn back!" Rodriguez screamed. He had quickly recovered from the blow and now was again pushing the black pistol at Jack.

The explosion of gunpowder in the confined cockpit was deafening. Jack, flying with his right hand and shooting with his left, got off one shot. There was a flurry of blood and confusion as the 185 sank lower. The brush line raced into the windshield. Jack pulled hard on the controls, but it was not enough.

It was too late.

They hit the first alder bush at 110 knots. Jack yanked again on the controls, then popped the flaps, but the plane refused to fly. The elevator had been severely twisted by the first contact with the bushes.

Cutting through the alders and willows, the ground raced into the windshield. With no control, Jack was no more than a passenger at that point—and he was the only one alive in the airplane.

Crashing hard into the ground, the 185 violently catapulted across the frozen tundra.

Then there was silence.

CHAPTER 53

My name is Jessi Torsen, but most people call me Jet. I'm a Fish and Wildlife Trooper, assigned to the Dillingham Post. I've remained silent about the search for Jack Blake for a long time. Now that it's over, I can tell the story. After a week and a half of some of the worst winter weather Alaska has to offer, most had given up any hope of Jack being alive. But there's a reason some people survive in desperate situations and some don't. I believe it has more to do with desire than abilities, but Jack had both. I always saw him as a survivor.

Since the first day we met—when Jack was a recruit in King Salmon—I knew we would always be together. Maybe it was his deep blue eyes, maybe it was his soothing voice, maybe just his presence, but I was immediately attracted to Jack. I never thought I could fall in love with a man so quickly, but I did. Our love only grew stronger over the years.

Jack has always shown compassion to those who needed and deserved it. His kindness was matched only by his strength, dealing with criminals fairly and handling the most violent the only way they understood. It was due solely to the forces of our jobs—pulling us in different directions and stealing hours, days, months, and years from our lives—that we hadn't wed.

The search for Jack lasted ten days. We had no idea where to start—there was no distress call and no ELT signal. Major Emery had come from Anchorage to run the search and rescue operation. Dave Daniels and Ted Herlihy were basing out of Saint Marys. They too, were stranded on the ground because of weather. But at least they had been able to get out on snowmachines for ground searching. Ronnie Torgy searched at least twelve hours a day. When he broke the trooper snowmachine, he used his own.

The rest of the Bethel troopers had been searching by snowmachines from Bethel. The weather on nine of the ten days prevented flying in a small plane. I started out seven of the days, turning back each time because of snow, ice, fog, and high winds. I hardly slept. My heart was aching with the frustration of not being able to do more.

The weather broke on the tenth day. I estimated I had four hours of searching before the skies came down again. VPSO Josh Luko met me at the Cub, as he had done each of the nine days before.

"Jet, I had a dream last night. I saw Jack. He's alive and I saw his camp. I'll go with you and show you where it is." Josh spoke anxiously.

"Are you sure?" Josh's word was gold, but it *was* just a dream.

"I know it sounds strange, Jet, but I saw his camp. Here, I drew a map." Josh pulled a scribbled map from his parka. He had drawn the Kuskokwim and Yukon Rivers, noting the villages of Tuluksak, Lower Kalskag, Russian Mission and Saint Marys. There was big X at a ninety-degree angle to Kalskag, about five miles across the Yukon from Russian Mission.

"Why there, Josh? That isn't in the flight path from Bethel to Saint Marys."

"I know, but the weather in the flats gets low this time of the year, so Jack may have dropped down and decided to pick up the Yukon and follow it downriver to Saint Marys." Josh's eyes were pleading now.

"Okay, Josh, I'll head directly to that spot. And I *believe* your dream. I always have known that Jack is alive. I'm going to ask you to stay here, so I can pick up Jack in the Cub and bring him home."

"Jet, you *will* find Jack. But don't bring him home. My dream also told me that someone is trying to kill him. You need to hide Jack for a while. You can use my trapping cabin. Keep him there until it's safe."

Josh's vision told him what I already knew. Dave Daniels had developed an informant within Denali Pipeline Security who told him that F-Rod wanted Jack dead. It was just a matter of figuring how they would do it, when, and with whom. Dave said he needed just a little more time to nail Rodriguez on a conspiracy charge.

"Thank you, Josh. I will let you know what I find."

"Better than that, Jet. I will get Oscar to fly me to my cabin on Nishlik Lake. I will meet you and Jack there with the fire going."

Josh was so sure of himself that he made me want to get to the X as fast as possible. I was over the village of Upper Kalskag an hour later. A layer of fog shrouded the flats, allowing for just occasional peeks of the tundra. I flew directly to the Yukon where the fog had lifted. Circling, I studied tracks in the snow. Fresh snowmachine tracks led to the south bank of the river, then through the brush towards Josh's X, where they slithered into the fog.

Backtracking above the tracks led me first to steam rising from the river. The steam came from a Volkswagen-size pool of open water in the otherwise frozen Yukon. The waters beneath the ice ran fast, even in the winter. Even in minus-fifty degrees, these pools were common on parts of that great waterway—sometimes resulting in certain death for unsuspecting winter travelers in the dark. The snowmachine had broken a trail along the ragged edge of the death pool.

The tracks continued across the mile-wide portion of the Yukon, then upstream along the north bank. There was something in the distance, tight against the bank. As I got closer, I made out the airplane. The radial engine and chunky fuselage identified it as a Beaver, black and fitted with skis. The snow around the cargo door had been heavily displaced. A ramp lay under the plane and snowmachine tracks led away, joining the ones that had led me there. I circled lower and read lettering on the tail: "Denali Pipeline Security."

My heart raced and I knew I had to get to the X before the snowmachine driver. Pushing the throttle forward, I sped past the steam, picking up the tracks again as they entered the brush. The fog had broken a bit, offering glimpses of the tundra. Straining my eyes, I could barely see something in the snow—it was the tail of an airplane! Circling, straining more, I saw the wreckage. Then I saw the machine.

The black snowmachine was plowing away from the crash site, towing a trailer with someone lying in the back. I pushed the Cub down through the fog, but I was too low, too close to the ground. I popped back up through the clouds, turning toward the Yukon.

The speeding machine broke out of the fog just before the river. Pushing the stick forward, I dove, applied flaps, reduced power, and slowed. Pulling alongside the escaping snowmachine, I wagged the wing at the driver and goosed the engine. He ignored me, so I dove even lower and cut in front of him. Staring straight ahead, he continued to the Yukon.

Then I saw Jack.

Covered with the trooper–issued parka and insulated overalls, Jack's face was open to the wind. His eyes were closed and he looked still and lifeless. But I saw something on the next pass. His gloved hand moved. I got lower, and no, it wasn't from the bouncing sled. He was giving me the "thumbs up" sign.

Circling back towards the south bank, I was buying time until the snowmachine got closer to the steamy pool of water. When it was within two hundred yards, I slammed the stick forward. Coming alongside the trailer, I motioned to Jack. When two people in love spend enough time together, they can communicate without speaking, and that's what we did.

Now fifty yards from the steam, the snowmachine followed the trail it had broken on the way in. Pushing the stick full left, I aimed for the front of the snowmachine.

Sheer terror overtook the driver's face. He jerked the handgrips hard. Jack used the momentum to roll from the sled onto the snow.

With a tremendous splash, the snowmachine and trailer disappeared into the steam.

I landed next to Jack. He never looked so good, or so bad. Blood was caked on his face. His parka and pants were torn, bloodstained and tainted with smoke. He was wrapped in silver duct tape.

Pulling himself up, he limped to me, a broken smile coming over his face. "Any chance I could get a lift?" Jack was barely audible, but his blue eyes glowed.

Jack passed out shortly after we lifted off the Yukon River. Looking around every few minutes to the backseat of the Cub, I wanted to first affirm he was still breathing with all he'd gone through. Secondly, I just wanted to make sure he was actually there. Finding him alive seemed unreal after the odds he was up against. Now I only wanted to get him to safety. Safety meant caring for his medical needs, but also secluding him where F-Rod or his men would not find him. Nishlik Lake was a perfect choice, as it was a quick trip from Josh's cabin down a series of lakes to the Wood River, then to my home at Dillingham. Even in bad weather, I could keep low and scud-run to the cabin with supplies.

Turning the Cub to the east, I followed the Tuluksak River up into the Kuskokwim Mountains, gliding over a ridge to where Josh's cabin was tucked between mountains protecting Nishlik Lake. Just as he'd promised, Josh had a fire going and the little log cabin was toasty warm. Josh and I pulled the still-unconscious Jack up the trail in a sled.

Jack was a mess. The badge on his fur hat had a severe indentation and was deformed. Beneath the cap was a deep bruise, but the skin was unbroken. You could tell that something had hit the badge hard. I learned later that it was a .22 bullet.

Recalling my EMT training, I examined Jack's pupils, first in low light, then with a penlight.

Each pupil constricted when hit by the light and the reactions were the same. So far, so good.

Josh cut the silver duct tape away from Jack's arm, which had been taped to his chest to immobilize what must have been a fracture. More good news—there was only minor swelling and his fingers had normal color. Jack also had taped his ankle, but, like the arm, it was not displaced. If it was broken, it was probably only a closed, or simple, fracture. We pulled off Jack's shirt. The redness surrounding his ribs probably meant those were fractured as well. Then we found the worst of his injuries—a bullet wound in his right shoulder. Again, if you consider crashing an airplane and being shot, he was lucky. The bleeding had stopped and the bullet had gone all the way through.

"Jack is going to make it." He'd lost a lot of weight and looked like hell, but I agreed with Josh's prognosis.

I cleaned the bullet wound and, since the bleeding had stopped, elected to let it drain uncovered to prevent an abscess. Josh made splints from cardboard that we fastened to Jack's arm and ankle with duct tape. We then taped his ribs.

In my med kit from the survival gear in the Cub, I found two bottles, one containing an antibiotic, and the other a painkiller. I kissed Jack on his lips and asked him to wake up. His eyelids fluttered and his blue eyes focused on me.

"Hey, beautiful, how are you?" Jack whispered.

"Hello, sleepyhead, what's your name?"

"Is this a trick question? Robert Redford, of course, but you can call me Sundance." Jack smiled and I knew he would be okay.

"How do you feel? Is your neck stiff?" I hoped he would be truthful.

"Like I've been in a plane crash, shot, sledded across a bumpy trail, then thrown into the back of a Cub. But, my neck is okay. I think it's the only thing that doesn't hurt."

Jack started to laugh, but held back when the pain from his ribs shot a message to his brain.

"Rest now, I'll be back shortly." I kissed Jack's forehead and gave him a cup of water to wash down the meds.

Jack eyes closed and he smiled as I walked to the door with Josh.

"I've got to go and do some damage control before things get out of hand. Please wake Jack every two or three hours, to make sure he's okay. If he starts vomiting, or seems to be disoriented, I will have to take the chance and fly him to the Dillingham hospital."

I hated to leave Jack, but I knew he was in good hands.

CHAPTER 54

Stabilized in good flying conditions on a cross-country flight always offers a good opportunity for sorting things out and making decisions. I had a big one to make on the flight back to Bethel—who could I trust to tell about Jack? We would have to account for his whereabouts. But, if the wrong person found out that he was alive, he would be hunted down. And he was in no condition to fight.

Jack trusted three of the men who had been searching for him over the past ten days, as did I. I'd known Rich Emery since I was hired on and always considered him to be of the highest integrity. He did all he could to help Jack and me, and he kept our relationship secret. He could be trusted for certain. Dave Daniels was a good friend of Jack's and he had been pulling out all the stops on the investigation of F-Rod. Jack was unsure about Ted Herlihy at first, but they had become close in Glennallen and even closer after the Manley shooting.

Yes, all three could be trusted with Jack's life.

"What have you heard about Jack?" It was the first time Ronnette had said more than two words in a row to me, ever. I never took it personally, just figured she didn't like anyone much.

"It doesn't look good, Ronnette," I answered. I think I saw tears well in her eyes. She had been coming in early, staying late, answering the radio and the phones since Jack's disappearance. It occurred me that, like most everyone I knew, Ronnette must have cared for Jack—she just hid it well. Maybe she was on our side after all, but I still didn't know if I could trust her. This wasn't the time to find out.

Major Emery was sitting behind Lutz's desk. Lutz had been abruptly transferred to Kotzebue the week before. Word was, the involuntary move was due to Lutz's delaying initiating the search for Jack. Of course, Lutz probably thought it had more to do with his offending the Natives in Hooper Bay by damaging the community center's plumbing system. Ronnie Torgy would soon be promoted to the Bethel first sergeant position. I closed the door and told the major everything.

"You did the right thing, Jet. I agree that Dave Daniels and Ted Herlihy should know, but no one else. I'll brief them. I'll have Oscar fly Rodriguez's Beaver back to Bethel and stash it in our hanger. We'll put out a press release, saying that Jack is still missing and believed deceased, as indicated by a snowmachine track leading from the crash site to open water in the Yukon. We will have to treat it as if Jack is dead until all this blows over, however long that takes. I'll have Daniels write a report.

"You'd better get back up to Josh's cabin and take care of your man. If you need anything—*anything* at all—you let me know personally. And please give Jack my best. I'm going to see that we get full resources on this investigation and get Roderick locked up as soon as possible."

I stopped by the Alaska Commercial Company and bought some provisions, heavy on the makings for chicken noodle soup. In the store's natural section, I found some Symphytum—a homeopathic remedy for helping broken bones to rejoin and heal.

Jack was sitting up on his bunk when I got back to the cabin.

"Where can I kiss you that it won't hurt?" Jack's lips were bruised and cut and his face was puffy.

"Jet, you look so good to me right now that nothing you could do would hurt me." Jack smiled and lifted his good arm to wrap around my waist. Josh purposely looked out the window as I kissed Jack's head, then his lips. At that point, there was no reason to keep our love secret.

"Josh, how's our patient?" I asked.

"No throwing up and his pupils are still working. I was worried he was having delusions when he talked about marrying you soon. Maybe those weren't delusions after all?" Josh gave his big teddy bear grin.

It snowed heavily for the next four days. Jack was healing quickly. He told me what he could remember about the crash. He recalled little about his survival afterwards, and he had lost all memory of the period from when he was shot until when he climbed into the Cub with me. The three of us played cards, Scrabble and chess, while the snow piled up outside. Josh entertained us with stories about his life growing up in his remote village. Jack and I planned our life after the troopers.

The storm broke on the fifth day.

"Josh, I think it's time I got you home. Your wife and kids must miss you," I said.

"I miss *them*. I will have to come up with a story why I'm not bringing any pelts home from the trapline and why a pretty girl is flying me."

I kissed Jack, promising I'd return as soon as I dropped Josh off in his village and bought more supplies.

"I love you, Jet. Please hurry back. Josh is great company, but I can't wait for us to be alone," he whispered.

"Me too, Jack. Now just lie here and rest. You have a long way to full recovery."

"I love you more," I added, as I opened the door to the cold air.

Josh spoke once we were outside. "Oh, one thing, Jet. I was working on some old traps, just before you got back a few days ago. I set a Newhouse #6, just to try it out, but left it when I heard Jack waking up in the cabin. That's a big ol' grizzly bear trap with steel teeth and the power to snap a leg bone. I'm sorry, but I can't find it—the big snowstorm covered it. It's somewhere over there." Josh pointed to the side of the cabin, near where some cut up wood was waiting to be chopped.

"Well, I don't think Jack is going to be wandering around out here while I'm gone. He's still in such bad shape that he can't come outside. This wind will probably blow the snow away and uncover it by the time I get back, so don't worry." I tried to reassure Josh, believing Jack would stay put. Then I decided to let Jack know, just in case.

I stuck my head in the cabin to warn Jack about the trap, but he had fallen back asleep, so I left a note by the door.

CHAPTER 55

The Cub floated in the water, just off Nishlik Lake. The wind had been blowing more than a hundred knots the night before. We had pulled the floatplane into a little creek, lashing the wings, two ropes per strut, to big rocks. The wind had died down to about twenty-five, and my fishing partner, of all people, was First Sergeant Lutz. I started to pull the inspection plate where the wing strut disappears into the wing. I'd heard horror stories of wings falling off after being tied down in high winds, and wanted to check for damage.

"Why check the wings? We're going anyway," Lutz yelled.

Despite the disturbing dream, when I woke up I felt the best I had since the crash. It took a minute to nail down why I felt so good, but then it was clear—my headache was gone. Earlier, even the slightest flash of light set off a sledgehammer inside my skull. Today, the sunlight blasting through the window called to me. My vision was still too blurry to read a note hanging by the door—I'd check that once the cobwebs cleared. I needed to get outside to the fresh air. The cane Josh carved helped me limp out the door.

The rush of wind and cold was stimulating. Finally, I could take a deep breath and barely feel my cracked ribs stabbing at my insides. Josh's cabin is on a hill overlooking Nishlik Lake. Below the lake is the valley leading to the Wood River and the Tikchik Lakes. It would be a treat to return in the summer with Jet and catch one of the monster lake trout that Josh talks about. Right then, I was just happy Jet would be back soon so we could be alone. I had decided to re-focus my life, making Jet my top priority. We would be together, no matter the cost. I guess, for a hardhead like me, I had to be shaken up a bit to realize what's really important in life. I thought of a bit of wisdom, shared with me by mountain guide Ray Genet: "We're here for a *good* time, not a *long* time."

I almost grabbed Josh's sawed-off .12 gauge that hung next to the door—a standard tool most Alaskans take when venturing into the Bush—but I ignored my mental checklist. I rationalized that it wouldn't be needed, as bears were hibernating at that time of the year. And, the only two humans who knew where I was were Jet and Josh.

A nice pile of sawn birch and spruce was scattered next to the cabin. I'd heard Josh chopping wood a few days ago so knew an axe had to be close by. I began to tromp around in the snow—maybe the axe had been covered in the storm.

It was tough going, wading through that deep frozen mess with a bum leg. I poked around with the cane, but no axe. It hurt when my injured ankle bumped against a metal object under the layer of snow. I slid my heel back and forth in the snow, trying to again find the object.

Contact! I had it.

I stopped and listened. It sounded like an airplane in the distance, but Jet couldn't be back so soon. I decided it must be the wind ripping through the mountains.

I could feel the metal again now with my foot. If I could just scoot it back a little, I could grab it with my cane. Sliding it back now, closer, it started to slip on the ice beneath the snow. I stomped with my good foot to stop it.

I heard something again. I stopped, hesitated, looking around and searching the snow and the sky. The wind blocked out whatever it was. Maybe I should get the shotgun from the cabin—no—no one is looking for me way out here. If it *is* an airplane, it's probably just wolf hunters, scouring the nearby ridges and flats for easy prey.

I pulled the axe up with my uninjured hand and rolled a log onto the stump. I'm not sure what hurt more, my ribs, my ankle, or my arm.

Swack.

With one quick chop, the birch round split in half. It was cold enough that the wood split easily. Although I was sore and each blow with the axe sent pain up my shoulder, it was good pain. It felt right to be using my body again. The air was clean, sun was breaking through the clouds, and it felt good to be alive.

Crunch.

I turned around to the tromping behind me.

I froze at what I saw.

"Hello, *amigo.*"

Even after thirty years, I recognized Felix Rodriguez. He had the same deep brown killer eyes. The same hatred on his face. The same .22 revolver in his hand.

Josh's shotgun would have been handy about then, but I hadn't listened to that little inner voice that told me to take it outside with me earlier. So there I was, bringing an axe to a gunfight.

"We meet again, Jack. I guess you thought you were safe out here—just like in Dallas and in Idaho. You wanted to be the big hero when we were kids and I gave you the chance to die a hero, first in Laos, then here in Alaska. But you blew it Jack, you somehow beat the odds. It's been fun, but the troopers are getting too close and this is my last chance. So, unlike a hero, you will die like a dog."

My uncle taught me to avoid the "Four Poisons of the Mind." He said that fear, confusion, hesitation and surprise were killers. Calmness had come over me and I accepted the situation, eliminating the fear. I couldn't let my instincts take over, that would lead to confusion. I wouldn't hesitate to take action when I saw an opening, but right then Rodriguez was taking his time to impress me before he killed me.

Surprise was the element to avoid. I needed to watch, focus, keep calm, and retain a clear head. I paced around the woodpile, with the axe hanging at my left side and my cane dragging from my right hand. Rodriguez mimicked my pacing, staying five feet away. Close enough for an easy kill shot, and far enough away from a swing of the axe.

"Why didn't you just kill me right way?" I asked calmly, although I already knew the answer.

"That would be no fun, amigo. You were just a game to me, nothing more, nothing less."

"And what about the innocent people who died because of the shell-shocked vets you unleashed?"

"Collateral damage," he shrugged. His eyes watched mine—his boots followed my steps—as I shuffled back along the side of the cabin. I thought I'd try to distract him, or at least to anger him. I wanted to change his focus. He kept coming.

"So, I guess it's unfortunate also that you tried to take advantage of some of the villagers' weakness for alcohol. You ruined the lives of some good people. By the way, don't you think it was a little sloppy to hand out expensive scotch when homebrew is the drink of choice in the Bush? Maybe even downright *stupid*?"

I dragged my leg faster. I gripped my weapon.

"Slow down, Blake, you're a cripple. You can't escape this time. Even if you could outrun me, my bullet would still find you. Are you afraid of dying, Blake?"

No, I'm afraid of getting *old*," I answered.

Behind my back, I re-gripped Josh's cane. Then, like a tonfa, I whipped the stick towards Rodriguez. He grabbed it in his glove. I swung him around, into the deeper snow. He dropped to one knee, taking the cane from my arms with him.

My injured ankle had failed me. The intense pain caused me to buckle onto the tundra.

"So now, it ends." Rodriguez rose from the ground, stomping towards me in the deep snow.

SNAP!

"What the hell?" Rodriguez screamed in pain.

He lifted his right leg. The teeth of a massive bear trap bit deeply into his shin. Ragged flesh and bone poked through his pants.

The .22 was leveled at my chest, quivering in his hand. "So long," he growled.

The axe uncoiled from my hand, rapidly whipping through the cold air. It found its mark—the center of Rodriguez's chest. Blood raced from his parka. His eyes stared at me in disbelief.

Felix Rodriguez flopped onto his back, dead before he hit the ground. Just like a schoolboy in Dallas, so many years ago.

Only now, there was justice.

CHAPTER 56

I hurt from my ankle to my head. Dragging myself back into the cabin, I collapsed onto the bunk. Blood was flowing from my bullet wound and my ankle felt like it was re-fractured. My head was pounding and my arm swelled around the splint. I reached for a painkiller, but stopped. I wanted to be alert in case Rodriguez had backup.

Super Cubs make a distinct sound—more like a flying tractor than an airplane. Sitting up in the bunk, I scraped frost from inside the window, scanning the lake as the unidentifiable ski plane silently touched down in the snow.

Pulling my tired and throbbing body from the bed, I painfully limped to the door. Someone was climbing the path to the cabin with a rifle in the ready position.

Silhouetted by the setting sun, the figure strode quickly towards the cabin. Squinting, I tried to focus as I chambered a shell into Josh's shotgun.

Then the most wonderful voice cut through the cold and the pain.

"Jack, it looks like you've had company. Is everything okay?"

Jet stopped when she saw Rodriguez bleeding into the snow. "Wood chopping accident?" Jet mused.

"Jet, I can't tell you how great it is to see you. Meet Felix Rodriguez."

"So that's the famous F-Rod," Jet said as she carefully walked around the body and pulled the .22 from its hand.

"I'm guessing he didn't drop by for a social visit. It will be dark soon, so I'm sure the investigative team won't come out until tomorrow. I'll get up in the Cub in the morning and call the major by radio. The body will be fine in this cold."

"Tomorrow works for me, Jet. I'd like to speak to you alone, anyway. We need to talk about a lot of things."

"Good, I'd like to hear the rest of the story on this, Jack, and I need to talk to you too. Here's your cane."

"Thanks, now I'm all better," I forced a smile.

"God, Jack, it looks like you have been bleeding again. You had better lie down and let me look at that."

"Later, Jet. First I'd like to look in Rodriguez's plane, if you don't mind helping me down to the lake."

I put my arm around Jet and we struggled down the trail.

"Jack, I only told the major. And he said he would confide only in Ted and Dave. Who do you think tipped off Rodriquez?"

"If my hunch is right, I don't think anyone leaked. I trust any of those men with my life."

The black Helio Courier dripped oil onto its skis and the frozen lake. In small white letters, "DPS" was scrolled on the tail.

Jet flung the plane's door open. A bottle of Gold Leaf Extra 18 Year Old Scotch fell into the snow. She grabbed a radio from the passenger seat.

"That booze looks familiar, Jack, but look at this."

Light was leaving the clear skies quickly and Jet could barely read the letters stamped on the face of the radio: "BIODIGTONICS."

"Biologists use these receivers to track wildlife. A transmitter attached to a collar is hung on the critter. The bear, wolf, moose, or whatever, moves around, beeping into the airwaves. The biologist can then track it anywhere. Why would Rodriguez need one of these?" Jet asked.

"Let's take a look at your Cub. Remember back in Hooper Bay, when the VPSO saw someone around your plane?"

"Yes, but nothing was out of the ordinary... except the loose inspection cover."

Jet popped the cover, reaching around in spaces she couldn't see. Her hand felt something attached to a wing rib with Velcro. She pulled it from the inspection hole and turned on her flashlight in the now total darkness.

"So, that's how he found you! One of his goons tagged me with this. They have been tracking me for more than six months!"

Blue and green northern lights crackled in the skies above us as she looked into my eyes.

"Jack, do you think it's *over?* Do you think our lives will now return to *normal?*"

I reached into the Cub and turned on the ADF radio receiver and tuned it the Dillingham AM radio station, "KDNG." "*To Share Our Love,*" by the Moody Blues crackled over the airwaves. I brought Jet in close and found my courage to say what I'd wanted to say for so long.

"I'm not sure if our lives will ever be *normal,* at least as long as we're in this business. 'The swift wings of time beat faster and faster'—I can't remember where I heard that, but it makes sense. As far as I know, we only go around once, so we should make the most of it. So, instead of a *normal* life, maybe we can at least have a *life.* A life together."

Searching for the right words, I knew I was rambling. I was trying to say what I'd wanted to say for so long.

"Jack Blake, are you suggesting what I think you are?"

"I hope so. I'd get down on one knee, but everything on my body hurts too much to bend. Will you marry me?"

The Northern Lights exploded above us like a Fourth of July fireworks show, now swirling red, yellow, and orange.

Jet said yes. We embraced, kissed, and stumbled back to the cabin. We threw another log on the stove and the fire came to life. Jet lit a candle and then we...

Wait a minute. I almost forgot to turn off my tape recorder.

"END OF TAPE."

Made in the USA
Middletown, DE
15 August 2023